MW01641585

ISBN: 979-8-9906197-9-1 (Paperback)

Edited by Red Adept Editing

CONTENTS

CHAPTER 1

James Ryder stepped off the Red Line train onto the elevated Thorndale station platform that stretched into darkness beyond the overhead lights. His footsteps echoed against the concrete platform surface as a handful of train passengers dispersed into the streets of Chicago on a late July night. The digital clock above the tracks read 10:17 PM.

Empty coffee cups tumbled across the tracks, pushed by wind from the departing train. Ryder adjusted the pharmacy bag in his left hand and scanned the platform, checking for threats and planning contingencies even on a pharmacy run. He noticed the young man trailing him toward the stairs in the empty station.

He was thin, in his early twenties, but his calculated steps had the cadence of someone who'd once marched in Army formations.

Ryder descended the metal stairs, his rubber soles silent against the ridged steps. The tree-lined streets of Andersonville stretched before him, mature oaks blocking streetlights and creating pools of shadow between islands of amber light. Nana's new prescriptions rattled in the bag—blood thinners and beta blockers to regulate her blood flow as she continued her recovery. Tomorrow, he'd fight the insurance company. Tonight, he just needed to get her stabilized.

The man on the platform had pulled a hoodie over his head and picked up his pace. Unusual for a warm summer night.

Footsteps behind him maintained a consistent distance. Not the random pace of someone heading home. Too deliberate. Too focused.

Ryder turned left, away from his intended route. The footsteps followed. He caught a reflection in a parked car's window—a thin man with hands shoved deep in a worn military surplus jacket.

The young man lunged forward in a blur, grabbing for the pharmacy bag.

"Hey!" The stranger's voice cracked. "I'll take that!"

Ryder's hand shot out, catching the man's wrist and twisting in one smooth motion. The attacker stumbled, his grip slipping, but he ripped the bag free before bolting down the street.

"Shit!" Ryder sprinted after him, boots finding purchase on the uneven sidewalk.

The thief was fast. Lean muscle and desperation carried him across four lanes of Broadway Avenue against the light, car horns blaring as vehicles swerved around him. Ryder followed, using stopped traffic as cover while keeping his target in sight.

The young man vaulted a chain-link fence into the parking lot behind vintage shops. Ryder scaled it in two quick movements, his body moving with fluid precision. The thief was already fifty yards ahead, cutting between parked cars toward the alley.

Ryder closed the distance. The thief had speed, but no strategy. His breathing was jagged, and his movements were becoming erratic.

They raced through backyards, past vegetable gardens and children's swing sets. A motion-sensor light flicked on, illuminating the chase for three seconds before darkness reclaimed the runners.

The thief stumbled over a garden hose but kept running, the pharmacy bag clutched against his chest.

Ryder tracked him by sight and sound—ragged breathing, sneakers slapping concrete, and the rustle of the paper bag. They emerged onto Clark Street, the thief darting between late-night pedestrians outside a corner bar. Shouts erupted behind them as startled patrons jumped aside.

The young man made his mistake at the wall behind the auto repair shop—eight feet of cinder blocks topped with razor wire. He tried anyway, fingers scrambling for purchase as Ryder closed the final twenty yards.

Ryder hit him low, driving his shoulder into the man's midsection and slamming him against the unforgiving wall. They both went down hard, rolling across oil-stained asphalt. The pharmacy bag scattered its contents, pill bottles bouncing and sliding into shadows.

The thief beat Ryder to his feet, securing a piece of a broken glass bottle on his way up. Ryder looked into the thief's eyes and saw fear, not the icy gaze of someone willing to take a life. He unleashed a lightning-quick right jab that knocked the glass out of his grasp and sent the skeletal man back to the pavement.

The former Delta Force operator was on him before he could recover, pinning the thief face-down and applying pressure between his shoulders.

The young man struggled for a moment, then went limp.

"Please," the stranger gasped, his voice muffled against the pavement. "Don't call the cops. I'm a veteran and served this country overseas. I didn't mean to steal anything."

Ryder held position, studying the man beneath him. He had an emaciated frame with track marks on visible skin. Military-issue dog tags hung from a chain around his neck. All familiar indicators of a story he'd heard too many times.

"What's your name?"

"Ricky. Ricky Nelson."

Ryder eased his grip and helped the man sit up against the wall. "Where did you serve?"

"Afghanistan. Two tours with the 10th Mountain Division." Ricky's hands shook as his fingers moved to his neck. "Got hit by an IED outside Kandahar. Got a Purple Heart and everything." He gestured to his left leg. "Doctors gave me pills for the pain. Lots of pills."

The broken record played again. Different name, same story. Overseas service, battlefield injury, prescription medication, addiction, homelessness. Ryder collected the scattered pill bottles, checking each label.

"What made you think I had what you needed?"

Ricky stared at the ground. "Pharmacy bag. Figured maybe you had some OxyContin or something." His voice dropped to a whisper. "Haven't had anything in two days. Feel like I'm dying."

"Why don't you get treatment instead of stealing?"

"Everything's overcrowded. The waitlists are months long." Ricky pulled his knees to his chest. "Been sleeping under the Wilson Avenue bridge since my girlfriend kicked me out. She said I wasn't the same person who came back."

Ryder studied the young man's face in the dim streetlight. Hollow cheeks, sunken eyes, but underneath the destruction, traces of his military past remained. The infantry soldier was still alive inside, though fading with each fix.

He pulled a business card from his wallet and held it out. "I may be able to help you. Stay out of trouble and call me in a week."

Ricky took the card with trembling fingers, squinting at it in the darkness. "Phoenix House Veteran Recovery Centers. You run this place?"

"Among other things." Ryder stood, brushing oily dirt from his shirt. "One week. Don't make me hunt you down again."

He left Ricky sitting against the fence and resumed his journey to Nana's house, the torn pharmacy bag secure in his grip. Existing recovery centers were overwhelmed, and too many veterans like Ricky Nelson were falling through the cracks. Chicago needed another Phoenix House.

By the time he reached Nana's front yard, his mind was calculating the critical components of a new center—cost, location, staffing, and funding. The Bitcoin account taken from Peter Richter's office before his demise could cover initial expenses, but sustainable operations would require additional resources.

"There you are." Nana appeared in the doorway before he could insert his key, her silver hair reflecting the porch light. She wore her favorite cotton robe with one hand on the doorframe for balance. "I was starting to worry."

"The pharmacy was busier than I expected." Ryder helped guide her back through the door and into the kitchen. The stroke had affected her coordination and subtly impacted her speech. "I got everything the doctor prescribed."

He handed her the bag and watched as she examined each bottle, reading labels with careful attention she'd once applied to his homework assignments.

"Too many pills," she muttered. "I don't know why I need to take so many."

"It's to prevent another stroke. You need to take everything your doctor prescribed."

"How much was all this? I'll pay you back," Nana said with a serious tone.

"Nothing," Ryder lied. "It was all covered under your insurance."

She shot him a look that could still make him feel twelve years old. "I know that's not true, James Ryder. My insurance company doesn't pay for my prescriptions."

Ryder laughed. "Okay, you caught me. It was only five dollars."

Nana must have sensed she would not win the argument, so she moved to sorting pills into daily containers while Ryder checked window locks and door security. The house smelled of lavender tea and wood oil, unchanged since his childhood. Family photos lined the hallway, including his military portraits and commendation certificates that Nana had framed despite his protests.

She capped the last bottle and turned to face him. "I'm pretty tired, so I'm heading to bed."

Ryder followed her to the bedroom. "Get some rest. I'll be in the guest room if you need anything."

"I'll be fine." Nana squeezed his arm. The grip was firm, easing some of the concern for the woman who had been his caregiver since he was twelve.

Ryder waited until she turned out the light on the nightstand before settling into the living room armchair. He pulled out his encrypted phone, scrolled to Will Cameron's contact information, and texted him.

The response came within minutes. *Still awake. What's up?*

Ryder typed, *How much is left of the Bitcoin account?*

The balance shot up over the past two weeks. You still have sixty percent of the original amount remaining. Market has been good to us.

Liquidate half.

The pause stretched longer this time. When Will's response appeared, Ryder could almost hear the curiosity in his voice. *That's a substantial amount. What's the play?*

New Phoenix House in Chicago.

Roger that. I'll have the funds transferred by noon tomorrow. Do you have a location in mind?

Ryder considered the question. Chicago's North Side had multiple neighborhoods that could work, areas with sufficient veteran populations but without the bureaucratic obstacles of downtown.

Not yet. Let me work on the preliminary planning first.

Copy. Anything else?

Negative. Get some sleep.

He set the phone aside and checked on Nana one final time. Her breathing was even, and the new medications on her nightstand were within easy reach. The TIA had been a warning shot. Her doctor's prognosis was optimistic, but Ryder knew how quickly things could change.

Tomorrow would bring new challenges. The unresolved battle with Nana's health insurance company. Location scouting for the Phoenix House expansion and finding resources to help Ricky Nelson, if he calls. But tonight, Nana was safe, and one more veteran could find his way back from the edge if he stayed out of trouble long enough to avoid prison or death.

Ryder settled into the guest bed and stared at the ceiling, his mind working through the logistics of opening another veteran recovery center. Chicago's veteran community deserved better than overcrowded facilities and months-long waitlists. They deserved the same dedication and resources they'd provided to their country. He had built Phoenix House centers twice before, turning them into a model for veteran recovery services across two states.

He could do it again.

Outside, the city continued its restless pulse. Traffic lights cycling through empty intersections, emergency sirens echoing between buildings, and the distant rumble of late-night trains carrying their cargo of shift workers. Chicago never slept, just shifted into a different rhythm.

Ryder closed his eyes and let the familiar sounds wash over him. Before he drifted toward sleep, scenes of the chase replayed in his mind. How many other veterans were sleeping under bridges tonight? How many would perish before he opened the doors to his next Phoenix House?

The question hung in the darkness, unanswered.

CHAPTER 2

Ryder's bedroom remained dark at zero five thirty when his internal clock pulled him from sleep. Dawn hadn't yet crept through the curtains as he rolled from bed and padded barefoot down the hallway.

Shadow's room stood empty.

Her dog bed lay undisturbed, water bowl full, and toys arranged where they'd been the night before. Ryder's pulse quickened. Shadow never left her room during the night. The Belgian Malinois operated with military precision, adhering to routines with the same discipline she'd maintained in Afghanistan.

He moved toward Nana's bedroom and found her door ajar. Ryder eased it open wider, and the pale morning light revealed Nana sleeping peacefully, her silver hair spread across the pillow. Shadow lay curled beside the bed, her dark eyes tracking Ryder's movement as he entered.

The dog's tail thumped once against the floor in greeting, but she didn't move from her position. Her muscular frame remained coiled in protective readiness, maintaining watch over the woman who'd welcomed her into the family.

Ryder crouched beside Shadow and scratched behind her ears. "Good girl," he whispered. "You knew she needed you."

Shadow's keen instincts had detected something Ryder missed. Whether it was Nana's irregular breathing, a change in her scent, or some other subtle indicator, the dog had recognized vulnerability and responded. Military working dogs possessed abilities that continued to amaze him, even after years of partnership.

He studied Nana's face in the dim light. Her color looked good, breathing steady and deep.

"Keep watching over her," Ryder murmured to Shadow before retreating to the kitchen.

The familiar ritual of morning coffee provided structure after a chaotic evening. Ryder opened his laptop and researched veteran recovery centers in Chicago. The VA's website painted a grim picture. It showed seven facilities with waiting lists exceeding six months. Four were not accepting new admissions. The remaining three operated at maximum capacity.

One facility caught his attention. Veteran's Haven on West Madison Street. Their website showed a converted warehouse. The photos looked recent enough to warrant investigation.

He checked his watch. Zero six forty-five. Time to head to the airport and pick up Will Cameron.

***

The tall and lean former intelligence analyst waited curbside with a single bag when Ryder pulled the white Toyota Camry to the pickup zone. Will jumped into the front seat and gripped Ryder's hand in greeting before securing his seat belt.

"Did you get a new car?"

"This is Nana's car. She let me borrow it, so I don't have to navigate a bus through the streets of Chicago."

Ryder turned to his lieutenant and friend as he pulled away from the curb. "You're looking better since the last time I saw you. How's the recovery from the fentanyl poisoning?"

"Going well," Will replied, straightening in his seat. "I'd say I'm back to ninety percent now."

"Good. Are you ready to check out some potential locations for the next Phoenix House?"

"Let's do it."

The drive through downtown Chicago revealed a city already humming with life. Veterans Haven occupied a converted warehouse squeezed between a tire shop and a discount furniture store. A small sign read "Veteran's Haven Recovery Center" in faded blue lettering.

Ryder entered first, and Will followed through the glass doors into a narrow lobby with fluorescent lighting.

"Here to see someone?" a security guard asked.

"We're looking into recovery services for a friend."

The guard pointed down a hallway. "Director's office. Third door on the right."

Ryder knocked on the half-open door. A woman in her fifties looked up from a computer screen, curly blonde hair extended to her shoulders. Dark circles under her eyes suggested long hours and sleepless nights.

"Margaret Sheehan. Can I help you?"

"I'm James Ryder, and this is Will Cameron. We run Phoenix House recovery centers. We're researching the current capacity situation in Chicago."

Her expression shifted from wariness to interest. "I've heard positive things about Phoenix House. What brings you to Chicago?"

"Family circumstances. Considering opening a facility here."

Margaret stood and walked to her window. "Come see what we're dealing with."

The warehouse floor below contained rows of beds separated by thin partitions. Men sat on narrow beds or gathered in small groups, their conversations creating a constant low murmur.

"That room there," Margaret pointed to a corner area, "is supposed to house twelve men in six double-occupancy rooms. We've got eighteen living there right now."

Ryder counted the visible occupants. All shared the hollow expression of people pushed beyond their limits.

"How long is a typical stay?"

"Three to six months, but we're extending that to accommodate overflow. Some guys have been here eight months because there's nowhere else for them to go."

She pulled a folder from her desk drawer. "Twenty-three veterans are requesting admission this week. I can take maybe six."

Ryder studied the applications. Different names, different units, different conflicts, but the underlying story remained consistent.

"What would help most?"

"More facilities. More bed space." Margaret closed the folder. "But mostly, more people who understand that these men served their country and deserve better than warehouse conditions."

Ryder handed her his business card. "We're looking at some locations today and would like to help once we're operational. Text me your number and I'll contact you when we have open beds."

"I can't tell you how much this city needs this," Margaret said.

Ryder nodded, and the duo returned to the car parked along the street. "Where to now?"

"The most promising location is in Logan Square," Will replied as he climbed into the car. "Near the corner of Kimball and Logan Boulevard."

Logan Square offered a different atmosphere from downtown. Tree-lined streets stretched between neighborhoods of bungalows and greystone buildings. Mature oaks provided canopy shade over sidewalks where residents walked dogs and pushed strollers.

They parked, and Will gestured toward a three-story brick building across the street. "They've been operating here for eighteen months but have run into financial problems. The owner wants to sell rather than declare bankruptcy."

The building showed promise with its solid construction, large windows, and a landscaped front area with space for parking.

"What's their current capacity?"

"Sixteen residents. Only housing seven right now. The owner says they've had trouble maintaining occupancy." Will consulted his tablet. "They're asking four hundred thousand, so it's priced to sell."

They crossed the street and examined the building's exterior. The brick facade was solid but needed cleaning. The windows appeared in workable condition. The surrounding neighborhood comprised similar buildings housing small businesses and residential apartments.

A middle-aged African American man emerged from the building's front entrance. He wore a rumpled polo shirt with the organization's logo and carried himself with the bearing of someone fighting a losing battle.

"Mr. Cameron?" The man extended his hand. "David Johnson. Thank you for coming."

Will made introductions before Johnson led them through the facility. The interior layout was functional but uninspiring. Common areas with donated furniture, dormitory-style rooms with basic amenities, and a kitchen adequate for meal preparation but lacking warmth.

"We started with such high hopes," Johnson explained as they toured the second floor. "My brother served in Iraq, struggled with addiction for years before getting clean. We thought we could help other veterans avoid his struggles."

"What happened?" Will asked.

"Funding. We underestimated operational costs and overestimated insurance reimbursements. The VA pays below our actual costs, private insurance is inconsistent, and most veterans can't afford to pay out of pocket."

They continued through the third floor to the administrative offices and additional dormitory space. The bones of the facility were solid, but everything needed updating.

Ryder exchanged glances with Will. The situation was familiar from their experience at Phoenix House Tampa.

"We're prepared to make a full-priced offer with an immediate close."

"I need to ask you something," Johnson said, fixing his stare on Ryder. "Are you going to take care of these men? Really take care of them?"

Ryder met his gaze. "I'm a veteran myself. This isn't a business investment, it's a mission."

Johnson nodded. "My brother died two years ago. Overdose. He was clean for eight months, then relapsed. I keep thinking that maybe if we'd done something differently—"

Will responded as Johnson trailed off. "You can't save everyone. But you can provide the foundation for people to save themselves."

“Deal,” Johnson said, extending his hand.

***

One week later, Ryder stood beside Will Cameron as the first residents from Veterans Haven arrived at Phoenix House Chicago. Six men carrying duffel bags and worn suitcases, combined with the previous seven residents.

The facility had undergone a remarkable transformation in just seven days—fresh paint throughout, new furniture in the TV room, and updated kitchen appliances. Most importantly, a sense of warmth that had been missing before was present in the common areas.

"Welcome to Phoenix House Chicago," Ryder addressed the group of thirteen as they gathered in the main common room. "This is your home for as long as you need it to rebuild your lives. We have three rules. Respect yourself, respect others, and commit to your recovery."

A new resident in a faded Army t-shirt stepped forward. "What's the catch?"

"No catch. You're here because you've served your country, and you deserve better than sleeping under bridges or in overcrowded warehouses."

The man studied Ryder's face. "You military?"

Ryder nodded. "Army Ranger and then Delta Force. Ten years."

The atmosphere in the room shifted. Military credentials carried weight with veterans who'd learned to distrust civilian administrators. Nods of understanding passed between the men.

"Will here served in SIGINT," Ryder continued. "Shadow, my K9 partner, is around somewhere getting familiar with the building. We understand what you've been through because we've been through it ourselves."

"When do we start the program?" another man asked.

"You started the program when you walked through the door. Recovery isn't something that happens to you. It's something you do. We provide the foundation, and you do the work."

As the residents dispersed to claim rooms and unpack belongings, Ryder set aside the corner room on the second floor. Ricky Nelson had been on his mind throughout the week. Nine days had passed since their encounter in the parking lot, and Ryder had heard nothing.

"Still thinking about the kid from the train station?" Will asked.

"He seemed different. Scared, desperate, but not beyond saving."

"Sometimes they're too far gone to accept help."

Ryder checked his watch. Sixteen thirty. If Ricky Nelson hadn't called by now, the chances of him calling at all were slim. Tomorrow, Ryder would offer the room to someone from Veterans Haven's waiting list.

He walked through the facility one final time. The kitchen hummed with activity as the new and old residents worked together to prepare dinner. Voices and laughter echoed through common areas where men played cards, watched television, and engaged in tentative conversations.

This was the original vision for Phoenix House. It wasn't just housing or recovery, but community and brotherhood.

Ryder headed toward the exit. He wanted to get home and check on Nana.

His phone buzzed as he reached the parking lot. The caller ID showed an unknown number from the Chicago area.

Ryder answered on the second ring. "Ryder."

Silence stretched across the connection, broken only by the ambient sounds of traffic and shaky breathing. Ryder waited, instinct telling him someone was there, someone who needed time to find words.

A raspy voice finally spoke. "Mr. Ryder, this is Ricky Nelson. We met at the train station last week. Do you still have a place for me to stay?"

CHAPTER 3

The forty-second floor of LifeCore Health Insurance's downtown Chicago headquarters hummed with the afternoon energy of a Fortune 500 corporation. Andre Atwood's Italian leather shoes clicked against polished marble as he strode toward the boardroom, his imposing six-foot-five frame cutting through clusters of executive assistants and junior analysts.

Atwood adjusted his silk tie and checked his Rolex. Two minutes early for the quarterly board presentation. Perfect timing to seize control before the CFO could bore everyone with his spreadsheets.

Twelve board members occupied leather chairs around a Brazilian rosewood table. Dr. Allison Lee sat at the far end of the table, her medical degree and ethics creating constant friction Atwood had learned to navigate. Chad Kline positioned himself near the presentation screen, with his tablet and clicker ready for action.

"Before we dive into standard financial reports, I want to share some exceptional news," Atwood announced, his voice filling the room with the authority that had carried him from college football linebacker to CEO in fifteen years.

Atwood's smile radiated confidence as he clicked to the first slide, revealing numbers that made even the most skeptical board members lean forward.

"Net income increased twenty-seven percent from last quarter." He paused for effect. "That's fourteen points above our most optimistic projections."

Murmurs of approval rippled around the table. Board members exchanged glances and nodded. Numbers danced on the screen, guaranteeing bonus checks and stock option exercises.

Margaret Hawthorne, CEO of Precision Medical Devices, raised her hand three chairs to Atwood's right. She was the pragmatist on the board.

"Andre, congratulations on the results. Was the increase driven by expanding the policyholder base?"

Atwood's smile widened. "Some of it, but the majority came from efficiency improvements implemented by our Chief Underwriting Officer and his team."

Chad Kline straightened in his chair, basking in the recognition.

Another board member started to speak, but the young woman recording the meeting stopped him with a raised hand. "Sir, please state your name and company for the transcript."

The man cleared his throat. "Tobias Richter, CEO of Richter Enterprises. I need to be sure I'm understanding the results correctly. You're growing revenue and increasing income through efficient management of policy decisions. Is that accurate, Mr. Atwood?"

The LifeCore CEO recognized the setup. Richter had suggested the efficiency improvements fifteen months ago during a post-board meeting conversation in the hotel bar that had sparked Kline's current initiatives. The older man was lobbing him a softball, expecting Atwood to hit a home run.

"Correct, sir. Chad Kline and his underwriting team are executing at the highest level. We expect continued improvement with program expansion."

Dr. Lee's audible sigh carried across the boardroom. Atwood stiffened, shooting her a menacing glare before forcing his attention back to the board members' approving nods.

The meeting concluded with handshakes and promises of continued excellence. Dr. Lee and Kline lingered as the room emptied.

Atwood waited until the last board member disappeared before turning toward his two department heads.

"Outstanding work, Chad." Atwood extended his hand for a high-five that echoed through the empty boardroom.

"That quarterly bonus is almost enough to finish my basement renovation," Kline said. "Maybe even add the pool table I've been wanting."

Dr. Lee remained seated, her expression combining professional disappointment with barely contained anger.

Atwood stepped toward her, using every inch of his one-foot height advantage to create the psychological pressure he'd learned on football fields and in corporate conference rooms. His shadow fell across her chair as he looked down.

"I appreciate your passion for patient care. That's why we made you chief medical officer." His voice dropped to a register that had intimidated opponents and competitors for two decades. "But never embarrass me in front of the board like that again." His words delivered the power of a physical slap.

"Do you understand me?"

Dr. Lee pushed her chair back and stood, creating distance between them. Her nod was quick.

"Good." Atwood's insincere smile returned. "Chad and I will handle the post-meeting analysis. You're dismissed."

Dr. Lee gathered her tablet and papers, her movements sharp with suppressed frustration. The boardroom door closed behind her with a soft click.

Kline shook his head. "I can't believe her attitude. She's actively undermining everything we've accomplished for this company. Maybe it's time to consider replacement options."

"She's harmless," Atwood chirped, shoving his hands into his pockets and casually rocking on his heels. "Firing her would attract attention from state regulators. It's bad timing with our efficiency improvements showing such positive results."

"You're right. We can't afford regulatory scrutiny right now."

"Of course I'm right," Atwood boasted. "Forget about Dr. Lee. We need to focus on what boosts the bottom line. I want you to expand the AI system that's eliminating inefficient treatments."

Kline's enthusiasm was immediate. "What kind of expansion are you thinking?"

Atwood turned from the window, his expression showing the tenacity that had made him millions. "Turn up the parameters. Eliminate more inefficiencies."

"What about Dr. Lee? Expanding the program will cause some negative outcomes and preventable deaths."

"Chad, do you want to finish the basement and buy the pool table?" Atwood moved closer, his physical presence reinforcing the question.

"Yes, sir. I just wanted to make sure we're considering all the implications."

Atwood raised his hand, cutting off any further discussion. "Business executives make tough decisions every day. This situation is no different. Focus on the thousands who will benefit from our efficiency."

He stared at Kline for a beat, then ambled to his executive leather office chair and sat.

"It's the right thing to do, Chad. Make it happen."

Atwood spun his chair toward the windows, dismissing Kline with the gesture. Lake Michigan shimmered in the distance like steel beaten by a thousand hammers.

For a moment, his own reflection floated in the glass. Not the man in a tailored suit, but the boy from West Columbia, South Carolina. Skinny, hungry-eyed, standing in a cold kitchen while his mother wept over another past-due notice. The smell of boiled cabbage and mildew persisted throughout the house. The thud of his older brothers fighting in the next room because there was never enough to go around.

That boy had made himself a promise before his tenth birthday. Never again.

Every quarterly gain, every denied claim, and every efficiency improvement pushed that promise further from fear and closer to control. Dr. Lee would never understand. She grew up in the Virginia suburbs outside Washington, and she'd never stood in a grocery line counting coins and praying they'd be enough.

Behind him, Kline cleared his throat, pulling Atwood back.

"The algorithm already flags high-cost treatments and sorts them by age. We can tighten thresholds and push it to scan more claims."

Atwood kept his gaze on the skyline. "And what happens to the policyholders flagged?"

"They lose coverage for those procedures, and the oldest policyholders will take the biggest hit."

Atwood's jaw tightened. "We're in a war with rising healthcare costs, and that's just collateral damage. As long as the system does the math right, the company stays strong."

"Yes, sir." Kline hesitated. "Dr. Lee won't stay quiet."

"She's manageable. She believes she can change my mind." His mouth twitched. "And I'll placate her enough to let her continue thinking she can sway me."

"Understood," Kline replied sharply.

"Inform me when the parameters go live."

"Yes, sir."

Kline gathered his tablet and backed toward the door, the leather soles of his shoes whispering across the carpet. The door clicked shut, and silence settled in.

Atwood exhaled, the tension easing. The revenue and industry-leading profit margins weren't just about bigger bonuses or the next vacation house. They were proof he'd beaten the odds that had nearly crushed his mother. Proof he could bend life to his will instead of the other way around.

He checked his phone. A message from his wife, Ruth. *Dinner at eight. Don't be late this time.*

Atwood smiled. Ruth had seen him fight his way from the streets in West Columbia to the gridiron at Appalachian State University, which earned him All-Sunbelt Conference accolades as a linebacker. His success on the football field earned him access to wealthy university boosters, especially after some NFL draft experts forecasted Atwood might be a day three pick.

The NFL never panned out for Atwood, but he took full advantage of his new relationships and admission into a club he had never even known existed. After college, he committed to winning in boardrooms instead of stadiums and traded ice baths and trainers' tables for tackling quarterly earnings.

He slipped the phone back into his pocket and returned to the window. The city glittered in the afternoon sun. Glass towers, buzzing traffic, a million people chasing something. Most of them would never catch it. They didn't have the spine to climb up. They didn't have the fear of falling back down the ladder of life.

His phone buzzed again with a message from Kline. *New parameters uploaded. Expect increased denial rates by week's end.*

Atwood thumbed a reply. *Maintain maximum discreetness. No surprises.*

He stood, straightened his tie, and glanced once at Dr. Lee's empty chair. His broad smile from the board meeting had long vanished, replaced by a deep scowl. The thought of Ruth and his son suffering like he did growing up in West Columbia was unfathomable. This was the fuel feeding the raging fire inside him to be wildly successful. If anyone tried to stop his climb, he would see them defeated and destroyed.

Chapter 4

The August evening sun filtered through the family room blinds of Nana's brownstone as Ryder turned his key in the front door. The familiar scent of lavender soap and lemon oil should have greeted him, but silence stretched through the hallway where Nana's radio often played soft jazz after dinner.

Shadow's behavior stopped him cold.

The Belgian Malinois paced in tight circles near the front door, her ears pinned back and tail tucked. Ryder recognized the health alert indicators from their deployments together.

"Shadow, what is it?"

The dog's amber eyes locked on his, then darted toward the kitchen. She sat at the entrance and barked once. Not the alert bark for strangers or the playful bark for morning greetings. The distress call Shadow used when lives hung in the balance.

Ryder moved across the living room and rounded the corner into the kitchen.

Nana lay motionless on the linoleum floor beside the kitchen table. Her body twisted at an unnatural angle with her left arm beneath her torso and her right leg bent at the knee.

"Nana!"

Ryder dropped to his knees beside her, fingertips finding her neck to check for a pulse—it was weak, but present. Her skin felt cool, indicating she'd been down for some time. Her breathing was shallow and irregular. The left side of her face showed visible drooping, her mouth slack.

Another stroke. Much more serious this time.

He pulled out his phone and dialed 9-1-1, cradling her head with his free hand.

"Emergency services, what's your emergency?"

"I need an ambulance. My grandmother appears to be having a stroke. She's unconscious but breathing," Ryder replied and gave the operator the home address.

"Sir, how old is your grandmother?"

"Sixty-eight years old. I found her on the kitchen floor. No idea how long she's been down."

"Is she responsive? Does she notice your voice or touch?"

"Negative. Visible facial drooping on the left side. Her pulse is weak but steady."

"An ambulance is on the way. The estimated arrival time is six minutes. Stay on the line with me."

Ryder shifted position to keep Nana's airway clear while Shadow pressed close against his leg. The dog's training included medical alerts, and her behavior confirmed what Ryder already knew. This was serious.

"Sir, do you know if she has any medical conditions or takes medications?"

"She had a TIA about two weeks ago. She's on blood thinners and beta blockers." Ryder's voice remained steady despite the fear clawing at his chest.

The operator continued gathering information while Ryder monitored Nana's breathing. Seven minutes stretched like hours before he heard sirens approaching. Shadow's ears perked up, and she moved toward the front door.

Two paramedics entered with urgency. The lead medic, a woman in her forties, kneeled beside Nana while her partner prepared equipment.

"When did you find her?"

"About ten minutes ago."

The medic checked vitals and pupil response. "Clear signs of a stroke. We need to get her to Northwestern Memorial."

They worked with practiced efficiency, establishing an IV line and securing Nana on a stretcher. Ryder shut the door behind them and followed them to the ambulance.

"Family member?" the medic asked.

"Guardian. She raised me."

"You can ride along."

The emergency room staff at Northwestern Memorial moved with fluid urgency. Ryder sat in the waiting room while doctors and nurses performed tests and evaluations.

Dr. Kendra Asher emerged from the treatment area after two hours. She was in her mid-forties, and her lips were pressed into a thin, grim line that foreshadowed difficult news.

"Mr. Ryder? I'm Dr. Asher, the attending neurologist."

Ryder stood. "How is she?"

"I treated your grandmother two weeks ago for the TIA. This one is much more serious. She's suffered a major ischemic stroke."

Dr. Asher pointed to her head. "A blood clot blocked circulation to a significant portion of her brain's left hemisphere. We dissolved the clot, but there's been substantial damage."

"You said she could make a full recovery from the TIA. What about this one?"

"She'll need extensive rehabilitation. Daily physical therapy, occupational therapy, and speech therapy. With intensive treatment starting as soon as possible, she might regain up to eighty percent of her pre-stroke abilities, but that could take a full year."

Ryder absorbed the information. "When do we start?"

"She'll remain here for stabilization. Then we'll recommend transferring her to a specialized stroke rehabilitation facility. The sooner we begin intensive therapy, the better her chances."

Ryder rubbed the back of his neck. He was determined to get Nana all the treatment she needed to recover but knew it would be expensive. "Will insurance cover that?"

Dr. Asher's expression shifted. "I'll connect you with someone in Billing who understands how rehabilitation claims work with all insurance providers. They can answer your questions, but I will say—"

She stopped mid-sentence.

"What is it?"

"I recall from her last visit that your grandmother has Medicare Advantage with LifeCore Health Insurance. They've been challenging to work with this year. They've denied a substantial number of rehabilitation claims."

The name hit him like ice water. He'd been fighting with LifeCore to pay for Nana's last hospital visit and had noticed more denials on her previous medical bills.

"Can I see her?"

“We’re admitting Mrs. Ryder and moving her to a private room on the fourth floor. Give us twenty minutes, and then you can see her.”

Nana looked fragile in the hospital bed, monitors beeping around her as Ryder crept in. The woman who'd raised him was covered in an array of tubes and wires. Her face still showed the effects of the stroke, but her breathing was stronger.

Ryder pulled a chair close to her bedside.

"We're going to get through this," he whispered. "Whatever it takes."

His phone buzzed with a text from Will Cameron. *Heading to Phoenix House in the morning. Do I need to pick anything up?*

Ryder typed back, *I'm at Northwestern Memorial with Nana. She had a major stroke.*

The response came seconds later. *On my way.*

Ryder stared at the monitors tracking Nana's vital signs. Each beep represented another moment of recovery time that LifeCore might try to deny. Every hour of delay could mean the difference between Nana regaining her independence or spending her remaining years dependent on others.

He thought about Dr. Asher's words. LifeCore had been denying rehabilitation claims. How many other families were facing the same impossible choice? How many seniors were being condemned to inadequate recovery because some corporate executive decided their lives weren't worth the expense?

Ryder's hand moved to the scar on his left temple, a physical reminder of what happened when systems failed the people they were supposed to protect. He'd founded Phoenix House to support veterans abandoned by powerful organizations that prioritized profits over people.

Now the same forces were targeting the woman who'd saved his life.

Dr. Asher returned with additional paperwork. "Mr. Ryder, I need to submit the rehabilitation recommendation to LifeCore within twenty-four hours. The sooner we get approval, the sooner we can begin the transfer process."

"What if they deny it?"

"We'll appeal, but that takes weeks. Every day we delay treatment reduces her potential for recovery."

Ryder stood and walked to the window overlooking the Chicago skyline. Somewhere in those glass towers, LifeCore executives were making decisions that destroyed lives. They hid behind corporate policies and actuarial tables while real people suffered the consequences.

The thought hollowed him out. The woman who'd raised him, who'd been his anchor through every crisis, might never recover.

"Doctor, submit the rehabilitation request. Include everything she needs for optimal recovery."

"I'll get that processed tonight."

After Dr. Asher left, Ryder returned to the chair next to Nana's bedside. He sat in the silence, watching her chest rise and fall. Her breathing was stronger now, but the left side of her face still showed the stroke's damage. How much function would she regain? Would she ever be able to live independently again?

Thirty-five minutes later, Will Cameron appeared in the doorway, his lanky frame rushing across the tile floor to Nana's bed.

"How is she?"

"She had a major stroke. They dissolved the clot, but there's been significant damage." Ryder's voice carried concern mixed with exhaustion. "She needs months of intensive rehabilitation to have any chance at recovery."

Will moved to the monitors tracking Nana's vital signs. "What are the doctors saying?"

"With immediate, intensive therapy, she might regain eighty percent function. But it could take a year, and insurance has to approve the treatment plan."

"Weren't you already fighting with her insurance provider?"

"Yeah." Ryder rubbed his face. "The neurologist says LifeCore has been denying rehabilitation claims recently."

Will turned to face Ryder. "What if they deny Nana?"

"I'll liquidate whatever we need from the Bitcoin accounts. But it's not just about the money."

"What do you mean?"

Ryder stood and walked to the window. The streetlights cast long shadows across the hospital parking lot as the sky turned from blue to black. "This is the third time we've had issues with LifeCore. First, they delayed approval of her blood thinners after the TIA. Then they denied coverage for the cardiac specialist follow-up. Now this."

"Sounds like every insurance company I've had. It's what health insurance companies do."

Ryder had limited experience with the health insurance industry after spending a decade in the Army. He didn't want to accept what Will said was true. "Three separate denials for legitimate medical care? That's not normal pushback, Will. That's a malicious pattern."

"You think they'd be that blatant about it?"

Ryder thought about the sequence. Three denials of three separate, legitimate medical needs, all necessary for Nana's health.

"Remember when we were dealing with the VA bureaucracy? How they'd delay and deny veteran benefits to avoid paying out? Same tactics, different organization."

Will nodded. "Corporate executives hiding behind policies while real people suffer."

"Exactly. And if LifeCore is doing this to Nana, they're doing it to other people who don't have the strength or financial means to fight the system."

"What do you want to do?"

Ryder looked at Nana's peaceful face. Right now, he needed to focus on her recovery, but the larger pattern was impossible to ignore.

"My first priority is making sure Nana gets the rehabilitation she needs, regardless of what LifeCore decides. But let's start paying attention to their decision-making process."

"You want me to look into their recent claim statistics?"

"Just some preliminary research. See if there's data available on their denial rates, any recent corporate changes, that kind of thing."

Will pulled out his laptop. "I can run some basic searches on their executive team and recent financial reports. Public information only."

"Nothing invasive yet. I could be wrong about this."

"But if you're right?"

Ryder's hand moved to the scar on his left temple. "If they're denying legitimate claims to vulnerable people, then someone needs to hold them accountable."

A nurse entered to check Nana's vitals. Her movements were professional, but her expression showed strain. After adjusting the IV and recording readings, she paused.

"Your grandmother is stable. The next twenty-four hours will tell us more about her recovery potential."

Ryder nodded.

Will stood and moved toward the door. "I can get more done at Phoenix House, so I'm heading out to start research on LifeCore."

"Thanks for coming, Will. Keep me posted."

Ryder studied Nana's face again. The drooping on the left side was less pronounced than earlier, but still visible. Every day of delayed treatment reduced her chances of full recovery.

As the night crew of doctors and nurses arrived, Ryder remained at Nana's bedside. The woman who'd raised him after his parents died deserved better than fighting corporate bureaucracy for basic medical care.

Someone needed to pay attention to what LifeCore was doing. Someone needed to ask the right questions.

A figure in a white lab coat appeared in the door, interrupting his thoughts. It was Dr. Asher.

"I'm heading out, but wanted to let you know the rehabilitation request was submitted to LifeCore. We should have a response within forty-eight hours."

"Thanks, Doctor."

"You should head home and get some sleep. She's going to be stable until tomorrow."

"Thanks, but I'm not leaving her side."

Dr. Asher left, and Ryder turned back to Nana. He would stay by her bed and fight alongside the strongest woman he'd ever known. Ryder sensed that a battle with the insurance company was looming soon. If his assumption was correct, the conflict might transition from phone calls and letters of appeal to a physical appearance at the LifeCore office. No matter the obstacles or the opponent, he was prepared to fight and win—at any cost.

CHAPTER 5

Ryder slept with his large frame folded into the small, padded chair beside Nana's hospital bed, his head tilted back against the faux leather headrest. Soft snores escaped his lips as morning light filtered through the venetian blinds. The rhythmic beeping of the monitors was a steady, military cadence, each pulse counting the minutes since Dr. Asher had submitted the rehabilitation request to LifeCore.

He sat up when Nana stirred, her eyelids fluttering open. The left side of her face still drooped, but her eyes held their familiar sharpness. She blinked, taking in the sterile white walls and the IV tube snaking from her arm.

"James." Her voice was clearer than yesterday, though still slurred. "You stayed all night."

"Where else would I be?"

She attempted a smile, the right side of her mouth lifting more than the left. "You look terrible."

"Thanks. You too."

A soft laugh escaped her lips, the sound lifting the weight that had settled in Ryder's chest. If she could joke, she was still fighting.

"How do you feel?"

Nana shifted against the pillows, testing her range of motion. Her left arm moved more slowly than her right, but it moved. "Frustrated. This old body used to do what I told it to do."

"Give it time."

"Time." She repeated the word as if she were tasting it. "How much time do I have, James?"

Before Ryder could answer, Dr. Asher entered carrying a tablet, her expression foreshadowing unwelcome news.

"Good morning, Mrs. Ryder. How are you feeling?"

"Better than yesterday. Ready to start working."

Dr. Asher glanced at Ryder before sitting in the chair beside the bed. "That's what I wanted to discuss. We heard from LifeCore about the rehabilitation authorization."

Ryder straightened. "And?"

"They've approved limited physical therapy. Enough to help Mrs. Ryder achieve basic mobility for discharge."

"That's not what you recommended."

"No. I submitted a plan for intensive rehabilitation. Daily physical therapy, occupational therapy, and speech therapy for at least three months, maybe more depending on progress." Dr. Asher's voice contained the restrained frustration of someone fighting a losing battle. "With intensive treatment, Mrs. Ryder could regain her previous quality of life. With what LifeCore approved, she'll achieve basic functionality."

Nana absorbed the information. "What's the difference?"

"Basic functionality means you can walk short distances with assistance, perform simple tasks like dressing and bathing with help, and communicate basic needs. It's enough to keep you out of a nursing home."

"And with the full treatment?"

Dr. Asher leaned forward. "You could do almost everything you did before the stroke, like drive a car, cook your own meals, and maintain your home. Quality of life versus basic survival."

Ryder felt heat building in his chest. "They're deciding between independence and dependence based on cost."

"I'm afraid that's true." Dr. Asher turned to Nana. "I've seen this pattern more often in the past year. LifeCore approves minimal care to meet regulatory and legal requirements while denying treatment that could restore meaningful function."

"But you're the doctor," Nana said. "Your medical opinion should matter."

"It used to." Dr. Asher's professional mask slipped, revealing exhaustion. "Now, insurance companies override medical decisions with actuarial tables and efficiency standards."

Ryder stood and walked to the window. Chicago's skyline stretched before him, glass towers reflecting the morning sunlight. Somewhere in one of those buildings, LifeCore executives were making decisions that destroyed lives.

"Let's appeal now."

Dr. Asher's eyebrows lifted. "The appeal process can take months. Mrs. Ryder needs to begin intensive therapy now for optimal results."

"Then we start with the limited rehab. I'll pay out of pocket for the rest if necessary," James added, unsure if he could afford it.

"James, that's expensive," Nana protested.

"Less expensive than watching you lose your independence because some corporate bureaucrat decided your life isn't worth the investment."

Dr. Asher stood. "I'll arrange for the physical therapist to start this afternoon. We can begin with the approved sessions while working through the appeal."

After Dr. Asher left, Ryder returned to his chair. Nana studied his face with the intensity of someone who'd raised him from childhood.

"You're angry."

"Yeah, I'm pissed."

"At my health insurance company or at yourself?"

The question hit him like a physical blow. "What do you mean?"

"You've spent your adult life protecting people. Your Delta Force team, veterans, Phoenix House residents, and people who can't protect themselves. Now the person who raised you needs protection, and you feel helpless."

Ryder clenched his jaw, his entire body tensing at the sound of the truth. Before he could respond, a physical therapist appeared in the doorway. A woman in her thirties with an athletic build that spoke of dedication to physical fitness.

"Mrs. Ryder? I'm Jasmine, your physical therapist. Dr. Asher said you're ready to get started."

Nana brightened. "More than ready."

Jasmine entered with a wheelchair and began explaining the day's goals. Simple movements to assess current function and establish baseline measurements. Watching Nana struggle with simple balance and coordination tore at Ryder, but her determined focus spoke volumes of the fight still burning within her.

Forty minutes later, Jasmine helped Nana back into bed. The session had exhausted her, but her eyes held satisfaction.

"How did I do?"

"You did great, Mrs. Ryder," Jasmine said with a genuine smile. "We'll work on balance and coordination tomorrow."

After Jasmine left, Nana fell asleep almost immediately.

His phone buzzed with a text from Will. *Found some interesting public information about LifeCore. Can you meet at Phoenix House later?*

Ryder typed back, *Meet you there in 1 hour.*

He kissed Nana's forehead, inhaling the faint scent of lavender soap that still clung to her skin. The woman who'd taught him that strength came from protecting others was fighting for her independence.

Fifty minutes later, Ryder pushed through the front door of Phoenix House. Will sat behind his laptop on the conference table, surrounded by empty coffee cups.

"What did you find?"

Will adjusted his laptop so the screen faced both of them. "LifeCore's financials are public since they're traded on the NASDAQ. Their earnings per share have skyrocketed over the past eighteen months."

Ryder studied the financial charts. Revenue growth, earnings increases, and stock price appreciation. "Should have bought their stock a year ago."

"Look at their medical loss ratio. It's the percentage of premium revenue they spend on actual medical care. The industry average is eighty-five percent, but LifeCore's ratio is sixty-two."

"They're spending less on medical care while charging the same premiums."

"Exactly. And here's where it gets interesting." Will pulled up another document. "I found online reviews from LifeCore policyholders. Take a look."

The reviews painted a disturbing picture. Denied cancer treatments, rejected surgeries, and delayed approvals for emergency care. Hundreds of complaints described the same pattern Nana was experiencing.

Ryder felt his jaw tighten. "How many reviews?"

"Over three thousand complaints in the past year. LifeCore approves minimal treatment and denies anything they deem expensive."

"Same thing they're doing to Nana."

"And they're getting away with it." Will pulled up another document. "The official appeals process on their website has multiple levels designed to exhaust people into giving up."

Ryder studied the appeals flowchart. It contained five complicated levels, along with mountains of forms and documentation, all while patients deteriorated.

"Most people can't navigate this while dying."

"That's the point." Will leaned back. "Deny, delay, profit."

Ryder walked to the window overlooking Logan Boulevard. His hands balled into fists as he considered the intentions behind LifeCore's actions.

"This doesn't feel like standard business practice for a health insurance company," Ryder murmured.

"What do you mean?"

"Look at these reviews. Seniors, cancer survivors, and stroke victims. People who are too sick or weak to fight back." Ryder turned. "LifeCore is targeting the most vulnerable policyholders."

Will's expression shifted. "You think it's intentional?"

"I think we need to find out. Can you get into their system?"

Will pushed back from the table and exhaled. "My first couple of attempts were blocked, but I'll keep trying until I find a way in."

"Once you're in, start with their executive team. Who's making these decisions? Who's designing the denial policies? I want to understand who we're really fighting." Ryder's hand moved to his scar. "If LifeCore is harming vulnerable people for profit, someone needs to hold them accountable."

A soft knock on the Phoenix House door interrupted them. Ryder looked up to see a thin young man standing on the front steps, shoulders hunched inside a worn Army surplus jacket.

Ricky Nelson.

Ryder's expression must have shown his surprise because Ricky's face shifted to defensive anger.

"You look shocked to see me."

"No, I—"

"Right." Ricky turned to leave. "This was stupid anyway."

"Wait." Ryder stood. "I forgot we agreed you'd come today. My grandmother had a stroke yesterday, and everything else went out of my head."

Ricky paused, his hand on the door frame. "Your grandmother?"

"She's stable, but fighting insurance for rehabilitation coverage. That's what Will and I were working on."

Will looked up from his laptop. "Ricky? I'm Will Cameron." He stood and extended his hand. "Ryder mentioned you might stop by."

Ricky's eyes moved between them, evaluating. "You're the one who runs this place?"

"We both do. I handle operations until we hire someone. Ryder handles the big picture." Will's voice carried understanding. "How long have you been clean?"

The question caught Ricky off guard. He shrugged. "Eight or nine days, I guess."

"Good work. The hardest part is behind you."

"How would you know?"

Will smiled. "Because I just broke triple digits myself. I met Ryder when I decided to get clean."

Something shifted in Ricky's posture. The defensive edge softened. "You were using?"

"Pills, mostly. Started after I got out, lasted a couple of years before I hit bottom." Will gestured toward the conference table. "Want to sit? We can talk about what Phoenix House offers."

Ricky glanced at Ryder, then back at Will. "I guess."

As Will explained the program structure and housing options, Ryder watched Ricky's body language gradually relax. The young veteran asked practical questions about rules, expectations, and timelines. His military bearing became more apparent as his guard dropped.

"What's the catch?" Ricky asked.

"No catch," Will said. "We've both been where you are. The system that trained us to fight abandoned us when we needed help most."

"So you fix people?"

"We help people fix themselves." Absolute conviction underscored Will's voice. "The only requirement is that you want to get better."

Ricky was quiet for a long moment. "I want to get better. I just don't know if I can."

"That's enough to start."

After Will walked Ricky through the paperwork and housing arrangements, the young veteran left with a move-in date in two days. The confidence in his stride was subtle, yet undeniable.

"Good kid," Will said after Ricky left.

"Yeah." Ryder stared at the LifeCore reviews scattered across the table. "How many Rickys are out there? How many people are getting crushed by systems that should protect them?"

"More than we can count."

Ryder leaned onto the table, palms down, imagining all the real people behind the reviews.

"What if someone fought back?"

CHAPTER 6

Ricky Nelson stood on the front steps of Phoenix House Chicago, his military duffel bag slung over one shoulder. The late morning sun filtered through oak leaves, casting shifting patterns across the brick facade of the converted recovery center. His hands trembled as he gripped the black iron railing. Nine days clean, but the withdrawal symptoms still hit in waves that left him nauseated and dizzy.

The building rose three stories above Logan Square's tree-lined streets. Fresh paint covered the peeling siding that had marked the previous owner's financial collapse. The American flag hung from a polished brass pole beside the front door, its fabric snapping in the summer breeze.

Ryder opened the door before Ricky could knock.

"Welcome to Phoenix House." Ryder's gaze swept over the young veteran's appearance—hollow cheeks, dark circles under his eyes, and clothes that hung loose on a skeletal frame. "How are you feeling?"

"Like hell," Ricky chirped.

"That's honest."

The interior smelled of sawdust and floor wax. Hardwood floors gleamed in the morning sunlight, and the walls displayed framed photographs of US military memorials in Washington, DC.

"Ready for the tour?" Ryder asked.

"Yes, sir."

They walked through the facility's common areas. The main floor contained a conference room, kitchen, and living area furnished with comfortable but functional furniture. A television mounted on the wall played local news with the volume low. Two veterans sat at a card table, playing cribbage and drinking coffee.

"This is Ricky Nelson. He's moving in today," Ryder announced.

The older of the two men, with a full beard and rough pink burn scars covering his hands and forearms, looked up from his cards. "Gabe Orosco. Welcome to Phoenix House."

Ricky's eyes lingered on the scars before he could stop himself.

Gabe noticed and held up his hands, turning them in the light. "Electronic countermeasure flares malfunctioned while I was loading them onto a Super Hornet. Burns went from my fingertips to my chest. I spent twenty-three days in the USS Nimitz infirmary crossing the South China Sea." He lowered his hands and returned to his cards. "Got out of the Navy and now I burn myself on my red wine reductions in the kitchen."

Ricky nodded in understanding.

The younger man, in his late twenties with a prosthetic right arm, nodded. "Steve Walsh. Army?"

"Tenth Mountain Division," Ricky said.

"No kidding. Afghanistan?"

"Two tours."

Steve's expression shifted. "I was there too. Helmand Province, 2019."

Something passed between them. Recognition that transcended words. A shared experience that civilians couldn't understand.

"You play cards?" Gabe asked.

"Some."

"Good. We play every morning after group session. Losers do the dishes."

Ryder watched the interaction with satisfaction. The veterans were already building connections, finding common ground through shared service. Phoenix House worked because it created a community among people who understood each other's battles.

They continued upstairs to the bedroom level.

"What were you on?" Ryder asked.

"Opioids."

"Which one?"

Ricky replied without hesitation. "All of them."

Ryder stopped in the hallway and turned to face his new resident. "This won't be easy, but you're doing the right thing."

Ricky nodded. "I know."

They continued down the hall until they reached a door marked with the number seven.

"This is yours." He opened the door to reveal a simple but clean room with a single bed, desk, dresser, and window overlooking the street. "You'll have your own room for now but will share a latrine with three other residents. Linens are in the closet."

Ricky set his duffel bag on the bed and looked around. "It's nice."

"Rules are simple. No drugs, no alcohol, no weapons. Group session every morning at zero eight hundred. Individual counseling twice a week. Kitchen privileges, but you're responsible for your own meals and dishes unless we're doing group dinners."

Ricky nodded, then sat on the bed. The movement seemed to drain whatever energy he'd been holding in reserve.

"You need to rest."

Ricky stretched and yawned. "Yeah, it's been a while since I've slept."

"We have a group dinner tonight at eighteen hundred if you're up for it."

Ryder left Ricky to settle in and walked downstairs to find Will at his laptop in the conference room. He'd volunteered to help Ryder with Nana's appeal process

"How's everything going?"

Will looked up, frustration clear in his expression. "LifeCore is digging in its heels. They're demanding additional medical documentation for Nana that Dr. Asher already provided twice."

Ryder's jaw tightened. Three days had passed since Nana's stroke, and LifeCore was playing games with her recovery while she struggled with basic motor functions.

His phone buzzed with a text message from CID Special Agent Jenna Kendrick.

Thanks for the heads up on the Galindo and Richter connection. Learned more about Michael. I have some news to share next time I'm in Tampa.

Ryder typed back, *Glad it helped, but I'm not in Tampa. I'm in Chicago.*

Are you serious? I'm leaving for Chicago in a day or two. Why are you there?

Nana had a stroke. Fighting with the insurance company.

I'm sorry about Nana. I'll look you up when I get there.

He stared at the last message for a moment. Kendrick was coming to Chicago. He didn't know why she was traveling to the Windy City, but he realized he was looking forward to seeing her. Their relationship had evolved from adversaries to something approaching a professional partnership, built on mutual respect and her willingness not to arrest him.

"Who's that?" Will asked.

"Special Agent Kendrick. She's coming to Chicago."

"The same Army CID investigator who has been hunting you down?"

"I've helped her with information about her fiancé's murder by Richter Pharmaceuticals and saved her from drowning in a sinking car in Florida. I hope she's not hunting me anymore."

Will raised an eyebrow but didn't pursue the topic.

A commotion upstairs interrupted their conversation—raised voices, and then the sound of someone retching violently. Ryder took the stairs two at a time, with Will close behind.

Ricky was in the bathroom, gripping the toilet while his body expelled what little he'd managed to eat for lunch. Sweat covered his face, and his entire frame shook with convulsions.

"Delayed withdrawal," Will mumbled. "Happens sometimes when stress triggers the physical symptoms."

Shadow appeared in the bathroom doorway. The Belgian Malinois had been downstairs in the kitchen but sensed the distress on the second floor. She approached with caution, her calm presence filling the small space.

Ricky's violent shaking subsided. He sat back against the bathroom wall, exhausted and embarrassed.

"I'm sorry. I thought I was past this."

"You are," Will said, leaning against the door frame. "Your body is just remembering what it went through. This is normal."

Shadow stepped closer and settled beside Ricky, her warm bulk providing comfort and stability. The dog's presence seemed to ease something in the young veteran's expression.

"Can I pet her?"

"Sure. Her name is Shadow. Former military K9."

They helped Ricky back to his room, Shadow following and settling on the floor beside the bed. The dog's protective instincts had extended to include Phoenix House's newest resident.

"Rest. Shadow will stay with you for a while," Ryder said as he closed Ricky's door.

Downstairs, Will had returned to his financial analysis.

"How many times did you go through withdrawal symptoms during your first month of recovery?"

Will shook his head as if trying to shake away a bad memory. "More than I wanted to admit."

"But you got through it."

"Yeah. The Appalachian Trail and Phoenix House saved my life."

Ryder nodded, his focus on the blank wall. "I remember."

"Hey, I found something interesting." Will flipped his laptop screen toward Ryder. "I still haven't been able to get past LifeCore's online firewalls, but I was able to get into the Illinois Department of Insurance server and found some interesting data. LifeCore's denial patterns for hip replacements, stroke recovery, and open-heart surgery post-op care are off the charts. All treatments that are most common among senior patients."

The spreadsheet displayed hundreds of denied claims, organized by medical condition and patient demographics.

Ryder studied the data and began pacing. "They're targeting specific populations."

Will returned to his analysis, so Ryder went upstairs to check on his new resident and found Ricky sleeping peacefully with Shadow curled beside the bed. The dog's presence had provided comfort during the afternoon's medical crisis.

The scene reminded him of why Phoenix House mattered. Veterans helping veterans, healing happening through community and understanding rather than bureaucratic systems. Ricky would recover because he was surrounded by people who understood his struggle and were committed to his success.

Unlike LifeCore, which profited from human suffering while hiding behind corporate policies.

Later that day, the residents gathered together in the kitchen for a group dinner. Nothing fancy, just spaghetti and garlic bread prepared by a small team of residents while conversation flowed around the table. Ricky took part, answering questions about his military service and listening to others share their recovery stories.

"How long have you been clean?" Steve asked during dessert.

"Ten days."

"Good work. I'm at ninety-six days."

"What's it like?"

Steve considered the question. "Some days are harder than others. But having people who understand makes all the difference."

Gabe nodded. "First month is about getting through each day. After that, you start thinking about what comes next."

"What came next for you?"

"Purpose. Phoenix House gave me something to fight for besides just staying clean."

After dinner, Ricky helped with the dishes while Shadow remained nearby. The dog's therapeutic presence was working exactly as Ryder had hoped.

Later, Ryder walked Shadow around the neighborhood before bedtime. The Logan Square streets were quiet except for distant traffic and the occasional L train rumbling past on elevated tracks. The area felt secure, residential enough to provide privacy while maintaining access to medical and employment resources.

Back inside Phoenix House, he checked on the residents one last time. Ricky was awake, reading a paperback novel while Shadow slept beside his bed.

"How are you feeling?"

"Better. The other guys helped me understand what to expect."

"Good. Tomorrow we'll start working on employment options and long-term goals."

"Mr. Ryder?"

"Yeah?"

"Why are you doing this? Phoenix House, helping people like me."

Ryder considered the question. The same one Nana had asked about his motivation for protecting others.

"Because somebody needs to."

It fell short of the full answer, though it rang true. Someone had to stand between predators and their prey.

"Get some rest. The real work starts tomorrow."

Ryder had spent his military career eliminating threats to America and its citizens. Since his return from Afghanistan, he'd already taken the lives of two powerful men who'd preyed on the most vulnerable in society, and the world was a better place for it. Those were clearly evil people, and killing them hadn't cost Ryder a minute of sleep, but he'd never expected to call a health insurance company an adversary. Yet here he was, uncovering programs and plots forged in a corner office in a skyscraper in downtown Chicago that were every bit as deadly as Alexander Novick's and Javier Galindo's offenses.

He'd promised his grandmother he'd deliver justice, not vengeance, and he intended to honor his word until it no longer generated the desired results to help Nana recover her quality of life.

If that occurred, Ryder would change tactics and do things his way.

Chapter 7

Will Cameron held his breath, running a hand through his hair as he waited for the VPN to connect. He tapped a new command while he peered at his laptop screen on the Phoenix House conference table and was eager to see if his latest attempt could infiltrate LifeCore's fortress-like servers. The only light in the room came from the screen, casting the edges of his face in a cold, electric glow. A wall clock above the door read twelve forty-two. The three-story brick building that housed the veterans recovery center sat quietly on Logan Square's tree-lined streets, its walls holding the warmth of the summer day.

Most residents had gone to bed hours ago. Ricky Nelson was on his third night at the facility, detox symptoms keeping him restless. Will had heard him pacing earlier, floorboards creaking on the upper level.

Ryder had stepped out twenty minutes ago with Shadow for their late-night stroll around the neighborhood.

Will jumped from his seat and pumped his fist. "I'm in!"

He returned to his seat as LifeCore's internal network unfolded, then he navigated to the claims processing section.

What he found made his stomach turn.

Their system automatically flagged patients over sixty-five for additional review, and several expensive treatments triggered automatic denials. He found dozens of internal transfers in the last week labeled as efficiency bonuses to be peculiar.

His screen flickered. "Unauthorized access detected. Session terminated."

"Son of a bitch," Will shouted. "You're not keeping me out today."

The former Army Intelligence analyst launched proxy connections, bouncing signals through servers across three continents. The cat-and-mouse game stretched for several minutes, each side deploying more advanced techniques until Will found himself inside LifeCore again.

"Yes!"

He moved from claims processing to the LifeCore email server.

The emails between Atwood and Kline spelled it out—deny expensive care to senior patients and hope they die before appealing.

Will copied the files to his encrypted drive, building a case that could expose LifeCore's practices to regulators. Dr. Lee's name appeared in several emails where she raised medical concerns, only to be overruled by Kline's financial calculations.

He dug deeper, following financial trails that led to unusual payments in the accounting system.

The screen turned bright blue and then black. LifeCore's resources outmatched his solo operation, and Will's access was terminated.

He slammed his fist on the table. "Damn it."

Will's mind raced through the implications of what he'd discovered. LifeCore wasn't just denying claims to maximize profits. The internal company efficiency transfers for no apparent reason suggested something darker.

The low rumble of a vehicle engine cut through the night silence.

Will moved to the window and peered through the blinds. A black SUV sat on the street outside Phoenix House, engine running, headlights dark. Tinted windows made it impossible to see inside, but something about its positioning triggered every tactical instinct he'd learned in military intelligence.

He grabbed his phone and activated the security camera system installed during the renovation. Multiple angles showed the SUV from different perspectives, revealing four silhouettes inside. The driver remained behind the wheel while the three passengers sat motionless.

The timing couldn't be coincidental. Less than thirty minutes after LifeCore's security team detected his intrusion, serious men were sitting outside Phoenix House. That level of coordination required planning, resources, and connections far beyond typical corporate cybersecurity.

Will's chest tightened as the pieces clicked into place. LifeCore had been denying care to its most vulnerable policyholders, generating billions in profits by refusing life-saving treatments. Now they'd discovered his digital intrusion and dispatched a team to eliminate the threat he represented. These weren't corporate security guards issuing a cease-and-desist notice. They were professional operators sent to silence him.

The SUV's rear doors opened.

Three men emerged in dark clothing, moving with military precision. They spread out as they approached the building, one bearing right while the other two stayed left. The driver remained in position, engine running for a quick escape.

Will's heart hammered against his ribs.

Ryder had taken Shadow for a walk and was somewhere in Logan Square's residential blocks, too far away to provide backup if these men breached Phoenix House.

Will was alone in a building full of recovering veterans who'd already survived more violence than most people could imagine. He couldn't let corporate assassins add to their trauma.

He moved through the main community room, checking on the residents. Steve Walsh and Gabe Orosco sat at their usual card table, late-night cribbage providing a distraction from the restlessness that plagued many veterans.

"Everything okay, Will?" Steve asked, his prosthetic arm resting beside his cards. Something in his voice suggested his combat instincts were picking up on Will's tension."

Will opened his mouth to speak but answered with a nod.

"You sure everything is okay?" Gabe asked, hazel eyes studying Will's face.

Will forced a smile. "Yeah, everything is fine."

As he climbed the stairs to check another floor, Will's mind churned with everything he needed to worry about. LifeCore had somehow connected his digital intrusion to Phoenix House's physical location. That meant they had intelligence capabilities far beyond typical corporate security.

The rhythmic breathing of deep sleep permeated the hallway from most rooms, but Ricky Nelson's door leaked soft light beneath it. The young veteran was awake, likely fighting the insomnia that came with early recovery.

Will heard Ricky moving inside, pacing again to burn off nervous energy. The kid was fighting his own war against addiction, showing more courage than most people ever mustered. He didn't need to know about the professionals gathering outside Phoenix House, preparing to execute whatever brutal orders LifeCore had given them.

Will descended to his room on the main floor, tactical mind calculating options. The building had multiple exits, but the men outside may have positioned themselves to cover the primary escape routes. They were either planning a coordinated assault or preparing to contain anyone who tried to flee. Either way, their intentions were clearly hostile.

He opened his gun safe and retrieved his Glock 17. The pistol felt familiar, its weight bringing back memories of Miami, when he'd stormed Galindo's compound with Ryder and Shadow.

Footsteps appeared behind him. Will spun, pistol rising.

"Easy," Gabe Orosco said as he raised both hands. Steve Walsh stood shoulder to shoulder beside him.

"'We heard voices outside, and they didn't sound friendly. You need help?' Gabe asked.

Will's first instinct was to send them back to safety. But these weren't civilians. They were former soldiers and sailors who volunteered to defend their countries against armed enemies. The duo could also help defend Phoenix House against armed thugs.

He looked back into the safe at three additional Glock 17s with full magazines. Ten seconds later, Orosco and Walsh held their weapons, and Phoenix House had enough firepower to defend its residents.

"I spotted three armed thugs headed toward Phoenix House with one more waiting in the SUV out front. Walsh, you take the back entrance," Will barked. "Orosco, position yourself in the kitchen so you can provide support to whichever entrance needs it. I'll take the front door."

The trio moved to their defensive positions. Will took the foyer, using the staircase banister as cover while maintaining sight lines on both the front door and the hallway leading to where Orosco and Walsh had positioned themselves. His military training kicked in, muscle memory guiding movements and tactical assessment of the space.

Footsteps creaked across the front porch.

Muffled voices discussed entry methods in tones too low to understand through the heavy wooden door. Will strained to catch fragments of their conversation. Were they planning to breach through multiple entrances or send everyone through one door?

Metallic scraping suggested someone was examining the door lock.

The deadbolt held firm.

Will's breathing steadied as he centered the pistol's sights on the entrance. These men had come to Phoenix House because of his digital intrusion into LifeCore's systems. The muscle sent to teach him a lesson may think he was just another hacker, some technical specialist who would surrender when faced with physical violence.

They would be wrong.

He'd taken lives in Miami when storming Galindo's compound, but Ryder had been with him. The memory of that night played through his mind. Ryder's calm voice directing the assault, Shadow's silent movement through hostile territory, and the certainty that came from fighting alongside someone who always made victory feel inevitable. Orosco and Walsh in the rear helped, but they weren't James Ryder. Nobody had given him the confidence to face any threat like the former Delta Force operator had.

Minutes passed in silence, each second stretching as Will waited for the assault to begin. His attention kept returning to the conversation taking place just feet away. Were they coordinating breach timing?

The weight of responsibility pressed against his chest. If the three veterans defending Phoenix House failed and these corporate killers breached the building, they could murder everyone inside—Ricky Nelson and all the other veterans who'd already survived more violence than most people could imagine. They deserved protection, not another betrayal by the system they'd served.

The sounds from the other side of the door intensified, a chorus of muffled thumps culminating in the hair-raising groan of wood bowing under the weight of men.

He tried to view the men on the security cameras.

"Damn it. Wrong angle."

Will had positioned cameras to watch the entrance to Phoenix House but had neglected to cover the front porch. He was operating blind.

His throat tightened as he imagined the tactical discussion happening beyond the door.

Will raised his pistol, centering sights on the entrance. His finger found the trigger as he prepared to fire upon anyone who came through the door.

CHAPTER 8

Ryder held the leash as Shadow sniffed the wheel of a parked sedan, her nose cataloging information that human senses couldn't process. The Belgian Malinois investigated every detail with the thoroughness that had kept them both alive during combat operations. Her methodical approach reminded Ryder of another investigator who shared the same attention to detail.

Special Agent Jenna Kendrick would arrive in Chicago soon. Her message had been brief but carried an urgency that suggested she'd uncovered something significant. Whatever she'd discovered was important enough to risk her career by sharing it with him.

Shadow stopped, her body tensing. The dog's amber eyes locked on something ahead, ears forward in an alert position. Ryder followed her gaze down the quiet residential street.

A black SUV sat parked along the curb fifty yards from Phoenix House's front entrance. The vehicle looked out of place among renovated bungalows and greystone buildings. Its polished chrome bumper and rims contrasted with the dusty trucks and cars that typically lined these streets.

Ryder counted three figures on Phoenix House's front porch. They moved with the rigid discipline of men who'd received military training.

He maintained his casual pace while his tactical mind logged all the details. The driver remained in the SUV, engine running based on the faint exhaust vapor. Standard procedure for a team expecting to withdraw soon. The three men had positioned themselves to control sight lines and escape routes, but their arrangement revealed impatience. They were preparing to enter Phoenix House.

Shadow's low growl confirmed his assessment. The dog's instincts had identified the same predatory energy that Ryder recognized from countless hostile encounters. These men hadn't come for conversation.

Ryder shortened Shadow's leash and approached the SUV first. The driver was compact, with dark hair and pale skin, suggesting regular indoor work. Ryder had never seen him before, but the man's alertness and positioning identified him as a security team driver rather than muscle.

He shortened his stride and pivoted to a stealth approach as the three men focused on breaking into Phoenix House. Shadow followed suit.

"Can I help you?" Ryder asked, his tone mockingly friendly as he climbed the front steps with Shadow at his side.

“Oh, shit!” the shortest of the three cried out. “It’s him.”

“He said only to proceed if we entered undetected. We have to abort,” the medium height operative replied.

A guttural growl came from the giant standing next to the door. He marched toward Ryder, his hand drifting toward his jacket. Shadow's response was immediate. The Belgian Malinois lunged forward with a snarl that promised violence. The massive man froze, his eyes wide as he stared into Shadow's bared teeth. Only Ryder's tight grip on the leather leash kept the dog from closing the final distance.

“I’m not leaving yet,” the giant hissed.

"Crane said no police or witnesses tonight, so we have to go," the medium-height guy repeated. "We'll come back another time."

The mention of Brandon Crane's name confirmed Ryder's suspicions. Tobias Richter's new head of security had found Phoenix House and deployed a team to send a message or complete the job they'd failed to finish in Tampa.

"Fine," the short guy said. "Let's go."

Ryder didn't move as the three men walked past him toward the waiting SUV. The giant couldn't resist a parting comment as he passed. "Today's your lucky day, but we'll be back soon to finish the job."

The throat punch that followed had the speed and precision of a rattlesnake strike. Ryder's knuckles connected with the man's larynx with surgical accuracy. The massive individual's eyes widened in shock as his airway collapsed. He dropped to his knees, both hands clutching his throat as he gasped for air. His face turned red, then purple, as he struggled to breathe through his damaged windpipe.

The man's two companions reacted instantly. The shorter operative's hand swept toward his jacket, fingers closing around the grip of a concealed pistol. Another man, of medium height with a military bearing, stepped left to create a crossfire angle.

"Big mistake," the shorter man snarled, his weapon clearing the leather holster.

A blur of fur and muscle flashed before Ryder as Shadow's jaws clamped down on the shooter's non-firing arm. Her razor-sharp teeth penetrated flesh and muscle, swinging him off balance. The shorter operative spun around and attempted to line up his sights on the Belgian Malinois, but Shadow kept him off balance.

However, ten seconds into the battle, Shadow made the mistake of trying to pull the man to the ground, giving the shooter time to aim at the former military dog. The operative's finger found the trigger and began to apply pressure.

The SIG Sauer appeared in Ryder's hand with no conscious thought, just muscle memory from thousands of hours of combat training. His first shot caught the shorter man center mass before the operative could fire. The hollow-point round punched through his sternum, the impact spinning him sideways. His unfired weapon clattered across the porch boards.

Ryder fired a second time, turning the gaping hole in the man's chest into a crimson canyon before he collapsed onto the front yard grass.

The medium height operative had his pistol halfway drawn when Ryder's muzzle tracked left. Fear blanched his face, visible even in the low light.

"Drop it, or you're next."

The operative complied.

“Why are you here?” Ryder demanded.

“We, we—” the medium height operative stammered. “We were told you were getting too close and had to be stopped.”

“Too close to what?”

Ryder noticed the giant move to his knees, so he rushed down the steps and stood over him to prevent any planned counterattacks. The giant's bloodshot eyes shifted between his dead companion and Ryder's unwavering pistol.

"You two have thirty seconds to grab your partner and get out of here."

Both men stared back at Ryder, as if unsure whether it was safe to move.

"Come on." Ryder delivered a kick to get the giant moving. "The cops will be here soon, and you don't want to be carrying a dead body when they get here. Crane would not be happy."

Footsteps pounded inside Phoenix House. The front door burst open, revealing Will with his Glock 17 raised in a two-handed grip. His eyes swept the scene—one limp body, one man with hands raised, and Ryder standing over the gasping giant.

"I heard shots. You okay?"

"Fine," Ryder barked. "Check the street."

Will moved to the edge of the porch, scanning for additional threats. The black SUV's engine revved as the driver realized the operation had gone sideways. Tires squealed against the pavement as the vehicle raced away from Phoenix House.

"Driver's fleeing. Should I pursue?"

"Negative. Grab a tarp from the backyard."

"Okay, but first I have to let Orosco and Walsh know we're all clear," Will announced.

"Tell them to make sure nobody comes out front."

"Got it."

After Will vanished through the front door, the giant managed to draw enough air to speak. "You killed Oleg," he wheezed.

"Oleg chose death when he pointed a weapon at my dog," Ryder replied. "Not something I recommend."

He kept his pistol trained on the giant operative. "When Will gets back with the tarp, get Oleg out of here."

"And you're going to deliver a message to Crane. Tell him Phoenix House is off limits. Tell him what happens when his people threaten my team."

The man struggled to his feet, still holding his throat. "This isn't over."

"It is for Oleg." Ryder gestured toward the body. "If I see you again, you'll be in the same position he's in now."

Will returned with a heavy-duty tarp and handed it to the giant. He waved the third operative down from the porch to help.

A minute later, the two operatives disappeared into the night. Ryder and Will began the methodical process of eliminating evidence. Shell casings went into a plastic bag, and blood was scrubbed from the porch boards.

"I can't believe they got here so fast," Will muttered as they walked through the front entrance of Phoenix House.

Ryder frowned. "What do you mean?"

"I was in LifeCore's secure server when they caught me. When they—"

"Hold on." Ryder closed the door behind him and engaged the deadbolt. "Tell me exactly what happened."

Will gestured toward the conference room, where his laptop still displayed LifeCore's online portal. "I got inside the LifeCore system. I found emails between Atwood and Kline that prove they're denying care to seniors and hoping they die before appeals are processed."

Ryder's jaw tightened as he absorbed the implications. "How deep did you go?"

"Deep enough to trigger their security protocols. Someone noticed the intrusion and traced it back here." Will ran his hands through his hair. "When I saw those men on the porch, the speed that LifeCore's security team got here surprised me."

"They weren't from LifeCore. Those were Tobias Richter's men." Ryder moved to the window to check the street. A Chicago Police cruiser rolled past Phoenix House without stopping. "They're led by Brandon Crane, his new head of security, who was with Galindo the night we took him out in Miami."

Will's expression shifted from relief to confusion. "How do you know that?"

"One of them mentioned Crane's name. Plus, they were military-trained operatives prepared to kill me... and maybe you."

The adrenaline that had sustained Will through the confrontation was beginning to fade, leaving exhaustion and anger in its wake. He slumped into a chair at the conference table, his laptop screen casting blue light across his features.

"Shit," Will exhaled. "Now we have two groups to worry about."

"I'll worry about security. What did you find out about LifeCore?"

"I found healthy young people getting approved for elective treatments while seniors are denied basic rehabilitation therapy." Will's voice was thick with disgust.

"This is solid intelligence, Will. This may be enough to expose their operations to federal regulators and trigger criminal investigations."

Will looked up from the laptop, his eyes bright with possibility. "Or enough to help you take Atwood out permanently. I can get you the building schematics of LifeCore's headquarters, security codes, and Atwood's penthouse on the fifty-second floor. Everything you need to deliver justice the way you delivered it to Novick and Peter Richter."

The offer hung in the air between them. Will's transformation from reluctant ally to eager partner mirrored the progression Ryder had observed in others who were pushed beyond their breaking point by institutional corruption. The system's failure to protect the innocent encouraged vigilantes to take matters into their own hands.

Will must have taken Ryder's silence as indecision. "These insurance executives are murdering people just as surely as any terrorist or cartel boss you've eliminated. They're just using denial letters instead of bullets."

Ryder couldn't argue with the logic. Andre Atwood and Chad Kline had weaponized bureaucracy to eliminate inconvenient patients, turning LifeCore's claims processing department into an instrument of systematic murder. Their victims died slowly and invisibly, abandoned by a system designed to profit from their suffering.

"I promised Nana I'd try legitimate channels first. I want to honor that promise, but more than that, I don't want to upset her while she's still recovering. The stress of knowing I've put myself in harm's way to help her could set back her rehabilitation."

Will's disappointment was evident, but he nodded. "What about Richter's people? They'll be back."

"Let them come. We'll protect Phoenix House and its residents from any threats, just like we did tonight."

He moved to the security panel near the front entrance. "Set up the additional monitoring protocols we discussed. Install cameras to capture license plates and facial recognition data for any hostile operatives who return to the area."

Will nodded. "I'm on it."

"Tomorrow we build a case that regulatory agencies can't ignore."

Will gathered his materials from the conference table, his movements slow as exhaustion claimed him. "What if the system fails again? What if they bury the evidence or buy their way out of consequences?"

Ryder's expression didn't change, but something cold and final flickered in his eyes. "Then we'll talk about those building schematics."

The former Delta Force operator would honor his promise to Nana and focus on her recovery, but he wouldn't wait forever. Atwood and Kline needed to be stopped before they killed more innocent victims, using any possible means.

CHAPTER 9

The late afternoon sun slanted through the windows of Nana's Andersonville brownstone, casting long shadows across the hardwood floors. Ryder watched from the doorway as Karla Sandoval helped Nana with her afternoon medications and light stretching exercises.

"Let's try moving that left arm a little more, Mrs. Ryder." Karla's voice was patient and soothing. "Small movements, nothing that hurts."

Nana sat in her recliner, her left side still weak and uncoordinated from the stroke. Sweat beaded on her forehead from the simple effort of lifting her arm.

"There you go," Karla encouraged. "Remember to take your blood thinner in four hours. I'll leave a note on the kitchen counter."

The insurance company had denied adequate physical therapy, approving only basic home healthcare for the first week out of the hospital. Nana would be on her own in one more day unless he could figure out another way to pay for her care.

Karla helped Nana adjust her position in the recliner, checking that her left leg was supported. The home healthcare nurse's movements were efficient and gentle, demonstrating her experience of both the physical and emotional challenges of stroke recovery.

"Perfect," Karla said, gathering her supplies. "I'll see you tomorrow morning at nine."

Ryder moved into the kitchen to give them space for their goodbyes. Through the window, he could see the yellow roses beside the front steps swaying in the warm August breeze. The coffee maker gurgled as it finished brewing, the sound mixing with Karla's gentle reminders from the next room about medication schedules and safety precautions.

Twenty minutes later, Karla emerged from the family room carrying her medical bag. Ryder noted the concern in her eyes.

"How's she doing?" he asked.

"Your grandmother is a fighter, but she's frustrated." Karla sighed. "The stroke affected her left side. Ordinary tasks like bathing or getting dressed are challenges now."

Ryder studied Karla's expression. "But?"

"She needs regular, intensive physical therapy to have any chance of regaining full independence. The basic care I'm providing helps with daily living, but it's not rehabilitation." Karla paused. "Without proper PT, she'll plateau at her current level of function."

"What would you recommend if insurance weren't a factor?"

"Based on what I've seen work well for most patients, she needs daily physical therapy sessions for at least two months. Balance training, coordination exercises, and strength building. The brain can rewire itself after a stroke, but only with ongoing therapy." Karla's voice carried professional frustration. "Home healthcare keeps her safe and comfortable, but it won't restore the independence she desires."

The reality hit Ryder like a physical blow. Nana's current level of care meant she could lose her independence. Everything she could do two weeks ago would be more difficult or require a monumental effort for the proud, independent woman. LifeCore's decision to deny adequate physical and occupational therapy condemned her to permanent dependency.

"How do you like working with her?" Ryder asked.

"Mrs. Ryder is one of my favorite patients. She never complains, follows all medical instructions, and maintains such a positive attitude despite everything." Karla's expression softened. "She reminds me of my grandmother."

"Would you be interested in continuing beyond what insurance covers?"

Karla's eyebrows lifted. "You mean a private arrangement for her home healthcare?"

"Exactly. Same schedule, same care, just outside the insurance system."

"I'd love to help her, but private home healthcare is expensive. My usual rate is one hundred and fifty dollars per day for two visits."

Ryder did the mental calculation. Thirty days would cost forty-five hundred dollars. It was a substantial amount after investing in Phoenix House Chicago, but he still had some reserves in his Bitcoin account—a small price to pay for Nana's recovery.

"I'll get you the full month in two days."

"Great," Karla said. "Same time tomorrow."

They shook hands, and Ryder felt some of the tension in his shoulders ease. Nana would have the basic care she needed, even if LifeCore continued denying her treatment.

After Karla left, Ryder found Nana resting in her recliner.

"Tough day?"

"Frustrating day," she corrected without opening her eyes. "I tried to make coffee this morning and spilled grounds all over the counter."

"Minor setbacks."

"Everything feels like a setback lately."

Ryder's phone buzzed with a text. The delivery driver was at the front door with dinner from Nana's favorite Italian restaurant.

"Dinner's here," he said.

Ryder stood close enough to assist if needed as she stood, her left arm trembling with the effort. Walking to the dining room required immense concentration, but she made it with the help of the wall. Her independence, even in small measures, was something to protect.

Nana ate slowly, her left hand still clumsy with the fork, but she cleaned half her plate.

"Karla's going to continue working with you after the insurance runs out," Ryder said.

Nana paused mid-bite. "Insurance is ending?"

"Yes, but I'm paying for her to continue for another month."

"James, that's too expensive."

"Less expensive than watching you lose your independence."

The same words he'd used with Dr. Asher a week ago. The situation hadn't changed, but his resolve had strengthened. Whatever it cost to keep Nana safe and on the road to recovery, he'd find a way to pay for it.

After dinner, he helped her to the family room, where she settled onto her favorite recliner. The evening news ritual had been part of their routine since he was a boy. Channel Seven at six o'clock, watching the world beyond Andersonville unfold across the television screen.

The lead story covered a warehouse fire on the south side of Chicago, then transitioned to a multiple-car accident that closed all inbound lanes of the Eisenhower Expressway for two hours. The third story made Ryder's blood run cold.

"Earlier today, LifeCore Health Insurance celebrated a major milestone," a reporter announced outside a gleaming glass tower overlooking State Street and the Chicago River. "The company officially opened its new headquarters, completing its move from the previous location near O'Hare Airport to the top thirty office floors of this fifty-two-story office tower in one of Chicago's most prestigious buildings."

Video footage panned across the building's facade, reflecting the late afternoon sun like a monument to corporate success. Ryder's jaw tightened as he recognized the building from his previous visits to downtown Chicago.

Andre Atwood appeared on screen in a tailored Navy blue suit, scissors in hand for the ribbon-cutting ceremony. His smile was broad and confident, the expression of a man who'd never doubted his right to occupy this space. Chad Kline stood at his side like a loyal lieutenant, serious and attentive.

"Mr. Atwood, what attracted LifeCore to this location?" a reporter asked as Atwood positioned his scissors over the ribbon.

His smile widened as he gestured to the surroundings. "Just look at this." He beamed with pride. "This building represents excellence, and that's what LifeCore delivers to our policyholders every day."

The camera captured the ribbon falling to the ground as applause echoed from the assembled crowd. City officials, business leaders, and media representatives celebrated LifeCore's arrival at the northern end of Chicago's financial district.

Atwood moved to the podium, his expression growing serious as he leaned toward the microphones. "LifeCore has experienced explosive growth because we focus on what matters most, delivering exceptional value to our policyholders. When you provide superior service, success always follows."

Ryder felt Nana's hand find his arm. Her grip was weak, but her message was clear. She was listening to the same lies that had condemned her to inadequate medical care.

A different reporter stepped forward. "Mr. Atwood, have you seen the recent comments in the Chicago Tribune regarding accusations that LifeCore denies care to seniors that other insurance providers often cover?"

Atwood's smile faltered for just a moment, a micro-expression that revealed his true feelings about the question from the newspaper article. He recovered quickly, the political mask sliding back into place.

"I haven't seen those specific comments, but LifeCore follows the highest medical standards. Our medical team reviews every case."

The reporter pressed further. "Are you aware that your denial rates for seniors are higher than industry averages?"

Atwood's jaw tightened. "Our decisions are based on medical necessity, not demographics. Every policyholder receives the same careful consideration regardless of age."

The lie hung in the air like smoke. Ryder had seen the evidence of LifeCore's targeting of vulnerable policyholders through Nana's case and Will's research.

The news segment ended with shots of the new headquarters lobby, showing Atwood and Kline shaking hands with Chicago's elite in politics and business.

Nana reached for the remote and muted the television. The silence in the room felt heavy with unspoken understanding.

"He's lying," she whispered.

"Yeah, I know."

"They're celebrating while people like me fight for basic medical care."

Ryder studied his grandmother's profile in the dim light from the television. The stroke had delivered a significant setback, but it hadn't broken her spirit. She understood what they were facing.

"The appeals process could take months," he said. "Even if we win, it might be too late to help your recovery."

"And if we lose?"

"Then we keep paying for your therapy ourselves."

Nana turned to look at him. "What about the other people they're denying? The families who can't afford to pay out of pocket?"

The question cut to the heart of what Ryder had been thinking since watching Atwood's performance. How many families were watching their loved ones deteriorate because some corporate algorithm had determined their lives weren't worth the investment?

"I don't know," he admitted.

"But you're thinking about finding out."

Ryder met her eyes. The woman who'd raised him could still read him like a book. She knew he was considering options beyond the appeals process.

"Whatever you're thinking, whatever you're planning, don't let your anger over what they're doing to me cloud your judgment."

Ryder nodded, but his mind was already moving beyond the appeals process. Atwood and Kline hid behind corporate policies and legal protections while real families faced impossible choices, and lawmakers and regulators had created the system to protect companies like LifeCore from accountability.

"I won't," Ryder assured her.

Ryder secured his grandmother's arm to steady her as she shuffled to her bedroom. Her steps were steadier this time, proving that the limited physical therapy was working. She settled into bed with Shadow curled at her feet.

"Get some rest," he said. "Karla will be here tomorrow morning."

"James?"

He paused in the doorway.

"Whatever you decide to do, be careful. I can't lose you, too."

"You won't."

Ryder made his way back downstairs and stepped onto the front porch. The yellow roses beside the steps released their fragrance into the warm night air. The street was quiet except for the distant sound of traffic.

His phone buzzed with a text from Will. *Just intercepted a press release from LifeCore's investor relations firm about their upcoming quarterly earnings report. It's unbelievable. Can you meet?*

He typed back, *Phoenix House tomorrow. Ten hundred.*

Ryder settled into the chair Nana used to watch the world from her front porch. He already knew what the press release would say and what the reaction would be from the financial community. Wall Street would heap praise on LifeCore executives for the efficient operation of their health insurance business. However, the financial news organizations wouldn't report that LifeCore had crossed the line from cold-hearted capitalism to systematic murder of their sickest and most vulnerable policyholders.

He was committed to honoring his promise to Nana and letting the appeals process play out a little longer, but she wasn't the only victim in this crime. Ryder's mental clock was ticking closer to the alarm he'd set, marking the deadline of his willingness to pursue justice within the system.

Once that alarm went off in his head, Atwood's days were numbered.

CHAPTER 10

Tobias Richter stood behind his mahogany desk on the sixty-second floor of Richter Tower, the Manhattan skyline stretching endlessly beyond the floor-to-ceiling windows. The air conditioning hummed against the humid morning air, mixing with the distant rumble of traffic below. Coffee steamed from a handmade Tuscan ceramic cup.

He adjusted his Ferragamo tie and tapped the video conference interface embedded in his desk. Two screens flickered to life, revealing faces he'd selected to rebuild what James Ryder had destroyed.

"Good morning." His voice held the executive authority that had built an empire. "Welcome to the Richter family of businesses."

The woman on the left screen sat in a sterile office in Tysons Corner, Virginia. Tracy Sutter, forty-nine, a former pharmaceutical executive with Pfizer. Behind her, diplomas from Johns Hopkins and Harvard Business School decorated the wall.

"Mr. Richter." Her voice was steady despite the weight of stepping into her first CEO role. "I'm honored to be leading Richter Pharmaceuticals forward."

The second screen displayed a man sitting in Peter Richter's former Dubai office. Mason Carter, fifty-four, retired Army colonel with extensive experience in defense contracting. A charcoal business suit had replaced his desert camouflage uniform, but his military bearing remained unmistakable. The office's panoramic view of Dubai's glittering towers provided an impressive backdrop.

"Sir." Carter's tone was crisp and professional. "I understand Richter Defense Systems has significant opportunities ahead."

Tobias nodded, studying the faces of the individuals who would turn around Richter Enterprises. The pharmaceutical division had lost Alexander Novick to Ryder's ruthless administration of justice. RDS was crippled after Peter's death, leaving a void that extended far beyond operational leadership. These replacements represented more than personnel changes. They were the foundation for rebuilding everything Ryder had torn down.

"You both have your work cut out for you." Tobias paced behind his desk. The movement helped him think, a habit developed during decades of high-stakes negotiations. "I have high expectations for both organizations and expect you to maintain our previous growth and profit results."

Sutter leaned forward. "The pharmaceutical division's revenue targets for Q4 appear aggressive given the recent... disruptions."

"Disruptions." Tobias let the word hang in the air, finding it inadequate for describing Ryder's assault on his empire. "That's one way to characterize the systematic murder of key personnel. But yes, Tracy, the targets remain firm. Our investors expect consistent performance regardless of temporary setbacks."

Carter's expression hardened. "Defense contracts in Afghanistan generated significant margins before the operation halted. Rebuilding those relationships will require substantial time and political capital."

"Time we don't have." His voice carried an edge that made both executives shift uncomfortably. "Which brings me to our immediate priorities."

The elevator's soft chime interrupted the conversation. Tobias glanced toward the polished steel doors as they parted to reveal Brandon Crane. The former Navy SEAL emerged with his characteristic measured stride, his black suit concealing the shoulder holster beneath his left arm. His pale blue eyes scanned the office with professional vigilance while his short strawberry-blond hair caught the morning sunlight streaming through the windows.

"Mr. Crane." Tobias gestured toward a leather chair positioned near the desk. "Please take a seat. We were just finishing our call about operational challenges."

Crane settled into the chair as Tobias turned back to the video screens.

"I expect to see turnaround plans on my desk from both of you at the end of next week. Questions?"

Sutter and Carter remained silent.

"Good. Now get to work." Tobias tapped the screen on his desk, and it turned black.

Crane sat expressionless throughout the exchange. His tactical background had prepared him for many scenarios, but corporate operations calls weren't among them.

"Now, for the reason I invited you here, Mr. Crane." Tobias moved to the window overlooking Central Park. The morning sun glinted off the Central Park Reservoir and painted the trees in shades of gold and green. "Richter Enterprises and I have made significant investments in LifeCore insurance. Based on the latest information I've received on earnings, we will get a substantial boost from those investments."

Crane's confusion deepened. "I thought the earnings for LifeCore wouldn't be released until tomorrow."

Tobias shook his head, allowing a thin smile to play across his lips. "You still have so much to learn, Mr. Crane. Inside information moves faster than press releases when you maintain the right relationships. We need to protect this investment, and once again, James Ryder is involved."

The name hung in the air like a physical presence. Crane's posture shifted from confusion to focused attention, his security instincts engaging.

"Ryder's grandmother is a policyholder of LifeCore." Richter's voice carried satisfaction at the symmetry of the situation. "When Chad Kline informed me of this connection, I asked him to eliminate as many benefits as possible to inflict additional pain on James Ryder."

Crane processed this information. "Denying medical coverage as psychological warfare is... creative."

"It's business." Tobias corrected, though he appreciated the compliment. "Ryder has cost us hundreds of millions in destroyed assets and eliminated personnel. Every pressure point we can identify becomes fair game."

Through the windows, a helicopter circled above Central Park, its rotors creating tiny shadows that danced across the manicured landscape. Tobias watched its path while organizing his thoughts about the next phase of operations.

"Do we have current intelligence on Ryder's location and knowledge of LifeCore?" the head of Richter Enterprises asked.

"I had a team testing the readiness of Ryder's new recovery house in Chicago, with orders to eliminate him as long as they left no connection to Richter Enterprises." Crane's tone became more confident as the conversation shifted to his area of expertise. "They made contact two days ago, and it didn't go well. We've already lost one man."

"Ryder?" Tobias asked.

"Yes. Oleg attempted to shoot his dog during a standoff, and Ryder killed him and disarmed the other two men."

Tobias noted the details. He did not know, nor had any concern about Oleg, but the aggressiveness to shut down Ryder pleased Tobias. His former head of security, Marcus Jensen, had been effective in his own brutal way, but Crane brought the hard-hitting approach of military special operations to their security challenges.

"We are beyond probing, given current circumstances." His voice hardened with decision. "I want you to escalate the mission to definitive personnel elimination."

The words descended like a death sentence pronounced from sixty-two floors above the city.

Crane's expression didn't change, though something predatory flickered behind his pale blue eyes. "Parameters?"

"I want that thorn in my side removed for good." The calm delivery made the order more chilling than any dramatic pronouncement could have achieved. "Whatever resources you require, whatever collateral complications arise, eliminate James Ryder permanently."

"Timeline?"

"Immediate. Kline's team caught Ryder's sidekick, Will Cameron, hacking into their systems, so they may already have incriminating information on LifeCore. Every day Ryder remains operational increases the risk of investment loss for me and the organization." Tobias moved to his desk. "Coordinate with our Chicago contacts for any local resources you require."

Crane stood, his movements carrying the coiled energy of a man transitioning from planning to execution. "I'll need detailed intelligencc on thc veterans facility and Ryder's operational patterns."

"Whatever you need. Our private investigation firm has comprehensive surveillance data. Financial resources are unlimited. Political protection is available if complications arise."

The security chief moved toward the elevator, and the steel doors closed behind him, leaving Tobias alone in his office overlooking the city that had made his fortune possible. Sixty-two floors below, millions of people conducted their daily business, unaware of the deadly chess game playing out in the corporate towers above them.

The reflection staring back from the window showed a man who had taken some recent losses but remained far from defeated. Ryder's quest for justice had inflicted severe damage, eliminating key personnel and disrupting established revenue streams. But Tobias Richter had survived worse setbacks during his climb to power.

The LifeCore investment would generate substantial returns when its quarterly earnings exceeded Wall Street expectations. Chad Kline's algorithm had eliminated medical expenses while maintaining legal compliance, creating the profit margins that would justify Richter's confidence in his investment partners.

Ryder's grandmother represented a brilliant form of psychological warfare. Every denied treatment authorization would remind the former Delta Force operator that his campaign against Richter Enterprises carried personal costs. The systematic cruelty of corporate healthcare denials would inflict emotional damage that physical threats could never achieve.

His phone buzzed with a text message from Crane. *Team realigned. Elimination mission engaged.*

Richter's coffee had grown cold during the conference call, the aroma no longer wafting from the cup and filling the room. Tobias touched his intercom.

"Please prepare fresh coffee and schedule lunch with Senator Morrison's chief of staff. I want to discuss defense appropriations for next year's budget cycle."

"Yes, sir," Richter's assistant replied. "Anything else?"

"Contact our legal department. I want a comprehensive review of our liability exposure regarding the pharmaceutical seizure in Florida. Assume federal attention will intensify."

"Understood."

The intercom clicked off, leaving Tobias alone with his thoughts and the city spreading beyond his windows. Somewhere in Chicago, James Ryder was continuing his methodical destruction of everything Tobias had built. But the former Delta Force operator had made a critical mistake by threatening Richter Enterprises while maintaining personal attachments.

Ryder's grandmother represented a vulnerability that tactical brilliance couldn't protect. The systematic denial of her medical care would inflict psychological damage while demonstrating the reach of Richter's influence. Every delayed treatment authorization would send a message about the consequences of challenging Richter's institutional power.

The morning sun climbed higher, filling the office with brilliant light that reflected off every polished surface. Tobias felt the familiar surge of confidence that came with decisive action, the satisfying sensation of chess pieces moving across a board with checkmate lining up perfectly.

James Ryder had chosen to wage war against an empire built on political connections, unlimited financial resources, and the willingness to eliminate any threat to its established power. The former soldier's tactical skills were impressive, but they couldn't overcome the institutional advantages that money and influence provided.

The battle lines were drawn, and Tobias Richter intended to end the menace to his empire and himself once and for all.

CHAPTER 11

The high-pitched whine of a leaf blower cut through the morning air as landscapers worked the front yard of Phoenix House's next door neighbor. The aroma of fresh-cut grass mixed with smoky bacon sizzling in the kitchen, where one resident perfected his new breakfast routine. Voices drifted from the dining room, residents discussing their plans for a group session later that morning.

Ryder returned from the shower after a morning run and found Will peering at his laptop on the conference room table, his lanky frame bent over spreadsheets displaying LifeCore's stock performance. Numbers telling a story of corporate success built on ruthless efficiency.

"Nice run?" Will asked without looking up from his screen.

"It's humid out, but I still got three miles in."

"How's Nana doing?"

"She's a fighter. Would be doing much better if she had more physical therapy." Ryder poured coffee from the machine in the adjacent kitchen. "How are the new Phoenix House residents adjusting?"

"Most are doing well, but I'm concerned about Ricky. He's trying hard, but he's struggling with sobriety more than the others."

Ryder studied his friend's face, noting the dark circles under his eyes. "You've been at this a while."

"Someone has to keep track of LifeCore's war against grandparents." Will gestured toward his laptop screen. "Check this out. Their stock jumped another four percent in pre-market trading. Investors are celebrating their quarterly earnings announcement."

The financial charts showed LifeCore's stock price in a steady climb over the past six months. Share values had increased from forty-two dollars to fifty-seven dollars, rewarding shareholders for the company's growing denials of medical care.

"We should have used some of the money left in the Bitcoin account and bought LifeCore stock." Will turned the screen toward Ryder. "We'd be up twenty-one percent on that money in just over a week."

Ryder sipped his coffee, tasting bitterness that had nothing to do with the brew. "Or we could short LifeCore stock now while the optimism is highest."

Will looked up from his laptop. "Shorting only makes sense if you think the stock will go down. It's betting against the company by selling shares at current prices, then buying them back later, at a lower price." He turned back to the chart displaying LifeCore's explosive growth. "Unless something changes at LifeCore, I don't see that stock dropping anytime soon. Are you sure you want me to short LifeCore?"

"Fair point. Hold off for now."

They moved toward the kitchen, where a steady dripping sound indicated a leak under the sink. Ryder crouched beside the cabinet, examining the plumbing. Water pooled beneath the primary supply line, requiring immediate attention to prevent damage to the floor.

"Hand me that wrench." Ryder pointed toward the toolbox on the counter.

As Will passed him the tool, Ryder continued, "We need to pull the job posting for a house manager. Money's getting tight. Can you stay a little longer?"

"I can handle operations until we hire someone here, but I can't stay forever," Will replied as he watched Ryder work under the sink. "They need me back at the Phoenix House in Falls Church. Plus, I'd like to see my girlfriend live and not just on a phone screen."

"I appreciate your help. We'll hire someone as soon as we can."

Ryder tightened the pipe connection, testing it for leaks. The temporary fix would hold until they could arrange for professional repairs. Phoenix House Chicago operated on lean budgets, requiring careful management of every dollar spent.

The silence stretched between them as Ryder considered the financial pressures mounting around their mission. Helping veterans required resources they couldn't always guarantee, especially while fighting government bureaucrats for grant money and insurance companies that deployed armies of lawyers to deny legitimate claims.

Ryder's phone buzzed against the kitchen counter. The caller ID showed Karla Sandoval, Nana's home healthcare nurse. It was unusual for her to call this early.

"Karla? Is everything okay?"

"Mr. Ryder, I'm in the emergency room with your grandmother." Karla's voice carried stress and fatigue. "She had a dangerous fall this morning while trying to get dressed. She hit her head on the dresser corner."

Ryder's grip tightened on the phone. "How bad?"

"She's conscious and talking, but there's significant bruising on the left side of her face. Dr. Asher wants to keep her overnight for observation, but LifeCore is refusing to cover admission."

The familiar pattern repeated itself. Nana needed medical care, LifeCore found reasons to deny coverage, and the system protected corporate profits while vulnerable people suffered.

"I'm on my way."

"Northwest Community Hospital. Emergency department."

Ryder ended the call and grabbed his keys from the counter. "Nana fell and hit her head. LifeCore is refusing to cover hospital admission."

Will closed his laptop. "Want me to come with you?"

"No, stay here and keep an eye on the residents. I'll handle this."

The drive to Northwest Community Hospital took twenty-two minutes through morning traffic. Ryder's mind raced through contingencies, calculating the cost of private payment for hospital admission while reviewing LifeCore's pattern of denying seniors the care they needed most.

He found Nana in a wheelchair near the emergency department's exit, wearing a hospital gown. Visible bruising covered the left side of her face from temple to jawline, and her hair was matted with dried blood from a scalp wound that had required three stitches.

Dr. Asher stood nearby, her expression radiating deep frustration. The physician's professional demeanor barely contained her disgust with the insurance company's decision.

"Mr. Ryder." Dr. Asher's voice was tight. "I feel like a broken record, but the insurance company has determined that your grandmother's injuries don't warrant hospital admission. They're classifying this as bumps and bruises managed through outpatient care, even though these injuries are directly related to her stroke recovery."

Ryder kneeled beside Nana's wheelchair, studying her condition. The bruising was extensive, and her left eye was swollen shut.

She needed medical observation to monitor for signs of concussion or internal bleeding.

"How are you feeling, Nana?"

"Like I got hit by a truck." Her voice was weak but steady. "Stupid dresser jumped out and attacked me."

Despite everything, she was making jokes. The woman who'd taught him to find humor in difficult situations was fighting to maintain her dignity while corporate executives counted profits from her denied care.

Karla appeared beside them, carrying discharge paperwork and a small bag of Nana's personal items. "I tried to get her case elevated to someone higher at LifeCore, but their medical reviewer said the injuries don't meet their criteria for inpatient care."

Ryder kept his expression neutral, but inside his chest, something cold and dangerous was crystallizing. LifeCore had crossed another line, endangering his grandmother's health to save money on hospital costs.

"We'll take her home."

Dr. Asher handed him a discharge instruction sheet. "Watch for signs of confusion, persistent headaches, or changes in vision. If any of those symptoms develop, bring her back right away."

"Understood."

Ryder helped Karla transfer Nana from the wheelchair to her vehicle, supporting her weight as she settled into the passenger seat. The process was slow and careful, requiring gentle movements to avoid aggravating her injuries.

"Thank you for calling me." He squeezed Karla's shoulder. "I'll follow you back to Nana's house."

"She's going to need extra attention for the next few days. Besides the physical injuries, her confidence also took a big hit."

Ryder nodded and walked to Nana's car, which he'd borrowed after parking his converted bus in an RV storage lot while she recovered. The two-year-old white Toyota Camry that Ryder had bought for Nana earlier that year started, its engine settling into a familiar idle.

Once they reached Nana's house on the north side of Chicago, Ryder sat alone in the car for a moment, his hands gripping the steering wheel. The cruelty LifeCore could inflict on innocent people was beyond comprehension.

His fist connected with the dashboard, leaving a dent in the plastic surface. The physical release felt inadequate compared to the rage building inside his chest. Someone needed to pay for what they were doing to Nana and thousands of other policyholders.

Ryder pulled out his phone and called Will.

"How is she?"

"Bruised and battered, but stable. LifeCore refused to cover hospital admission for observation."

"That's criminal."

"It gets worse. They're calling it bumps and bruises that don't warrant inpatient care."

Will was quiet for several seconds. "Is there anything I can do?"

"Watch LifeCore's stock run up after the market opens and then short as much as we can afford."

"Ryder, I get you're pissed at LifeCore right now, but they just blew away earnings expectations. Something dramatic would have to happen to the company to reverse that upward trend."

"Just short LifeCore." Ryder's voice was ice.

Will paused, understanding the implications. "Does that mean what I think it means? When?"

"Short it before the market closes today." Ryder hung up.

He stared through the windshield at Nana's house, where yellow roses bloomed beside the front steps despite the late summer heat. They were the same flowers she'd tended since he was a boy, representing beauty and resilience in a world that often showed neither quality.

The mental alarm in his head was ringing like a piercing siren, screaming a primal, bone-deep warning. Appeals processes, regulatory oversight, and legal challenges move at a glacier's pace for people who need immediate care. By the time justice worked its way through official channels, more vulnerable patients would suffer or die.

LifeCore, under the guidance of Andre Atwood, had crossed the line from aggressive business practices to something approaching murder, using artificial intelligence and bureaucratic processes to deny medical care to the people who needed it most.

It was nearing the time for solutions outside the system.

Ryder climbed the stairs and entered Nana's house through the front door. He'd leave the management of Phoenix House up to his Army veteran partner for a few days. Will also had to place the bet against LifeCore's stock price by shorting it before the market closes.

Soon, the executives would learn their critical mistake. They hadn't wounded vulnerable prey, but had instead awakened an apex predator that handles threats the only way it knows how—it destroys them.

Justice always finds its way home.

CHAPTER 12

The rented Toyota SUV vibrated beneath Special Agent Jenna Kendrick as she navigated the washboard streets of Chicago's northwest side. She drove with her windows down after a recent storm had brought cooler temperatures. A black sedan puttered ahead of her below the speed limit until Kendrick passed the lost or confused motorist.

Her auburn hair, pulled into a tight bun, had loosened during the two-hour flight from Virginia, with strands escaping around her temples. The tan line on her left ring finger stood out against the steering wheel, a visible reminder of Michael York's engagement ring that she'd removed for the first time. Losing her Navy SEAL fiancé to an experimental drug still stung like a recent slap.

Logan Square emerged around her as she followed the GPS directions. Mature oak trees formed a canopy over streets lined with brick bungalows and three-story greystone buildings. The neighborhood felt established yet transforming, like a butterfly emerging from its cocoon.

Phoenix House Chicago occupied a converted recovery center in the middle of a block, its fresh paint and new windows standing out among the weathered buildings. A simple yard sign near the sidewalk read, "Phoenix House Veteran Recovery Center."

Kendrick parked two blocks away, positioning the SUV to maintain visual contact. She pulled out her binoculars and began her assessment.

Movement in her peripheral vision caught her attention. The black sedan she'd passed earlier parked down the street with the driver's attention focused on Phoenix House. A dark blue Ford Explorer sat across from Phoenix House with two occupants visible.

At least three parties were conducting surveillance on Ryder's new facility.

Her phone buzzed with a text from Sergeant Major Atkins. *Are you on site with Specialist Geller yet?*

She stared at the message. For months, Atkins had been relentless about pursuing Ryder. Now he was acting as if the fugitive Delta Force operator was an afterthought.

She typed back, *I have solid intel that Ryder is in the area. Conducting surveillance to confirm.*

The response came quickly. *Negative. Focus on the Geller shooting investigation. We'll deal with Ryder later.*

Kendrick frowned at her phone. Something had changed in Atkins' priorities, and the shift felt wrong. She typed, *Understood. Proceeding with the Geller case.*

Kendrick set the phone aside. The shooting investigation of former Army Specialist Geller provided convenient cover for her real purpose in Chicago—sharing her intel with former Sergeant First Class James Ryder to get his input. He'd know if her suspicions are warranted or a case of unfounded paranoia.

An hour passed with minimal activity at Phoenix House. Residents came and went, most moving with the careful deliberation of people rebuilding their lives. Kendrick debated whether she should warn Ryder about the surveillance on his property.

At sixteen thirty, she made her decision.

Kendrick started the Toyota SUV and drove away from Phoenix House, taking a circuitous route through Logan Square's residential streets. The GPS guided her to a familiar address she'd visited four months earlier.

Nana's house sat on a tree-lined street in Andersonville, a three-story brownstone with yellow roses climbing the wrought-iron trellis beside the front steps. The meticulously maintained property radiated decades of careful attention.

She parked and approached the front door. Her knock was answered by the sound of metallic clicks of locks being disengaged.

The door opened to reveal an unfamiliar woman in forest green scrubs.

"Hi, I'm Special Agent Kendrick. Is Jill Ryder here?"

The young lady's brows furrowed.

"I'm friends with her grandson. We had tea here earlier this year."

The door opened wider. "I'm Karla, and I'm the home healthcare nurse helping Mrs. Ryder until she gets back on her feet. She's in the kitchen."

Kendrick strode down the familiar hallway, where the same family photos lined the wall.

She entered the kitchen, and when Nana looked up from her magazine to see her guest, Kendrick gasped.

"Are you okay, Mrs. Ryder?"

Nana's hand moved to her face as her fingers patted her swollen eye. Then confusion flashed across her face. "Where's Karla?"

"I'm sorry, Mrs. Ryder. I'm Special Agent Kendrick. We met a few months ago. I'm friends with James."

Recognition flickered across Nana's features. "Of course. You're the young woman investigating those pharmaceutical companies." Her voice carried warmth despite slight slurring from the stroke.

Karla stuck her head into the kitchen. "Are you okay, Mrs. Ryder?"

"Yes, Karla. Can you stay for coffee?"

"No, Mrs. Ryder, I have to get to my next appointment."

"Okay, I'll see you tomorrow."

After Karla left, Nana felt compelled to explain her to Kendrick.

"That was Karla. She's helping me get back on my feet after the stroke."

"I'm sorry, Mrs. Ryder. Your grandson told me, and that was one reason I wanted to stop by."

Nana attempted a smile, but only raised the right corner of her lips. "That's nice of you."

In the kitchen, Kendrick helped prepare coffee while Nana settled at the kitchen table overlooking the backyard. The window offered a view of a garden where yellow roses bloomed alongside tomato plants.

Kendrick noted the careful way she moved her left arm. "How are you feeling?"

"Better than I was, but not as good as I hope to be." Her smile was wry. "I still have left side weakness and balance problems from the stroke."

Kendrick poured coffee into ceramic mugs. "The same thing happened to my grandpa. What kind of rehabilitation are you receiving?"

"Whatever we can afford to pay out of pocket." Nana's expression darkened. "My insurance company decided that physical therapy was a luxury they couldn't afford to cover."

"They denied coverage?" Kendrick asked with a hint of shock in her voice.

"Multiple times. Each with a different excuse." Nana sipped her coffee, her left hand trembling. "James is paying for Karla's services now."

Kendrick felt familiar anger at corporate bureaucracy but kept her expression neutral. "I'm sorry you're dealing with that."

Nana studied Kendrick's face. "I appreciate the concern about me, but that's not why you're really here, is it?"

Kendrick met Nana's penetrating gaze. The woman had raised a Delta Force operator. She understood deception.

"I have information to share with James, but I can't approach him in public."

"Because you have orders to arrest him?"

"Yes."

Nana nodded. "But something has changed?"

Kendrick considered her response. "Let's just say I'm not sure I'd be arresting the right person if I take your grandson into custody."

"You're a smart woman." Nana patted Kendrick's hand.

Silence stretched between them, broken only by the gentle ticking of a grandfather clock. Nana studied Kendrick's face with the intensity of someone who had spent years reading people's intentions.

The sound of a key turning in the front door interrupted their conversation. Footsteps echoed in the hallway, accompanied by the distinctive clicking of Shadow's claws across the hardwood floor.

"That's James."

Kendrick's pulse quickened as footsteps approached the kitchen. James Ryder appeared in the doorway, halting when he saw her sitting at his grandmother's table.

His square jaw and close-cropped hair were the same as she remembered, but seeing him in this domestic setting created an odd disconnect. The man who had eliminated corporate executives was hanging car keys beside the refrigerator with a pink keychain that said *I'm still hot, it just comes in flashes now.*

"Special Agent Kendrick." His voice was neutral, controlled. "This is unexpected."

"James." Nana's voice carried mild reproach. "Don't be rude. Agent Kendrick has been helping me make coffee."

Ryder's eyes moved between them. "Not trying to be rude, but why are you here?"

Kendrick stood. "I'm in Chicago on official business, but I have information that I want to share with you."

"Sit down, James," Nana commanded. "Both of you. We're having a civilized conversation."

Ryder pulled out a chair across from Kendrick, skepticism evident in his movements.

"How long have you been watching Phoenix House?"

"Since this afternoon. I'm not the only one."

His jaw tightened. "Who else?"

"At least two other surveillance teams. Professional setups."

Nana looked between them with growing concern. "Someone is watching Phoenix House?"

"I guess we're a popular venue now." Ryder's gaze locked on Kendrick. "What's your official business in Chicago?"

"Investigating a justified shooting incident from Kandahar six months ago. Army Specialist claimed self-defense when he killed an Afghan civilian, but witnesses came forward after his discharge saying it was personal." Kendrick paused. "The specialist returned to Chicago last month. I'm here to question him and verify witness testimony."

"Love triangle?"

"That's what the witnesses claim. Between the specialist and the victim's wife."

Ryder's hand moved to the scar along his left temple. "Unrelated to anything with me?"

"Not related at all. But it gave me cover to come to Chicago."

Ryder seemed to relax in his chair. "Okay, I'm listening."

The conversation continued through dinner until daylight faded outside. She shared information about surveillance teams and the high-level details regarding the wrap-up of the Javier Galindo case in Florida.

Around twenty hundred, Nana stretched and rubbed her neck. "I think I'm ready for bed. You two have more to discuss."

As Nana prepared to leave, she paused beside Kendrick's chair. "You know, you two would make a cute couple."

Both Kendrick and Ryder turned red, the unexpected comment cutting through their professional tension.

"Nana."

"I'm just saying." She patted Kendrick's shoulder. "It's nice to see James talking to someone who understands."

Ryder stood. "Let me help you to your room."

After helping his grandmother upstairs, Ryder returned with a neutral expression.

"Sorry about Nana. That was inappropriate."

"Completely inappropriate," Kendrick lied.

"Want to continue this on the front porch?"

They moved outside, where the evening air smacked them with the sounds of crickets and traffic in the distance. Streetlights created pools of amber light between mature oak trees.

Kendrick settled onto the top step while Ryder leaned against the railing, positioning himself to observe both directions. Even here, his tactical awareness remained constant.

"You here to arrest me?"

Kendrick's finger felt the emptiness where her engagement ring once occupied. "No, I'm not here to arrest you."

"Why not?"

"I'm not sure you're the one who deserves to be behind bars."

They sat in comfortable silence, watching occasional cars pass under streetlights. The discussion regarding the surveillance of Phoenix House was important, but this moment of shared understanding felt significant.

"Nana told me about all the insurance company denials. She said you were frustrated with their games. What are you planning to do about the insurance company?"

"What can I do? Keep appealing the claims, I guess."

Kendrick nodded but wasn't buying it. "Don't forget why I first tried to arrest you. I know James Ryder won't file appeals forever."

The Army CID special agent caught the brief curl of his lips skyward that she would have missed if she weren't studying his face.

"I'm not sure yet. The tools available to work within the system don't seem to be working."

Kendrick examined his profile in the darkness, noting how the streetlight two houses down highlighted his square jaw. For a moment, the similarity to Michael's features was striking.

She quickly changed the subject. "Oh, I have something to tell you."

Before she could continue, Ryder's phone rang. He glanced at the screen, and his expression shifted.

"I have to get this."

He answered. "Hey, Will."

Kendrick could hear the urgency in the voice on the other end. Ryder's posture tensed.

"How bad?"

More urgent conversation.

"I'll be right there." Ryder ended the call and was already moving toward the street. "Ricky relapsed. I need to get to Phoenix House."

"Ricky?"

"One of our residents. A young veteran who arrived last week." His voice carried frustration and concern. "Will says it's bad."

He was jogging toward a white sedan. "Can we finish this tomorrow?"

"Of course. Go."

Kendrick watched him drive away, tires squealing as he took the corner toward Logan Square. The urgency reminded her that behind all their tactical discussions, real people were fighting personal battles every day.

She remained on the porch for several minutes, processing the evening's revelations.

Kendrick noticed she'd missed a message from Atkins during her conversation with Ryder. *Any progress on the Geller case?*

She typed back, *Still investigating. The Ryder connection may be significant.*

The response from Atkins was immediate. *Focus on Geller. I want a full report by noon tomorrow.*

Kendrick stared at the response. The sudden urgency to switch from a murder suspect of a prominent defense contractor to verify a justified shooting case felt odd.

As she walked back to her car, Kendrick thought about Nana's comment. It may have been inappropriate to say, but it wasn't one-hundred percent inaccurate. They understood each other's battles. They had both lost people to corporate predators.

Kendrick shook off the fleeting thought. She had a job to do in Chicago, but couldn't help thinking that the surveillance teams meant imminent trouble for Phoenix House or James Ryder.

The desire to ignore the Geller case and help Ryder was stronger than she'd anticipated. She could feel the weight of a career-ending decision settling upon her, one she knew was now unavoidable.

CHAPTER 13

Will Cameron's footsteps echoed through Phoenix House Chicago's hardwood hallways as he made his final rounds at twenty-one hundred hours. The evening carried a palpable tension. Ricky Nelson had picked at his dinner, barely taking part in conversation, his eyes distant and unfocused. After the other residents gathered in the living room to watch television, Ricky had excused himself early.

Something felt wrong.

Will knocked softly on Ricky Nelson's door. No response.

He knocked again, harder this time. "Ricky? Everything okay in there?"

Silence.

The hair on the back of his neck stood up. His intel analyst training had taught him to recognize when patterns shifted, when something felt wrong. Ricky had been at Phoenix House for over a week, attending every group session, taking part in evening dinners, and even joining the morning card games with Gabe and Steve. The young veteran had shown steady progress, the soldier who defended his country overseas returning as his confidence grew.

Will tested the door handle. It was unlocked.

He pushed the door open and smelled something that shouldn't be there. Sweet, acrid smoke that he recognized from his own darkest days. The scent hit his stomach like a physical blow, triggering memories of needles and spoons in dark corners.

Ricky lay on his bed, fully clothed, his breathing shallow and labored. A burned spoon sat on the nightstand beside a small baggie and a syringe. Track marks dotted his left forearm.

"Damn it."

Will checked Ricky's pulse. Weak but steady. He searched for any signs of an overdose. The young veteran's pupils were pinpoints, his skin clammy and pale. Breathing remained regular, which meant he wasn't in immediate danger, but the heroin left him semi-conscious.

"Ricky?" Will shook his shoulder.

The young veteran's eyes fluttered open, unfocused and glassy. "Will?"

"Yeah, it's me. Did you overdose?"

Ricky shook his head. "Not too much. Just a little bit."

Will pulled out his phone and called Ryder.

"Will?"

"Ricky relapsed. Found him semiconscious in his room with heroin. He's breathing, stable, but he's in awful shape."

"Should we call 9-1-1?"

Will looked at Ricky, who was shaking his head frantically. "No," Ricky whispered. "Please. No ambulance."

"He's conscious and his breathing is normal," Will told Ryder. "Pupils are responsive. I think he's past the danger zone."

The silence stretched for three seconds. "I'm on my way."

Twenty minutes later, Ryder's footsteps thundered up the stairs two at a time. Will met him in the hallway outside Ricky's room, the confiscated drugs secured in a plastic evidence bag.

"How is he?"

"Conscious, coherent, but shaky. I've been sitting with him."

They entered thc room where Ricky sat on the edge of his bed, head in his hands, his entire body trembling. The young veteran looked up when they entered, his eyes red-rimmed and filled with shame.

"Mr. Ryder, I—"

"Don't!" Ryder commanded. "You violated the most basic rule of Phoenix House. No drugs. Ever."

Ricky's face crumpled. "I know. I'm sorry."

He wiped his nose with the back of his hand. "I couldn't sleep. Started thinking about Afghanistan, about the guys who didn't make it home. I told myself I'd just buy a little, keep it as insurance. But once I had it..."

"You used it," Will said, completing his sentence.

Ricky's gaze dropped to the floor. "I let everyone down."

"You let down nine veterans who are depending on Phoenix House to stay clean," Ryder said as he moved to the window. "Men who trusted you to respect the program."

Will cleared his throat. "Ryder."

The message was subtle but clear. Ryder turned back to Ricky. "Phoenix House helps veterans who are already clean maintain their sobriety. We're not a detox center."

"I want to get clean again. I'll do whatever it takes."

"Getting clean isn't something we can do for you," Will said. "It's something you have to do for yourself."

"What do I need to do?"

Will studied the young veteran's face. "Are you committed to getting clean for good?"

Ricky wiped his nose again with the back of his hand and nodded.

"Then do it," Will said.

"Can I do it here?"

Will looked at Ryder, who was pacing near the door. He could tell frustration was pulsing through his veins.

"Ryder and I will discuss whether we give you one more chance."

***

The next morning, Ryder sat in Phoenix House's community room while the other residents processed the morning's events. Word had spread quickly through the tight-knit community. Ricky Nelson had relapsed and was still in Phoenix House.

The reactions were as varied as the men themselves.

"He broke the rules," said another Marine veteran, who'd been clean for five months. "Phoenix House only works if everyone respects the program."

"The kid was struggling," Gabe Orosco countered. "We've all been there. Sometimes you fall down."

Walsh sat at the end of the table, his prosthetic arm resting on the polished wood surface. "What happens now?"

Ryder had been dreading this question. Phoenix House operated on trust and mutual accountability. One person's relapse could trigger a cascade of doubt and temptation throughout the community.

"Ricky says he's committed to his recovery now and will stay clean as long as he's in Phoenix House."

"And if he doesn't?"

"Then he can't stay here."

The stark simplicity of the answer reflected the harsh reality of addiction recovery. Programs could provide structure and support, but they couldn't force the internal commitment required for lasting sobriety.

"Are you changing the rules because of this?" asked a former Navy corpsman.

"No. The rules remain the same. Respect yourself, respect others, commit to your recovery."

"Then why are we even talking about letting him stay?"

Ryder looked around the table at thirteen men who'd all faced similar crossroads in their own lives—veterans who'd served their country with honor then struggled to find purpose and meaning when they returned home to a civilian world that didn't understand their experiences.

"Because we've all made mistakes. The question is whether someone learns from their mistakes or repeats them."

The Marine vet shook his head. "That's a hell of a risk."

"Recovery is always a risk. Every day, you choose sobriety over the temporary relief that comes from using. Every day you choose to trust each other to honor that choice."

Will entered the conference room carrying two cups of coffee and handed one to Ryder.

"How's Ricky?"

"Scared and ashamed but determined to prove he can do better." Will sat down across from Ryder. "It's the standard mixture of emotions for someone who just watched their world collapse."

Gabe Orosco leaned forward. "So he's staying even after last night?"

Footsteps in the hallway interrupted the conversation. Ricky entered the community room, his eyes clearer than the night before, but his voice still shaky.

"I wanted to apologize to everyone. What I did last night put all of you at risk. That wasn't fair, and it wasn't the action of someone committed to recovery."

Steve Walsh studied the young veteran's face. "Are you sure you're done using?"

Ricky hesitated. "I'm going to try."

"Try isn't good enough," the Marine vet said. "Either you're committed to recovery or you're not."

"I'm committed. I just... I know that saying that doesn't mean much after what happened."

Will stood and walked to where Ricky stood in the doorway. "Words are easy, but actions are what matter. The next few days will show us whether you're serious about changing your life."

"I understand."

"Do you? Because this is your last second chance. There won't be any more."

Will's voice held the finality of personal experience. He'd seen other veterans cycle through recovery programs, making promises they couldn't keep, burning bridges with people who'd tried to help them.

"Yes, I understand."

Ryder watched Ricky disappear up the stairs. Phoenix House had given Ricky Nelson tools and community, but those advantages meant nothing without the internal resolve to use them.

He turned back toward the nine other veterans who were counting on him to maintain a program that could turn around their lives. The weight of that responsibility felt heavier now, complicated by the knowledge that even the best intentions couldn't guarantee success.

Will moved from the community room to the office and was already back at his laptop, working on LifeCore's latest denial of Nana's rehabilitation coverage. The insurance company's bureaucratic warfare continued while Ricky Nelson fought a more personal battle for survival.

Both conflicts would test whether good people could overcome systems designed to defeat them. Bullets and brute force could conquer some predators, while others required the internal strength to fight demons that whispered the most convincing lies when lying awake at night.

In many ways, the battle to keep Ricky sober would be more difficult for Ryder to win.

CHAPTER 14

James Ryder's converted school bus loomed in front of Nana's brownstone, its imposing white frame stark against the tree-lined street. He adjusted the wireless camera feed on his tablet, monitoring the house's interior while Karla helped Nana with her morning exercises. Through the bus's tinted windows, he could observe both his grandmother's recovery efforts and any threats approaching from either direction along the sleepy Andersonville block.

Will Cameron climbed the bus steps carrying two cups of coffee and a backpack with his laptop. The mobile command center hummed with white noise from multiple computer systems, their screens casting blue and white light across the workspace Ryder had constructed earlier that year.

Ryder took the coffee, his eyes glued to the tablet where Nana's steps were shaky but purposeful. Her every move was a battle of concentration, yet she was reclaiming her mobility, one small, unsteady victory at a time.

"She's making progress. I wish she had regular physical therapy."

Will leaned closer to the tablet. "I hate that she has to fight her insurance company while trying to recover."

"Any word from LifeCore's appeals department?"

Will opened his laptop and scrolled to a message. "Same response every time. Denied pending additional review. They want more documentation from Dr. Asher proving the medical necessity of physical therapy."

The insurance company's strategy was obvious. Delay approval until Nana's recovery window closed, then claim the medical treatment was no longer justified. Corporate efficiency designed to eliminate expensive claims through confusion and stall tactics.

Will synced his laptop screen with the main monitor inside the command center. Financial reports, corporate organizational charts, and email communications flashed across the screens as he gathered evidence against LifeCore's executive leadership.

"I've been digging deeper into their corporate structure." Will pointed to a complex diagram showing shareholders and minority owners. "LifeCore has direct investment deals with hedge funds and healthcare industry titans. Many are connected to politicians and Wall Street CEOs, but one name stands out."

Ryder studied the chart, his eyes following ownership lines and investments. One name dominated as LifeCore's largest single shareholder.

"Richter Enterprises."

"Fourteen percent ownership stake, according to their most recent SEC filings." Will displayed additional documents showing financial transactions between the companies. "Tobias Richter sits on LifeCore's board and has significant influence over their strategic direction."

The connection explained everything. The professional surveillance teams outside Phoenix House, the military-trained operative who had died on his porch three nights ago, and the escalating pressure on his grandmother's care. Tobias Richter wasn't just seeking revenge for his son's death. He was protecting a billion-dollar healthcare fraud operation.

"Motion detected." Will pointed to one of the perimeter monitors.

Ryder swiveled his chair toward the surveillance feeds. A dark sedan had appeared on the residential street, moving slower than normal traffic. It passed Nana's house once, then circled the block and parked two hundred yards away with a clear sight line to both the brownstone and the mobile command center.

"How long has it been there?"

"Just arrived." Will zoomed in on the vehicle. "Two males. Upper twenties to low thirties."

Ryder's tactical mind processed the information. After taking multiple casualties at the Phoenix House encounter, Richter appeared to have shifted from direct assault to surveillance of Nana. Another way to intimidate him, like they did after he eliminated Peter Richter.

"Can you jam their communications?"

"Already on it." Will typed a few keys on his laptop. "Blocking cellular and radio frequencies in a two-block radius."

The sedan's occupants would know their communications were being disrupted, but they couldn't call for immediate backup or report real-time intelligence to their handlers. Ryder had a brief window to act.

"Stay here and monitor Nana's house. I'm going to have a quick chat with them."

Ryder descended from the bus and walked toward Nana's front door, appearing to be making a normal visit. Shadow stayed with Will, her ears forward and eyes locked on her handler's movements, sensing the predatory shift to an active hunt.

Once inside, he moved to the back door and slipped into the alley behind the brownstone. The residential blocks of Andersonville provided excellent cover. Mature trees, parked cars, and narrow gangways between buildings created multiple concealment opportunities.

Through a gap between houses, he observed the sedan. Two men sat motionless in the front seats, their attention focused on Nana's house. The driver lifted binoculars every few minutes while the passenger took notes on a pad.

Ryder circled wide, approaching from their rear blind spot. He crept closer, using parked cars for cover, until he was twenty feet from their vehicle.

A Harley-Davidson roared down the street, its exhaust echoing between houses. Both surveillance operatives turned toward the noise.

The driver spotted Ryder. "Contact rear!"

Both men bolted from the sedan in opposite directions. The driver sprinted west toward the residential blocks while the passenger ran east toward Clark Street.

Ryder chose the driver.

The man vaulted a chain-link fence into someone's backyard with athletic precision. Ryder followed, his boots finding purchase on the metal links. A Rottweiler exploded into barking fury, lunging against its fence next door as the two men crashed through its territory.

The driver weaved between garbage cans and a children's swing set, his breathing already labored. He wasn't built for sustained pursuit. Ryder closed the distance, his Delta Force conditioning giving him the advantage in a foot chase.

The operative stumbled over a garden hose, his momentum carrying him forward but destroying his rhythm. Ryder launched himself in a flying tackle that drove both men into the soft earth of a vegetable garden.

They rolled between tomato plants, trading vicious punches. The operative was skilled, his strikes precise and powerful, but Ryder's ground fighting experience overwhelmed him. A submission hold around the man's throat ended the struggle.

Ryder stood and dragged the man from the yard through a gate that led into the alley. Tall, well-manicured shrubs on both sides blocked the view of neighbors while Ryder questioned his captive.

"Who else is watching my family?" Ryder applied pressure to the man's throat, making breathing difficult.

The operative gasped for air. "Just... just the two of us. Crane's keeping it small after Phoenix House."

"Why is Crane watching my grandmother?"

"Leverage. He wants information on how to make her condition worse to distract you from LifeCore."

Heat flashed through Ryder's chest. "What are you looking for?"

"He said to watch her and see if we can disrupt anything that could make her sicker, like medications or equipment."

The admission was everything Ryder needed to know. Richter's organization had crossed every moral boundary by targeting his grandmother. They would use Nana's vulnerability as a weapon against him.

"What else?"

The operative's eyes hardened. "That's all you're getting."

Ryder tightened his grip, cutting off the man's airway completely. "Wrong answer."

But the operative remained silent, his face turning red as oxygen deprivation set in. Professional discipline, even under extreme duress. He would pass out before revealing additional operational details.

Ryder released the hold and drew his suppressed SIG Sauer. The operative sucked in desperate breaths while staring down the pistol's barrel.

"Last chance. When is Crane planning to strike?"

The man panted, his eyes unfocused. He was finished talking and of no use to Ryder, so the former Delta Force operator slid his index finger inside the trigger guard.

A heavy branch struck Ryder across his upper back with stunning force. Stars exploded across his vision as he pitched forward, the SIG Sauer tumbling from his grip. The impact sent waves of disorientation through his head, scrambling his coordination.

The passenger had circled back, armed with a thick oak branch. His partner was already scrambling to his feet as Ryder gathered himself on all fours.

"Move! Now!"

Both operatives sprinted away through the residential backyards, leaving Ryder dazed and alone in the alley. He rose to give chase, but his legs wouldn't cooperate. The branch had connected with surgical precision, exactly where it would cause maximum disorientation without permanent damage.

By the time Ryder's vision cleared, they were gone.

He retrieved his pistol and checked for witnesses. The Rottweiler two houses down continued barking, but no neighbors had emerged to investigate the commotion. He walked toward the command bus, his back and neck throbbing with each step.

Fifteen minutes later, Ryder climbed into the mobile command center, where Will was monitoring multiple screens.

"How'd it go? Do I need to find another tarp?”

"Not this time, but I sent Crane another message." Ryder settled into his chair and checked the surveillance feeds. "They're planning to target Nana with medical sabotage."

Will's expression darkened. "Then we need to move faster on LifeCore. I'm ready to go in as an insurance inspector to gather more intel."

Ryder nodded, his jaw tightening with resolve. The surveillance team had been a probe, testing his defenses and gathering intelligence for a more sophisticated attack. But they'd also revealed Atwood and Richter's escalating desperation.

Time was running out. If he couldn't expose LifeCore's crimes through legal channels, he would have to deliver justice through more direct methods.

His grandmother's life depended on it.

CHAPTER 15

Will Cameron posing as William Harper stepped through the revolving glass doors into LifeCore's soaring lobby, his shoes clicking against polished marble that reflected the morning sun streaming through floor-to-ceiling windows. The sound of fountain water trickling over black river rock provided a subtle backdrop to the steady rhythm of business.

His fake Illinois Department of Insurance credentials felt solid in his breast pocket. Twenty-four hours of preparation had produced a convincing cover identity complete with regulatory database access and official letterhead. If anyone called to verify his authority, they'd find William Harper conducting routine compliance audits for the state insurance commission.

The building's security desk occupied a cherrywood island in the center of the lobby. A single guard in a standard contracted security company uniform looked up from his computer screen as Will approached.

"I'm William Harper with the Illinois Department of Insurance here for scheduled compliance interviews at LifeCore Insurance."

The guard examined Will's credentials with casual interest. "Sign in here, please." He handed over a temporary pass. "Data processing is on the thirty-second floor, but you have to go through a second security point on twenty-four to get there. Elevators on the right will take you to twenty-four."

Will clipped the badge to his jacket and walked toward the elevator bank. So far, everything was proceeding according to plan. Building security had accepted his cover without question, treating him like any other government inspector conducting routine business.

The elevator climbed toward the twenty-fourth floor, digital numbers counting upward while soft jazz played through hidden speakers. Will straightened his crisp navy tie and reviewed his planned questions one last time.

The doors opened with a soft chime.

Will exited and noted the second security checkpoint blocked access to the office area. Three guards in tactical-style uniforms examined visitor badges and checked identification against appointment schedules. Their equipment included metal detectors, X-ray machines, and multiple facial recognition cameras that captured every person from different angles.

Will's confidence waned as he neared the checkpoint. This level of security seemed excessive for an insurance company conducting legitimate business. The guards moved with military precision, their eyes tracking every visitor with suspicious intensity. Their positioning and alertness suggested people expecting trouble.

"William Harper, Illinois Department of Insurance." Will produced his credentials. "I'm here for compliance interviews with your data processing team."

The lead guard studied his identification with the thoroughness of someone at a border crossing. A second guard ran his credentials through a scanner while typing commands into his computer terminal. The third positioned himself to block any retreat while surveillance cameras recorded everything from multiple angles.

"Step through the metal detector, sir."

Will complied, maintaining calm despite the paranoid atmosphere. The scanner beeped as he passed through, triggering additional scrutiny of his briefcase contents. They examined his legal pad, pens, and voice recorder with suspicious intensity.

"The facial recognition database is down, but appointment verification shows William Harper scheduled for ten-thirty," the second guard announced after a full minute of database queries.

Will did his best to suppress a smile regarding the temporary outage of the facial recognition database.

"Mr. Harper, welcome to LifeCore. Please sign in here and wear this visitor badge at all times." The lead guard handed him a plastic badge with his name and a timestamp. "Take the hallway on your right. Ms. Soto in cubicle forty-seven will escort you to the interview rooms."

The guards' eyes followed him as he walked away from the checkpoint. Their vigilance suggested people protecting unscrupulous activities, not employees processing routine insurance claims. LifeCore's executives understood they had secrets to protect.

Will walked past workstations where employees reviewed claim files. Each line represented a patient whose approval or denial determined survival.

Emma Soto stood when he approached her cubicle. She was a young woman in her upper twenties with stylish, thick black glasses that matched the color of her curly locks.

"Mr. Harper? I'm Emma. They told me you'd be interviewing some of us about our procedures."

"That's correct. Just routine compliance verification."

She led him to a small conference room with a round table and four chairs.

"I've been here eighteen months processing rehab claims. The system flags anything questionable."

"What's your average approval rate?"

"Maybe twenty percent? The algorithms are pretty strict."

Will took notes on a legal pad. Emma's answers confirmed what he'd found—LifeCore had weaponized bureaucracy to eliminate expensive patients.

"Do you ever question the denial decisions?"

"Sometimes, but I don't have medical training. If the system says a treatment isn't necessary, I process the denial and move to the next case."

Twenty minutes of questioning revealed Emma to be another cog in LifeCore's machine. She processed denials without understanding their medical consequences, insulated from the human cost of each rejection letter.

"Thank you for your time, Ms. Soto. Could you arrange for me to speak with your supervisor next?"

The supervisor, Shawn Callahan, had processed claims for seven years. He knew rehabilitation therapy meant independence for senior patients.

"The system's gotten more restrictive. Everything over a few thousand goes to medical review now."

"Medical review, meaning Dr. Lee's department?"

"Right. She's the chief medical officer. She's supposed to make the final call on complex cases, but her recommendations always get overruled anyway."

Will's pulse quickened. Dr. Lee was fighting the same battle from inside the system, her medical expertise ignored in favor of financial calculations.

"I'd like to speak with Dr. Lee if possible."

Shawn checked his computer. "She's got an opening at eleven-thirty. Conference room B down the hall."

Will spent the intervening time reviewing LifeCore's official policies, building his understanding of how they presented their denial practices to regulators.

Dr. Allison Lee entered conference room B carrying a tablet and a coffee mug that read "World's Most Caffeinated Doctor." A woman in her late forties, with a single streak of gray interrupting her long raven hair, strode to the open chair and sat.

"Mr. Harper? I was told you're reviewing our treatment protocols."

"That's correct. I want to understand LifeCore's methodology for determining the appropriate care for its policyholders."

Dr. Lee sipped her coffee and studied him. Something in her expression suggested she was evaluating more than his credentials.

"Are you a new inspector?"

"No, why?"

"I used to get questions about medical treatments at previous companies, but ever since I started at LifeCore, my discussions with the IDOI have always been about record keeping."

Will's stomach tightened as the pieces clicked into place. The Illinois Department of Insurance wasn't investigating LifeCore's medical decisions because they were paid off or intimidated into focusing on paperwork compliance instead of patient care. The corruption extended far beyond LifeCore's walls, reaching into the regulatory agencies charged with protecting consumers.

"Dr. Lee, I'd like to ask about your treatment recommendation for—"

The conference room door burst open.

Four massive security guards filled the doorway, their bulk blocking any escape route. The lead guard stepped forward, his hand resting on the taser clipped to his belt.

"Sir, we need you to come with us."

Will remained seated, staying in character despite his racing pulse. "Excuse me? I'm conducting an official state inspection. This behavior is out of line, and I will report it to my supervisors at IDOI."

"We ran your ID through another facial recognition database," the lead guard said flatly. "It came back as William Cameron, former Army Intelligence and currently an unemployed junkie."

The words hit like a physical blow. LifeCore's security system had unveiled his well-designed cover identity in minutes. Dr. Lee's eyes widened as she realized the man sitting across from her wasn't a government inspector.

"So you aren't here to get my professional opinion on medical treatments?"

Before Will could answer, the guards yanked him from his chair with excessive force. The contents of his briefcase scattered across the table as they zip-tied his wrists behind his back and marched him toward the elevator.

"This is assault!" Will protested loud enough for other employees to hear. "I'm filing a complaint with the state attorney general's office!"

The elevator ride to the ground floor felt like an eternity. Four guards surrounded him in the small space, their hot breath on his neck adding to the heat building in his chest. Will's mind raced through escape scenarios, but zip-ties and overwhelming numbers eliminated most options.

They bypassed the main lobby, instead exiting through a service corridor that led to the building's loading dock. Concrete walls and harsh lighting replaced the polished marble and designer fixtures of the main lobby.

"Where are you taking me?"

"Shut up." One guard shoved him with enough force to make him stumble and use the wall to prevent himself from falling to the ground.

The deserted loading dock smelled of diesel exhaust and garbage. There were no witnesses to what the LifeCore security guards planned to do with a captured infiltrator.

The guards shoved him against a concrete wall, the impact sending pain through his shoulder blades. One guard cut the zip-ties while the others formed a semicircle that blocked his escape routes.

"You've got ten seconds to disappear." The lead guard drove his fist into Will's stomach. "If we see you anywhere near this building again, you won't be walking away."

The blow doubled Will over, gasping for air while the other guards delivered punches to his ribs and face. It was professional violence designed to send a message without causing serious damage that would require medical care.

They stepped back, allowing him to stumble toward the street.

Will forced himself to walk normally despite the pain radiating through his torso. Each step felt like broken glass grinding against his ribs, but showing weakness would invite further violence. He made it to the sidewalk before allowing himself to lean against a building wall.

Blood dripped from his split lip onto his shirt. His ribs ached with each breath, and his left eye was already swelling shut. But he was alive and free, which meant LifeCore had chosen intimidation over elimination—this time.

The taxi ride back to Logan Square gave him time to process what had happened. Dr. Lee's comment about the Illinois Department of Insurance focusing on record-keeping instead of medical decisions revealed corruption that reached into state regulatory agencies. LifeCore had neutralized oversight through political influence or financial pressure.

But Dr. Lee herself was clean. He saw it in her eyes when he asked about medical procedures instead of mundane record keeping.

The taxi stopped outside Phoenix House. Will paid the driver and ambled toward the front entrance, each step sending fresh waves of pain through his battered body.

Ryder was waiting in the main community room with Shadow lying at his feet. The Belgian Malinois lifted her head as Will entered, her dark eyes taking in his condition.

"What the hell happened to you?"

Will collapsed into an armchair, exhaustion overwhelming the adrenaline that had carried him through the beating. "LifeCore happened."

"What?"

Will recounted the entire operation, from his successful entry through the final beating in the loading dock. Ryder's expression grew darker with each detail, his hands clenching into fists as he absorbed the details of Will's treatment.

"Which floor is Atwood on?"

"Ryder, wait." Will straightened despite the pain. "I think Dr. Lee wants to talk. She's the key to taking down LifeCore."

The words stopped Ryder's movement toward the door. He turned back, studying Will's bruised face while weighing options.

"She's frustrated, and I get the impression she wants to tell her story but is unsure who to turn to for help or is afraid of retaliation. I'm not sure which. It may be both, but I am confident she's on our side."

Ryder settled back into his chair, the predatory tension leaving his shoulders. Shadow sensed the change and rested her head against his leg.

"We need a discreet way to reach Dr. Lee that won't get anyone killed, and I think I know the right person to do it."

CHAPTER 16

The sharp crack of gunfire echoed through the underground firing range as Brandon Crane squeezed the trigger in measured sequence. Brass casings clinked against concrete, their metallic percussion mixing with the acrid smell of gunpowder that hung in the recycled air. Through his safety glasses, he observed the tight cluster of holes punched through the paper target's center mass at twenty-five yards.

Fifteen rounds. Fifteen holes within a two-inch grouping.

Crane set the SIG Sauer P226 on the metal stand and activated the mechanical target retrieval system. The whir of cables and pulleys filled the shooting lane as his target traveled toward him along the overhead track.

Lunch hour training sessions kept his Navy SEAL skills sharp, even though corporate security work rarely required marksmanship at this level. Muscle memory and tactical reflexes required constant use to stay at their peak effectiveness. The day he stopped training was the day he became vulnerable to someone better and more dedicated.

He examined the target, noting the precise placement of each round. Satisfactory, but not exceptional. His instructors at SEAL Team Three would have demanded better consistency under stress conditions.

Crane returned his eye and ear protection to the front counter, packed his weapon into his range bag, and headed to street level, where a driver waited.

His secure phone buzzed as he settled into the back seat of the black Mercedes. The partition between the driver and passenger compartments provided privacy for sensitive conversations, while tinted windows shielded him from surveillance.

"Crane."

"This is Mason Carter at Richter Defense Systems." The voice carried tension that put Crane on alert. "We have a significant security breach that requires your immediate attention."

Crane activated the phone's encryption protocol and gestured for the driver to take a longer route back to the office.

"What's the nature of the breach?"

"Our counterintelligence team caught one of our senior sales managers, Josh Edelman, sharing classified weapons schematics with the Houthis in Yemen. They discovered the breach during routine monitoring of international correspondence."

The implications settled like a bitter weight in Crane's chest. Selling weapons technology to hostile regimes was the greatest offense for an employee at a defense contractor.

"How long has this been going on?"

"At least six months, maybe longer. The counterintelligence team found his offshore bank account with three deposits over that period, each one for one hundred and fifty thousand dollars."

Crane's jaw tightened as he processed the scope of Edelman's betrayal. Navy SEALs died when enemy forces gained access to American tactical advantages. Every weapons system Edelman had compromised represented blood that American servicemen facing unexpectedly capable enemies would spill. His boss, Tobias Richter, might sell out the troops for enough profit from an enemy of the United States, but Crane still gave a damn about his brothers and sisters in uniform.

"Send me Edelman's complete personnel file, financial records, and communication logs. I want everything documented before we move forward."

"Should I terminate his employment and coordinate with federal authorities?"

"No." Crane's voice carried cold certainty. "I have a more permanent solution in mind."

Carter's silence suggested he understood the implication without requiring additional explanation. Individuals who committed offenses as serious as Edelman's while working in the defense industry rarely survived to face trial in federal court. Crane's background included specialized training for eliminating threats that were best handled outside the public eye.

"Understood. The files will be in your secure inbox within the hour."

The call ended, leaving Crane staring through tinted windows at Manhattan's towering skyline while calculating the resources required to eliminate Edelman without creating complications for Richter Defense Systems. Executing permanent solutions required careful planning to avoid unwanted attention from federal investigators.

His phone buzzed again, this time displaying an unfamiliar number with a Chicago area code.

"This is Crane."

"Sir, this is Jabari at LifeCore Security." The voice carried urgency despite its professional tone. "We've had a breach of our systems. Unauthorized access to classified executive communications and financial records."

Crane leaned forward in the Mercedes's leather seat, his attention shifting from the Edelman situation to this new threat. He could handle multiple security crises in a single day, but the amount of classified information lost would justify an extra finger of bourbon after work.

"How significant?"

"The hacker penetrated deep into the internal correspondence between senior executives. Sensitive materials accessed."

Someone with serious cyber capabilities had targeted LifeCore's most sensitive operations, the kind of information that could destroy the company if it fell into the wrong hands.

"Do we have identification of the hacker?"

"Yes, sir. He entered the building under the alias William Harper from the Illinois Department of Insurance."

Crane's jaw tightened as he gestured for the driver to return to Richter Enterprises. The name was unfamiliar and meant nothing to him, but the timing suggested coordination between physical and digital infiltration.

"What's his real name?"

"Will Cameron, according to facial recognition. Former Army intelligence analyst with a current address in Falls Church, Virginia."

Crane recognized the name instantly. The connection to James Ryder hit him like a physical blow. He'd battled Ryder and Cameron, along with their Phoenix House Tampa crew, in Miami a month earlier. He understood their capabilities, which meant LifeCore and Richter Enterprises were in for a hell of a fight.

His fingers drummed against the sedan's armrest as implications cascaded through his mind. Ryder wasn't just reacting to his grandmother's medical situation. He was mounting a coordinated intelligence gathering operation against LifeCore, the same systematic approach he'd used to dismantle criminal organizations in Tampa and Virginia.

"Did Cameron get access to sensitive material?"

"He was able to access executive email threads discussing claim denial strategies and internal financial systems. We terminated his access before he could download everything, but he saw enough to understand our operational priorities."

The Mercedes pulled into Richter Enterprises' underground garage, where security cameras monitored every vehicle. Crane exited the sedan and headed toward the private elevator that would carry him to the executive floors, his mind already calculating tactical responses to Ryder's intelligence operation.

"I want the entire LifeCore Security team on high alert. Assume Ryder is planning follow-up operations and prepare accordingly. This was reconnaissance, not their main assault."

"Understood, sir. Should we coordinate with local law enforcement?"

"Negative. This stays internal. Ryder operates outside legal constraints, which means traditional law enforcement won't be effective against him." Crane paused, considering tactical options. "But keep documenting everything. We need a paper trail showing that he's the aggressor in this situation."

"Yes, sir."

Crane ended the call and dialed Tobias Richter's private line. Three rings later, the familiar voice answered with its characteristic controlled tone.

"Mr. Crane. I assume you have something urgent to discuss."

"Sir, we have a situation with James Ryder. He's initiated an assault against LifeCore using sophisticated intelligence-gathering techniques. One of his associates penetrated their corporate security and accessed executive communications."

Silence stretched across the connection while Tobias processed the information. In the background, Crane could hear the faint sound of classical music from Richter's corner office.

"How much did they learn?"

"Enough to understand LifeCore's claim denial strategies and possibly identify the bounty program. The cybersecurity team disrupted the breach before complete data extraction, but Ryder now has operational intelligence about sensitive operations."

"I see. And your assessment of next steps?"

Crane weighed Ryder's capabilities, countermeasures, and potential objectives. "Ryder is transitioning from defensive to offensive operations. He's gathering intelligence for a coordinated assault on LifeCore's leadership. We should consider preemptive action to eliminate the threat before he can execute whatever he's planning."

"Come to my office. This requires a face-to-face discussion."

The line went dead, leaving Crane staring at the phone. Ten minutes later, he stepped off the private elevator into Tobias Richter's domain.

Sunlight streamed through massive windows that offered panoramic views of Manhattan's skyline. Tobias sat behind his enormous desk, reviewing financial documents with the same focused attention he applied to all business matters.

"Mr. Crane." Tobias gestured toward the leather chair positioned across from his desk. "Please sit."

Crane settled into the chair, noting how Tobias continued reviewing documents for several seconds before acknowledging his presence. Power games and psychological positioning, even during crisis situations.

"Tell me about the breach." Tobias set aside his papers and fixed Crane with steady eyes. "Specifics, not generalizations."

"Will Cameron, former Army intelligence, conducted digital reconnaissance on LifeCore executive communications and financial systems. Then he used false credentials to gain physical access to LifeCore's offices. We uncovered his real identity before he could interview anyone of significance."

"What did he find?"

"Email threads between Atwood and Kline discussing claim denial strategies and financial records showing the bounty transfers from Kline's ledger to Human Resources."

Tobias leaned back in his chair, his expression revealing neither concern nor surprise. The revelation that his carefully constructed business relationships might face exposure seemed to generate no more emotional response than routine quarterly reports.

"Your recommendation?"

Crane leaned forward, his military training driving him toward decisive action. "We mount an offensive operation against Ryder's Chicago facility before he can utilize the intelligence he's gathered. A coordinated assault to eliminate the threat."

Tobias rose from his chair and moved to the windows overlooking Central Park. His silhouette stood motionless against the bright sky, hands clasped behind his back. "How did that work out for Galindo's men when they tried that in Tampa?"

The question jolted Crane like a splash of ice water to the face. Galindo's cartel operatives were trained security professionals with significant resources and tactical experience. Yet Ryder had eliminated them during their assault on the Florida Phoenix House location.

"Sir, Galindo's men were cartel hitmen operating outside their area of expertise. My team consists of former US Special Forces operators with extensive combat experience. We understand Ryder's training and tactical mindset. We can generate different results."

Tobias remained at the window, his eyes scanning pedestrians navigating Central Park's walkways sixty floors below. The silence stretched for a full minute.

"Get the team prepared for an assault, but not at the veteran's house," he said, turning back to face Crane. "First, I'm going to make a few phone calls to soften the target."

Crane's brows furrowed. "Sir? I don't follow."

A sinister smile formed on Tobias Richter's face, transforming his typically composed features into something predatory. His eyes held the cold calculation of someone who had identified an opponent's weakness and intended to exploit it.

"Let's see just how concerned he is about the recovery of his precious grandmother."

CHAPTER 17

Ryder pushed through the front door of Phoenix House, his boots silent on the hardwood floors. Sweat still clung to his forehead from helping set up the new hospital bed in Nana's family room that LifeCore had approved two weeks after Dr. Asher had prescribed it. Ryder had rearranged the furniture so his grandmother could move from the hospital bed to the bathroom without help.

He found Will at the conference room table, hunched over his laptop, surveillance footage frozen on the screen.

"Thought you might want to see this." Will gestured toward his laptop.

Ryder moved behind Will's chair, studying the black-and-white surveillance footage. The timestamp showed fifteen forty-three, approximately four hours earlier. A sedan idled across the street from Phoenix House while two figures sat motionless in the front seats.

"How long?"

"Three hours. Different car than yesterday, but same basic surveillance pattern."

Whoever was watching Phoenix House understood operational security and had access to multiple vehicles. These weren't curious neighbors or random criminals casing the property.

"LifeCore or Richter?"

"Hard to tell. The surveillance increased after LifeCore caught me in their system, so I'd guess it was them." Will closed the laptop. "They know we're onto them."

Ryder studied the empty conference room. The room's single window offered a clear view of the street where the surveillance team had positioned themselves. They'd chosen their spot well, maximizing visibility while maintaining escape routes.

"They're going to make a move soon."

Will nodded. "We need to expose LifeCore soon to redirect their attention away from us."

The weight of the situation pressed against Ryder's chest. Phoenix House represented hope for veterans who'd exhausted other options. The residents who called this place home had already survived combat, addiction, and the bureaucratic indifference of a system that promised care but delivered disappointment. They deserved protection from corporate predators, who viewed their recovery as an inconvenience.

"Next steps on reaching Dr. Lee?"

"I've been thinking about that." Will opened a different browser window, revealing the American Medical Association's website. "She's speaking at their conference in two days at a hotel near Grant Park. Perfect time for me to try again to make contact."

Ryder's phone buzzed against his hip. The caller ID showed Karla Sandoval. She'd left Nana's house hours ago after helping with dinner, so the late call triggered immediate concern.

"Karla? Is everything okay?"

"Mr. Ryder, I'm sorry to bother you, but I wanted to let you know what happened today." Her voice was a cocktail of stress and anger. "My boss called and said they'd suspended me from my day job."

Ryder's grip tightened on the phone. "Why?"

"They said they got a complaint from a health inspector that I was abusing senior patients under my care. My boss said they have to suspend me without pay pending investigation." Karla's voice wavered. "She said I have to cease working with all clients, even freelance patients like Mrs. Ryder, or I could face jail time for the unauthorized practice of medicine since my license is suspended."

Rage flowed through Ryder's veins like molten metal. Karla was the only lifeline Nana had for potential recovery. Without her daily care and exercises, Nana would plateau at her current level of dependence, confined to her walker and new hospital bed while her independence slipped away.

"That's LifeCore. They don't like how I'm about to expose their inhumane insurance process." His voice remained controlled despite the fury building in his chest. "Can you still come help Nana tomorrow so I can get something else lined up?"

"Yeah, I was calling to tell you I have more time now to spend with your grandmother."

A slow breath escaped Ryder, his mind trying to reconcile what he had just heard. "What about your boss? What about jail?"

Karla let out a soft chuckle. "Mr. Ryder, I grew up on the south side of Chicago. It takes a lot more than some corporate asshole hiding behind a health inspector to scare me."

Despite everything, Ryder couldn't help but smile. Karla was a warrior like him, but instead of tactical gear and a Glock, she wore scrubs and carried a blood pressure monitor. Her battlefield was different, but her courage was identical.

"Thank you, Karla. I'll take the extra hours and pay you double if you can try to help Nana with some physical therapy. She's slipping after her initial progress."

"She is slipping and desperately needs PT. I used to work in a rehab clinic six years ago, so I can help Mrs. Ryder with a few exercises I saw there."

The connection ended, leaving Ryder staring out the window. LifeCore, with Tobias Richter's help, was sending a message that they could inflict damage on their rivals. Nana was caught in the crossfire of a shot intended for him.

Will studied Ryder's expression. "What happened?"

"LifeCore got Karla suspended from her day job. False complaint from a health inspector about abusing patients." Ryder's voice carried deadly calm. "They're trying to cut off Nana's care."

"This is escalating fast."

"Too fast." Ryder moved to the window, scanning the street for surveillance vehicles. The block appeared quiet, but that meant nothing. Professional watchers knew how to remain invisible until they sprang into action. "Our timeline to stop LifeCore just got more urgent."

Will opened his laptop again, navigating to the AMA conference website. The screen displayed speaker schedules and venue information for the medical association's annual gathering.

"Dr. Lee is the first speaker after dinner at the AMA meeting in two days." He pointed to the conference agenda. "Healthcare policy panel at nineteen hundred hours. It's the perfect time for me to attempt contact with Dr. Lee again."

"No." Ryder's response was immediate. "LifeCore security knows your face now, and I'm sure they know mine. You won't get within fifty feet of that hotel without triggering their countermeasures."

"Then how do we reach her?"

Ryder considered their options. The insurance company had deployed surveillance teams, corrupted health inspectors, and demonstrated its willingness to destroy innocent people's careers to protect its criminal enterprise. Any approach to Dr. Lee would require someone LifeCore wouldn't recognize as a threat.

"I'm bringing Kendrick on board."

Will's expression shifted to concern. "I thought we agreed she couldn't be trusted."

Ryder turned from the window to face Will. "She's the only one who won't draw the attention of LifeCore security to reach Dr. Lee at the AMA event."

"And if she arrests us instead?"

The question hung in the air between them. Kendrick had spent months investigating Ryder's activities, convinced he was operating outside legal boundaries.

"She won't."

"How can you be so sure?"

"I know her pain. When someone turns your life upside down and you feel helpless to do anything about it, you'll do anything to avoid that feeling again. She'll help."

Will stared at his laptop screen, the conference website still displaying Dr. Lee's scheduled appearance. His fingers drummed against the table as he processed the implications of involving an Army CID agent in their plans.

"If that's what you want, but I don't like it."

"I don't like that big corporations are picking on home healthcare nurses and that families across America are scheduling funerals for their grandparents instead of making vacation plans together." Ryder's voice contained the sharp edge of a man pushed beyond his limits. "This needs to end, and Kendrick has the skills and willingness to help us do it."

After a long moment, Will nodded. "You're right. Let's get Kendrick to help us."

Ryder stood and patted Will on the shoulder. "I'm going to check on everyone and then head out. I'll call Kendrick when I get home."

The main room buzzed with conversation as residents settled into their evening routines. Steve Walsh and Gabe Orosco sat at their usual table, playing cards while the television provided background noise. Their casual demeanor couldn't mask the alertness that all combat veterans carried, the subtle awareness of exits and potential threats that never disappeared.

Ricky Nelson emerged from the kitchen carrying a sandwich and a glass of milk. The former soldier had been clean for two days straight, attending group sessions and participating in Phoenix House's structured program. His improvement was steady but fragile, requiring constant support to prevent another relapse.

"How are you feeling tonight, Ricky?"

"I'm fantastic, Mr. Ryder." Ricky's smile was genuine. "I talked to my mom today. First time in three months. She wants me to come visit when I'm ready."

"That's progress."

"Yeah. Will told me about taking things one day at a time. Today was a good day."

Ryder clasped Ricky's shoulder. "Keep it up. Tomorrow will be an even better day."

As he moved through the building, Ryder checked each common area and verified that security protocols were being followed. The residents had embraced their role as informal sentries, maintaining awareness of their surroundings while supporting each other's recovery. Their vigilance would provide early warning if threats materialized against Phoenix House.

Shadow waited by the front door, her instincts alert to Ryder's preparations for departure. The dog's ears pricked forward, and her dark eyes tracked every movement with unwavering focus.

"Ready to go home, girl?"

Shadow's tail wagged once, a controlled expression of enthusiasm that matched her disciplined training. She'd learned to balance affection with tactical readiness during their years of serving together in hostile environments.

The walk to Ryder's borrowed car took them past the surveillance position Will had identified. Ryder's eyes swept the street without appearing to search, cataloging parked vehicles and potential observation points. The block seemed to be normal, but professional watchers adapted to avoid detection.

Shadow's behavior remained relaxed as they approached Nana's sedan, indicating no immediate threats in the area. Her sensitive nose and acute hearing provided early warning systems that human senses couldn't match. If hostile surveillance were present, she would alert him through subtle changes in posture or movement.

The drive back to Andersonville took twelve minutes through light evening traffic. Streetlights flickered on as Chicago transitioned from day to night.

Nana's house sat quiet and secure behind its wrought-iron fence. The yellow roses beside the front steps had closed their petals for the evening, waiting for tomorrow's sunlight to bloom again. Ryder parked in front of the house and let Shadow out.

Inside, the house was silent except for the grandfather clock and Nana snoring softly in her hospital bed. Her breathing was steady and deep, the sleep of someone who'd worked hard trying to regain her independence and had earned her rest.

Shadow settled beside Nana's bed. The dog had appointed herself as Nana's guardian, providing comfort and protection with the loyalty that defined her breed.

In the kitchen, Ryder brewed coffee while considering his approach to Kendrick. Their relationship had evolved from adversarial to neutral over the past months, but asking her to participate in activities that skirted federal law would test whatever trust they'd built.

His phone displayed Kendrick's contact information. Special Agent Jenna Kendrick, Army Criminal Investigation Division. The woman who'd once been determined to arrest him might be the key to exposing LifeCore's systematic slaying of vulnerable patients.

The call connected on the second ring. "Special Agent Kendrick."

"It's Ryder. Are you still in Chicago?"

"Yeah," Kendrick sighed. "This case is taking longer than I expected."

"Are you still willing to help me bring a company preying on military veterans and seniors to justice?"

The silence stretched longer than he expected, and he wondered if she'd changed her mind.

CHAPTER 18

Bedroom windows supporting old air-conditioning units droned like tired engines as Ryder made his final sweep through Phoenix House. Box fans hummed behind half-shut doors, pushing the heavy August air in lazy circles. Crickets carried on in the backyard, their chorus cut by the low rumble of distant thunder and the scent of rain pushing in through the screens.

On the upper floors, residents filled the halls with their own restless soundtrack—a cough muffled under a pillow, the rattle of pill bottles on nightstands, and laughter leaking from the TV room. Someone dragged a prosthetic foot across the hardwood floor, slow and uneven, before retreating behind his door.

Ryder paused at the corner and scanned the corridor. Nothing was out of place. Still, every hum, click, and shuffle kept him sharp, tuned for any sound that didn't belong.

He returned to the conference room to find Will leaning over his laptop, charts and jagged graphs spilling blue light across his face. His eyes lingered on the hallway behind Ryder before returning to the screen.

"Everything solid with Kendrick's intercept plan?"

Will's fingers moved across the keyboard, pulling up the hotel floor plan. "Dr. Lee's presentation should end around nineteen thirty, which gives Kendrick a window to approach her in the hotel lobby before LifeCore's security detail escorts her back upstairs."

"My concern is that Dr. Lee may be too afraid to talk," Will continued. "It would be best if we could get her out of the hotel."

Ryder nodded, studying the screen. "Fear keeps people compliant, but it also makes them desperate for someone to trust. Kendrick can read people. If Dr. Lee wants to help, she'll recognize the opportunity."

Will closed the laptop and stretched. "I'm heading upstairs. Long day tomorrow."

"Same." Ryder stood and moved toward the hallway.

Will climbed two steps and turned around. "What time is Kendrick coming tomorrow?"

"After her morning briefing, so around ten hundred."

Ryder left the conference room and sensed the unusual quiet. He moved through the common areas, noting the residents who'd gathered in the living room to watch the late news. Orosco and Walsh were playing their nightly card game, their conversation punctuated by the soft slap of cards against the wooden table.

The second-floor hallway stretched before him, illuminated only by emergency exit lighting at both ends. Each door was closed, and residents settled into their private spaces for the night.

Ricky Nelson's room sat at the end of the hall, a corner location that provided maximum privacy for someone still struggling with the demons of withdrawal and recovery. Ryder approached the door, listening for any sounds that might indicate distress or relapse.

Silence.

Complete, unnatural silence.

Ryder knocked softly on the door frame. "Ricky? Everything okay in there?"

No response.

He knocked again, harder this time. "Ricky?"

The hair on the back of his neck stood up. His tactical instincts, honed through years of Delta Force kill team operations, screamed warnings about the stillness beyond the door.

Ryder pushed the door open and immediately knew Ricky Nelson was gone.

The bed sat empty, covers pulled back as if someone had left in a hurry. The window stood open, allowing the night air to flow into the room and carry the distant sounds of traffic from Logan Boulevard.

Ryder flipped on the light, revealing details that told the story of Ricky's departure. A small baggie on the nightstand, with white powder residue visible in the bottom. A burned spoon beside it. A rubber tourniquet dangled over the lamp base.

"Damn it."

The evidence painted a clear picture. Ricky had scored drugs, brought them back to Phoenix House, and used them in his room before disappearing into the night. The window had provided his escape route, allowing him to avoid the main entrance, where other residents might have seen him leave.

Ryder pulled out his phone and called Will.

"Everything okay?" Will answered.

"Ricky's gone. Left through his window, and there's evidence of drug use in his room."

"How long?"

Ryder checked the nightstand. The spoon was still warm. "Less than an hour. Maybe thirty minutes."

"Where would he go?"

Ryder recalled his conversation with Ricky the night they first met. The struggling Army veteran said he used to sleep under the

Wilson Avenue Bridge. He moved toward the window, assessing the drop to the alley below. "I think I know where he might go. I'm going to look for him."

"The kinds of places he'd go aren't safe for anyone, even someone with your training."

"That's why I need to find him."

Ryder ended the call and pocketed the phone. He secured the room, removing the drug evidence to prevent other residents from discovering it in the morning. Phoenix House's reputation and the recovery of nine other veterans depended on maintaining the community's trust and focus.

The drop from Ricky's window to the alley below was manageable for someone with military training and desperate enough to risk injury. Ryder retraced the likely path, following the alley toward Logan Boulevard, where public transportation would provide Ricky with quick access to his next destination.

Ryder considered bringing Shadow. Her tracking skills could help locate Ricky in the maze of Chicago's seedy underground. But finding someone who'd relapsed meant dealing with dealers and users who would scatter at the first sign of law enforcement. A tactical dog would spook the people whose cooperation he needed.

Shadow would have to stay home tonight.

Ryder entered "Wilson Avenue" into his phone's GPS as he walked to Nana's sedan and found a single bridge over the North Branch of the Chicago River. He started the engine and headed north.

Fifteen minutes later, he parked and slid down the muddy bank to the water's edge. Light from the Wilson Avenue streetlights above glinted off the dark sliver of river snaking through the north side of Chicago.

There was no sign of Ricky or anyone else in the area. Ryder headed back up the bank when he saw an L train rumble over a bridge a hundred yards north. It was more secluded than the Wilson Avenue bridge, so Ryder made his way to the L train bridge. A small park sat in the shadows.

His eyes caught movement below the bridge.

He approached a group of people huddled around an overflowing trash bin in the park.

"I'm looking for someone. A young Army veteran, early twenties, probably looking to score."

A woman with matted hair and hollow cheeks looked up from a shopping cart filled with aluminum cans. "Lots of young people come through here, looking for all kinds of things."

"This one would have been here within the last hour. Maybe he's still here."

"Might be under the bridge. That's where the fresh faces usually go first."

Ryder followed her gesture toward the structure with another L train passing over it. The area beneath the bridge was dark, lit only by the occasional flicker of lighters or the glow of cell phone screens.

Three men emerged from the shadows as Ryder approached. The point man was tall and gaunt, with the predatory smile of someone who specialized in exploiting vulnerability. His companions flanked him, creating a triangle formation that blocked Ryder's access to the bridge.

"You lost, man?" the apparent leader asked. "This ain't your neighborhood."

"Looking for a friend. A young Army veteran who might have come through here tonight."

"Information costs money."

Ryder tilted his head. "Come again?"

"You want information I have, I need to get paid."

"Fine, how much?"

The leader's smile widened, revealing missing teeth. "Everything you got."

The two flankers moved closer, revealing knives in their hands. They were crude street weapons, but sharp enough to cause serious damage in close quarters. Their positioning was amateur but eager, desperation-fueled aggression that made them unpredictable opponents.

Ryder assessed the tactical situation in a matter of seconds—three attackers with edged weapons in a confined space. No cover was available, but concrete walls would limit their mobility. His advantage lay in his training and experience, which he could use against opponents whose only skills were desperation and street violence.

"Easy way or hard way. Your choice."

"My choice?" Ryder confirmed.

"Yeah. Your choice," the leader hissed.

"Definitely the hard way."

Ryder's next move was instantaneous, his body in motion while the men remained flat-footed.

His left hand shot out, catching the leader's wrist and twisting until the knife clattered against gravel. Before the man could react, Ryder's right elbow connected with his temple, dropping him unconscious to the ground.

The first flanker lunged forward with his blade extended. Ryder sidestepped, grabbed the attacker's wrist, and used his momentum to drive him face-first into the concrete pillar. The knife skittered away into the darkness.

The third man hesitated, realizing he was facing someone far more dangerous than the typical victim who wandered into their territory. His hesitation cost him.

Ryder closed the distance in two quick steps. A precise strike to the man's solar plexus doubled him over, gasping for breath. A controlled blow to the back of his head sent him to the ground beside his unconscious companions.

The entire encounter lasted less than fifteen seconds.

Ryder collected the dropped knives and searched the area under the bridge. No sign of Ricky Nelson, but fresh needle debris showed recent drug activity. The young veteran may have been there earlier, but he'd moved on.

He drove around the area for another hour. No sign of Ricky. It was futile to search a city of three million people for one man who didn't want to be found.

Ryder stopped at the police station before returning to Phoenix House.

"Recovery isn't a straight line. A lot of people fall off the path before they find their way." The sergeant handed Ryder a case number. "We'll keep an eye out, but most of these guys turn up when they're ready or when they're forced to by circumstances."

***

Special Agent Jenna Kendrick rounded the corner and found Ryder sitting at Phoenix House's kitchen table, staring into a half-empty cup of coffee. Dark circles under his eyes and the stubble covering his jaw told the story of a sleepless night. Shadow lay at his feet, her head resting against his boot in silent support.

Ryder looked up, surprised.

"Sorry for just dropping in. One of your residents let me in."

He shrugged. "It's alright."

Kendrick set her briefcase on the counter. "Something wrong?"

Ryder ran his fingers through his short hair. "We lost someone last night. Ricky Nelson relapsed and disappeared from the facility."

Kendrick pulled out a chair and sat across from him. "I'm sorry. Do we need to look for him?"

"No. I filed a police report, but Ricky knows he's in the wrong. He doesn't want to be found right now." Ryder looked up, meeting her eyes.

"You sure? I know some people at CPD."

"He'll come back when he's ready, but until then, we have to focus on Dr. Lee."

Will emerged carrying his laptop and a mug of coffee. "Special Agent Kendrick. Ready for tonight's operation?"

"We'll see." Kendrick studied both men's faces. "Walk me through the plan one more time."

Will opened his laptop and pulled up the hotel layout. "Dr. Lee's presentation ends around nineteen thirty. It's customary at AMA events for speakers to meet with attendees in the lobby afterward to shake hands and answer questions."

"Where do I intercept her?"

"In the line to meet her after the speech."

Kendrick nodded. "And then?"

"Gain her trust. Get her away from LifeCore's security so you can have a private conversation." Will's fingers moved across the keyboard, highlighting sections of the hotel floor plan.

Kendrick took two steps back and threw her hands up. "I don't like the idea of manipulating someone to get their trust."

"Dr. Lee might represent our only chance to gather evidence that saves lives," Ryder promptly replied.

Kendrick looked at both men, her green eyes reflecting the internal struggle between duty and justice that had been building since their investigation began. Federal agents were supposed to work within legal boundaries, following established procedures and respecting corporate rights.

However, when the system failed to protect individuals like Michael York and Nana, those boundaries became obstacles to justice rather than protections for those who needed them.

She stood up, shouldering her bag. "I guess some risks are worth taking."

The words carried the weight of a career-ending decision. Once Kendrick committed to operating outside federal authority, there would be no path back to her previous life as a by-the-book CID agent.

"Let's do it."

CHAPTER 19

The revolving doors at the hotel and conference center spun with business executives, weary travelers, and medical professionals as Special Agent Jenna Kendrick positioned herself beside a marble pillar in the bustling lobby. Conversations and corporate networking echoed off polished floors and the high ceiling. Through floor-to-ceiling windows, Michigan Avenue stretched north and south, with Lake Michigan visible in the early evening sunlight.

Kendrick's tactical training easily identified the LifeCore security team trying to blend into the crowd. Three men in navy blazers stood near the elevators, their earpieces visible above their collars. A fourth operative positioned himself beside the concierge desk, his eyes scanning the lobby while pretending to read a newspaper. Professional placement, but obvious to anyone who knew what to look for.

The elevator chimed as Dr. Allison Lee emerged from the conference level, surrounded by a small group of admirers clutching conference folders and business cards. Her presentation on "Ethical Healthcare Delivery in the Modern Era" had drawn applause from the American Medical Association crowd downstairs. Kendrick recognized her from Will's intelligence briefings—a mid-fifties woman with raven hair and a pointy chin, wearing a charcoal blazer that projected authority and competence.

A line formed as conference attendees waited their turn to shake hands with the speaker. Kendrick joined the queue behind a dozen medical professionals eager to exchange pleasantries with LifeCore's chief medical officer. Will Cameron's extensive research armed the CID special agent with essential information on LifeCore, which she used to entice Dr. Lee into a private conversation.

The LifeCore security detail maintained their perimeter, alert but not aggressive. Their job was protection, not intimidation, at least in public view. Kendrick knew their role was to protect LifeCore from a potential internal whistleblower, not Dr. Lee from aggressive radiologists or pediatric nurses.

Dr. Lee's interactions were brief but genuine, the charm of someone accustomed to corporate events and public speaking. She offered the same professional smile and firm handshake to each attendee, her responses polished but personal enough to make each interaction feel meaningful.

"Dr. Lee." Kendrick stepped forward, extending her hand. "Brilliant presentation. I'm Jennifer Kennedy from Chicago General Hospital."

"Thank you so much." Dr. Lee's handshake was firm, her eyes making brief but direct contact. "What brings you to the AMA conference?"

"Professional development." Kendrick lowered her voice, forcing Dr. Lee to lean closer to hear over the lobby's background noise. "I've also been following some interesting developments at LifeCore. I think you might want to hear what I've learned."

Dr. Lee's expression shifted almost imperceptibly. Her professional smile remained intact, but Kendrick detected the wariness of someone operating under pressure.

"I'm not sure what you mean."

"The Carol Hanson case," Kendrick said while carefully observing Dr. Lee. "I know what they're really doing."

The color drained from Dr. Lee's cheeks. She swallowed hard as her eyes darted to the LifeCore security team, then back to Kendrick.

"I can't discuss company business with the public."

Kendrick glanced at the security operatives, who were taking notice of the extended conversation. Time was running short before they intervened to move Dr. Lee out of the lobby.

"Lose your security detail," Kendrick whispered. "Meet me at Cloud Gate in Grant Park in thirty minutes. I'm with people who can help you do the right thing."

Without waiting for a response, Kendrick stepped away from Dr. Lee and melted into the lobby crowd. She didn't look back as she pushed through the revolving doors onto Michigan Avenue, but she could feel the weight of desperate eyes following her toward the street.

The late summer humidity hit her like a wall as she crossed the busy intersection toward Grant Park. Traffic moved in sluggish waves, air conditioning units humming behind tinted windows as commuters sought relief from the August heat.

Grant Park stretched before her, an oasis of green space bordered by the towering skyline of downtown Chicago. Office buildings reflected the setting sun in geometric patterns of glass and steel.

Cloud Gate, also known as "The Bean," dominated the northwest corner of Millennium Park like a giant liquid mercury drop frozen in time. The polished stainless steel sculpture curved and twisted, reflecting the city skyline in distorted patterns that shifted with the viewer's perspective. Tourists clustered around its base, taking selfies and marveling at their warped reflections in the seamless surface. Children ran beneath the arch, their laughter echoing off the curved metal overhead.

Kendrick found a position behind a cluster of oak trees thirty yards from the sculpture, where she could observe the entire plaza while remaining concealed.

Minutes ticked past with no sign of Dr. Lee. Families pushed strollers along the pathways. Joggers passed on the trail, their footsteps rhythmic against the concrete. The evening crowd around the sculpture thinned as darkness approached.

Kendrick checked her watch—thirty-eight minutes since their conversation in the hotel lobby. Either Dr. Lee had decided the risk was too great, or LifeCore's security had prevented her from leaving the building.

A slender figure approached from the north path, moving with the careful gait of someone trying to appear casual. Dr. Lee wore sunglasses and had exchanged her conference blazer for a short-sleeved blouse.

Kendrick waited until Dr. Lee reached the sculpture before emerging from her concealed position.

"Dr. Lee."

The LifeCore CMO turned to face the voice. "I shouldn't be here."

"But you came anyway." Kendrick positioned herself so they could speak while appearing to admire the sculpture like any other tourists. "That tells me something."

"It tells you I might be making a terrible mistake."

"Or it tells me you're tired of watching people die for corporate profits." Kendrick kept her voice gentle but direct. "I'm a federal agent, Dr. Lee. I'm working with people who know about the corruption at LifeCore, and we're going to take them down."

Dr. Lee removed her sunglasses, revealing red-rimmed eyes that spoke of sleepless nights and moral anguish. "You don't understand what you're asking. These aren't just aggressive business practices. They've built a system designed to kill people."

"Then help us stop it."

"If they find out I've talked to federal agents, they'll fire me and blacklist me from the industry. I'm sure they'll attempt to destroy me, or maybe worse," Dr. Lee said as her voice cracked and trailed off.

"We know you've been trying to do the right thing. You're not our target. You're the solution."

The words seemed to break something inside Dr. Lee. Her shoulders sagged as suppressed guilt and frustration found an outlet.

"Andre Atwood wasn't always like this. When I first met him fifteen years ago, he had brilliant ideas about revolutionizing health insurance for the most vulnerable populations. Coverage for pre-existing conditions, expanded mental health benefits, and prescription assistance programs."

"What changed?"

"Bonuses. Stock payouts. Shareholder pressure." Dr. Lee's laugh was bitter. "The company went public, and then every decision was about quarterly earnings instead of patient outcomes."

"Tell me about the targeting system."

Dr. Lee glanced in both directions, then focused on Cloud Gate's reflective surface as if the distorted cityscape might provide answers to impossible questions.

"Chad Kline's algorithms target vulnerable populations. Seniors, disabled veterans, and low-income families. The system flags them as 'high-cost, low-yield' and prioritizes denials."

Kendrick scanned the bean, using its reflection to search for LifeCore security without turning around.

"The internal transfers we found. What are they?"

"Those are bounties. Employees get paid for denying claims." Dr. Lee's voice fell to a whisper. "Some of them double their salary."

"How much?"

"Fifty to a hundred for routine denials. Major cases pay two thousand or more." Dr. Lee wiped at her eyes. "The adjuster got twenty-five hundred for denying Carol Hanson's cancer treatment."

The number hit Kendrick like a physical blow. Someone was paid twenty-five hundred dollars to condemn Carol Hanson to death.

"She could have lived another decade. Stage two breast cancer with an excellent prognosis for a full recovery. But Kline's system flagged her as an economic liability, the adjuster collected her bounty after issuing the denial, and Atwood approved it without looking up from his profit projections."

"How many of these bounties do they pay out each year?"

Dr. Lee shook her head. "Tens of thousands. Maybe more. Kline's department processes them like assembly line work. They're coded as efficiency bonuses to avoid regulatory scrutiny."

The scope was staggering. Not dozens of isolated cases, but an industrial-scale system designed to profit from human suffering—thousands of families destroyed by deliberate corporate policy while executives celebrate their quarterly earnings.

Kendrick's hands clenched into fists. Her investigation had begun with questions about Michael York's death, but it had led to something far more extensive than individual corruption. This was systematic murder disguised as business efficiency.

"I need documentation. Files, emails, anything that proves what you've told me."

"I can't access Kline's systems directly. He maintains separate databases with restricted security protocols." Dr. Lee looked around the park again, her concern about crossing LifeCore security clear in every movement. "But I can ask around. I know a few other people who are concerned with our policies and may be willing to help."

"We appreciate any evidence you can gather for us and understand that it comes with personal risk for you and your co-workers. Be careful."

Dr. Lee replaced her sunglasses, preparing to leave as the setting sun reflected off the glass buildings. "I'll be careful. These people have already killed to protect their profits. They won't hesitate to kill again."

Kendrick absorbed the warning. The revelation made her uneasy about the danger Dr. Lee would face in gathering evidence. "Will you be safe?"

"For now. They need me to maintain their medical credibility with regulatory agencies. But if they discover I've talked to federal agents..." She didn't finish the sentence.

"We're going to stop them. All of them."

Dr. Lee managed a partial smile. "I hope you succeed. Thousands of people are counting on it, whether they know it or not."

She walked away without looking back, her figure disappearing into the evening crowd of tourists. Kendrick remained beside Cloud Gate for another ten minutes, watching for any signs of surveillance or pursuit. The park seemed normal, but her training kept her alert for threats that might not be obvious.

Her phone buzzed with a text from Ryder. *How did it go?*

Better than expected, she replied. *Dr. Lee confirmed everything. This is bigger than we thought.*

How much bigger?

Kendrick stared across Lake Michigan as it disappeared into the darkness, processing the full implications of what she'd learned.

Tens of thousands of people, she typed back. *They're killing tens of thousands of people.*

The response came immediately. *Then we stop them.*

Kendrick pocketed her phone and started walking toward her car. The investigation had crossed a threshold from which there would be no return.

Special Agent Kendrick, Army CID, had just committed to stopping the bureaucratic killing of innocent people on a case she had zero jurisdiction or authority over. If Sergeant Major Atkins ever found out, she'd face court-martial and jail time. She didn't care. LifeCore had to be stopped—at any cost.

CHAPTER 20

Ryder raised his finger to pause Kendrick's recap as laughter from the Phoenix House kitchen caught his attention. Three residents were giving Orosco grief about his experimental breakfast creation, their voices carrying the easy camaraderie of men who'd learned to find humor in difficult circumstances.

"What the hell is that supposed to be, Orosco?" one resident called out. "Looks like something my dog threw up after eating garbage." More laughter followed, punctuated by plates clattering and spoons clinking inside porcelain coffee cups.

Orosco's voice rose above the noise. "It's called creativity, you knuckle-dragging door kickers. Just because you're used to MREs and cafeteria slop doesn't mean the rest of us can't appreciate fine cuisine." The good-natured ribbing continued until a former Marine crossed the line. "Keep it up, Orosco, you'll make someone a good wife someday."

The kitchen went quiet. Chair legs scraped against the floor as Orosco shot back, "Well, your mama seemed to be fine with my cooking when she invited me over." Voices shifted from playful to hard, with an edge that often preceded fistfights in barracks and barrooms.

Ryder was through the kitchen doorway before the situation could escalate further. "Everyone, chill out and eat your breakfast."

His calm authority cut through the tension like a blade. He moved to Orosco's side and patted him on the back. "I think your food is amazing, and top chefs can make over six figures. Don't let anyone discourage you from your passion."

The residents dispersed with mumbled apologies and resumed their morning routines. Ryder returned to the conference room, where Kendrick and Will had witnessed the entire exchange from their seats at the table.

"Impressive," Kendrick said, noting how quickly Ryder had defused the situation. "Now, back to what I was saying about Dr. Lee. She seemed genuinely fearful yesterday. When I mentioned we knew about LifeCore's patient targeting, she looked like someone had pointed a gun at her head."

Ryder studied the steam rising from his black coffee. "Did she give you anything concrete?"

"She confirmed everything Will found in their financial records. Atwood and Kline are paying bounties for denying care to high-risk patients. But she doesn't have direct access to the documentation." Kendrick paused for a beat. "Dr. Lee also said she knew Atwood and Kline would destroy her career if they ever suspected her of talking to outsiders."

Will looked up from his laptop. "Did she mention any specific cases or examples?"

"I mentioned the case you shared with me, Carol Hanson, and I heard the emotion in her voice when she described the way LifeCore screwed her over. Dr. Lee then said that Atwood wasn't always like this, but bonuses and shareholder pressure changed him."

The conversation was interrupted by the distant sound of a lawnmower starting up next door, followed by voices from the kitchen as more residents began their morning routines. Phoenix

House was waking up around them, but the trio remained focused on their growing case against LifeCore.

"What's our next move?" Ryder asked.

"We wait," Kendrick replied. "Dr. Lee said she would contact me if she accessed information that could help us. Pushing too hard could spook her."

Will closed his laptop and leaned back in his chair. "The ball is in Dr. Lee's court now. We have to see if she can provide concrete evidence of LifeCore's operations."

Ryder nodded, but frustration simmered beneath his controlled exterior. Waiting meant more patients would suffer while LifeCore executives paid more bounties. Every delayed decision meant more people like Nana would lose their independence or their lives to bureaucratic cruelty disguised as business efficiency.

They worked in silence throughout the morning until Kendrick's phone dinged with an incoming message. Ryder noticed her expression harden as she read the text.

"Is that Dr. Lee?"

"No, it's my boss, Sergeant Major Atkins." Her jaw tightened as she typed a quick response. "He told me to wrap up my case in Chicago and get back to DC."

Will leaned back in his chair. "How long do you have?"

"As long as it takes," Kendrick said without hesitation. "I'm not leaving until LifeCore is held accountable."

Ryder studied her face, recognizing the determination he'd seen in mirrors during his own campaigns against corrupt institutions. "Does he know you're with me?"

"Oh, hell no. He'd flip his lid if he knew I was with you."

"Would he command you to arrest me?"

Kendrick's laugh held no humor. "No, quite the opposite. He seems to have developed an allergy to arresting James Ryder over the past month. He's been all over the board with you since he assigned me to this case."

The actions of her boss seemed unusual to Ryder, but he didn't know Atkins personally. The military hierarchy operated by different rules than civilian organizations, and superior officers sometimes had motivations that remained hidden from their subordinates.

"How about lunch?" Ryder suggested, changing the subject. "Downtown has some decent restaurants with outdoor seating."

Will declined, citing his need to continue analyzing LifeCore's financial records for additional evidence. But Kendrick accepted, and twenty minutes later, they parked on the eleventh floor of a parking garage near the heart of the city.

The restaurant Ryder selected occupied a corner location with a patio overlooking the Chicago River. The midday sun filtered through market umbrellas, creating a pleasant atmosphere despite the escalating heat of the day. Office workers and tourists filled the surrounding tables, their conversations creating a steady background murmur that would mask their discussion of federal investigations and corporate corruption.

They ordered and enjoyed a brief moment of downtime. Ryder found himself studying Kendrick's face as she watched pedestrians cross the bridge above the river.

"You're taking an enormous risk staying in Chicago against orders."

"So are you." She turned to meet his gaze. "At least I have federal credentials and backup if things go wrong. You're operating alone."

"Not alone. Will's become more valuable than I expected. And Shadow's always watching my back."

"Speaking of Shadow, how's she adjusting to city life after Afghanistan?"

Ryder smiled at the thought of his canine friend and protector of Nana. "Better than I expected. She loves Nana, and the Phoenix House residents treat her like a celebrity. Turns out Belgian Malinois enjoy being the center of attention."

Their food arrived, and they ate in comfortable silence. Ryder appreciated Kendrick's straightforward approach to their unusual partnership. No games, no hidden agendas, just professional competence focused on a shared objective.

Kendrick was starting the second half of her sandwich when her phone chirped again.

"Atkins again?"

"No, it's Dr. Lee." Kendrick's voice carried excitement mixed with apprehension. "She has some files to give us. She says it's urgent and wants to know if we can meet her now on the Riverwalk below State Street."

Ryder calculated the distance. "That's only eight blocks away. We can be there in ten minutes."

They paid and hurried through the crowded sidewalks along the river.

The Chicago Riverwalk stretched below street level, offering pedestrian access along the water's edge with views of the city's architectural landmarks. Trees provided shade along the walking path, where tourists moved at a leisurely pace despite the afternoon heat.

Kendrick spotted Dr. Lee near the State Street bridge. She wore sunglasses and casual clothes, but her nervous energy was visible from fifty feet away. Her head turned constantly, scanning for threats or unwanted observers.

"Dr. Lee," Kendrick called as they approached.

The LifeCore chief medical officer turned toward their voices. She clutched a leather portfolio and a small USB drive in her right hand. Wrinkles stretched across her forehead as she noticed the imposing former Delta Force operator striding beside Kendrick.

The CID special agent must have spotted the concern and immediately introduced him. "This is Sergeant James Ryder. We're working together on this case."

The quick thinking impressed him. Her omission that Ryder was a former sergeant in the US Army, intended to make him sound more like a law enforcement officer, was especially crafty.

"This is all I could get without raising suspicions," Dr. Lee said quickly, pressing both items into Kendrick's hands. "But it should be enough to shut down LifeCore's patient targeting system completely."

Ryder stepped closer, using his body to shield their exchange from casual observers. "What's on the drive?"

"Financial records showing bounty payments. Emails between Atwood and board members. Patient files with overruled medical recommendations." Dr. Lee's words came rapidly. "Internal memos on demographic targeting."

Kendrick secured the items in the inner pocket of her blazer. "This is incredibly valuable evidence."

"It's also incredibly dangerous for me." Dr. Lee's voice shook. "I had to be very careful getting this information, and I can't speak to either of you anymore. If they discover what I've done, they'll destroy my career and have me arrested for corporate espionage."

"We understand," Ryder said. "This took courage."

Dr. Lee removed her sunglasses. "You now have the information you requested. Please use it to stop them before more people die."

She turned and rushed back toward the street level, leaving Ryder and Kendrick alone beside the river with evidence that could bring down LifeCore's executive leadership.

They returned to Phoenix House to find Will still hunched over his laptop next to empty coffee cups. His lanky frame was bent in concentration as he cross-referenced financial data with patient files.

"Dr. Lee delivered," Kendrick announced, producing the USB drive.

Will's eyes lit up as he inserted the drive into his laptop. The screen filled with folder after folder of documents, emails, and financial records. He opened several files, scanning their contents with growing excitement.

"This USB is a gold mine," he said after several minutes of examination. "We have pages and pages of information that must break a dozen laws and hundreds of ethics violations with the Illinois Department of Insurance."

"Who should we turn it into?" Ryder asked. "The police or the Illinois Department of Insurance?"

Will leaned back in his chair and pursed his lips, his background in intelligence helping him evaluate the options. "White collar crime doesn't get much attention from law enforcement unless it's the FBI, and I don't know if this falls under their jurisdiction for insurance fraud. On the other hand, the Illinois Department of Insurance can shut down LifeCore operations in Illinois, which would be a good start to taking down Atwood and his cronies. I can file a report with their enforcement division."

Ryder debated whether bureaucratic punishment was sufficient justice for systematic murder. His instincts told him that corporate executives who profited from patient deaths deserved more severe consequences than regulatory fines and license revocations.

But thousands of LifeCore policyholders would benefit from state intervention, even if the ultimate punishment failed to match the severity of the crimes. Sometimes incremental justice was better than no justice at all.

"Do it."

Will spent the next hour preparing a comprehensive report to accompany Dr. Lee's evidence. Every piece of evidence painted a picture of institutional murder disguised as efficient business operations.

When Will clicked send, transmitting the report and evidence to the Illinois Department of Insurance's enforcement division, Ryder felt something he hadn't experienced since discovering LifeCore's targeting of Nana—cautious optimism.

For the first time since James Ryder became aware of LifeCore's ruthless history of denials, he believed they might face some form of justice through official channels. The evidence was overwhelming, the violations were clear, and regulatory authorities had the power to shut down the company's Illinois operations within days.

Shadow appeared at Ryder's side, the former military canine sensing his handler's change in demeanor. The dog's presence served as a reminder that battles are won through intelligence, planning, and execution, then improvising when the first three strategies didn't work, ensuring victory.

Ryder hoped that their hard work and efforts to gather evidence on Atwood, Kline, and LifeCore would pay off with a swift resolution and lead to accountability. Still, he was prepared to improvise if needed.

CHAPTER 21

Brandon Crane adjusted his earpiece as he stood in the surveillance van parked three blocks from Nana's Andersonville brownstone. Rain drummed against the vehicle's tinted windows while he studied the residential street through high-powered binoculars.

"The veteran recovery center is too well defended," Crane shared over the radio. "Ryder's expecting trouble there, but we can still exploit the grandmother's house."

"Copy. Eyes on the residence," Glenn replied from the alley.

"Two individuals inside. The grandma and another adult female."

Crane checked his watch. Eighteen twenty-three. The former Delta Force operator's devotion to family created the tactical opening they needed.

"When Ryder arrives, give him a few minutes to go upstairs. Once inside, you have authorization to eliminate the primary target." Crane's instructions carried the weight of a death sentence. "Collateral damage is acceptable. Make it look like a home invasion gone wrong. Ryder will fight back once he's engaged, so that shouldn't be a problem."

"Rules of engagement for civilians?" Glenn asked.

"No witnesses." The order hung in the humid air like a blade. "Tobias Richter wants this problem resolved permanently."

Crane watched the white Toyota Camry pass his van and park in front of the target house. Ryder jogged inside and closed the door behind him.

“Ryder’s inside. Move out.”

The rain turned into a light mist as Crane's team moved into final positions around the brownstone. The medium-height operative who'd escaped Ryder's questioning days earlier crouched beside the back door, lock picks ready. His two companions flanked the property's rear entrance, their suppressed weapons drawn.

"Breach in thirty seconds," Glenn whispered through the comm system.

Crane watched through his scope as the team approached the house. Yellow roses climbed the wrought-iron trellis beside the front steps, their petals closed against the evening moisture. The peaceful domestic scene would soon become a battlefield.

"Go!"

***

Ryder's key turned the handle of Nana’s front door, and he stepped inside from the rain. He shook the moisture off his jacket and hung it on a hook behind the front door. The grandfather clock in the hallway chimed six-thirty, its steady rhythm providing comfort after another difficult day at Phoenix House. Shadow padded beside him and accepted the scratches behind her neck.

"Nana?" he called softly.

"In here, James." Her voice carried from the family room.

She’d worked over two hours with Karla, and the latest session had been a grueling effort for Jill Ryder. The left side of Nana's face continued to droop, and her speech still slurred. The stroke's grip on her body was tightening rather than loosening.

Karla met him in the kitchen, her medical bag already packed. Dark circles under her eyes matched the concern etched into her features.

"How was she today?"

"She's losing ground." Karla's professional mask couldn't hide her frustration. "The basic physical therapy sessions aren't enough. Without intensive rehabilitation, she's going to plateau far below where she could be."

Ryder snagged a can of Liquid Death Sparkling Mountain Water from the refrigerator, buying time to process the implications. "What would intensive therapy look like?"

"Daily sessions with a licensed physical therapist. Occupational therapy to rebuild fine motor skills. Speech therapy to ensure she can communicate adequately." Karla took a deep breath. "She needs specialized equipment, targeted exercises, and professional expertise I can't provide."

The numbers ran through Ryder's mind like a tactical battle plan. His Bitcoin account, already strained from Phoenix House operations and Nana's private care, wouldn't cover the expense.

"I can continue the basic care as long as you need, but I want you to understand what we're up against."

Ryder studied his grandmother's caretaker. Karla genuinely cared about Nana's recovery, not just the paycheck. Her dedication reminded him of the medics he'd served alongside in Delta Force, professionals who fought for every life regardless of the odds.

"Keep working with her. I'll figure out the rest."

Karla went into the family room to make her final check on Nana.

“I’m going to change. I’ll be right back to help with my grandmother,” Ryder said as he climbed the stairs two steps at a time.

He opened his phone and the trading app to check prices after the market closed. LifeCore's stock price had climbed another three percent that day, rewarding shareholders for the company's systematic denial of medical care. The short position he'd established was bleeding money as investor optimism pushed share prices higher.

He could close the position, cut his losses, and use those funds for Nana's therapy. The Illinois Department of Insurance investigation might never materialize, and even if regulators took action, the process could drag on for months while LifeCore's stock continued climbing.

But closing the short position felt like surrender. Somewhere in LifeCore's glass tower, Andre Atwood was celebrating future bonuses built on the suffering of vulnerable patients. The evidence Will had gathered through Dr. Lee painted a clear picture of institutional murder disguised as business efficiency.

The IDOI case against LifeCore had to succeed.

Ryder closed the trading app. Justice required patience, even when patience felt like surrender.

A scream shattered the house's peaceful silence.

Karla's voice, filled with terror and pain, cut through the night like a blade. Shadow's ears snapped forward as she bolted toward the stairs, her military training recognizing the sound of immediate danger.

Ryder's SIG Sauer appeared in his hand with muscle memory that bypassed conscious thought. He moved down the staircase with Shadow at his side, his tactical mind processing threats and countermeasures.

The scene in the family room sent a chill down his spine.

A tall operative in tactical gear held a suppressed pistol against Karla's temple, her body rigid with fear as his arm encircled her throat. Two more armed men flanked the room's entrances, their weapons sweeping for additional targets.

"Drop it or—"

The hollow-point round from Ryder's weapon punched through the gunman's forehead before he could complete his threat. Brain matter and blood sprayed across the family room wall as his body crumpled, releasing Karla to dive behind a couch.

Ryder searched for Nana as his barrel tracked left toward the second operative, who stood frozen by the sudden violence. Shadow launched herself across the room, seventy pounds of muscle and razor teeth clamping down on the man's firing arm. Her jaws found flesh and bone with crushing force, swinging him off balance as his weapon discharged into the ceiling.

Two rounds center mass, and then one to the head. The second operative collapsed beside his partner as Shadow released her grip and bounded away from the falling body.

The third gunman was ready.

Ryder recognized him immediately. The same operative he'd questioned in the alley behind Nana's House, now armed and positioned with a clear shot across the family room. Muzzle flash erupted from his suppressor as the bullet grazed Ryder's left collarbone, spinning him sideways.

Shadow yelped as a second round sparked off the hardwood floor where she'd been standing. The Belgian Malinois vanished around the corner, deploying her survival instincts that had kept them both alive through multiple deployments.

Ryder dove behind the heavy wooden coffee table he remembered from his youth, overturning it to create an improvised cover as more rounds punched through the air where he'd been standing. The thick oak absorbed several slugs, but wouldn't withstand sustained fire.

He was pinned.

The operative held a perfect firing position, able to shoot Ryder the moment he emerged from cover. No movement was possible without exposing himself to lethal fire.

Where was Nana? Would she hear the gunshots and try to investigate? The thought of his grandmother wandering into this battlefield sent ice through his veins.

Ryder considered calling Will or Kendrick for backup, but neither could arrive in time. His survival would be decided in the next sixty seconds by tactical skill and the creative deployment of resources.

A Spartan war cry, followed by a high-pitched yelp, echoed through the room.

"You bitch!"

Ryder peered over the coffee table's edge with one eye to see Karla standing beside the surviving operative, her fist wrapped around a surgical scalpel buried deep in the side of his neck. Blood poured between her fingers as the man clawed at the blade, his weapon forgotten.

The SIG Sauer's muzzle found its target. One round through the heart ended the threat.

Ryder vaulted over his cover, sweeping the room for additional hostiles before rushing to Karla's side. Blood covered her scrubs and hands, but her eyes held the fierce satisfaction of someone who'd fought back against overwhelming odds.

"Are you okay?"

"Yeah." Karla wiped blood from her hands with clinical detachment. "I told you I was tough."

"Yes, you are." Ryder's respect for the home healthcare nurse had exploded. "Where's Nana?"

"Your shoulder is bleeding. Hold on, and I'll get my medical bag," the nurse stated.

"Not until I know Nana is safe. Where is she?"

"She was headed toward the bathroom when they showed up."

The bathroom door remained closed at the end of the hallway. Ryder approached carefully, his weapon lowered but ready. The silence behind the door could mean anything.

He knocked softly. No response.

"Nana?" He tried again, louder this time. "It's James. The bad guys are all gone."

A shaky voice emerged from the other side. "Come in."

Ryder found his grandmother sitting on the toilet seat with the lid down, and her Smith & Wesson revolver gripped in her good hand with the muzzle pointed at the door.

"Nana." He removed the pistol from her grasp. "Are you okay?"

"No, I'm not hurt, but what the hell was that?" The strength in her voice that had sustained her through seven decades returned. "Who were those men?"

"Just some people who want me dead."

Nana studied his face, unblinking. "Are they with the insurance company?"

"I suspect they're tied to LifeCore, so yeah."

The admission hung between them like a bridge spanning the gap between corporate boardrooms and domestic terrorism. Andre Atwood's systematic murder of patients had escalated to a direct assault on Ryder's family.

Nana reached out with her good hand, squeezing his fingers with surprising strength. "I think it's time for you to handle this your way now."

Ryder met her eyes, seeing the same moral clarity that had guided him from a wounded boy to the man he is today. The woman who'd taught him that justice heals while vengeance wounds was giving him permission to cross whatever lines were necessary to protect innocent people.

He nodded. No other words were required.

CHAPTER 22

Ryder touched the bandage on his shoulder as he leaned back in the recliner two days after the assault by three Richter security operatives. He put his feet up and scrolled through his phone after helping Nana to bed. She was still weak and tired after witnessing an assault in her family room and dealing with days of police, paramedics, and cleanup crews in her house. He had stayed at Nana's house over the last forty-eight hours to ensure she was okay after the traumatic event that had unfolded in her family room. Now he wanted to know if Will had heard anything from the IDOI enforcement division.

His phone rang, the display showing a downtown Chicago number.

"James Ryder?"

"Speaking."

"This is Detective Morrison, CPD. We have a situation involving one of your Phoenix House residents. We found a young man named Ricky Nelson unconscious in an alley near the Kennedy Expressway and Addison Street about thirty minutes ago."

The words hit Ryder like a rogue wave. "Where is he?"

"Northwestern Memorial. I recommend getting there as soon as possible."

Ryder grabbed his keys and wallet, his mind racing with possibilities of what he might find.

The emergency room buzzed with controlled chaos. Nurses moved between treatment bays while monitors beeped in the background.

"I'm looking for Ricky Nelson. The ambulance brought him here about forty-five minutes ago."

The admissions clerk checked her computer. "Are you family?"

"He's a resident at my veterans recovery facility. I'm his emergency contact."

She directed him to the third-floor ICU, where Dr. Stacy Robbins met him outside Ricky's room.

"I'm Dr. Robbins, the attending physician. Mr. Nelson suffered a severe drug overdose. We've administered naloxone and stabilized his vital signs, but the damage is extensive."

Through the room's glass wall, Ryder could see Ricky connected to multiple machines. Tubes and wires surrounded his pale form, the mechanical sounds of life support providing artificial breath and circulation.

"What happened?"

"Heroin overdose combined with fentanyl contamination. The mixture stopped his breathing for an unknown period. We've restored oxygen flow, but there may be permanent neurological effects."

Ryder absorbed the information. "What's his prognosis?"

"It's too early to determine the extent of brain damage. We're monitoring for signs of cognitive function, but the next seventy-two hours will be critical."

Dr. Robbins gestured toward Ricky. "There's something else you should know. Mr. Nelson has Medicaid insurance through the Illinois Department of Healthcare and Family Services, and the provider initially denied coverage for the overdose treatment protocol. They classified it as 'self-inflicted injury' and refused to authorize the medications we needed to save his life."

"Who is the provider?" Ryder asked, already sensing the answer.

"LifeCore Health Insurance."

The familiar name triggered a surge of rage that Ryder forced down through years of practice. "Initially denied?"

"After multiple requests, the insurance company granted authorization, but the delay cost us precious time. If we'd been able to administer the full treatment when Mr. Nelson first arrived, his chances of recovery would have been much higher."

The bureaucratic cruelty was staggering. LifeCore had added a military veteran to its long list of casualties.

"Can I see him?"

"Yes, but just understand that he may not be responsive."

Ryder entered the ICU room where machines maintained Ricky's life. The young veteran's face was pale and drawn, his chest rising and falling in rhythm with the ventilator. Track marks dotted his arms, evidence of the battle he'd lost against his demons.

"Ricky, I wish we'd met sooner. Maybe you wouldn't be here right now."

Guilt settled in his gut and twisted into a knot.

Ryder remained beside Ricky's bed for the rest of the night, watching the monitors track vital signs that grew weaker every hour. Dr. Robbins returned often with updates that painted an increasingly grim picture. Brain scans showed extensive damage from oxygen deprivation. Even if Ricky survived, he was facing lifelong care.

At six forty-seven AM, the monitors flatlined.

Dr. Robbins and her team worked for eighteen minutes, pushing medications and performing compressions that turned more and more desperate. But Ricky Nelson's body had endured too much trauma. The combination of drug toxicity and delayed treatment had overwhelmed his body's capacity for recovery.

"Time of death, seven-oh-five AM."

The machines fell silent. Ryder stood beside the bed where a young soldier had lost his last battle, this time against an enemy that hid behind corporate policies and profit margins. Another veteran who'd served his country with honor, only to be abandoned by the systems that should have protected him.

***

The Phoenix House common room felt hollow when Ryder returned at seven-thirty in the morning. Will sat alone at the dining table, staring at an empty coffee mug. The other residents were still asleep, leaving the building in heavy silence.

"Ricky?" Will asked with hope in his voice.

"He's gone."

Will closed his eyes and exhaled. "Damn it. I should have seen it coming."

"We both should have." Ryder dropped into the chair across from him. "He was fighting demons we couldn't reach."

They sat in silence, weighed down by the burden of failure.

"The other guys know?"

"I told them it wasn't looking good for Ricky before they went to bed. They won't be surprised. I saw it in their eyes last night."

The truth cut deep. Ricky Nelson had survived multiple deployments in Afghanistan, only to lose his life to enemies he'd brought home with him. The young soldier had died fighting a battle that should have been winnable with proper support and medical care.

"Dr. Robbins said LifeCore delayed his overdose treatment. Called it a self-inflicted injury."

Will's hands clenched into fists. "They killed him."

"As surely as if they'd injected the heroin themselves."

The anger in the room was palpable but controlled. They'd both seen too many good people die from systemic failures that should have been preventable.

"I'll tell the residents after they wake up."

"And then what? We just accept that this is how the system works?"

Will's phone buzzed on the table between them. He glanced at the notification, and his expression changed.

"It's from the Illinois Department of Insurance. Hopefully, this is good news. We're due for some."

He opened the lengthy message, and the color drained from his face as he read. “Let’s go into the conference room.”

"What is it?" Ryder asked after closing the conference room door behind him.

"IDOI let LifeCore off easy."

A jolt of cold realization shot through Ryder. "We gave them everything Dr. Lee provided."

Will read the bureaucratic language in the IDOI response and provided a summary to Ryder.

"The Illinois Department of Insurance issued LifeCore a formal reprimand and a $500,000 fine for 'procedural irregularities in claims processing,' which is nothing more than a rounding error in their quarterly earnings,” Will shared as he shook his head. “The IDOI acknowledged 'concerns about denial rate patterns' but cited insufficient evidence of intentional wrongdoing. They concluded that the algorithm's complexity made it impossible to prove discriminatory intent. The case is now closed."

"What about Dr. Lee?" Ryder inquired. "She stuck her neck out to get us information."

"That's the worst part." Will's voice cracked. During the investigation, LifeCore claimed that the information in the complaint was obtained through an unauthorized breach, so IDOI is investigating LifeCore employees for potential violations of corporate data security laws. I have no doubt that Atwood and Kline will point investigators to Dr. Lee and paint her as a suspect rather than a whistleblower."

The betrayal was complete. Dr. Lee had risked her career to expose LifeCore's systematic targeting of vulnerable patients, only to face criminal charges while the executives she'd tried to stop celebrated their immunity.

Ryder stared at the evidence spread across the conference table. At the outset, they assumed that it would be enough to bury Atwood in federal court. Enough to let the system work the way it was supposed to.

Except that the system had already failed. The Illinois DOI had slapped LifeCore on the wrist. Federal regulators moved at a glacial pace while people like Ricky Nelson died in alleys.

'Justice heals; vengeance wounds.' Nana's voice echoed in his mind.

But what was justice for tens of thousands of denied claims? For Ricky to die in the ER because some algorithm decided lifesaving treatment wasn't cost-effective?

The law said to wait and let the system work. Trust the process.

Ryder's hands curled into fists. He'd trusted the judicial system after he'd buried his parents when he was twelve. He'd trusted the process in Afghanistan when he identified war crimes and reported them through the proper channels.

Trust in the system hadn't benefited James Ryder, but pursuing justice had never failed him.

"They've thought of everything," Will murmured.

"Not everything," Ryder corrected his lieutenant. "They've prepared for lawyers and regulators and congressional hearings. They haven't prepared for justice."

The room fell silent except for the distant sound of an L train passing. Both men understood the implications of what Ryder had just said.

"LifeCore executives think their money and connections make them untouchable," Ryder added.

Will closed his laptop, keeping his focus on Ryder. "What are you thinking?"

The former Delta Force operator turned to face his friend, Nana's words of support for his brand of justice playing in his mind. "I'm thinking that Andre Atwood has been hunting vulnerable patients for years. It's time for him to discover what it feels like to become prey."

CHAPTER 23

Sunlight spilled across the LifeCore conference room, reflecting off Lake Michigan's surface in waves of silver. Andre Atwood claimed the leather chair at the head of the table, his imposing frame filling the space with a sense of corporate authority.

"Conference call ready, Mr. Atwood." His assistant departed, closing the heavy doors behind her.

Chad Kline sat to his right, eager to discuss his latest efficiency results.

"Good morning, gentlemen." Atwood's voice filled the room as the secure video connection rendered. Two faces appeared on the split screen: Tobias Richter from his Manhattan office overlooking Central Park, and Brandon Crane from Richter's Chicago operations center.

"Andre, I trust the quarterly results continue to exceed expectations?"

"Results are growing as planned, maybe even better." Atwood allowed satisfaction to color his voice. "Chad's algorithms are performing exactly as you suggested fifteen months ago."

"Excellent. But before we discuss operational matters, I want to provide further clarity about our relationship," Tobias stated. "Richter Enterprises' interest in LifeCore extends beyond the fourteen percent minority position disclosed in public filings. It's a true partnership."

Atwood's eyebrows rose. "I'm not sure I understand."

"Richter Pharmaceuticals has developed a breakthrough medication called NeuraNox. Clinical trials show exceptional promise for treating traumatic brain injury and pain management," Tobias explained. "I see a tremendous opportunity for LifeCore to become the first major insurance provider to approve NeuraNox coverage once FDA authorization is complete."

Atwood's interest sharpened. "What's the FDA approval timeline?"

"Six to nine months for final approval, assuming no complications during Phase Three trials."

The strategic advantage was obvious. Early approval of a revolutionary medication would position LifeCore as an innovative leader in pain management while generating positive publicity to counter potential regulatory criticism. The partnership would also create substantial profit opportunities for both organizations.

"Who serves as liaison between our organizations in this partnership?"

Tobias steepled his fingers and paused for a moment. "All business matters come directly to me, and Brandon Crane will handle coordination between Richter and LifeCore security matters."

Crane's unblinking gaze remained fixed on the camera, and he nodded acknowledgment. "I've been monitoring potential risks to LifeCore's business model. Recent intelligence suggests increasing regulatory scrutiny and a possible federal investigation."

The words sent a chill through the conference room. Atwood's jaw tightened as he absorbed the implications of federal attention focusing on their operations.

"What kind of federal involvement?"

"Nothing confirmed yet, but patterns suggest coordination between a whistleblower and multiple agencies. We need to keep a tight lid on all LifeCore sensitive data from external and internal interests."

The video conference continued for another twenty minutes, covering operational details and strategic coordination between the organizations. When the call ended, Atwood felt energized by possibilities while also concerned about the risks of investigation.

"Interesting developments." He turned to Kline as the screens went dark.

"The NeuraNox opportunity could transform our market position, but Crane's warning about investigator scrutiny is concerning."

Atwood stood and moved to the window, looking down at Chicago's financial district. Workers moved between office buildings like ants from a steel and glass colony.

"Schedule a staff meeting for this afternoon. I want department heads to review current operations and address any potential compliance issues."

***

The afternoon meeting convened in LifeCore's main boardroom with twelve department heads arranged around the Brazilian rosewood table. Dr. Allison Lee sat at the far end, while Chad Kline positioned himself near the presentation screen.

"Good afternoon, everyone." Atwood's booming voice echoed throughout the room.

He clicked to the first slide, revealing numbers that made even skeptical faces around the table brighten with approval.

"Chad's algorithmic approach to risk assessment has generated exceptional results for us and our policyholders. We can—"

"The financial results are impressive," Dr. Lee interrupted. "However, I'm concerned about the increased mortality rates among our most vulnerable policyholders."

The room fell silent. Atwood's expression hardened before his corporate smile returned. He'd learned to manage Dr. Lee's ethical concerns through a combination of deflection and intimidation.

"What Dr. Lee refers to are unfortunate coincidences. Our medical review follows industry standards."

"That's not accurate." Dr. Lee pressed. "I've witnessed dozens of cases where we denied medically necessary treatments for financial rather than medical reasons. Patients are dying because of our policies."

The department heads shifted uncomfortably under the weight of the tension in the room.

"Dr. Lee, your passion for patient advocacy is admirable, but our decisions are based on evidence-based medicine and actuarial analysis." Atwood's voice held an edge. "If you have specific concerns about individual cases, we can discuss those in a one-on-one meeting."

The chief medical officer's jaw tightened as if she planned to continue her protest but then recognized the dismissal.

"I'd also like to express concern about our growing reliance on external security consultants. The presence of armed personnel in our building creates an atmosphere of intimidation rather than healthcare."

Atwood's eyes flashed with irritation. Dr. Lee was pushing boundaries that could threaten operational security if her concerns spread to other employees or reached regulatory attention.

"Security measures reflect the reality of corporate operations in today's environment. Schedule a meeting through my assistant if you have further concerns."

The meeting concluded with standard reports from other departments and promises of continued excellence. As the room emptied, Atwood gestured for Kline to remain behind. The two men waited until the last department head departed before speaking.

"Dr. Lee is becoming a problem." Kline's voice was low but urgent. "Her questioning in front of the staff could encourage other employees to raise similar concerns."

"Agreed," Atwood replied through his clenched jaw.

"IT and LifeCore security have uncovered that someone in data processing accessed sensitive materials from servers, and that information was passed along to Dr. Lee. Financial records, executive communications, and algorithmic specifications that could expose our entire operational model."

The revelation hit Atwood like a blindside block by a tight end. Dr. Lee now had access to information that could destroy LifeCore and send him to prison.

"How certain are they?"

"One hundred percent."

Atwood drifted behind the table, his fingers drumming a quick, anxious rhythm before he caught himself and stopped.

"We need to contain this situation before it spreads." His voice carried the menace that had intimidated opponents throughout his career. "Dr. Lee cannot be allowed to leak sensitive information to federal authorities."

"Should we involve Crane? His security capabilities extend beyond corporate protection."

Atwood considered the option. Crane's military background and connection to Richter Enterprises suggested capabilities that extended into darker territories. But involving Tobias Richter's organization in domestic security matters could create complications.

"I don't know how Tobias would react to direct involvement in employee matters. This needs to be handled without creating additional exposure for Richter."

Kline was quiet for several seconds, his analytical mind weighing options and calculating risks. His expression shifted as he reached a decision.

"I know somebody who can help. Someone with specialized capabilities who does this type of work on a contract basis. It would take a couple of days to set up, but it would be a permanent solution to our problem."

The euphemism hung in the air between them. Atwood understood what Kline was suggesting. The methodical murder of patients through denial letters had been an abstract business decision, but this would be the direct elimination of a specific threat.

"Are you certain this person can handle the situation without creating links back to LifeCore or Richter?"

"I won't do it if I'm not one hundred percent certain. All connections would be severed. Nobody could prove we were involved with anything that happened to Dr. Lee."

Atwood stared out at Lake Michigan, watching sailboats navigate the afternoon waters while his mind processed the magnitude of what they were discussing. Dr. Allison Lee had been a colleague for seven years, a brilliant physician who'd joined LifeCore with genuine intentions to improve patient care.

But she'd become a threat to everything he'd built. Dr. Lee's evidence could destroy his life and send him to prison.

"Set it up."

The two men gathered their materials and departed the boardroom, each carrying the weight of the decision they'd made.

Instead of retreating to his company-provided penthouse suite ten floors above LifeCore offices, Atwood navigated Chicago's evening traffic toward his suburban home in Winnetka. Manicured lawns and quiet tree-lined streets replaced soaring office towers, taxis, and the rumble of L trains. The forty-minute drive gave him time to transition from LifeCore CEO to devoted family man.

His eight-year-old son, Malik, was waiting in the driveway with a baseball glove and a grin that could melt the hardest heart. The boy launched himself into his father's arms as Atwood emerged from the car, their embrace a ritual that reminded him why every difficult decision was worthwhile.

"Dad! Coach canceled practice, so we get to play catch before dinner!" Malik's enthusiasm was infectious.

Atwood's wife, Ruth, appeared in the doorway, her smile warming his chest the way it had for twelve years of marriage.

"How was your day?" She kissed his cheek as he balanced Malik in one arm.

"Challenging, but productive." The standard response that protected his family from the darker realities of his professional life. "What's for dinner?"

"Malik requested brisket with cheesy macaroni, so that's what we're having. But first, you two have serious baseball business to conduct."

The next thirty minutes were pure joy. Father and son played catch on their expanse of green grass while their golden retriever, Max, chased every errant throw with boundless energy. Malik's pitching accuracy was improving, and his enthusiasm for the game reminded Atwood of his own childhood dreams of a professional athletic career.

"Dad, do you think I could play in the major leagues someday?" Malik asked as they collected baseballs scattered across the grass.

"If you work hard and never give up, you can accomplish anything. The most important thing is always to do your best and take care of the people you love."

After dinner, he helped Malik with homework while Ruth prepared for her evening run through their neighborhood. The domestic tranquility was precisely what he'd worked so hard to achieve. Financial security, family happiness, and community respect validated every difficult business decision he'd made.

At nine thirty, as Ruth tucked Malik into bed, Atwood's phone buzzed with a text message from Chad Kline: *My contact confirmed a permanent solution to our problem. Should I proceed?*

Atwood stared at the message while the sounds of his family's bedtime routine continued around him. Everything he'd built could disappear if Dr. Lee exposed LifeCore's systematic targeting of vulnerable patients.

His mind drifted back to his own childhood, spent in a cramped apartment with his mom and brothers. Wearing secondhand clothes to school, working after-school jobs to help with rent, and watching his mom worry about money every night until exhaustion granted her a few hours of sleep.

He'd sworn his son would never experience that uncertainty. He would have every advantage his father's hard work and strategic thinking could provide.

Dr. Allison Lee threatened all of that.

Atwood typed his response: *Do it.*

He deleted the message thread and powered off his phone, then climbed the stairs to join his wife for adult conversation in the stately bedroom. It was a perfect evening for the LifeCore CEO. Whatever happened to Dr. Lee was a necessary business decision to protect his family's future.

CHAPTER 24

The screech of tires against wet asphalt jolted Ryder from sleep, his body already moving before his mind caught up. In the dream, he was twelve again, watching his parents' sedan spin through the intersection a week before Christmas. The drunk driver's Mercedes didn't even slow down—its wealthy owner was unconcerned that his reckless actions would lead to real consequences. Two years in minimum security for destroying a family, while Ryder learned that justice and law weren't the same thing.

He sat up in his bed at Nana's house, sweat cooling on his skin. The grandfather clock in the hallway chimed five thirty, its familiar rhythm grounding him in the present. The dream continued to linger, as it often did. James Ryder hadn't been there to witness the death of his parents, but he'd relived it in his mind a million times. The pain was still raw, like a fresh wound.

Shadow arrived from Nana's room, her intelligent eyes reflecting concern for her handler's distress. The Belgian Malinois had learned to recognize the signs of his recurring nightmares, providing the silent comfort he needed.

Ryder dressed, checked on Nana, and drove to Phoenix House, arriving as the morning sun painted Logan Square's tree-lined streets in golden light. Will Cameron arrived in the conference room after Ryder finished his third cup of coffee.

"When did you get here?" Will asked, opening his laptop.

"A few hours ago," Ryder replied. "What are you working on?"

"I've been trying to get access to more LifeCore encrypted communications."

"Any word from Dr. Lee?"

"Nothing. Kendrick says her texts go unread and her calls go straight to voicemail," Will said with a sigh, frustration woven throughout his words. "Either she's been discovered by LifeCore security, or she's gone underground until the heat dies down."

Ryder nodded, his attention split between Will's update and the weight of decisions pressing against his chest. It was three days after the Illinois Department of Insurance had given LifeCore a slap on the wrist for its long list of infractions. Three days since the system had revealed its complete corruption.

Will closed his laptop and leaned back in his chair. "After our last conversation, I've been researching Andre Atwood, Chad Kline, and the LifeCore building."

"What did you find?"

"We can do this." Will's voice remained calm despite the serious implications of his suggestion. "I can provide everything you need. Building schematics, security protocols, and executive schedules."

The offer hung in the air between them, representing a point of no return that transformed their mission from investigation to execution. Ryder had crossed similar thresholds before, but this time, it felt different. The system hadn't just failed; it had protected the criminals while prosecuting the whistleblowers.

"Show me what you have."

Will reopened his laptop and began displaying the intelligence he'd gathered over the past seventy-two hours. Architectural drawings revealed LifeCore's headquarters in precise detail, from parking garage access points to rooftop helicopter landing pads.

The fortress mentality revealed everything about LifeCore's executives. They understood that their organized murder of vulnerable patients had created enemies who might seek justice outside legal channels. Atwood and his team designed their corporate tower to protect them from the consequences of their crimes.

The tactical challenges were significant but not insurmountable. Ryder had infiltrated more secure facilities during Delta Force operations, eliminating high-value targets who believed their wealth and connections made them untouchable. Andre Atwood would discover the same lesson Peter Richter and Alexander Novick had learned about the reach of justice.

"Atwood's executive protection team consists of former military operators with extensive close protection experience." Will highlighted the top floor of the building. "He also has a residential penthouse on the fifty-second floor, where he stays several nights each week."

Will switched to a satellite image of Winnetka with hundreds of mansions visible from the aerial view. "This is Atwood's home with his wife and son. It's a similar setup to the Novick property we penetrated in Tysons Corner but embedded deeper within the community. I'm confident we can get in, but not so sure we can get out undetected."

Ryder rubbed his chin as he studied the landscape on the screen. "Let's focus on the LifeCore building downtown. What about Kline?"

"Kline's office is on the same floor as Atwood's but on the opposite side of the building."

Ryder studied the layouts, his tactical mind processing entry points, sight lines, and contingency routes. The mission would require precise timing and overwhelming force to penetrate three layers of professional security. Not impossible, but challenging enough to demand careful planning.

"Are the members of his security team contractors or LifeCore employees?"

Will pulled up personnel files on LifeCore's protection details. "They're all on the LifeCore payroll. Most are former SEALs, Rangers, and Marines. They report—"

Will stopped mid-sentence and leaned closer to his screen.

"What is it?"

"They report to the head of LifeCore security but also have a dotted line to Brandon Crane at Richter Enterprises. These guys are all in on what LifeCore is doing."

That answered the question lingering in the back of Ryder's mind. He knew many veterans found work with security firms after leaving the military. Eliminating security contractors just trying to make a living wasn't something he wanted to do. Penetrating LifeCore without harming the security team would have been a monumental challenge, but that was no longer a concern.

Footsteps in the hallway interrupted Ryder's tactical analysis. Special Agent Jenna Kendrick appeared in the conference room doorway, her green eyes turning to the building schematics displayed across Will's laptop screen. She entered while studying the architectural drawings and security protocols with the trained attention of a federal investigator.

"What exactly are you planning?"

Will's fingers moved to close the laptop, but Ryder gestured for him to leave the displays visible. "Dr. Lee provided evidence of organizational murder. The regulatory system dismissed it as fabricated. We're considering a more direct approach to justice."

Kendrick approached the table, her eyes scanning the detailed intelligence Will had assembled. The LifeCore corporate logo was visible on multiple documents, making their target unmistakable.

"You're planning to assassinate Andre Atwood." The statement carried no question, just recognition of their intentions.

"I'm planning to eliminate a threat that kills vulnerable patients for profit." Ryder corrected. "Atwood and Kline have blood on their hands. They're no different from the Taliban leaders who killed Americans that I hunted daily over in the sandbox. The system won't hold them accountable, so someone else has to."

Kendrick studied his face, searching for something in his expression. "I don't approve of murder, Ryder. Even when the targets deserve it."

"Do you approve of innocent victims dying every day so Atwood can afford a fourth vacation home?" The question carried an edge that reflected Ryder's growing frustration with moral absolutes. "Do you approve of stroke patients being denied rehabilitation while corporate executives celebrate quarterly bonuses?"

"Of course not."

"Then what do you suggest? We've tried regulatory complaints. We've tried working within the system." Ryder gestured toward Will's screen filled with evidence tabs. "Every legitimate channel has been corrupted or compromised. How many more people have to die while we file paperwork and hope for justice?"

Kendrick remained silent for several seconds, her internal struggle visible in her eyes. The weight of choosing between law and justice had been building since she first learned about LifeCore's crimes. Federal agents trust institutional processes, but those same institutions had failed LifeCore's victims.

"We need more intelligence first. Direct action should be a last resort, not a first option."

Will looked up from his laptop. "You said Dr. Lee won't respond to any of your messages. She's either been silenced or she's too afraid to maintain contact. We can't gather additional evidence without inside access."

"Then I'll go in." Kendrick's words surprised even her. "I can use my federal credentials to gain access to LifeCore's executive offices. An official investigation cover provides legal justification for asking questions that would otherwise raise suspicions."

Ryder felt something unexpected tighten in his chest. The thought of Kendrick infiltrating LifeCore's corporate fortress, surrounded by security personnel who have demonstrated their willingness to use violence, triggered protective instincts he hadn't expected.

"I don't like it." His response was immediate. "LifeCore's security team includes Richter operatives. We know they've killed to protect their operations. I don't want you going into that environment alone."

"Why not?" Kendrick's jaw tightened, and her chin lifted defiantly. "I've been in the Army Criminal Investigation Division for nine years, with some of that time in combat zones. I can handle myself in dangerous situations."

"This isn't about your skills or competence. It's about unnecessary risk." Ryder stood and moved to the window, using the motion to process his emotional reaction. "Will's intelligence gathering provides everything we need for a direct assault. Why complicate the mission with additional infiltration attempts?"

"Because eliminating targets should be the last option, not the preferred solution." Kendrick's conviction was clear. "If I can gather enough evidence to trigger legitimate federal prosecution, we can achieve justice without adding to the body count."

Will closed his laptop with deliberate force. "Federal prosecution? The same federal system that's allowed Richter Enterprises to operate for over a decade? The same system that's ignored LifeCore's patient targeting while rewarding their executives with tax breaks?"

Kendrick's face flushed red as she spun to face Will. "Not every federal agency is compromised. Some parts of the system still work when presented with overwhelming evidence."

The conference room fell silent except for the distant sounds of Phoenix House residents preparing for their morning group session. Voices drifted through the hallway, veterans supporting each other through the daily battles of recovery and reintegration. Men who'd served their country with honor, only to be abandoned by the same systems that now protected corporate murderers.

Ryder turned back to face Kendrick, studying her expression in the morning light. Her determination was genuine, but full of the dangerous optimism of someone who still believed institutional justice was possible. Dr. Lee had possessed similar faith before discovering that whistleblowers faced prosecution while criminals received protection.

"How long?" Ryder inquired.

"How long what?"

"How long do you need to gather evidence before we move to direct action?"

Kendrick considered the question. She knew that every day of delay meant more vulnerable patients would not receive lifesaving care while executives paid more bounties.

"Less than a week. Give me three to four days to infiltrate LifeCore and document their operations. If I can't produce evidence sufficient for federal prosecution within that timeframe, I'll support whatever action you decide to take."

The compromise felt inadequate to Ryder's sense of justice, but it represented progress toward Kendrick's moral evolution. She was choosing to operate outside her federal authority, accepting personal and professional risks to pursue truth over institutional loyalty.

"I have two conditions." Ryder underscored his statement by holding up two fingers. "You maintain constant communication with Will, and if there's any sign of compromise or threat, you extract immediately. We're not losing anyone else to LifeCore's corporate brutality."

"Agreed."

Will reopened his laptop and began typing commands that would establish secure communication protocols for Kendrick's infiltration mission. "I'll need twelve hours to create bulletproof federal credentials and operational cover."

He turned to face Kendrick. "Can you create a cover story that would justify an Army CID investigation inside LifeCore?"

Kendrick paused before responding. "Yeah, I'll have to do some research on LifeCore personnel, but I can come up with something convincing."

"Can you get your supervisor to corroborate if called to confirm your presence at LifeCore?"

"Oh, hell no."

"What about having someone else act as Sergeant Major Atkins if called by LifeCore?" Ryder asked. "Maybe another special agent you trust."

Kendrick pursed her lips. "I know someone who will do it."

"Confirm with him before we proceed. If LifeCore's security discovers the deception, they won't hesitate to eliminate the threat."

Kendrick nodded. Ryder knew the CID special agent understood the stakes involved in her decision to operate outside federal authority. Once she entered LifeCore's headquarters under false pretenses, there would be no backup or official support if the mission went wrong.

"One more chance to do things the right way. But if institutional justice fails again, we can discuss doing things your way."

It wasn't a commitment to the justice Ryder desired, but the words carried weight that transcended their budding partnership. Kendrick was on the verge of crossing the same moral threshold Ryder had crossed years earlier, choosing truth over law when the two became incompatible.

"Four days," Ryder stated. "After that, we solve this problem my way."

CHAPTER 25

Special Agent Jenna Kendrick moved beside Will in the Phoenix House conference room, poring over LifeCore human resource files while Ryder handled Phoenix House business. The coffee in her mug had gone cold an hour ago, but she didn't notice. Somewhere in LifeCore's employee database was her entry point.

"There." Will pointed to a profile photo of a woman in Army dress blues. "Elena Grabowski. Former Army medic, discharged three years ago."

Kendrick leaned closer, studying the file. Twenty-nine years old, raised in Evanston, Illinois, served eight years in the Army without incident. But the discharge documentation told a different story.

"General discharge under other than honorable conditions." Will continued reading. "Accused of stealing medical supplies from the aid station in Kandahar. She denied it, but her commanding officer didn't believe her."

"Perfect." Kendrick straightened in her chair. "That gives me legitimate justification for a CID investigation."

Will's fingers moved across the keyboard, pulling up additional records. "She works in LifeCore's data processing department. Ms. Grabowski has access to claim files, denial patterns, and internal communications."

The irony wasn't lost on Kendrick. A veteran accused of stealing medical supplies now processes insurance denials that withhold medical care from others. The system's cruelty extended in directions she hadn't expected.

"Did you find someone to verify your investigation once you reach LifeCore Security?" Will asked.

Kendrick pulled out her encrypted phone. "I know someone who'll help. I'll call and confirm now."

Special Agent Derek Thompson answered on the second ring.

"Special Agent Kendrick, great to hear from you. What kind of trouble are you stirring up now?"

"The good kind. I need you to impersonate our commander for a phone verification."

"Sergeant Major Atkins?" Thompson confirmed.

"Yeah."

The pause stretched long enough for Thompson to process the implications of impersonating their commander. They'd worked together investigating cases in Afghanistan over the past two years, building trust through shared risks and moral clarity.

"This related to the pharmaceutical case we worked on in Kabul?"

"Connected, but bigger. Corporate executives are killing patients for profit."

"How big are we talking?"

"Thousands of victims. Bounty payments for successful denials of veteran care. AI algorithms targeting the most vulnerable populations."

"Atkins better never find out we did this behind his back," Thompson said. "Or we're both toast."

"He won't."

Thompson's exhale was audible through the phone. "Send me whatever details I need to stay in character."

***

Ninety minutes later, Kendrick stood before LifeCore's sleek headquarters, its glass facade reflecting the Chicago skyline like a monument to corporate ambition. The building's grand stature spoke of wealth and influence, power concentrated in the hands of executives who viewed human suffering as a business opportunity.

The lobby hummed with morning energy. Employees moved between elevators with the purposeful strides of people convinced their work mattered. Marble floors and abstract art created an atmosphere of prosperity that masked the cruelty occurring on the floors above.

Kendrick timed her entry when the LifeCore security guard assigned to assist the lobby was on break and breezed through building security. Ten minutes later, she emerged from the elevator on LifeCore's twenty-third floor and approached the security checkpoint.

"Special Agent Kendrick, Army Criminal Investigation Division." She presented her credentials to the security officer in his crisp uniform with the LifeCore logo above his heart. She noted the well-stocked service belt: a Glock pistol, Taser, and nightstick. "I'm investigating former Army Specialist Elena Grabowski regarding the theft of military medical supplies."

The guard examined her identification with professional skepticism.

"I'll need to verify your credentials with your commanding officer."

"Of course."

The verification call connected Thompson to LifeCore security. Kendrick listened as he assumed Atkins' gruff demeanor with frightening accuracy.

"Special Agent Kendrick is investigating medical supply theft by former personnel now working in the private sector." The fake Sergeant Major Atkins barked through the phone. "She has my full authorization to interview witnesses and review relevant documentation."

"Thank you, Sergeant Major. We'll provide full cooperation."

LifeCore Security escorted Kendrick to the twenty-fourth floor, where Elena Grabowski processed insurance claims in a cubicle farm that stretched across half the building. Under the sterile light, dozens of employees sat confined in uniform workstations, reviewing medical files like assembly-line workers.

Elena looked up from her computer screen as Kendrick approached. Recognition flickered across her features, the wariness of someone who'd built a solid wall of distrust.

"Ms. Grabowski? Special Agent Kendrick, Army CID. I need to ask you some questions about your service record."

"I didn't steal anything." The response was immediate and defensive. "I told them that three years ago."

"I'm not here to re-litigate past accusations. I'm investigating irregularities in medical supply chains that may have affected multiple personnel."

Elena's expression shifted from defensive to curious. "You mean other people were affected?"

"That's what I'm trying to determine. Can we find somewhere private to talk?"

They moved to a small conference room where Elena's story unfolded with painful familiarity. Medical supplies disappearing from the aid station, accusations without evidence, and a commanding officer eager to find a scapegoat. It became clear to Kendrick that the actual thieves had been selling supplies to local contractors while an honest medic took the blame. She made a mental note to look into former Army Specialist Grabowski's case once LifeCore was brought to justice.

"Why are you asking about this now?" Elena's question carried hope that justice might finally reach her case.

"Because we have more information now. People who tried to do the right thing got blamed while the real criminals escaped consequences."

The interview continued for forty minutes, long enough to establish Kendrick's legitimate presence in the building while providing cover for her real mission. Elena's access codes and system knowledge created opportunities for intelligence gathering that formal requests could never achieve.

"I need to review some personnel files to understand the scope of the investigation." Kendrick followed Elena through the data processing department.

"Anything you need. It feels good to finally talk to someone who believes me."

Elena's access revealed structured targeting. Seniors, veterans, and low-income families. Rejection rates that defied medical necessity.

Kendrick leaned closer to the screen and shook her head in disgust as her phone buzzed with a message from Will: *They're tracking you. Be careful.*

She glanced toward the ceiling, noting the cameras that monitored the workstations.

"Elena, I need to use the restroom. Can you show me where it is?"

The hallway provided temporary respite from surveillance while Kendrick processed what she'd discovered. LifeCore's claim processing system wasn't just aggressive. It was weaponized and designed to eliminate expensive patients while maintaining plausible deniability for executives.

Kendrick returned to Elena's workstation, her mind balancing the delicate act of gathering intelligence and avoiding detection. Will's surveillance had confirmed what she'd suspected—LifeCore security was tracking her movements with increasing attention.

The rest of the afternoon passed in careful intelligence gathering. Elena's access provided glimpses into executive communications, financial records showing irregular bounty payments, and patient files documenting the human cost of corporate efficiency.

As five o'clock approached, Kendrick prepared to extract herself from LifeCore Tower with enough evidence to build a case while maintaining her cover for future operations. Elena walked her to the elevator bank, their conversation focused on the fictional medical supply investigation.

"Thank you for listening." Elena's voice carried genuine gratitude. "It means more than you know."

"Justice takes time, but the truth always prevails."

Kendrick stepped into the elevator, her mind cataloging the intelligence she'd gathered. Evidence that could expose LifeCore's corporate murder machine.

The elevator descended one floor before stopping. The doors opened to reveal Dr. Allison Lee stepping inside, her expression shifting from routine distraction to shock as she recognized the federal agent who'd approached her at Cloud Gate.

They stared at each other as the elevator doors closed. Dr. Lee's eyes darted toward the security camera mounted in the corner, then back to Kendrick's face. Recognition flashed across her features, followed by fear.

"You shouldn't be here." Dr. Lee's voice was barely a whisper.

Kendrick's pulse quickened. The chief medical officer's expression revealed an internal struggle between self-preservation and the desperate hope that someone might finally expose LifeCore's crimes.

The elevator descended in silence, each floor bringing them closer to the lobby, where LifeCore security waited. Kendrick watched Dr. Lee's face, searching for any sign of her intentions. Would she help expose the systematic murder of patients, or would fear drive her to alert Atwood's security team about the federal agent who'd infiltrated their operations?

The floor indicator counted down—fifteen, fourteen, thirteen.

A half-dozen LifeCore employees joined their co-worker and Kendrick on the twelfth floor. Several offered smiles and nods to their chief medical officer.

Kendrick knew she'd never make it out of the elevator if Dr. Lee shared her true intentions with the faithful LifeCore workers. She watched Dr. Lee's face for any tells that could determine whether Kendrick walked out of the building or disappeared into corporate security's custody.

The elevator resumed its descent—ten, nine, eight.

The silent tension stretched between them like a taut wire, ready to snap in either direction.

When the doors opened in the lobby, the elevators emptied except for Dr. Lee and Kendrick. Neither woman moved. Dr. Lee made eye contact with the LifeCore security guard, who then focused his stare on the CID special agent. Kendrick held her breath as Dr. Lee debated life-altering decisions in her mind.

CHAPTER 26

Rays from the descending sun reflected off nearby buildings into the elevator, highlighting the standoff between Dr. Lee and Kendrick. Dr. Lee's eyes darted between the LifeCore security officer in the lobby and Kendrick's face. The chief medical officer's breath quickened, and Kendrick could almost feel the frantic thrum of her heartbeat in the still air.

"You shouldn't be here," Dr. Lee whispered, her voice tight with fear.

Kendrick remained silent, watching Dr. Lee's internal struggle play out across her features. She felt the eyes of the LifeCore security guard watching them with increased interest.

Dr. Lee stepped forward, her heels clicking against the marble as she approached the security checkpoint. The LifeCore guard maintained his gaze as she passed, recognizing the chief medical officer with a respectful nod.

"Evening, Dr. Lee. Have a great night."

"You too." Her voice carried forced casualness.

Kendrick moved past the security desk toward the revolving glass doors, her pulse hammering against her throat. Each step felt deliberate, calculated to appear routine while her tactical mind cataloged exit routes and potential threats.

"Have a good evening, ma'am," the guard called after her.

The Chicago summer air hit her like a warm blanket as she pushed through the doors onto Dearborn Street. The distinct scent of diesel exhaust from a city bus mixed with the lake breeze from the east.

Kendrick walked three blocks before allowing herself to breathe normally. Dr. Lee had chosen silence over self-preservation, protecting a federal agent she barely knew rather than securing her own position with LifeCore's executives. The courage required for that decision spoke volumes about the physician's moral clarity.

Her phone buzzed with a text from Will: *Clear the building?*

Yes. Dr. Lee kept quiet, she replied.

Return to Phoenix House. We need to debrief.

The taxi ride to Logan Square took twenty-five minutes through evening traffic. Kendrick's mind processed the intelligence she'd gathered throughout the day, cataloging evidence that painted a damning picture of LifeCore's operations. Elena Grabowski's access had provided glimpses into the intentional targeting of vulnerable patients, but deeper intelligence would require additional infiltration.

Ryder met her at the front door before she could knock. His square jaw and close-cropped hair caught the porch light as he gestured for her to enter. Shadow appeared at his side, the Belgian Malinois offering a tail wag of recognition before returning to her protective vigilance.

"How did it go?"

"Better than expected, but not as much as we need."

They moved into the conference room, where Will was waiting with his laptop open.

"Elena Grabowski was the entry point we needed." Kendrick settled into a chair across from Ryder. "Former Army medic, railroaded by her commanding officer for supply theft she didn't commit. She's eager to help anyone investigating military injustice."

Will looked up from his keyboard. "Did you access their internal systems?"

"I was able to confirm the targeting algorithms and denial patterns from Elana's workstation." Kendrick showed her phone, displaying the photos she'd captured. "But the real evidence is deeper."

Ryder studied the images. "This confirms Dr. Lee's story."

"It's enough," Will said, closing his laptop. "We have sufficient evidence to justify direct action against Atwood and Kline."

"Not quite." Kendrick's response surprised both men. "Elena mentioned she's seen internal memos authored by Atwood and Kline that made her uncomfortable with the blatant disregard for policyholder health. She needs more time to find them. If I can spend one more day gathering intelligence, we'll have everything needed for a federal case."

Ryder's jaw tightened. "You're pushing your luck. LifeCore Security is already tracking your movements inside the building."

"One more day. Elena trusts me now, and I can leverage that relationship to access sensitive files without raising additional suspicions." Kendrick met his gaze. "This intelligence could help us, no matter which route we ultimately take."

The room fell silent except for the distant sound of Phoenix House residents mingling in the community room.

"Twenty-four hours," Ryder said. "After that, we move forward with whatever intelligence we have."

***

Gray light on a rainy morning penetrated LifeCore's windows as Kendrick returned to the data processing floor. Elena Grabowski looked up from her computer screen with genuine warmth, her demeanor reflecting the trust they'd built during the previous day's conversations.

"Special Agent Kendrick. I was hoping you'd return."

"Good morning, Elena. I need to expand the investigation to include command structure analysis." Kendrick settled into the chair beside Elena's workstation.

Elena's eyebrows furrowed. "For a medical supply theft investigation?"

Kendrick knew she could lose Elena's trust. "Understanding the chain of command similarities here and at your old unit could help me identify patterns."

Elena's expression shifted. "Mr. Atwood's personal files are restricted access. I'm not supposed to view executive information without specific authorization."

The internal struggle played across Elena's features as she weighed professional obligations against her desire for justice. Her fingers hovered over the keyboard while she debated accessing information that could cost her job.

Kendrick pulled out all the stops with her next statement. "I think someone set you up on those theft charges, and it came from the top."

That broke through Elena's resistance. Her fingers flew across the keyboard, navigating through security protocols and accessing executive personnel files that revealed intimate details about Andre Atwood's life.

The screen filled with information that made Kendrick's pulse quicken. Atwood's home address in Winnetka, complete with property layout and security system specifications. His wife Ruth's employment at a local art gallery, his son Malik's school schedule, and extracurricular activities. Financial records showing offshore accounts and investment portfolios worth millions.

"He has a penthouse apartment here in the building, too," Elena said, pointing to additional residential information. "Top floor with private elevator access. I've heard he stays there several nights a week when he's working late."

Kendrick memorized every detail while maintaining her investigative cover. Atwood's patterns of movement, his family's vulnerabilities, and his corporate security arrangements painted a comprehensive picture of potential vulnerabilities. She knew that the personal information would not aid a federal investigation, but it provided vital intelligence for direct action.

"Are we done here?" Elena asked.

"Not yet, why?"

"I have another meeting to attend with underwriting."

Kendrick saw another opportunity to tap into LifeCore employees on the front line. "Can I attend?"

Elena bit her lower lip. "I guess that would be okay."

Once Kendrick settled into the conference room for Elena's meeting, her phone buzzed with a text from Will that made her blood freeze. *Exfil now. Atwood is coming!*

Someone had detected her infiltration.

***

Brandon Crane's office occupied a corner suite in Richter Enterprises' Chicago operations center, its floor-to-ceiling windows offering views of the city's financial district.

Security monitors covered one wall, each screen cycling through feeds from various Richter properties and allied organizations. Crane reviewed the day's visitor logs with methodical attention, scanning faces and credentials for anything that might represent a threat to their operations.

The LifeCore visitor database appeared on his primary monitor, showing every person who'd accessed the building over the past forty-eight hours. Delivery personnel, maintenance contractors, and business visitors moved across the screen in chronological order.

One face made him lean forward and pause.

Auburn hair pulled into a professional bun, green eyes that held intelligence and determination, and high cheekbones. The facial recognition software had identified her as Special Agent Jenna Kendrick, Army Criminal Investigation Division.

The name and face triggered immediate memory recall. Special Agent Kendrick had assisted the DEA in the investigation into NeuraNox smuggling operations in Miami. The same case had cost Galindo his life and disrupted months of careful planning.

He stared at the image, seeing past her natural beauty to the predator lurking behind those emerald eyes. This wasn't a desk-bound detective following routine leads. Kendrick was a seasoned investigator who'd infiltrated hostile territory with specific intelligence objectives.

The security report accompanying her photograph claimed she was investigating former Army Specialist Elena Grabowski for medical supply theft. Crane's military experience told him that the explanation was fabricated. CID agents didn't conduct company-wide investigations for minor theft cases involving discharged personnel.

Kendrick was hunting LifeCore from within.

Crane reached for his secure phone and dialed LifeCore security.

"This is Brandon Crane. I need to speak with the shift supervisor."

A moment later, a deep voice came on the line. "This is Jabari. How can I assist you, Mr. Crane?"

"You have a federal agent named Kendrick conducting interviews in your data processing department. Under no circumstances is she to leave the building without my direct authorization."

"Sir, she presented valid credentials for a legitimate investigation."

"Her credentials may be valid, but her investigation isn't. Detain her and await my arrival." Cold authority solidified in Crane's voice. "If she attempts to leave, use whatever force is necessary to prevent it."

"Understood, sir."

Crane ended the call and dialed Andre Atwood's private line. Three rings later, the familiar voice answered with obvious irritation.

"What is it, Crane? I'm in meetings until six."

"We have another mole inside LifeCore. A federal agent conducting unauthorized surveillance of your operations."

Crane pulled up Kendrick's photograph on his secondary monitor. "Army CID agent Jenna Kendrick, the same agent who disrupted another Richter Enterprises operation in Miami last month."

The silence stretched long enough for Atwood to process the implications. A federal investigation inside LifeCore could expose not just the efficiency algorithms and patient targeting system, but everything he'd built.

"How much has she uncovered?"

"Unknown. She's been inside the building for two days under the cover of investigating a discharged veteran. That's not something an Army CID agent would do. The security team is detaining her now." Crane checked his watch. "I'll be there in thirty minutes to conduct the interrogation myself."

"No!" Atwood's voice carried a dangerous edge. "This is my company, and I'll handle the situation myself."

"Sir, with respect, interrogating federal agents requires specialized expertise. Let my team handle the technical aspects while you focus on corporate damage control."

"I'm capable of interrogating someone." Atwood's tone grew darker. "I built LifeCore from nothing, and I won't have federal agents thinking they can walk into my building and threaten everything I've worked for."

Crane recognized the stubborn pride that had made Atwood successful as a CEO but could prove disastrous when dealing with trained federal operatives. Kendrick wasn't a junior investigator who would fold under executive pressure.

"At least wait until I arrive. Kendrick has tactical training that makes her dangerous when cornered."

"This is my company, and I'll handle it."

The line went dead, leaving Crane staring at Kendrick's photograph. Atwood's emotional reaction could compromise operational security and create a public incident that would bring unwanted attention to all their activities.

But orders were orders, even when they came from prideful executives who didn't understand the difference between corporate intimidation and tactical interrogation.

Crane gathered his weapons and headed for the door.

***

Andre Atwood's footsteps echoed through LifeCore's data processing department as he approached the conference room where his security team had surrounded the federal agent. Chad Kline followed close behind, his nervous energy evident in his fingers drumming against his tablet computer.

The afternoon sun slanted through office windows, casting long shadows across cubicles where employees continued processing insurance claims. Their routine work of denying medical care to vulnerable patients proceeded without interruption.

Atwood paused outside the conference room door, observing the scene through its glass wall. Special Agent Kendrick sat at the round table surrounded by an underwriter and two data entry personnel, maintaining the facade of her fictional investigation into Elena Grabowski's military service.

"Everyone out." Atwood's voice cut through the room as he pushed through the door with Kline close behind. "Now."

The LifeCore employees scattered, their chairs scraping against the carpet as they fled the conference room. Elena Grabowski shot a worried glance toward Kendrick before joining the exodus, leaving the federal agent alone with LifeCore's two most powerful executives.

Atwood closed the door behind him and activated the conference room's privacy screens, blocking external observation. The sudden isolation created an atmosphere of corporate menace that had intimidated countless business rivals and regulatory officials.

"Special Agent Kendrick." Atwood's six-foot-five frame filled the doorway as he studied her with calculating eyes. "What are you really doing in my building?"

Kendrick's expression remained neutral despite the obvious shift in circumstances. "I'm investigating the military service record of former Army Specialist Elena Grabowski, as I explained to your security team."

"Bullshit!" Atwood moved closer, using every inch of his physical presence to create psychological pressure. "Army CID doesn't conduct building-wide investigations for supply theft involving discharged personnel."

Kline positioned himself near the conference room's phone, his finger hovering over the security extension. "Should I call security?"

Atwood's ruthless grin foreshadowed his ill intentions as he continued toward Kendrick's chair.

"No." His voice dropped to a register that had terrified opponents throughout his climb to corporate power. "I'm going to handle this myself."

CHAPTER 27

The conference room's recessed lighting framed Andre Atwood as an intimidating silhouette as he towered over Kendrick's chair. Kline shifted his weight near the door, his tablet clutched against his chest like a shield.

"Let's try this again," Atwood growled. "What are you looking for in my building?"

Kendrick kept her expression neutral despite the adrenaline coursing through her. "I've already explained my investigation. Former Army Specialist Grabowski's service record contains irregularities that require—"

Atwood's massive hand shot out, wrapping around her left wrist with crushing force. His fingers dug into the delicate flesh as he applied steady pressure, his linebacker's grip designed to inflict maximum pain without leaving noticeable marks.

"Wrong answer." His grip tightened. "I know you're not here about a discharged Army medic. You're fishing for information about LifeCore's operations."

Pain shot up Kendrick's arm, but she forced her voice to remain steady. "You're assaulting a federal agent conducting an official investigation. Release me now, or you'll face federal charges for obstruction of justice."

Atwood's laugh was bitter. "Federal agent? You think that badge makes you untouchable in my building?" His grip tightened another degree, sending fresh waves of agony through her wrist. "I've been dealing with government bureaucrats since before you graduated high school."

Kendrick couldn't suppress the quick yelp that escaped her lips as bones ground against each other. Her tactical training screamed for her to fight back, to use Atwood's proximity against him, but four security guards flanked the conference room entrance with their hands resting on holstered weapons.

"Andre." Kline's voice carried obvious discomfort as he watched the interrogation escalate. "Maybe we should let security—"

"Let security do what?" Atwood snapped without releasing his grip on Kendrick's wrist. "Let some federal spy walk out of here with whatever she's gathered?"

Kline's face had gone pale, his eyes darting between Atwood's intimidation tactics and the security cameras he knew were recording everything. "This could create serious legal complications."

"Get security in here." Atwood's command cut through Kline's protests as he dropped Kendrick's wrist, leaving red marks where his fingers had squeezed her flesh. She cradled her throbbing arm against her chest while blood flow returned.

Kline darted from the room and rushed to the security supervisor waiting outside.

While Kline spoke to security, Kendrick used Atwood's distraction to slip her phone from her jacket pocket. She kept the phone below the table, sending a rapid text to both Will and Ryder: *Compromised at LifeCore. 24th floor Conf Room B. Need extraction now.*

The conference room door burst open as four LifeCore security guards entered. Each carried a sidearm, a Taser, and restraint gear.

"Detain this federal agent until Brandon Crane arrives." Atwood moved toward the door. "Search her and confiscate any recording devices or weapons."

The lead guard, Jabari, stepped forward, his hand moving to the zip ties on his belt. "Ma'am, we need you to stand and place your hands behind your back."

Kendrick remained seated, calculating options. Surrounded by four armed men, the odds seemed hopeless. She had to buy time for Will and Ryder.

"I'm a federal agent conducting an authorized investigation, and any interference with my duties constitutes a federal crime."

"Stand up," Jabari barked.

Atwood paused in the doorway. "Keep her secure until Crane gets here. He'll know what to do with this spy."

The emphasis he placed on the last word carried implications that made Kendrick's blood run cold. Brandon Crane's reputation extended far beyond corporate security, into territories where opponents disappeared without a trace or explanation.

Jabari took another step closer to Kendrick. "Ma'am, I need you to stand and keep your hands visible. I will not ask again."

Kendrick complied, rising from her seat while holding her injured wrist.

The search that followed was thorough. The guards located her backup magazine, the two USB drives containing Elena's intelligence downloads, and her encrypted phone. Each item was catalogued and secured in evidence bags.

"These USB drives weren't declared during your entry interview." The lead guard held up the devices with obvious suspicion. "What's on them?"

"Documentation related to my investigation into former Army Specialist Grabowski."

The guard's expression suggested he wasn't buying her cover story, but he secured the drives without further comment. Kendrick saw her hard-earned intelligence disappear into LifeCore's custody, knowing those files represented the only concrete evidence of the corporation's blatant patient targeting.

Jabari and another guard left the room, while the remaining two flanked her chair, their attention focused on preventing any sudden movements that might threaten their control of the situation.

Kendrick's tactical mind processed the deteriorating situation while her wrist continued throbbing from Atwood's assault. Her phone buzzed against the table where the guards had placed it after their search. The message notification was visible through the device's lock screen. *Got your message. On my way.*

The response came from Will's number, offering the first hope she'd felt since Atwood had grabbed her wrist.

***

Will Cameron's phone buzzed against his hip as he reviewed Phoenix House's financial statements in the conference room. The message from Kendrick made his blood freeze. *Compromised at LifeCore. 24th floor Conf Room B. Need extraction now.*

He dialed Ryder's number, listening to the phone ring before transferring to voicemail. The hospital where Nana was finally receiving her long-delayed CT scan was a dead zone for cellular signals, leaving Ryder unreachable when Kendrick needed rescue.

Will opened his phone and accessed the tracking software he'd insisted Kendrick activate before her infiltration mission. Her stationary position in LifeCore's headquarters appeared on his map as a blue dot, confirming she was trapped inside the building.

The tactical situation was desperate. Professional security personnel surrounded Kendrick inside a corporate fortress, and they viewed her as a threat. Each minute of delay made it more probable that the CID agent would face harsh interrogation or worse.

The building's lobby was almost empty when Will arrived, most employees having departed for the evening. He approached the security desk with the confident bearing of someone conducting legitimate business.

"Lyle Morrison from Northgate Security Solutions." Will presented his fabricated credentials to the building's guard. "I'm here for the consultation meeting on twenty-four."

The guard examined his identification with casual interest before waving him toward the elevators. "Sign in here and take any elevator to your floor."

Will's pulse hammered as the elevator climbed toward LifeCore's floors. The fake identity had passed initial scrutiny, but corporate security would possess more sophisticated verification systems that could expose his deception.

The elevator doors opened on the twenty-fourth floor to reveal two LifeCore guards positioned near the checkpoint counter. Their eyes tracked Will's movement as he emerged, professional suspicion evident in their posture.

"Can we help you?" The taller guard stepped forward.

"Lyle Morrison, Northgate Security. I'm here for the consultation meeting with Brandon Crane."

"Mr. Crane isn't here yet." The guard's voice carried suspicion. "Why did he tell you to meet him here?"

"I don't know. That's just what his assistant told me."

Both guards exchanged glances that confirmed Will's worst fears.

"I'm going to need to see some identification." The shorter guard moved to flank Will's position.

Will's hand moved with lightning speed, drawing his Glock 17 and centering it on the lead guard's chest. "Both of you, on the ground. Now."

The guards froze, their training warring with the reality of a drawn weapon pointed at center mass.

"Keep your hands visible and move slowly."

Both guards complied, lowering themselves to the carpeted floor with their hands extended. Will checked his phone's tracking display, confirming Kendrick's position past the checkpoint and down the hallway to his left.

"On your stomach with your hands behind your back."

As soon as they were down, Will removed zip ties and secured both guards.

"If you yell or sound an alarm, this will get messy."

Will sprinted down the corridor, following the indicator on his phone toward Conference Room B. The door was locked, but his size eleven boot made quick work of the reinforced handle. The crash of splintering wood echoed through the hallway as he burst into the room.

Kendrick sat surrounded by two LifeCore security guards, fresh defensive bruises visible on her arms. The evidence of physical interrogation sent rage pulsing through Will's veins.

"Everyone on the ground." Will's Glock swept across the room.

The guards backed away and froze but remained standing. Will sensed they would not comply and turned to Kendrick. "Are you okay to run?"

"Yes." Kendrick's voice carried a mix of pain and determination. "Let's get the hell out of here."

The security guards recovered from their initial shock, moving to block the conference room exit. Will's weapon swung back and forth between the security team, and they parted to let Kendrick and Cameron escape.

They moved through the hallway together, but the two original guards by the entrance had broken free from their restraints, and the two from the conference room followed. The narrow corridor became a battlefield as four armed men converged on their position.

The first guard reached Will with surprising speed, driving a powerful right hook toward his jaw. Will ducked under the punch and drove his elbow into the man's solar plexus, doubling him over. But two more guards grabbed Will's arms, wrestling for control of his weapon.

Kendrick moved with unflinching purpose despite her injury, using her CID training to devastating effect. A guard reached for her injured wrist, but she pivoted away and drove her knee into his groin. As he doubled over in pain, she snatched the Taser from his utility belt.

The electrical weapon discharged with a sharp crack, dropping a guard attempting to subdue Will with fifty thousand volts. His muscles seized as he toppled backward, creating an opening in their defensive line.

Will broke free from the other guard and grabbed Kendrick's good hand. "Elevator!"

They sprinted down the hallway as security guards shouted orders behind them.

The elevator doors stood open like a portal to safety. They dove inside as footsteps thundered down the corridor behind them. Will hammered the lobby button while Kendrick gasped for breath beside him.

Neither spoke during the quick descent to the lobby. As soon as they reached the ground floor, they bolted from the elevator. Will caught a glimpse of a person he recognized and paused. A tall man with short strawberry-blond hair and blue eyes vanished behind closing elevator doors.

The floor indicator on the lobby wall showed the other car ascending toward the floors they'd just left.

"Brandon Crane." Will's recognition hit him like ice water. They had evaded the most lethal person defending LifeCore secrets by seconds.

CHAPTER 28

Special Agent Jenna Kendrick sat alone in Phoenix House's conference room, sipping coffee in the early morning quiet. She'd arrived at dawn after a sleepless night, examining the purple and pink bruises on her left wrist—virtual fingerprints of Andre Atwood's rage.

Atwood's fiery eyes flashed through her mind. She'd seen that look before in Afghanistan, on the faces of enemies who wanted her dead. The LifeCore CEO hadn't just been intimidating her during their confrontation. He'd been calculating whether eliminating a federal agent was worth the risk.

If Will hadn't arrived when he did, she wouldn't be sitting here drinking coffee. She'd be another missing person, another unsolved case disappearing into bureaucratic files. The thought made her shudder.

Footsteps echoed in the hallway as Ryder and Will entered the conference room. Will looked exhausted, dark circles under his eyes from the adrenaline crash that followed their violent extraction from LifeCore's headquarters.

"How are you feeling this morning?" Ryder settled into the chair across from her.

Kendrick looked up from the table. "I've been better, but I'll survive."

She rolled the coffee mug between her palms, considering her next words.

"We do it your way now. I tried to work within the system one last time, and it almost got me killed. Will saved my life."

The admission hung between them, marking her transition from federal agent to vigilante. Ryder nodded once, understanding the weight of her decision without requiring explanation.

Kendrick's phone rang. The display showed a Chicago area code she recognized.

"Special Agent Kendrick."

"Jenna, it's Rebecca Mitchell with the FBI. I have news about the Geller case."

FBI Special Agent Mitchell's voice carried excitement that cut through Kendrick's brooding about LifeCore's persistent crimes. The war crimes investigation represented everything still functioning within the federal system—a case where evidence mattered and criminals faced consequences.

"What did you find?"

"The DNA evidence from the wife's undergarments is a perfect match to Specialist Geller. Plus, blood spatter analysis confirms he was present during the civilian's death, and witness testimony contradicts his self-defense claims."

The news provided welcome relief from corporate corruption. Christopher Geller had murdered an innocent Afghan civilian over a personal relationship, then lied about it to avoid consequences. Unlike LifeCore's crimes, this case offered legitimate prosecution through official channels.

"Where is he now?"

"Chicago PD has his current address from DMV records. He's living in Bucktown, working as a personal trainer."

Kendrick checked her watch. Zero eight hundred. "I'll pick him up within the hour."

"Perfect. The US Attorney's office is standing by for arraignment once you have him in custody."

The call ended, leaving Kendrick staring at her phone. Here was a case where the system still functioned, where evidence led to prosecution. The contrast with LifeCore's protected status highlighted how selective institutional accountability had become.

"Another case?" Ryder asked.

"It's that war crimes investigation from Afghanistan I told you about. An Army specialist who allegedly murdered a civilian, but he's claiming self-defense." Kendrick gathered her materials. "The DNA evidence is telling a different story."

Will closed his laptop. "Isn't that the case that brought you to Chicago?"

"Yeah. It'll be nice to work on something where evidence leads to arrests and prosecution." The irony wasn't lost on her. A single murder by a discharged soldier would result in federal charges, while LifeCore's elimination of thousands of patients remained protected by corporate and political influence.

***

An hour later, Kendrick sat in her car outside Peak Performance Fitness in Bucktown, watching the entrance. Mature oak trees lined the residential streets, their summer foliage creating pools of shade between converted warehouses and modern condominiums.

Christopher Geller emerged from the gym's front entrance at nine seventeen. Twenty-six years old with the lean build of someone who lived in the weight room, he moved with the confident stride of a man who believed his lies had protected him from accountability.

Kendrick approached as he reached his blue Honda Civic.

"Christopher Geller?"

He turned, taking in her professional appearance and federal credentials, confusion giving way to recognition.

"I'm Special Agent Kendrick, Army Criminal Investigation Division. You're under arrest for the murder of Tariq Hassan in Kandahar Province, Afghanistan."

"I don't know what you're talking about." Geller's voice carried forced confusion, but his body language revealed guilt. "That was self-defense. I filed a complete report with my commanding officer."

"We have your DNA on the victim's wife. Turn around and place your hands behind your back."

Geller's shoulders sagged as the weight of evidence caught up with his lies.

The arrest proceeded without incident. Geller offered no resistance as Kendrick secured him in handcuffs and read his Miranda rights.

FBI Agent Sarah Mitchell met them in the intake garage of the Chicago FBI office.

"Clean arrest?" Mitchell asked as they transferred Geller to two agents.

"No complications. He came quietly once he realized we had solid evidence."

They processed Geller through FBI intake procedures while coordinating with the US Attorney's office for formal charges. The machinery of justice operated smoothly, each step following established protocols that protected both the accused and the victims.

This was how the system was supposed to work when investigators had support and evidence drove decisions.

"What else are you working on while you're in Chicago?" Mitchell asked as they completed the paperwork.

Kendrick hesitated, considering whether to share information about LifeCore's systematic targeting of patients. The FBI agent represented institutional support that could legitimize their investigation.

But revealing LifeCore's crimes would expose her unauthorized infiltration of their corporate headquarters and cooperation with James Ryder. Her career would end, and a jury would never hear the evidence they'd gathered.

"I'm investigating veteran abuse by a health insurance company."

Mitchell's expression hardened. "What kind of abuse?"

"The calculated denial of medical care to service members and veterans. This company targets vulnerable populations to boost corporate profits while people die from treatable conditions."

"That's disgusting." The FBI agent's voice cracked with genuine anger. "I hope you get the bastards if they're hurting veterans. If you need any support, call me. We don't tolerate corporations that prey on people who served our country."

The words validated that Kendrick's mission aligned with broader law enforcement values, even if her methods had strayed from official procedures.

"Thanks. It's a complex case, but we're making progress."

They shook hands as Kendrick departed the building. The successful arrest provided momentum for the challenging conversation ahead with Sergeant Major Atkins.

***

The secure call connected after two rings, Atkins' familiar gruff voice carrying across the encrypted channel.

"Special Agent Kendrick. I trust the Geller arrest went smoothly?"

"Yes, the DNA evidence was conclusive, and he's in federal custody awaiting arraignment." Kendrick found a parking spot in a city park overlooking Lake Michigan, where she could speak freely. "The case is solid. Prosecution should be straightforward."

"Outstanding work. When will you return to Virginia?"

The question carried an edge of urgency.

"I need a few more days to complete the investigation. There are additional witnesses to interview and evidence to document for the prosecution team."

"Negative. The primary target is in custody, and the DOJ can complete the investigation. I need you back in Virginia for reassignment."

Kendrick felt the familiar unease that had been building around Atkins' recent behavior. His dismissive attitude toward thorough investigation contradicted everything she'd learned about his leadership style during their previous cases together. The man who'd trained her to pursue justice regardless of political convenience was now prioritizing bureaucratic efficiency over investigative integrity. She felt pressure to leave the city because of her proximity to James Ryder.

Kendrick tested her suspicions.

"There is something else. I've located James Ryder in Chicago, and I'd like some additional time to investigate his intentions. I believe he may have another target in mind."

"I thought I told you, no more James Ryder!" Atkins shouted through the phone. His tone contained anger that Kendrick had never heard from her commander.

"I want you on a plane and back to Virginia tonight, Special Agent Kendrick. That's a direct order."

The line went dead, leaving Kendrick staring at her phone while waves rolled against the lakefront.

Atkins' behavior pattern was becoming impossible to ignore. His sudden shift from thorough investigator to careless supervisor suggested external pressures or hidden motivations that compromised his judgment. The timing of his urgency to recall her from Chicago coincided with her investigation into LifeCore's corporate crimes.

Rather than book a return flight to Virginia, Kendrick drove to her hotel, her mind processing everything she'd observed. The CID agent had one more case to investigate through official channels.

Elena Grabowski's personnel file contained enough irregularities to justify a formal CID investigation into the medical supply theft allegations that had destroyed her military career. Three years of delayed justice was better than no justice at all, and proving Elena's innocence might provide some redemption for the system's failures.

Kendrick felt the weight of institutional betrayal pressing against her chest like a physical burden. Elena Grabowski's case represented everything wrong with systems that prioritized convenience over accuracy, speed over justice, and bureaucratic efficiency over human dignity.

The successful arrest of Christopher Geller proved that justice remained possible when evidence aligned with institutional interests and investigators had adequate support. But Elena's case demonstrated how those same institutions could be corrupted and abandon their responsibilities.

"Nobody will ever hold LifeCore accountable," Kendrick said into the empty hotel room. "We must do it ourselves, outside the system."

The words marked her final transition from federal agent to vigilante, choosing justice over law when the two became incompatible. Whatever happened next, she would face the consequences alongside Ryder and Will, united in their commitment to protecting innocent people from institutional predators who believed themselves untouchable.

CHAPTER 29

The muffled sound of Will's laughter drifted through the thin wall separating the Phoenix House office from the conference room where Ryder read more claim denials for Nana. Afternoon sunlight slanted through the west windows, causing shadows to expand across hardwood floors like a rising tide.

"I know, I know. It's not the same as me being there, but I hope you liked the flowers and gift I had delivered." Will's voice carried through the drywall, his tone lighter than Ryder had heard in weeks. "I promise I'll make it up to you when I get back to Virginia."

Ryder set down the letter he'd been reading and listened. The conversation reminded him that Will Cameron had a life beyond Phoenix House, beyond their mission against LifeCore, and beyond the endless cycle of helping broken veterans rebuild their shattered lives.

"Shelby, I wish I could be there with you right now. You deserve more than a phone call from your boyfriend six hundred miles away on your birthday." Will's voice dropped to something approaching tenderness. "I'll take you somewhere special when this is over. Maybe that Thai place in Georgetown you've been wanting to try."

The guilt hit Ryder like a sledgehammer to the chest. Will had been in Chicago for three weeks, managing Phoenix House operations while Ryder took care of Nana and fought with LifeCore. Three weeks away from his girlfriend, his life, and his own recovery program that had kept him clean for over six months.

"I know. I miss you, too." The wall couldn't hide Will's smile.

Silence settled over the adjacent room.

Ryder knocked softly on the office door frame.

"Come in." Will closed his laptop, but not before Ryder caught a glimpse of Shelby's smiling face on the screen background.

"Sorry. I wasn't trying to eavesdrop."

"It's fine." Will rubbed his face with both hands. "Shelby's birthday is today. She's twenty-six, and I'm six hundred miles away helping run a veteran recovery center while she celebrates with her friends."

Ryder settled into the chair across from Will's desk, studying his friend's expression. The young man who'd transformed from reluctant ally to dedicated partner balanced the weight of divided loyalties. Phoenix House needed his technical skills and operational oversight, while his personal life withered with each additional day away from home.

"She deserves better than this. Better than a boyfriend who disappears for weeks at a time to work on classified projects he can't explain."

"What do you want to do?"

The question hung between them like a bridge spanning the gap between duty and personal happiness. Will stared through the office window at Logan Square's tree-lined streets, where people lived predictable but normal lives.

"It's time for me to go home to Virginia. I want to take Shelby to dinner and hold her hand while she tells me about her day. I want to wake up next to someone who isn't traumatized by combat or struggling with addiction." Will's voice filled with exhaustion that went beyond physical fatigue.

Ryder understood the weight of that admission. Will Cameron had sacrificed his personal happiness to help establish Phoenix House Chicago, staying far longer than initially planned. But sacrifice had limits, and Will was approaching his.

"We need to find a permanent house manager."

"I've been thinking the same thing." Will opened his laptop and pulled up employment websites. "The problem is finding someone with the right combination of skills. Military background, addiction counseling experience, administrative capabilities, and the mental strength to handle residents who relapse or disappear."

"Let's take a walk around the house."

Together, they moved through Phoenix House, observing the afternoon routines that had become second nature to both staff and residents. The building hummed with quiet productivity as men who'd lost their way found purpose in small daily victories.

In the kitchen, Orosco supervised two newer residents as they prepared dinner for the entire house. His experimental cuisine had evolved from questionable breakfast creations to impressive meals that brought the community together around shared tables.

"Smells incredible in here." Ryder entered the warm space.

"Chicken marsala with roasted vegetables. Nothing too fancy, but better than MREs." Orosco's pride in his culinary skills was evident as he stirred the sauce. "These guys are learning that recovery doesn't mean giving up everything good in life."

In the living room, Walsh worked with a newer resident on job interview preparation. The former soldier's prosthetic arm rested on the table between them as he reviewed resume formatting and discussed responses to common questions.

"Eye contact is crucial. Employers want to see confidence, not desperation. You're not asking for charity. You're offering skills and experience they need."

The young veteran nodded, taking notes on a legal pad.

"What happens if they ask about my discharge?"

"You tell the truth. Medical discharge due to combat-related PTSD. No criminal history, no disciplinary issues, just an honest soldier who served his country and needs a second chance," Walsh advised. "Most employers respect military service, especially when you're honest about the challenges."

They continued through the building, observing scenes of recovery and mutual support that validated everything Phoenix House represented. Men teaching each other skills, sharing stories that broke through isolation, and building the trust necessary for lasting sobriety.

"This is why we're here." Ryder paused on the second-floor landing. "Not just to provide housing or counseling, but to create community among people who understand each other's battles."

"I know." Will's expression reflected the internal struggle between mission and personal needs. "That's what makes leaving so difficult. These guys depend on stability, and I feel like I'm abandoning them."

"You're not abandoning anyone. You're ensuring Phoenix House has sustainable leadership instead of running yourself into the ground trying to do everything."

They checked the upper floors, noting residents engaged in reading, exercising, and writing letters to family members they'd lost contact with during their worst periods. Small actions that represented enormous progress for some of the men who'd been sleeping under bridges or in overcrowded shelters weeks earlier.

"What about our other mission? LifeCore?" Will asked as they returned to the main floor.

"LifeCore executives will face justice no matter who is managing Phoenix House." Ryder's words carried certainty. "Andre Atwood and Chad Kline will be held accountable for their actions. That outcome doesn't depend on your presence in Chicago."

They settled into the conference room where their conversation had begun. Evening shadows stretched across Logan Square as the sun descended toward the western horizon. Streetlights began to flicker on, creating pools of amber light beneath the mature oak trees.

"Start the hiring process. Screen candidates, conduct interviews, and identify someone who can maintain Phoenix House's mission without compromising its values."

Will opened his laptop and began drafting a job posting that would attract qualified candidates.

"Timeline?"

"As soon as you find the right candidate. I want you back in Virginia with Shelby before LifeCore realizes what's coming for them."

Will nodded. "What about ongoing coordination among all three Phoenix House locations? Communication protocols, resource sharing, policy updates?"

"We'll establish remote management systems that allow you to oversee operations from Falls Church." Ryder leaned back in his chair, processing the logistics of Will's transition. "Phoenix House Chicago will also connect to the broader network in the near future."

"And after the LifeCore mission is complete?"

The question touched on futures neither man had considered. They had forged their partnership through shared combat against corporate predators, but what happened when those battles came to an end? Would Will return to a normal life with Shelby, or would new threats emerge that required their unique combination of skills?

"I'd like to focus on Nana's recovery and expand Phoenix House even more." Ryder stared at the blank wall, visualizing a time when that would be possible. "But there's never a shortage of powerful people who prey on the vulnerable."

Silence fell over the two men.

"Will, thank you for everything you've sacrificed to make Phoenix House possible. These men are alive because you chose to help them instead of focusing on yourself."

Will's expression softened. "They saved me as much as I saved them. But it's time for both of us to move forward. They need permanent leadership, and I need to rebuild my relationship with Shelby."

Ryder watched as Will gathered his materials and headed toward the stairs that led to his temporary quarters on the second floor. The young man who'd evolved from reluctant technical support to a dedicated partner deserved happiness beyond their mission against institutional predators.

Tomorrow would bring new challenges in their campaign against LifeCore, but tonight was about recognizing that victory required sustainable leadership rather than individual sacrifice. Phoenix House would continue its mission with or without Will Cameron, but his personal life couldn't survive continued neglect.

Ryder observed residents gathering in the dining room for Orosco's chicken marsala. Voices and laughter echoed through the building as men who'd lost everything found community among others who understood their struggles. The scene validated every difficult decision required to establish Phoenix House Chicago.

CHAPTER 30

Sirens wailed past Nana's house for the second time in five minutes, the sound cutting through the open kitchen window. Ryder glanced up from his phone, where he'd been checking emails and stock prices, then returned his attention to the screen as coffee steam rose from his mug.

Shadow lay beside Nana's hospital bed in the living room, her alert ears tracking every sound from the street. The Belgian Malinois had appointed herself as guardian, leaving her post only for essential needs.

Ryder's phone buzzed with an incoming call from Kendrick.

"Ryder."

"We need to warn Dr. Lee." Kendrick's voice was urgent. "I've been thinking about it all night, and she's not safe at LifeCore."

Ryder nodded. "I was thinking the same thing. She deserves to know what kind of man she's working for."

"I'll call her now. Hopefully, she'll take my—"

"Hold on," Ryder interrupted. "I have a different idea."

"What is it?"

"Let's invite her somewhere she'll feel safe so we can explain everything that's happened to you and Will inside LifeCore. I'm worried about her safety."

"Makes sense," Kendrick replied. "Where should we meet?"

Ryder glanced toward the living room, where Nana dozed in her hospital bed, unbothered by the commotion outside. "Here. Nana's house is private, and after what happened to the last Richter crew, I don't think LifeCore security will target this place."

"Sounds good. I'll see if she can come over this afternoon."

Twenty minutes later, Kendrick called back with confirmation. "She agreed to meet at two o'clock. I told her we had sensitive information about LifeCore's operations she needed to know for her own safety."

"Did she sound nervous?"

"Terrified. But she's coming."

At one fifty-five, Kendrick's sedan parked on the street a block from Nana's house. Ryder checked the security cameras he'd installed to monitor the street. Dr. Lee had insisted on taking the L, and he wanted to be sure nobody was tailing her.

Dr. Lee appeared on the monitor. She wore dark slacks and a professional blouse that suggested she'd come straight from LifeCore's offices. Her eyes darted up and down the quiet residential street, checking for unwanted observers.

Ryder opened the door before both women reached the front steps. "Dr. Lee, thank you for coming. I know this wasn't an easy decision."

"Agent Kendrick said you had information about my safety." Her voice was strained and shaky.

Ryder stepped aside and let Kendrick and Dr. Lee into the living room, where Nana watched TV from her recliner. Shadow lifted her head from beside Nana, studying the newcomer with cautious acceptance.

Dr. Lee stopped mid-stride when she saw her. "Is this your grandmother?"

"Yes, this is Jill Ryder, my nana. Nana, this is Dr. Lee." Ryder announced.

"James, you didn't tell me we were having company."

"Sorry, Nana. Special Agent Kendrick and I need to talk to Dr. Lee in private, and this was the best place to meet."

"Okay, I'm happy to see all of you." Nana's smile was warm despite her obvious fatigue. "Sorry, I'm not up to proper hosting today."

Ryder noticed Dr. Lee studying Nana's movements and speech patterns. The physician pulled a chair closer to the recliner, her medical instincts engaged. "Mrs. Ryder, how are you feeling to-day?"

"Oh, some days are better than others. I had a stroke—" Nana paused. "How long ago was it, James?"

"About four weeks ago, Nana."

"It's been a tough month since the stroke, and this morning was especially difficult."

"Can you tell me about the difficulties?"

"My left hand is always curled into a fist, and my balance is terrible. Yesterday I almost fell in the bathroom."

Ryder felt his jaw tighten as he listened to Nana describe struggles he hadn't fully comprehended. She'd been protecting him from the worst of her decline, maintaining cheerful conversations while battling the stroke's devastating effects.

Dr. Lee conducted an impromptu assessment, asking Nana to perform simple tasks that revealed the extent of her deficits. Fine motor control, spatial awareness, and cognitive processing all showed significant impairment from the stroke damage.

"Mrs. Ryder, can you lean forward for me?"

Nana struggled, requiring help to reach an upright position. Her left side showed significant weakness, and her coordination remained compromised.

"Does someone come here daily for your rehabilitation, or do you go to one of the nearby facilities?"

A soft chuckle escaped Nana. "Honey, I haven't had rehabilitation since I left the hospital a few days after my stroke. That's all my insurance company would cover."

"What?" Dr. Lee sounded genuinely mortified.

"Thankfully, James is covering Karla, the nice young nurse who comes over every day, so I don't end up in a nursing home."

Dr. Lee's expression darkened as she helped Nana settle back into a comfortable position. She turned to Ryder with restrained anger. "Can we speak... alone?"

They moved to the kitchen, leaving Kendrick with Nana and Shadow.

"Your grandmother is in serious trouble," Dr. Lee said, shaken. "She needs immediate intensive rehabilitation. Doesn't she have Medicare?"

"She has Medicare Advantage. LifeCore is the provider."

Dr. Lee shook her head and looked down at the table, shame evident in her expression. "I was afraid that was the case."

Ryder's plan to let Dr. Lee see the harm caused by LifeCore's policies had worked. Now he wanted to see how he could help Nana while protecting Dr. Lee. "What are we looking at if she doesn't get proper care?"

The LifeCore CMO sat up straight and exhaled. "Progressive deterioration. Within six to eight weeks, she may lose the ability to live independently. The stroke affected her balance, fine motor skills, and spatial processing. Those deficits will worsen without proper intervention."

The diagnosis hit Ryder like an icy wave. He'd known Nana was struggling, but hearing the clinical reality from a medical professional made the situation more urgent.

"How do we get LifeCore to cover all that?" Ryder whispered.

Shame returned to Dr. Lee's eyes as she shook her head. "I don't know. Andre has given Chad so much autonomy with his efficiency algorithms that I'm not sure I can even help, but I'll try."

"Thank you," Ryder replied. "I'd appreciate it, but that's not why we asked you to come up to Andersonville. Let's get Kendrick in here."

Special Agent Kendrick joined them in the kitchen and sat between Ryder and Dr. Lee.

"Show Dr. Lee your arm."

Kendrick rolled up her sleeve and revealed the dark bruises on her forearms with purple and yellow marks that formed a distinct pattern of finger grips.

Dr. Lee gasped when she saw the injuries. "What happened to your arm?"

Kendrick glanced at Ryder, who nodded his permission to explain. "Andre Atwood grabbed me during my investigation with Elena Grabowski. He accused me of being a spy and became very agitated and physically aggressive."

Dr. Lee approached for a closer examination of the bruises. "These are severe. He could have fractured your wrist if he'd applied more pressure."

"The encounter would have escalated further if security hadn't interrupted us."

"Andre did this?" Dr. Lee's voice carried a mix of disbelief and recognition.

"You've seen him lose his temper before," Ryder said.

"Not like this. He can be demanding, even harsh with subordinates, but I never expected physical violence..." She trailed off, perhaps remembering incidents that made more sense in this new context.

Ryder knew it was time to reveal why they'd brought her to Nana's house.

"Atwood and his associates are targeting people who threaten their operation. They've already made attempts on my life, threatened my grandmother's caregiver's job, and now assaulted a federal agent." Ryder's tone remained steady, but his words carried an unmistakable warning. "You need to be careful."

The physician sank into a chair, processing the implications of what she'd learned. "What do you want from me?"

"We want you to stay safe. Atwood knows you have access to patient files and financial records that could expose their targeting of vulnerable people. That makes you dangerous to them."

Ryder wrote his cell phone number on a piece of paper and slid it across the table to Dr. Lee.

"What's this?"

"My number. Put it in your phone now and call me if you notice anything suspicious. Cars following you home, unusual interest in your activities, threats of any kind."

Dr. Lee took the paper and stared at the numbers. "What if they're already watching me?"

"You should assume they are."

The room fell silent except for the rhythmic ticking of the grandfather clock and the distant sound of traffic. Shadow had moved closer to Dr. Lee, the dog's protective instincts extending to anyone showing kindness to Nana.

Dr. Lee gathered her purse and paused at the front door. "Your grandmother is a remarkable woman, Mr. Ryder. She deserves every chance to recover her independence. I'll do what I can, but Andre and Chad are ruthless when their bonuses are threatened."

Ryder held the door open for the LifeCore CMO. "I appreciate any help you can provide, but I also want you to stay safe. Call me if you ever feel threatened or sense something isn't right."

Dr. Lee passed through the door and turned back to face the former Delta Force operator. "I will."

Kendrick remained in the kitchen while Ryder checked on Nana. Shadow had resumed her post beside the recliner, chin resting on her front paws as she maintained her vigil.

"Thank you for looking out for Dr. Lee," Kendrick said when Ryder returned. "I don't trust Atwood or anyone else at LifeCore."

"She's been an ally in all this, so I'll do everything I can to protect her."

The CID agent moved to the kitchen window. Ryder noticed that her shoulders and jaw were tense. "What's wrong?"

Kendrick turned back to face the man she once hunted. "My way didn't work, and now we solve LifeCore your way, so what's next?"

The question hung in the air between them, carrying the weight of Ryder's certainty that law enforcement channels would never deliver justice to LifeCore, alongside Kendrick's apprehension about abandoning the system. The system had failed Nana, the veterans at Phoenix House, and every patient who died because of LifeCore's policies. Ryder sensed Kendrick was reluctant to proceed with his brand of justice.

"You don't have to do this. It's my way of ensuring everyone in our society still faces justice and accountability. I'd understand if you preferred to walk away now."

Kendrick joined him at the counter. "What if Dr. Lee comes back to us with evidence that breaks the case open? What if we can expose the entire operation without you having to cross lines you can't uncross?"

"Then Atwood likely beats the charges in court. That's not justice."

They stood in comfortable silence, both understanding that events had moved beyond their ability to control outcomes through careful planning. Forces larger than their investigation were pushing toward confrontation, and Ryder's patience for half-measures was reaching its limits.

"I should get back to Phoenix House," Kendrick said. "Will is expecting an update on the meeting."

"Tell him to work on LifeCore's building schematics. Floor layouts, security protocols, infil and exfil options."

"Are you sure about this direction?"

"I'm open to all outcomes that ensure Atwood and his associates face appropriate consequences for their crimes."

Kendrick nodded, understanding his careful phrasing. Ryder wasn't abandoning the system, but he was preparing contingencies that operated outside of it. The distinction mattered to both of them, even if the outcome might be the same.

After Kendrick left, Ryder moved to the front porch. He sat on the top step with his elbows on his knees and his chin resting on his knuckles. The residents of Logan Square passed on foot and in vehicles, but he didn't see them.

The former Delta Force kill team member never shied away from taking a life, but he also understood the enormous responsibility of acting as judge, jury, and executioner. Kendrick might not be comfortable with his sentence for the guilty parties, but he was. It was time to deliver terminal justice to the cruel and calculating healthcare executives.

CHAPTER 31

The early evening light had faded, leaving the floor-to-ceiling windows of Dr. Allison Lee's office dark against Chicago's glittering skyline. Outside the forty-second-floor window of LifeCore Tower, the city's lights stretched endlessly into the night. She massaged her temples, fighting the tension headache that had been building since her morning meeting with Andre Atwood.

The executive brief on their latest efficiency metrics sat open before her. Three hundred and forty-seven denied treatment authorizations in the past month alone. She'd tried to override sixteen of them, but the algorithm had flagged them all for additional review.

Her coffee had gone cold hours ago, but she sipped it anyway. The bitter taste matched her mood as she reviewed patient files that would never receive the care they needed. Carol Hanson's case haunted her thoughts. An eighty-one-year-old woman with stage two breast cancer was denied treatment because the actuarial assessment determined her life expectancy didn't justify the expense.

She typed a name into her computer terminal that had been weighing on her mind: Jill Ryder. Dr. Lee wanted to review the patient file and search for anything she might have missed that could help James Ryder and his grandmother fight the denials. The record appeared on her screen, and she leaned closer to ensure she was reading correctly.

The system had flagged Jill Ryder as unauthorized to receive any further treatments. All claims required direct routing to Chad Kline for review and approval.

Dr. Lee had never seen such restrictions in her seven years at LifeCore. The company's chief medical officer was supposed to have oversight on complex cases, but Kline had bypassed her authority. The systematic targeting was more personal than she'd realized.

Ryder's warning about being careful echoed in her thoughts. Atwood and Kline were no longer just pursuing profits. They were waging war against anyone who threatened their operations.

Dr. Lee glanced at her phone—seven thirty-eight. The financial district had emptied hours ago, leaving LifeCore Tower populated by cleaning crews and security personnel. Another twelve-hour day for a company that didn't appreciate her medical expertise or dedication to patient health.

Time to leave.

The elevator descended through empty floors, each ding of the indicator reminding her how isolated she was in the corporate fortress. At this hour, the building belonged to security teams loyal to Atwood and his executive circle.

The parking garage stretched beneath the building like a concrete cavern, harsh fluorescent lighting creating pools of brightness between dark shadows. Her heels clicked against the polished floor as she walked toward her silver sedan.

Dr. Lee fumbled with her key fob, nervous energy making her movements jerky. The car chirped as the doors unlocked, and the interior lights illuminated the empty vehicle. She slid behind the wheel and locked the doors, a habit developed over years of working late in downtown Chicago.

She exhaled and stared at the concrete wall before her. "Stop it! You're going to drive yourself crazy."

The words helped, and the tension eased from her shoulders. She exited the parking garage and drove north toward her historic brick row home in Lincoln Park.

Traffic was light on the northbound lanes of Lake Shore Drive. She settled into the rhythm of city driving, traffic lights, and lane changes requiring just enough attention to quiet her racing thoughts.

In her rearview mirror, headlights followed at a steady distance—nothing unusual about that. Thousands of people traveled Lake Shore Drive every evening. But as she turned west onto Fullerton Avenue, the same headlights remained behind her.

Dr. Lee's pulse quickened. She made another turn, this time north on Lincoln Avenue toward her neighborhood. The headlights followed, maintaining the same distance.

She reached for her phone and scrolled through the contacts until she found the number Ryder had given her two days earlier. Her finger hovered over the call button as she debated whether to involve him in what might be nothing more than coincidental traffic patterns.

Dr. Lee pressed Ryder's number and waited through two rings before his voice answered.

"Dr. Lee?"

"I think someone may be following me." Her voice was steady despite the fear crawling up her spine.

"Where are you now?"

"Two blocks from my house." She rechecked the mirror. The headlights had fallen back, but she thought the same car was still there. "What if they know about the files I gave you?"

"Don't go to your house. Drive to a police station or pull over and call 9-1-1."

Dr. Lee checked her mirror several times and no longer saw the suspicious vehicle behind her. "I turned into my neighborhood, and I don't see the car anymore. Just paranoid, I guess."

"You're not paranoid. Someone could still be following you."

"Nobody is behind me, so I think it's okay now. Sorry I called and alarmed you."

"I'm headed your way. Don't go to your house until I get there. I'm ten minutes out."

The conversation ended as she turned onto her street. Elm trees lined both sides of the narrow roadway, their thick canopies creating pools of darkness between streetlights. She drove past her house twice, looking for a closer spot, but at this time of night, she'd be lucky to find anything.

Dr. Lee parked half a block away from her house. She could see the steps leading to her red brick row home, which comforted her.

The car that had been following her was nowhere to be seen.

She climbed out of the sedan and locked the doors, her keys jangling in the quiet neighborhood air. Porch lights glowed from surrounding houses, and the distant sound of a television drifted from an open window. Normal urban evening sounds that should have been comforting but felt ominous.

Each step toward her front door stretched like the length of a football field. The sound of her heels on the cooling concrete echoed like cannon blasts, announcing her presence to every predator lurking in the shadows.

Her porch light cast a welcoming, warm yellow circle around her front door, which had never looked so inviting. It was like a lighthouse for a wayward ship in a storm.

Once she crossed the street, she could run up her stairs and push through the door into the safety of her home. The street lined with parallel-parked cars on both sides was her last obstacle.

Dr. Lee passed between the bumper of a windowless van and a blue hatchback and hesitated. The eeriness of the van made her uncomfortable, and she tried to peer inside the darkness, but could not see anything in the pitch-black interior.

She wasn't sure why the twenty feet of asphalt that she'd crossed a thousand times over the years was the cause of extreme anxiety. The LifeCore CMO checked her phone. Ten minutes had passed since she had spoken to Ryder.

This gave her a fresh wave of confidence. Dr. Lee removed her house keys, ready to unlock her front door as fast as possible, and started toward her home.

Halfway across the street, Dr. Lee dropped her house keys. She bent over to retrieve them when the sound of squealing tires cut through the silence like a scream.

A dark sedan raced down her street with its headlights off, engine roaring as it accelerated straight toward her. Her fingers found her house keys as two tons of steel barreled toward her with no intention of stopping.

She saw the whites of two eyes behind the wheel just before impact. Dr. Lee dove away from the sedan toward the parked cars on her side of the street. She wasn't fast enough. The speeding vehicle collided with her airborne body. First, she bounced off the hood, then smashed into the windshield and tumbled over the roof until she slammed into the pavement, sending lightning bolts of agony through her nervous system.

The sedan's brakes locked, rubber screaming against pavement as the driver brought the vehicle to a stop fifty feet past where she lay.

Dr. Lee gasped for air. Once her lungs filled with oxygen, she tried to push herself upright, but her left leg wouldn't support her weight. Bone fragments shifted beneath torn muscle, and each movement sent fresh waves of nausea through her core. The medical doctor understood she had a badly broken leg.

The car door slammed shut with purposeful anger.

Footsteps approached across the asphalt, measured and deliberate. Not someone rushing to help an injured pedestrian, but a predator closing in on wounded prey. Dr. Lee lifted her head enough to see a man's silhouette approaching, his face obscured by shadows and a dark mask covering everything but his eyes.

In his right hand, the dull gleam of a pistol caught the streetlight.

Dr. Lee propped herself up on one arm and focused on his eyes. They were cold, empty, and radiated the kind of evil that could kill an innocent person and feel nothing.

The assassin raised the pistol, its barrel pointing at her chest. Dr. Lee closed her eyes, expecting the sound of the gunshot and then the pain that would end her life for the crime of caring about patients more than profit margins.

CHAPTER 32

The aroma of grilled peppers and seasoned beef drifted through Ryder's car window as he waited in the drive-through line for dinner in Andersonville. He'd missed Orosco's dinner at Phoenix House and was looking forward to a classic Chicago Italian beef sandwich before settling in for the night at Nana's house.

His phone buzzed against the dashboard.

"Ryder."

"I think someone may be following me." Dr. Lee's fear cut through the ambient noise around him.

Ryder threw Nana's Camry into drive and pulled out of the line, tires squealing against asphalt as he accelerated toward the street.

"Where are you now?"

"Two blocks from my house." Her voice tightened. "What if they know about the files I gave you?"

“Don’t go to your house. Drive to a police station or pull over and call 9-1-1.”

A long pause stretched before Dr. Lee answered. “I turned onto my street and I don’t see the car anymore. Just paranoid, I guess.”

“You're not paranoid. Someone could still be following you.”

"Nobody is behind me, so I think it’s okay now. Sorry I called and alarmed you.”

"I'm headed your way. Don't go to your house until I get there. I'm ten minutes out."

Ryder ran two red lights and took the turn onto Clark Street at a dangerous speed. The digital clock on his dashboard read seven forty-one as he pushed through evening traffic toward Lincoln Park.

Dr. Lee hung up as Ryder merged onto Lake Shore Drive, weaving between slower vehicles while simultaneously scanning every dark sedan for potential secondary threats.

Traffic thickened near the Fullerton exit, forcing him to use the shoulder to maintain speed. Horn blasts and angry gestures followed in his wake, but Ryder ignored them. Nothing mattered except reaching Dr. Lee before anyone from LifeCore could harm her.

He took the turn onto Lincoln Avenue too fast, his sedan nearly sideswiping a parked delivery truck before the tires found purchase again. Residential streets meant slower speeds but also more hiding places for potential ambushes. Ryder scanned ahead for threats while calculating the fastest route to Greenview Avenue.

The tree-lined neighborhood streets of Lincoln Park stretched before him, dotted with parked cars and glowing porch lights. Dr. Lee lived somewhere in this maze of narrow roads and brick row houses, hopefully still safe and waiting for his arrival.

Ryder parked half a block away and rushed to the address Dr. Lee had provided. He stopped at the bottom step of the target house two minutes late. He didn't know if Dr. Lee had pulled over and called the police, as instructed, or if she was hiding inside her home, because it was dark inside and the shades were drawn.

The sound of squealing tires drew his attention to the street on his left. Ryder watched in horror as a dark sedan sped up down Greenview Avenue with its headlights off, engine roaring as it raced toward a figure crossing the street. It was Dr. Lee, and Ryder saw her picking something up from the street in the vehicle's path, her body outlined against the streetlights.

The impact sent her airborne, her body bouncing off the hood before crashing into the windshield and tumbling over the roof. She slammed onto the pavement with sickening force as the sedan's brakes locked, rubber screeching against asphalt.

Ryder was already moving, his suppressed SIG Sauer in his hand as he sprinted toward the scene. The sedan had stopped fifty feet past Dr. Lee's motionless form, and a car door slammed shut.

Dr. Lee lifted her head, clearly injured but alive. Her left leg was twisted at an unnatural angle, and blood covered her face from multiple lacerations. She tried to push herself upright but couldn't support her weight.

A tall figure marched toward Dr. Lee, his face obscured by a mask. In his right hand, the dull gleam of a pistol caught the streetlight as he walked toward his intended victim with measured steps.

Ryder sprinted along the sidewalk, using parked cars for concealment while closing the distance. The assassin's attention was focused on his wounded target, his pace deliberate and unhurried. A professional who believed he had control over the situation.

The assassin raised his weapon, pointing it at Dr. Lee's chest. Her eyes widened at the approaching shooter until she seemed to accept the outcome and closed her eyes.

Ryder was two car lengths away when he fired four times in rapid succession, each suppressed round finding its target center mass. The assassin stumbled backward, his unfired weapon clattering against the asphalt. He collapsed beside a parked car, blood spreading across his dark jacket as his life drained away.

Ryder approached with his weapon trained on the downed man, ready to fire again if necessary. The assassin's eyes were open, but vacant, and his breathing was shallow and irregular. Within seconds, the breathing stopped.

"Dr. Lee, you're safe now," Ryder called. "I'll be there in a few seconds."

She opened her eyes and turned her head toward his voice. "Is he dead?"

"Yes." Ryder kneeled beside the assassin's body and snatched his wallet and car keys.

He moved to Dr. Lee's side and conducted a rapid assessment of her injuries. Her left leg was bent at an awkward angle and was fractured below the knee. Blood covered her hands and face from multiple lacerations, but her breathing was steady, and her eyes remained focused.

"Can you feel your toes?"

"Yes, I can feel my toes. I don't have a spinal injury. It's a proximal tibial fracture," Dr. Lee announced as if she were diagnosing an accident patient in the emergency room and not herself. "I also have a bone contusion on my hip, multiple lacerations that will require stitches, and a grade 2 dorsal carpal ligament sprain."

"I'm glad you're going to be okay." Ryder pulled out his phone and dialed nine-one-one, providing the dispatcher with Dr. Lee's address and a description of her injuries. Hit-and-run accident, he told them. The driver fled the scene after striking a pedestrian.

"Ambulance is five minutes out."

The former Delta Force operator looked around the quiet residential street, checking for witnesses or additional threats. Porch lights glowed from surrounding houses, but no curious neighbors had emerged to investigate the commotion.

He had one or two minutes before someone called the police or came outside to investigate the strange noises. Ryder had to clean up the scene before the ambulance arrived.

"I have to move the body. I'll be right back."

Ryder dragged the assassin's corpse to the dark sedan, popping the trunk with the dead man's keys. The interior was empty except for a spare tire and basic tools. He hoisted the body inside, slammed the lid shut, then drove the vehicle thirty yards down the street and parked it between two other cars where it wouldn't be noticed.

The walk back to Dr. Lee took less than a minute, and he found her conscious and alert.

"How bad is the leg?"

"Not good." Her voice was tinged with the clinical detachment of a physician examining her own trauma. "I need that ambulance to drive faster."

He kneeled beside her again, using his jacket to cover her upper body. "What happened before the car hit you?"

"I had my house keys out so I could get inside as soon as I got to my door, but I dropped my keys rushing across the street. I bent down to pick them up, and that's when I heard the engine. The car came straight at me with no headlights." Dr. Lee's eyes filled with tears, whether from pain or frustration, Ryder couldn't tell. "They tried to kill me just for trying to help patients."

Red and blue lights appeared at the end of Greenview Avenue as the first ambulance turned onto the street. Ryder helped Dr. Lee maintain pressure on her lacerations while they waited for the paramedics to reach them.

"I can't believe Atwood and Kline would stoop this low." Dr. Lee's voice cracked. "We're supposed to be healing people, not intentionally hurting them."

The ambulance pulled beside them, followed by a Chicago Police patrol car. Two paramedics jumped out and began working on Dr. Lee while uniformed officers secured the scene.

"Ma'am, can you tell us what happened?" The lead paramedic attached a blood pressure cuff while his partner established an IV line.

"A male driver in a dark sedan hit me crossing the street and then fled north."

Ryder stepped back as the paramedics worked, watching them stabilize her broken leg and clean the worst lacerations. Their professional competence reminded him why people like Dr. Lee mattered in a world dominated by corporate executives who saw patients as profit centers.

The police officers took his statement while the paramedics prepared Dr. Lee for transport. He hadn't seen it, but he'd heard the screeching tires, he told them. The veterans recovery center owner happened to be driving by when he saw the impact. No, he didn't get a good look at the driver. No, he didn't hear any gunshots or see anyone else in the area. Yes, he'd be available for follow-up questions if needed.

Dr. Lee remained conscious throughout the treatment process, her eyes finding Ryder's as they loaded her onto the stretcher.

"Thank you for coming so fast. I don't want to think about what would have happened if—"

"Then don't," Ryder interrupted. "Focus on getting better and nothing else right now."

The ambulance pulled away with lights flashing and sirens wailing, disappearing into the night toward Northwestern Memorial Hospital. Ryder watched until the red taillights vanished around a corner, processing the evening's events and their implications.

They both knew that if he'd arrived thirty seconds later, Dr. Lee would be dead. Her knowledge, her evidence, and her potential testimony would have died with her on Greenview Avenue. The thought sent heat through his chest and up his neck as he considered how close they'd come to losing their most valuable ally inside LifeCore.

Ryder wouldn't know the identity of the assassin until Will did his research, but he was sure Atwood or Richter had sent the man. They'd crossed a line that proved they would kill anyone who threatened their profitable operation. No amount of evidence or regulatory pressure would stop people willing to murder for quarterly bonuses.

The police officers finished their investigation and departed, leaving Greenview Avenue quiet except for the distant sound of traffic and the occasional bark of a neighborhood dog.

Ryder returned to his car and sat behind the wheel, watching the empty street where Dr. Lee had almost died for the crime of caring about patients more than quarterly earnings. The woman who'd dedicated her life to healing people had been targeted for elimination by executives who'd forgotten their original mission.

Tonight, only his intervention and willingness to use lethal force had saved her life. The realization crystallized his thinking about LifeCore and the next steps in handling them using his methods.

Men like Atwood, Kline, and Richter understood only one kind of justice—the kind that came from the barrel of a gun wielded by someone with the skills to hunt predators and the willingness to look them in the eye and pull the trigger. That someone was James Ryder.

CHAPTER 33

Keyboard clicks echoed through Phoenix House's conference room as Ryder reviewed resident applications on his laptop. It was difficult to scroll through the veterans suffering from PTSD or substance abuse because each one deserved a place to recover, but Phoenix House didn't have the resources to take them all. His second cup of coffee that morning had gone cold as the former Delta Force operator focused on each man and woman behind the application.

Will Cameron sat across from him, hunched over his own screen. The acting Phoenix House manager had interviewed five candidates to replace him over the past two days, thinning the field down to one strong prospect who'd impressed him enough to warrant Ryder's attention.

"I have a good candidate to replace me here," Will said as he closed his laptop and leaned back in his chair. "Alex Serrano is a former Army Logistics Officer who retired three years ago. He's been running a halfway house in Austin for three years with zero recidivism among his residents."

"What's his motivation to help veterans?" Ryder asked. "We both know it's not for the money."

"He lost his brother to an overdose while he was deployed. Came home and decided to make a difference," Will shared. "He's got experience, intelligence, and the right motivation. I think he'd be perfect for Phoenix House Chicago."

Ryder closed his laptop and met Will's eyes. The young man who'd started as simple technical support had grown into someone capable of making critical operational decisions. His judgment had proven sound during their campaign against LifeCore, and his commitment to Phoenix House's mission was beyond question.

"If you think he's the right choice, make him an offer."

Will blinked. "You don't want to interview him yourself?"

"I trust your judgment." Ryder stood and walked to the window, watching residents move about their day. "You've been running this place since it opened. You know what leadership qualities matter more than I do."

The words hung in the air between them, marking another milestone in Will's evolving role in their operation and an acknowledgment that sustainable leadership required delegation rather than centralized control.

"I'll share the good news with him this afternoon."

Will opened his laptop again, but his fingers didn't touch the keys. "Ryder, is everything okay?"

"Yeah, why?"

"You've been staring at that same application for fifteen minutes without reading it. Something's bothering you."

Will was using the observational and pattern identification skills that made him a standout in Army Intelligence before an Afghan who blew himself up in Kandahar injured him.

"I'd prefer to wait until Kendrick arrives to discuss it."

Will opened his mouth, then thought better of it and returned his attention to his laptop.

The front door chimed downstairs, followed by Kendrick's voice greeting one of the residents. Footsteps ascended the staircase, and moments later, the CID special agent appeared in the doorway. She wore dark jeans and a black tactical jacket, her auburn hair pulled back in a ponytail.

"I came as soon as I got your message." She crossed the threshold. "What happened?"

Ryder gestured toward the conference room door. Kendrick and Will followed him inside, and he closed the door behind them. The morning sounds from the street below faded to background noise as the three of them settled into chairs around the table.

"Dr. Lee was attacked last night outside her home in Lincoln Park."

Kendrick's jaw tightened. "Is she okay?"

"Injured, but alive. A failed hit-and-run attempt that would have succeeded if I'd arrived seconds later. The driver tried to finish her with a pistol, but I intervened." Ryder's voice remained steady, clinical. "She's at Northwestern Memorial with a broken leg and multiple lacerations."

"You killed the assassin?" Will asked.

"Yeah." Ryder pulled the wallet and keys he'd recovered from his jacket pocket and tossed them onto the table. "Here's his keys and ID. Will, I want you to see who this guy was working for."

Will snatched the wallet and looked inside. "Brian Lyons. I'll see what I can find."

He opened his laptop and started typing. Kendrick stared at the wallet, her green eyes reflecting the controlled fury that could soon erupt in explosive anger.

"Richter or Atwood?" Kendrick asked, venom dripping from her voice.

"Don't know, but Will can find out. I suspect Richter because he's already sent his attack dogs after me twice, but if it's Atwood, it would indicate he's getting desperate."

"That's despicable, no matter who's behind it. They tried to kill a doctor simply for caring about their patients." Her words were quiet, but they carried weight.

"That's who we're dealing with." Ryder's voice trailed off.

His shoulders slumped as he leaned back in his chair and stared at the ceiling. The textured surface offered no answers, just the same questions that had plagued him since he'd decided to take on LifeCore. How many more people would be harmed? Was it worth the fight?

"You can't blame yourself for what happened last night," Kendrick stated.

"First Ricky, now Dr. Lee." Ryder brought his gaze back to the conference table. "Too many innocent people are dying or getting injured while I attempt to bring LifeCore to justice. Maybe my way eliminates the top executive, but at the expense of others. How many more people at LifeCore are in danger because of me?"

Will's chair scraped against the floor as he slid closer to Ryder, his laptop forgotten. Fire burned in the younger man's eyes.

"Ryder, I'm not former Delta Force or Army Ranger, but I've learned a lot from you in the last six months, and I can say with one hundred percent certainty that now is not the time to pull back." Will's voice rose, his confidence building. "Now is the time to go for the jugular if you want this madness to stop. Nana needs this to end. Dr. Lee needs this to end. Ricky needs this to end. It's time for direct action."

Ryder stared back at Will. Heat rose in his chest as protective instincts warred with tactical reality. He stood and stepped toward Will. His lieutenant jumped to his feet and leaned back reflexively until he realized Ryder wasn't trying to hurt him.

The former Delta Force operator pulled Will in for a brief bear hug with two slaps on his back.

"Thanks for bringing me back to reality."

Ryder shook his head. "I hate seeing innocent people get hurt, but I agree with everything you said. We eliminate Atwood in three days."

"Why three days?" Kendrick asked.

"Atwood and Kline present to analysts in two days, so they'll be working late with their teams over the next forty-eight hours. We hit them the day after their presentation."

They finally had a firm target date.

"It was Kline." Will blurted the words out as he stared at his laptop.

"What did Kline do?" Kendrick asked.

"He hired Brian Lyons. The man who tried to run down Dr. Lee had a long rap sheet in Wisconsin, so I compared his last known addresses with our usual suspects. Nothing correlated, but then I noticed that both Lyons and Kline attended Providence Catholic High School after Kline moved from Chicago to live with his uncle in Milwaukee. I bet Kline thought nobody would ever make that connection."

"They're escalating. We need to be ready in three days." Ryder's words came out as a growl.

Will opened multiple windows with LifeCore building schematics, security camera placements, and a list of approved vendors for the building. Kendrick moved her chair closer to review the intelligence that would inform their plans for direct action.

"Executive offices are on the forty-second floor, but they've portioned off their key departments like underwriting, IT, claims and the executive offices behind their secondary security entrance on the twenty-fourth floor. Atwood, Kline, and Dr. Lee are all on forty-two."

"Security checkpoints?" Ryder asked.

"Main checkpoint in the lobby, but the secondary access point at twenty-four controls access to executive levels. Badge readers are on every floor, but I can override those from my laptop. The real problem is the physical security team. Six guards minimum at the secondary entrance and the executive floor during business hours. Former military contractors, well-trained and well-armed."

Kendrick studied the screen. "What about after hours?"

"Reduces to three guards. Better but still formidable."

Ryder processed the information, his tactical training calculating approach vectors, engagement zones, and exit strategies. The mission was feasible, but complex.

"We need to consider how we cover our tracks afterward." Ryder leaned forward. "Chicago PD will have a hundred detectives hunting whoever takes down a Fortune 500 CEO. The feds will get involved within hours. We can't just disappear and hope nobody connects the dots."

Kendrick nodded. "They'll need to make an arrest or at least name a suspect. I recommend misdirection. We need someone else to take the fall."

"Who could that be?" Will asked.

"Crane." Ryder's voice carried satisfaction as the pieces fell into place. "Brandon Crane."

"How?" Will looked up from his screen.

"Don't you have footage of him in the LifeCore building multiple times?"

"Yeah. He meets with LifeCore's security operations."

"Start manipulating the video you have now to make Crane look like he's casing the place." Ryder stood and began pacing the conference room. "We'll also need to lure him into LifeCore Tower the night of our ambush to put him at the scene."

Will stared back for a beat, his analytical mind processing the implications. Then he nodded, a smile spreading across his face. "That may actually work. I can edit the footage to make his time in LifeCore look like reconnaissance rather than a legitimate security consultation."

He returned his attention to the laptop. "Give me forty-eight hours to edit the surveillance footage and map Crane's access patterns. I'll create a narrative that shows increasing suspicion and paranoid behavior."

"What about motive?" Kendrick asked. "Investigators will want to understand why Crane would target Atwood and Kline."

Ryder moved to the window and peered out at the world outside. Joggers, men in delivery vehicles, and dog walkers all went about their lives, unconcerned that a wrong move could be deadly. The former Delta Force operator didn't have that luxury. He had to solve the problem of LifeCore and Richter Enterprises, or people would die.

"Let's go all in and frame Tobias Richter." Ryder left the window and stood next to the conference room table, excitement clear in his body language.

Will and Kendrick exchanged a glance as if to confirm they both heard him correctly.

"How do we do that?" Will asked.

"Tobias Richter and his company are the largest shareholders of LifeCore. If he got wind that Andre Atwood and Chad Kline were cooperating with insurance regulators, it would be plausible for him to send his head of security to eliminate their problem."

Ryder continued pacing. "Perhaps Atwood and Kline were planning to testify to regulators that the algorithm was Richter's idea. Then, investigators can find a memo penned by Crane outlining the financial risk and possible solutions on Tobias Richter's computer."

A wide smile spread across Will's face. "You're evil, James Ryder. I hope I never cross you."

The former intelligence analyst's fingers flew across the keyboard. "I can forge emails and plant documents in both LifeCore's and Richter's systems that support that narrative. It'll take time, but it's doable."

Ryder leaned forward, his palms spread across the conference room table. "I need one more thing from both of you before we get started."

"What is it?" Kendrick asked.

"I need Will to take the vehicle with Brian Lyons stuffed in the trunk and park it somewhere on the opposite side of the city. Preferably, some place that's frequently in the news for drug or gang violence. Kendrick, you follow him, and ensure neither of you leaves any hair, prints, or fibers."

Kendrick stepped forward and answered on behalf of both of them. "We'll do it right away."

Ryder's phone buzzed in his hand. He glanced at the screen and saw a message from the contact he'd established at Northwestern Memorial, a nurse who'd agreed to keep him updated on Dr. Lee's condition.

Surgery was successful. Dr. Lee is stable in recovery. The doctor says she can see visitors tomorrow afternoon.

Relief washed over him. Dr. Lee would recover. The woman who'd risked everything to help them expose LifeCore's crimes would survive the assassination attempt and live to see justice delivered.

"Dr. Lee's surgery was successful." Ryder shared the message with Kendrick and Will. "She's in recovery and can have visitors tomorrow."

"I'd like to go with you when you visit," Kendrick requested. "She deserves to know she's not alone in this fight."

Ryder nodded.

Kendrick's transition into an ally was almost complete, and he was glad the Army CID special agent would be on his side during the operation instead of plotting against him.

CHAPTER 34

Andre Atwood's feet pounded against the treadmill belt as the LifeCore Tower's fifty-second-floor penthouse gym windows revealed downtown Chicago still cloaked in predawn darkness. His heart rate monitor showed one-sixty, pushing past the comfortable zone into territory that burned away stress and tension. It was five thirty in the morning, and he'd been running for forty minutes, chasing something that would forever remain out of reach.

The phone on the treadmill console vibrated with another message from Tobias Richter's office. Another request for updated quarterly projections. The second in less than a week. The pressure from Richter never stopped, never eased, and never allowed him a moment to breathe without worrying about topping last quarter's earnings.

Sweat soaked through his gray athletic shirt as he increased the incline to twelve percent, attacking the mechanical hill with the same intensity that had once earned him All-Sunbelt Conference accolades as Appalachian State's linebacker. The physical pain was a welcome escape from the mounting tension of maintaining LifeCore's growth trajectory.

Three miles turned into four and soon became five.

The treadmill slowed to a stop, bringing his punishing session to a close. Atwood grabbed a towel and wiped his face, staring at his reflection in the floor-to-ceiling windows. He maintained the physique of a man twenty years younger, but the face looking back showed the cost of corporate warfare. The lines around his eyes had deepened over recent months. Gray streaked through his temples more prominently than last quarter.

He walked through the penthouse toward the primary bathroom, passing through rooms filled with furniture that cost more than most people's houses. The morning light was beginning to creep over Lake Michigan, painting the water in shades of purple and gold.

Atwood showered and dressed in his usual uniform, a tailored charcoal suit that projected the authority expected from LifeCore's chief executive.

His phone buzzed on the bathroom counter. A text message from Chad Kline appeared on the screen.

Can you talk?

Something about those three words triggered alarm bells. Kline never contacted him this early unless the situation demanded immediate attention. Atwood dried his hands and called his chief underwriting officer.

"What's up?"

Kline's voice carried strain. "The contractor failed. His target is still alive."

The words dismantled Atwood's morning routine, sending it into chaos. He gripped the marble countertop, knuckles whitening as he processed the implications.

"What? How?"

"The contractor was killed before he could complete the assignment. When the police found his body, it was in the trunk of his car parked in a South Side neighborhood. She is in the hospital, but alive."

Atwood spoke through gritted teeth. "Someone obviously killed him and moved the body. What are the police saying?"

"They haven't made any connection to a hit-and-run and believe the killing was drug-related because of the contractor's long rap sheet. There are no connections to LifeCore or Richter."

"There better not be!"

The LifeCore CEO's reflection stared back at him from the bathroom mirror, showing a man whose control over his corporate empire was slipping away one catastrophic failure at a time. Failing to eliminate Dr. Lee meant someone had evidence and could testify against him. Everything he'd built was in jeopardy.

"Where is she now?"

"Northwestern Memorial Hospital. Stable condition. Broken leg and some lacerations, but she'll recover."

"Who killed the contractor?"

"Unknown. But based on the precision..." Kline paused. "It was professional work. Four center-mass shots with a suppressed weapon. Whoever it was knew what they were doing."

Ryder. The name crystallized in Atwood's mind with absolute certainty. A former Delta Force operator who'd destroyed every security team sent against him. The man who'd killed three of Richter's best operatives in his grandmother's house without breaking a sweat.

"Call Brandon Crane and come clean about our plan and the outcome. He'll be angry, but we need him now to get out of this," Atwood commanded Kline. "Conference call in five minutes."

Atwood paced through his penthouse, the morning ritual completely abandoned as crisis management protocols took over.

The conference call was connected with Brandon Crane, who joined from his hotel room in Chicago.

"What the hell were you thinking?" Crane demanded.

"We wanted to ensure there was no tie to Richter Enterprises in case something like this happened," Atwood replied.

"That's the only smart thing you did in this whole cluster of an operation. If you had come to me, none of this would have happened."

Atwood was not used to being reprimanded and didn't like Crane's tone, but knew he didn't have the leverage to push back. He wanted to move forward to a solution.

"I understand, but it happened, so what should we do now?"

"It's clear that James Ryder is involved, which complicates everything."

Atwood moved to the windows overlooking the city he'd conquered through corporate ruthlessness and algorithmic efficiency. The buildings, traffic, and people seemed more distant than usual.

"What do you recommend?"

"Double your personal security by the end of the day. Reinforce all access points to the executive floor. And prepare to defend yourself against direct assault."

The suggestion seemed absurd. "Ryder will never get through all the security in this building."

Crane's response carried a chill that penetrated Atwood's veil of composure. "I've seen him in action before. You'd better be prepared for him to kill everyone on your security team."

The line went silent for several seconds. Atwood processed the security contractor's assessment of James Ryder's capabilities, weighing it against his confidence in LifeCore's defensive measures. Armored glass. Reinforced doors. Biometric access controls. Two dozen security personnel with military and law enforcement backgrounds.

"He's one man."

"He's former Delta Force. And he's been preparing for this operation since you put his grandmother in a hospital bed." Crane's voice remained steady, professional, devoid of emotion. "Don't underestimate him because you have superior numbers. I did that in Miami, and it cost me most of my team."

Atwood stared at his reflection again and sighed.

"Double security on the twenty-fourth and the executive floor, effective immediately."

"I'll coordinate with LifeCore security," Crane confirmed. "But remember what I said. Be prepared to defend yourself. When Ryder comes, and he will come, you may be the only thing standing between him and your obituary."

The call ended, leaving Atwood alone in his penthouse fortress that felt less secure than it had thirty minutes earlier. He walked to his private office and opened the safe hidden behind a framed photograph of his family. Inside, a Glock 19 pistol and three loaded magazines waited alongside legal documents and emergency cash.

Atwood had owned the weapon for years, part of his executive protection protocols, but he'd never imagined needing it.

He set the weapon on his desk and stared at it, processing how his meteoric ascent to the chief executive of one of the largest health insurers in the country had deteriorated into preparing for a gunfight in his own office.

***

The Phoenix House conference room smelled of stale coffee as morning light filtered through windows overlooking Logan Square. Will scrolled through the information on his display, absorbing new data with the skill of a former intelligence analyst.

Ryder sat across from him with his laptop open, clicking the down arrow as he reviewed resident applications for Phoenix House.

Will closed his laptop and studied his friend with concern.

"You okay?"

Ryder's eyes focused slowly, as if returning from somewhere distant. "I'm fine."

"You don't seem fine."

A ghost of a smile touched Ryder's lips before fading. "I've been thinking about collateral damage."

Will leaned back in his chair, waiting for an elaboration that took several seconds to arrive.

"Ricky's dead because I didn't get him to a detox facility when he needed it. Dr. Lee almost died because she helped us expose LifeCore's crimes. Nana is regressing, and then we have all the countless names we don't know, who are suffering from LifeCore's tactics every day they are still in business. How many more innocent people will get hurt because of me?"

The question hung in the air between them, carrying genuine doubt that surprised Will. Ryder projected unwavering certainty in his mission, unshakeable conviction that his methods served justice better than corrupt institutions. Hearing him question those fundamental assumptions suggested a deeper crisis.

"You weren't responsible for Ricky. Detox is a choice that he never made for himself."

"I could have put him in a better environment at a facility that specializes in detox."

"You gave him a chance at recovery that nobody else offered," Will countered.

Ryder stood and moved to the window, hands shoved deep in his pockets as he watched residents arrive for their morning routines.

"And Dr. Lee? She's lying in a hospital bed with a broken leg because we involved her in our investigation. We could have gathered that information without involving innocent people."

"She involved herself," Will countered. "Dr. Lee was fighting LifeCore's corruption long before we arrived. We just gave her an ally who wouldn't abandon her when things got dangerous."

"An ally who nearly got her killed."

Will stepped beside Ryder. "Now is not the time to pull back."

Ryder turned to face his friend, eyebrows raised.

"Now is the time to go for the jugular." Fire ignited in Will's eyes, an intensity that matched Ryder's own mission focus on his best days. "Nana's stuck in a hospital bed because LifeCore denied care to boost quarterly earnings. Dr. Lee almost died trying to protect patients. Ricky never got the help he deserved because the system failed him."

Will took a sip of coffee as he let those words sink in.

"Every hour we hesitate, more people are suffering. More denials are being processed. More families are losing loved ones to corporate greed disguised as actuarial necessity. You want to honor Ricky's memory? You want to justify Dr. Lee's sacrifice? Then finish what we started."

He grabbed Ryder's shoulder, forcing direct eye contact. "I don't know if it's justice, vengeance, or what we call it. I just know it's about stopping predators who've weaponized healthcare for profit. You're the only one with the skills and willingness to deliver the justice they've earned."

Ryder held Will's gaze for several seconds before pulling him into a brief side hug that surprised them both. The physical contact lasted only moments, but it carried weight that transcended words.

"Thanks for bringing me back to reality."

"That's what partners do." Will stepped back, ready to change the subject. "So, what's the plan?"

Something shifted in Ryder's expression, and the hard look of a predator on the hunt returned to his eyes.

"We continue with our plan to eliminate Atwood in two days."

The statement carried absolute finality, a decision made and commitment locked. No more doubt. No more questioning. Just focused preparation for the justice that Andre Atwood had earned.

CHAPTER 35

Lake Michigan stretched beyond the horizon, blue-gray water meeting pale sky in a line that blurred under the morning haze. Ryder stood at the edge of Montrose Dog Beach, wind tussling his hair, which had grown over an inch since he had arrived in Chicago. Waves rolled against the shore in a steady rhythm, white foam dissolving across smooth stones and broken shells.

Shadow sat beside him, her muscular body relaxed yet ready for action. Her dark eyes tracked joggers on the paved path behind them, cataloging every movement with the focus of a trained sentinel. The beach stretched empty to the south, unmarked sand waiting for dogs and their owners to arrive.

"Go on, girl." Ryder unclipped the leash from her collar. "You earned this."

The Belgian Malinois sat as if awaiting a command.

Ryder picked up a stick and threw it toward the shoreline. Shadow's ears tracked the arc of wood through the air, but her body stayed locked beside his leg.

The stick landed twenty yards away.

"Go get it. Fetch."

She stood. Her tail twitched once, then she settled back into position. Shadow's focus returned to Ryder's face, searching for something more important than play.

A Golden Retriever bounded past them, chasing a tennis ball into shallow water. Its owner waved apologetically as the dog kicked up sand. Shadow tracked the retriever's movement but showed no interest in joining the game. Her military discipline had evolved into something deeper during their years together. She sensed the danger he was walking into.

Ryder crouched beside her, scratching behind her ears right where she liked it.

"I know." His voice was quiet beneath the sound of waves. "You're not wrong to worry."

Shadow's nose pressed against his hand. The gesture carried weight beyond simple affection.

They walked north along the shoreline, Ryder's boots leaving prints in the wet sand that waves erased within seconds. Shadow maintained position at his left side, her gait matching his. Other dogs ran free across the beach, their joy evident in their racing circles and splashing through the shallow water. Shadow watched them without interest. She had a singular purpose—to protect and defend.

The morning sun climbed higher, burning off the haze and revealing the Chicago skyline to the south. Somewhere in that steel and concrete maze, Andre Atwood and Brandon Crane were preparing for the confrontation that would soon come.

None of their efforts mattered. Justice would be served.

Ryder turned back toward the parking area. They loaded into Nana's sedan, Shadow settling into the back seat with her attention focused through the windows. Her ears remained pricked forward during the entire drive to Andersonville, tracking every sound and movement.

Nana's house stood quiet in the morning light when they arrived. Yellow roses climbed the wrought-iron trellis on both sides of the front steps, their blooms opening to catch the sunshine. Ryder led Shadow through the front door, her nails clicking against the hardwood floors as they moved through the entryway. Everything appeared normal, like he'd left it two hours earlier.

Nana's recliner sat empty in the family room.

Ryder found her still in her hospital bed hours later than he'd expected. Her silver hair spread across the pillow while her face held a serene expression of deep sleep. Nana's hands rested on the blanket, fingers curled into loose fists. She looked peaceful.

Too peaceful.

The stillness triggered something in Ryder's gut, an alarm that screamed warning despite the tranquil scene. He'd seen death in enough forms to recognize its signature. The absolute absence of movement, the way light fell across skin that seemed somehow different, the quality of silence that felt too complete.

"Nana?"

No response. No flutter of eyelids, no shift in breathing, no acknowledgment of his voice.

His heart hammered against his ribs. "Nana."

He moved to the bedside, hand reaching for her shoulder. The first shake was gentle, respectful of her age and the careful balance required after her stroke.

Nothing.

"Nana!" His voice cut through the quiet house with sharp edges. Shadow appeared in the doorway, her body tense with alarm at his tone.

Ryder grabbed her shoulders with both hands, shaking harder than he should, harder than was safe, but terror had replaced rational thinking. The woman who'd raised him, who'd welcomed him into her home when the world collapsed around his twelve-year-old shoulders, who'd provided stability through years of military service, now lay unresponsive beneath his desperate grip.

Nana's eyes opened.

She blinked twice, confusion replacing the peace of deep sleep. Her gaze found his face, taking in the terror he couldn't hide, the fear that had broken through every defense he'd built over decades of combat.

"James?" Her voice was uneven and thick from interrupted sleep. "What's wrong?"

Relief flooded through him with enough force to weaken his knees. He released her shoulders, stepping back to give her space.

"You wouldn't wake up." The explanation sounded inadequate even as he spoke it. "I thought..."

Understanding crossed her face. She reached for his hand, her grip weaker than before the stroke but steady enough to ground him.

"I was up most of the night." Nana's words came slowly, with extra effort. "I'm worried that I'll never fully recover, and that was running through my mind all night. When exhaustion finally caught up, I went deep."

Ryder nodded, working to slow his breathing and regain the composure that had shattered. Shadow moved to the bedside, pressing her nose against Nana's free hand in greeting and reassurance.

"I'm sorry for frightening you." Nana squeezed his fingers. "But I'm fine. Just tired."

Nana's eyes tracked his face, reading the thoughts he hadn't spoken. She'd always possessed that ability, seeing past his mask to the emotions he kept locked away. Her expression shifted, sadness mixing with pride and acceptance.

"Will you help me to my chair?" Nana gestured toward the recliner that she had sat in daily since Ryder had moved in fifteen years ago.

Ryder steadied her, supporting her weight as she transferred from bed to chair. The process revealed how much the stroke had stolen from her independence. Each movement required conscious effort, coordination that had once been automatic now demanding full attention. She settled into the recliner with visible relief.

"There's a binder on the bookshelf." Nana pointed to the wall unit across the room. "Third shelf, blue cover. Would you bring it to me?"

He found the binder where she'd indicated, with its blue vinyl cover and neat label across the spine in her careful handwriting. The title stopped him cold—Jill Ryder Estate Plan.

The weight of those words pressed against his chest. Nana was preparing for the inevitable, organizing details that would matter after she was gone. Documents that would govern the distribution of her modest possessions, instructions for final arrangements, all the practical considerations that death required.

He delivered the binder to her chair, holding it without opening the cover.

"I know it's not much." Nana's voice carried quiet determination. "The house will need work before it sells, and there's not a lot of savings after all the medical expenses. But I wanted everything in order, so you wouldn't have to worry about..."

"Not now, Nana." Ryder cut her off with gentle firmness. He set the binder on the side table without looking at its contents. "It's time to fight and make things right. We focus on that first, and then we can talk about estate planning."

Her eyes searched his face, finding whatever confirmation she needed. "You're going after them."

It wasn't a question. She knew her grandson well enough to predict his response to organizational injustice.

Ryder stared back at his grandmother without blinking. His silence affirmed her question, but he had vowed never to involve Nana in his administration of justice. She knew his plans without having to utter a word.

Nana reached for his hand again, her grip stronger this time. "Justice heals, vengeance wounds."

The words were familiar, a philosophy she'd shared throughout his life. The distinction between righteous action and destructive revenge, the line that separated necessary force from unnecessary cruelty.

Ryder crouched beside her chair, bringing himself to eye level. The woman who'd raised him deserved honesty, especially now.

"I'm choosing justice, Nana. Real, lasting justice." His voice dropped to a low register, heavy with conviction. "You deserve better. Everyone hurt deserves better."

Nana's free hand touched his face, fingers tracing the scar along his left temple. The gesture was tender and maternal.

"I know you will do what needs to be done." Her acceptance carried no judgment. "Just promise me you'll come back."

The promise stuck in his throat. Professional honesty demanded he acknowledge the possibility of failure, the reality that some missions ended without the operator returning home. Delta Force had taught him never to make promises that he couldn't guarantee with one hundred percent certainty.

But Nana wasn't asking for a tactical assessment. She was asking for hope, for something to hold during the days ahead while uncertainty gnawed at her peace.

"I'll do everything in my power to walk back through that door."

It was the best truth he could offer. Nana seemed to understand the distinction, recognizing the limits of what he could promise while appreciating the commitment behind careful words.

Shadow moved closer, pressing against both of them. The Belgian Malinois had witnessed their exchange with the attention she gave to all significant moments.

Ryder stood, reluctance heavy in his movements. Two days of preparation waited at Phoenix House, plans that required his focus and expertise.

Shadow didn't follow him toward the door.

The dog remained beside Nana's chair, her body positioned for protection and comfort. She'd made her choice, appointed her new mission with the same clarity that had guided her through combat deployments.

Protecting Nana.

"Good girl." Ryder's voice carried approval mixed with gratitude. "Stay with her."

Ryder took one final look at the scene. Late morning light streamed through the window, illuminating his grandmother in her recliner with a Belgian Malinois standing guard. The blue binder sat on the side table, its contents irrelevant for the time being. Everything that mattered was alive, present, and worth fighting for.

He walked through the house, cataloging details he'd taken for granted. Family photos on the walls, documenting decades of life and love. The grandfather clock ticking its endless rhythm. Jill Ryder's brownstone held more value than any corporate balance sheet could measure, more worth than Atwood's entire empire.

The front door closed behind him with a solid click.

Ryder stood on the front steps, breathing August air that carried the scent of roses and distant rain. Chicago spread around him in all directions, millions of lives intersecting in patterns too complex to map. Somewhere in that vast city, Andre Atwood was preparing his defenses, Brandon Crane was positioning his assets and Chad Kline was calculating his odds.

None of them understood what was coming.

Ryder descended the steps and moved toward Nana's sedan. The panic that had seized him minutes earlier had burned away, leaving only focused determination. Two more days of preparation with Will and Kendrick, then justice.

CHAPTER 36

Brandon Crane stood at the window of his Chicago office, watching dawn break over the city skyline. Sleep had become a luxury he couldn't afford, not when James Ryder was preparing to strike.

His encrypted phone buzzed with an incoming message from Tobias Richter: *Status update?*

Crane typed his response: *Surveillance reestablished. Will advise.*

The failed assault on the grandmother's house had taught him valuable lessons about underestimating Ryder's tactical capabilities. He had four operators dead, another wounded, and nothing to show for it except a clearer understanding of the threat they faced. Crane had survived over two decades in the Navy SEALs and private military contracting by adapting his tactics, and James Ryder demanded a complete revision.

He scrolled through his contact list, pausing at a name he hadn't used in years—Ben Hartman. Retired Mossad, age sixty-seven, living in Skokie under deep cover after forty years of intelligence work. The kind of asset that became invisible through sheer ordinariness.

Crane sent Hartman a message through their encrypted app, detailing the mission.

Minutes after sending the message, he received a response. The Israeli operative accepted the mission.

Ben Hartman would succeed where others had failed because he understood that the most effective surveillance came from operators who became part of the landscape itself.

Four hours later, Crane's phone displayed live footage from Hartman's concealed body camera. The retired Mossad agent moved past Phoenix House with a slow, deliberate saunter, the gait of someone with nowhere else to be and a scruffy terrier mix pulling at its leash. He looked like thousands of Chicagoans who walked their dogs in similar neighborhoods every day.

Crane watched the feed with professional appreciation. Hartman's surveillance technique was flawless, each pause natural and unremarkable. The former Israeli spy continued his route, documenting Phoenix House activities without ever appearing to do anything except walk his dog. The head of security for Richter Enterprises had adapted his approach, replacing door-kickers with a ghost who could observe without detection.

"First pass complete." Hartman's voice came through the encrypted channel. "Heavy activity inside. Multiple individuals are visible through windows, gathering in a small room for intense discussion. Looks like they're planning something."

Over the next three days, Hartman's reports intensified the potential problem. Ryder, Will Cameron, and Special Agent Jenna Kendrick spent hours in the same small room, surrounded by laptops and coffee mugs.

Crane forwarded the surveillance footage to LifeCore security with specific instructions—double the guard presence on floors twenty-four and forty-two, implement additional access controls, and prepare for a potential assault.

He returned to the window overlooking the city. The surge of adrenaline he'd experienced before his missions as a Navy SEAL was building in his chest. Crane understood the significance of what was about to happen inside the walls of LifeCore.

Brandon Crane couldn't hold his primary concern in his head any longer, so he let it escape into the empty room like a secret confession. "They're coming soon."

***

The LifeCore tower gleamed in the afternoon sunlight, its glass and steel facade reflecting across Chicago's financial district. The day before the planned assault, Ryder stood beside Will on the plaza across State Street, watching employees stream through the main entrance during their lunch break.

"Three visible cameras covering the main entrance." Ryder kept his voice low. "Badge readers at the doors, and a security desk with two guards inside the lobby."

Will pretended to take a selfie as he snapped photos with his phone. "Delivery entrance on the east side. Service vehicles only with separate badge access."

They completed their circuit of LifeCore Tower, returning to the plaza where lunch crowds provided natural cover for extended observation. Ryder cataloged every approach vector and exfil routes.

"That's Emma Soto and Elena Grabowski." Will gestured toward two women emerging from the building's revolving doors.

Ryder recognized the names from Will and Kendrick's intelligence reports. The two women moved toward a nearby sandwich shop, their body language growing more relaxed with each step away from the building.

"They may have new information about what's going on inside. I'll make contact." Will started across the plaza before Ryder could object.

Ryder maintained his position, scanning for LifeCore security while Will intercepted the two women near the sandwich shop entrance. Their relaxed shoulders and instant smiles upon Will's arrival told Ryder they were allies. Will's animated gestures suggested he was deploying the charm that had convinced countless people to share information they shouldn't.

Elena Grabowski pulled out her phone, showing Will something on the screen. Emma Soto leaned in, adding her own observations to whatever intelligence they were sharing.

When Will returned, his expression was grim. "We've got problems."

They moved away from the tower, walking north along State Street until the crowd thinned enough for private conversation.

"Security doubled on both target floors. Elena says the change happened yesterday, and the guards are carrying different weapons. She said it was military-grade hardware." The former Army Medic's knowledge of military weapons and gear was critical to the assessment. "Emma confirmed that Brandon Crane spent four hours at LifeCore this morning, briefing security supervisors on enhanced protocols."

Ryder processed the information while watching pedestrians flow around them like water around rocks in a river. The landscape had shifted. Their original plan assumed existing security protocols, with success achievable through stealth, speed, and surprise. The hardening of LifeCore security had foiled their existing plan.

"We need a new plan."

"Agreed," Will replied as he scrolled through the images on his phone.

"Call Kendrick and tell her to meet us at Phoenix House. We don't have much time."

They returned to Phoenix House thirty minutes later, where Special Agent Jenna Kendrick waited in the conference room. She had pulled her auburn hair into a loose ponytail, and the tactical pants and shirt she wore suggested she had already begun preparing for direct action.

"What security enhancements?" Kendrick asked before they could speak.

"They doubled guard presence on both target floors, and Brandon Crane is supervising defensive preparations."

Kendrick studied the building schematics that Will projected onto the wall. "What about alternate entry points?"

Ryder leaned forward, studying the rooftop access points. "We could rappel down from the roof to the forty-second floor and cut through the glass. I've done it before."

"How do we get to the roof?" Kendrick asked.

After a brief pause, Ryder shrugged. "I don't know."

The conference room fell silent until Will shouted out, "Wait!"

Both Ryder and Kendrick turned toward him.

"The server room." Will pulled up a different schematic, highlighting the thirty-eighth floor. "LifeCore's algorithm servers generate massive heat. They have dedicated HVAC equipment on thirty-eight just for cooling the data center."

"So?" Kendrick moved closer to the screen.

"So the server room has so much specialized cooling equipment that it requires its own service elevator." Will's excitement built as he traced the elevator shaft on the schematic. "Separate from the main elevators, accessible from the lobby. HVAC contractors use it to service the cooling equipment without going through LifeCore security checkpoints."

Ryder leaned over Will's shoulder, studying the layout. "That bypasses the entire security checkpoint on twenty-four."

"Exactly. We can pose as HVAC contractors, take the service elevator to thirty-eight, and we're inside the building above their main security presence."

Kendrick's crossed arms unfolded. "That actually makes sense." The Army CID agent looked at her watch. "How do we get HVAC contractor credentials in under thirty hours?"

"Leave that to me." Will was already typing commands. "I can forge work orders, create employee records in the building management system, and generate access badges. Give me twelve hours."

The tactical landscape shifted from impossible to achievable in the span of two minutes. Ryder felt the familiar sensation of a mission plan coming together, pieces falling into place through intelligence and adaptation.

Ryder leaned over the conference room table and looked Will and Kendrick in their eyes. The time for debates and alternative options was over. The team needed to finalize the mission plan and move to the execution phase.

"It appears that the HVAC contractor option is our new infil plan. Are we all in agreement?"

Will and Kendrick exchanged a glance and nodded in unison.

It was the commitment and consensus Ryder wanted for his small but lethal team. They were also putting their lives on the line for justice.

Ryder straightened and faced the shapes and notes written in dry-erase marker on the whiteboard. "It's settled. Now let's execute."

CHAPTER 37

Ryder stood over the conference room table, admiring the new weapons he had acquired for their specialized mission. Three SIG Sauer MCX-Rattler short-barreled rifles with integrated suppressors and folding stocks rested beside magazines loaded with 300 Blackout rounds. They provided the firepower in a close-quarters environment against an opponent with superior numbers, in the compact size required to get past building security.

His friend Brian Buckner, a former teammate with the 75th Ranger Regiment, had come through. The call to the owner of Tactical Edge Armory in Florida led to a discreet contact with a gun shop owner in Joliet, who specialized in supplying federal tactical teams.

The man had his hat pulled low, and his long, black hair and beard concealed his appearance when he arrived that morning in an unmarked panel van. He was small framed but surprisingly strong as he delivered the weapons in one trip in three leather utility bags with false bottoms. Nods and grunts were his only responses during the transaction, and he left the moment Ryder's cash was in his pocket.

Will Cameron sat hunched over his laptop, fingers flying across keys as he worked on fabricating the final credentials they'd need for building security. He saw the new weapons and moved to the table, hands on his hips.

"Wow, what are these?"

"Sig Rattlers. They are small enough to sneak into LifeCore, but still pack a punch."

"Who are they registered to?"

"Nobody." Ryder waved his hand across the rifles and pistols on the table. "They're all unregistered, so investigators using ballistics to identify the shooters will go down an endless rabbit hole."

The former Delta Force operator pulled more gear from the weathered leather bag.

"What else is in there?" Will asked.

"The latest night optical devices." Ryder's lips curled up as he moved to the second bag. "And level three body armor."

"That won't stop armor-piercing rounds." The former Army intelligence analyst stated to the room.

"No, but I doubt a security team defending a corporate office has armor-piercing rounds."

"I hope not."

Kendrick arrived and scanned the hardware on the conference room table. "Nice."

"Are the uniforms coming?" Will asked.

"I'm so screwed if anyone finds out how I got them, but yes, the uniforms are on the way."

"Why? What did you do?"

Kendrick swallowed hard and took a sip of the bottled water in her hand. "I found out the FBI uses Windy City Uniforms for some of their undercover work. I may have impersonated Special Agent Rebecca Mitchell from the Chicago FBI office and told them it was an urgent order, so they'll be here at fourteen hundred."

Will opened his mouth to respond, but Ryder beat him to it.

"You're toast," Ryder taunted.

Kendrick spun around, ready for a fight, but then her expression softened as her gaze swept across Ryder's face. She noticed his playful grin. "I'm what?"

"Hang around me long enough and trouble will always find you."

The CID special agent pushed Ryder and knocked him off balance before stomping away. Will let out a quick belly laugh, and even though Ryder couldn't see Kendrick's face, he could tell she was smiling.

The laughter was precisely what Ryder wanted to hear. It broke the tension in the room. He'd seen fellow operators freeze up before a mission because of mental stress and anxiety. It was deadly for even the best operators over in the sandbox, and it could be just as lethal in LifeCore Tower.

The front door opened with its familiar squeak. Footsteps approached the conference room, and Alex Serrano, the new house manager, appeared carrying three large duffel bags emblazoned with "Dearborn Climate Control Services" logos. The Phoenix House assistant manager dropped the bags beside the weapons cache.

"The driver said these are for Rebecca Mitchell." Alex looked at the group. "I figured one of you would know what that meant."

Will and Kendrick exchanged glances while Ryder unzipped one bag and examined the navy-blue coveralls inside. The Dearborn Climate Control logo looked legitimate, and it matched the company Will had identified in LifeCore's vendor database. He held the uniform up, confirming the size would accommodate his muscular frame plus the body armor beneath.

"Perfect." He tossed the uniform back into the bag. "What about the work order?"

Will spun his laptop around, displaying an official-looking document complete with LifeCore's letterhead and security watermarks. "Emergency service call logged at zero seven hundred this morning. Cooling tower number six failed in the server room on the thirty-eighth floor. Our aliases are listed as the responding technicians from Dearborn Climate Control."

"Will LifeCore's security verify the company?"

"Already handled." Will's smile carried satisfaction. "I created a complete digital footprint. Website, state registration, contractor licensing. If security calls, they'll reach my automated system."

"Walk me through the infil plan again."

Will pulled up building schematics on his laptop. "Service elevator accesses the thirty-eighth floor directly from the lobby. We arrive at seventeen hundred when the building is still busy enough that we don't stand out. I hope they don't get suspicious of our false bottoms and decide to search the tool bags more thoroughly."

"They won't." Kendrick's voice carried certainty. "I've studied building security both days I was onsite. They're most thorough with visitor credentials, but service contractors with legitimate work orders get expedited through. The real gauntlet is on the twenty-fourth floor that we'll bypass."

Will nodded and continued. "Once we reach the server room, I tap into LifeCore's camera system and confirm Atwood and Kline's location. We'll short one of the servers to trigger an alarm. Kline will receive the notification on his phone, and we eliminate him and anyone else who comes down to investigate."

"Are you sure Kline will come to investigate and not send someone else?" Kendrick asked.

"Positive." Ryder picked up one of the suppressed pistols and verified that it had a full magazine. "At that hour, Kline is the only option. Plus, he designed those systems himself and believes he's the only person qualified to fix them."

"What if Kline comes with an army of LifeCore security?" Kendrick's question hung in the air.

Ryder met her gaze across the weapons-laden table. "Then we adapt. I've conducted enough combat operations to know plans rarely survive first contact. Expect the unexpected."

The unspoken reality sat between them. They were a capable force of three, but they were infiltrating enemy territory protected by five times more well-trained security personnel. Success was not guaranteed.

Kendrick's phone buzzed. She glanced at the screen, and her expression softened. "Dr. Lee is out of the hospital. She's going home with crutches and plenty of pain medication."

"Good." Ryder felt genuine relief. Dr. Lee's near-death experience had reminded him of why they were doing this. How many other innocent people would Atwood and Kline order killed to protect their profits?

Will uncoiled from the chair with a stretch and extracted himself from the chair where he'd spent hours crafting their digital cover story. "I need to make one final check on the work order."

Ryder's phone vibrated against his hip with Nana's number on the screen.

"Hey, Nana."

"James." Her voice sounded tired but stronger than it had been in weeks. "I saw I missed your call when I was in the bathroom. Everything alright?"

Ryder walked to the window, putting distance between himself and the arsenal spread across the conference table. Outside, Logan

Square's tree-lined streets looked peaceful in the afternoon light. Normal people going about their everyday lives, unaware that three people inside the brownstone were planning to commit acts that would forever alter the health insurance industry across the country.

"Everything's fine. I was checking in to see how you're doing."

"If you're calling me to check in, you must be going on one of those missions you can't tell me about." Nana knew him too well. "Whatever it is, I hope you stay safe and remember everything I taught you."

Ryder closed his eyes, remembering countless conversations around her kitchen table. Her wisdom had guided him through his parents' deaths, adolescence, and his military service. But some situations existed beyond the simple moral framework she'd taught him.

"I'll be safe." The promise felt hollow given what they planned, but he meant it. "And Nana? After tonight, things will get better."

"If anyone can make this mess better, it's you, James." The warmth in her voice almost broke his composure.

They said goodbye, and Ryder returned to the conference table. Will had finished his work order check and was reviewing the building schematics. Kendrick continued to twirl her hair as she stood over the weapons cache.

The next hour passed in methodical preparation. They donned the HVAC coveralls over their body armor, adjusting straps and testing their range of motion. The suppressed Rattler submachine guns nestled inside the modified tool bags, their profiles disguised beneath false bottoms and legitimate HVAC equipment.

Ryder studied himself in the hallway mirror. The navy-blue coveralls and Dearborn Climate Control logo transformed him from a former Delta Force operator into an anonymous service contractor. The disguise was perfect.

He returned to the conference room where Will and Kendrick waited in their matching uniforms. They were perfect replicas of what they were supposed to be—technicians responding to an emergency service call. Nothing about their appearance suggested that they carried enough firepower to fight their way through LifeCore security to the executive floor.

Ryder checked his watch. Fifteen forty-three. They had seventeen minutes before they passed the point of no return. He secured a Rattler and began his final preparations.

“If this goes wrong,” Kendrick began, then stopped.

Ryder continued threading the suppressor onto his Rattler. “It won't.”

“But if it does.” She met his eyes. “I want you to know I chose this. Nobody forced me. This isn't on you.”

The words hung between them, carrying weight beyond their critical mission.

“Same,” Ryder said after an extended pause. “You've become someone I trust to watch my six. That doesn't happen often.”

Kendrick's smile was brief but genuine. “High praise from James Ryder.”

“The highest.”

The conference room fell silent except for the zipping of gear bags and the distant sounds of Phoenix House residents moving through their afternoon routines.

"Listen. Once we leave Phoenix House, we're committed,” Ryder announced. “No second thoughts, no hesitation. We go in, we complete the mission, and we get out alive. Everything we've worked for depends on executing this plan."

Will nodded, his usual nervous energy replaced by focused determination.

Kendrick took a deep breath and squared her shoulders. "I'm ready."

"Good." Ryder began breaking down the short-barreled rifles and packing them in the tool bags. "Let's finish this."

CHAPTER 38

The descending sun reflected off LifeCore Tower's glass facade as their white contractor van merged into traffic on State Street. Ryder sat alone in the backseat, keeping watch over the tool bags that rattled with legitimate HVAC equipment arranged over false bottoms concealing their weapons. Will drove while Kendrick sat beside him, her auburn hair pulled into a ponytail beneath a matching baseball cap.

Ryder checked his watch. Sixteen fifty-seven. Three minutes ahead of schedule.

"Everyone good?" Will's voice carried steady determination despite the mission's risks.

"Ready," Kendrick responded.

Ryder met Will's eyes in the rearview mirror. "Let's do this."

The van pulled into LifeCore's service entrance, where a middle-aged, uniformed security guard stepped from the booth beside the barrier gate. He was professional but relaxed while confronting HVAC contractors.

Will lowered his window and produced the fabricated work order. "Emergency service call for cooling tower six on thirty-eight."

The guard scanned the document, his expression revealing nothing. One wrong detail in Will's forgery could derail their infiltration before they'd even entered the building.

"Pull forward to the loading dock." The guard returned the paperwork and lifted the barrier. "Security will check your equipment."

The van rolled into the loading area, where two additional guards waited beside the service entrance. Ryder recognized the increased personnel as excessive for vendor access, evidence that Crane's enhanced defensive preparations were already in place.

They exited the vehicle and pulled the heavy tool bags from the cargo area.

"Bags on the table." The lead guard gestured toward an inspection station.

Ryder placed his bag first, watching the guard as he unzipped the main compartment. Multimeters, pressure gauges, spare parts, and diagnostic tablets filled the bag. The false bottom remained invisible beneath the legitimate gear.

The guard's hands moved through the tools with focused intensity. Thirty seconds. Forty-five. Ryder inched closer to the second bag as each passing moment increased the risk of discovery.

"You guys have a lot of equipment." The guard lifted a refrigerant manifold, examining its weight and construction.

"Server room cooling systems require specialized tools," Will said with the confidence of someone who'd researched all the technical requirements.

The guard returned the manifold and zipped the bag closed. Ryder maintained his neutral expression as he calculated the steps needed to eliminate all three guards, should the inspection reveal their weapons.

But the guard was already moving to Kendrick's bag.

The inspection was repeated with the same methodical attention to detail. Tools were examined, weights assessed, and compartments probed.

The inspection of the third bag was completed without incident. The lead guard stepped back and gestured toward the service elevator. "Thirty-eighth floor. Stay in the designated maintenance areas."

"Understood." Ryder collected his bag and moved toward the elevator with Will and Kendrick following. The doors closed on the guards' watchful expressions, and the elevator began its ascent.

Silence filled the enclosed space as the elevator climbed higher into LifeCore Tower. Ryder welcomed the burst of adrenaline pulsing through his veins as they passed the main security checkpoint without stopping. His body sensed the looming clash with LifeCore security and prepared for the intense action ahead.

"That was tense," Kendrick whispered.

"It's not over yet." Ryder unzipped his bag and verified the weapons remained secure beneath the false bottom.

Once the floor indicator illuminated floor thirty-eight, the elevator chimed. Doors opened into a sea of chirping and humming electronics. The temperature dropped as they stepped into the server room's climate-controlled environment. Banks of servers stretched across the space, their cooling fans creating constant white noise that would mask conversation and muffle weapon reports.

Will connected his laptop to a diagnostic terminal and accessed LifeCore's cameras. Multiple feeds appeared.

"Both targets on forty-two." He zoomed in. "Atwood's in his office. Kline's in the conference room."

Ryder studied the layouts, memorizing guard positions and movement patterns. Three security personnel on forty-two. He spotted at least five more patrolling the other floors and stairwells. The numbers were manageable if they could draw their targets down to the server room rather than fighting through LifeCore's defensive positions.

"Now let's see if we can draw them to us, so we don't have to fight through a half dozen security personnel."

Will nodded and accessed the server monitoring systems. His fingers paused over the keyboard. "Are you ready?"

"Ready," Ryder said.

The command sent electricity surging through the servers in the next row. Sparks erupted from the rear panel as components shorted in sequence. Alarms triggered throughout the building's management system, sending urgent notifications to facilities personnel and executive monitors.

Will's camera feeds showed Kline checking his phone seconds after the notification. The chief underwriting officer's expression transformed from indifference to focused urgency as he read the malfunction notification.

"He's taking the bait." Will tracked Kline's movements through multiple camera angles. "Leaving his office now. Heading toward the elevator alone."

Ryder felt the familiar sensation of mission progress settling over him. The planning phase had ended. Now they operated in the fluid reality where adaptation mattered more than perfect preparation. He moved to a position behind a server rack that offered concealment and clear sight lines to the entrance.

Kendrick took a position on the opposite side of the room, her suppressed pistol drawn and ready. Will remained at the diagnostic terminal, monitoring camera feeds while preparing to provide covering fire if the situation escalated.

The elevator chimed.

Chad Kline entered the server room with the urgency of someone determined to fix the problem as fast as possible. His attention focused on the smoking server, his diagnostic tablet already displaying error codes and system failures.

"What the hell?" Kline moved toward the damaged equipment, his complete focus on the technical problem rather than awareness of his surroundings.

Ryder emerged from behind the server rack with his unregistered suppressed pistol extended. The weapon's barrel pressed against Kline's chest. "Don't move."

Kline froze, his tablet clattering to the floor. His breath came in quick gasps as panic replaced the confidence he'd carried into the room.

"Why did you do it, Chad?"

"I... I don't... I don't know what you're talking about." Kline's voice cracked. His hands trembled as he raised them.

"Why did you design an algorithm to kill people?" Ryder's voice was even and calm, like someone who'd decided the fate of men before. "Why did you target vulnerable patients who trusted you with their healthcare?"

"It wasn't my idea!" The words tumbled out in desperate panic. "Atwood designed the targeting parameters. I just implemented the technical specifications. He's the one who increased the denial rates for maximum profitability regardless of patient outcomes."

The scent of ammonia mingled with burned circuitry as Ryder noticed Kline's tailored slacks dampen with urine, his bladder releasing under the pressure of confronting his mortality. The chief underwriting officer, who'd celebrated quarterly bonuses built on patient suffering, now stood trembling in his own cooling piss, facing justice he'd never expected to encounter.

"Atwood made me do it." Kline's voice rose to a pleading whine. "He said the board demanded better financial performance. I was just following orders."

"Just following orders." Ryder's finger tightened on the trigger. "How many times in history has that excuse justified evil?"

"Please!" Kline's desperation reached a crescendo. "I'm a victim too in all this, and I'll testify against Atwood. I'll give you everything. Just please don't..."

The suppressed weapon's report was only slightly louder than the server fans. Kline's chest erupted as the round punched through his sternum and obliterated his heart. His body crumpled to the floor, legs folding beneath him as gravity claimed his weight.

The chief underwriting officer's mouth opened and closed like a fish gasping for oxygen on dry land. His eyes held the terrified awareness that death had arrived despite his pleas. The movements slowed, then stopped. His final expression was one of disbelief that consequences had finally found him.

Ryder lowered his weapon and turned to the server banks. "Will, get the Rattlers from the bags. I'm going to blow some of these servers and take that algorithm offline for a while."

He extracted three blocks of C-4 from his tool bag, then cut them in half with his knife and attached the malleable explosives to six different servers. Each block represented the destruction of systems that had killed thousands through the calculated denial of necessary healthcare.

Kendrick approached from her position, her weapon still drawn but pointed at the floor. Her expression revealed confusion and conflict. "You didn't have to kill him. He said he would help us nail the man really behind all this."

Ryder paused in attaching a blasting cap to the shaped charge. "What should I have done differently?"

"We could have arrested him." Her voice was steady despite the obvious moral crisis. "The FBI would have taken him, and Kline still would have faced justice."

Ryder secured the final blasting cap and stepped back from the servers. He turned to face Kendrick.

"That's not justice." Ryder pointed at Kline's body sprawled on the floor in its final undignified pose. "That's justice."

The words hung between them. Federal agent and vigilante. Law and consequence. Different philosophies intersecting in the shared mission to stop corporate predators from claiming more victims.

Ryder unzipped his uniform to access his vest, took a Rattler from Will, and then activated the detonation timer for five minutes. It was enough time to reach the stairwell and begin their ascent to forty-two, where Andre Atwood waited.

"Move toward the stairwell for forty-two." Ryder collected his weapon and moved toward the exit. "We're not finished yet."

The elevator chimed again as they approached the stairwell door. Instinct kicked in, and Ryder's weapon rose toward the elevator, trained on the entrance as the doors opened.

Two LifeCore security guards emerged and stepped into the server room. The first guard's eyes widened as he processed the scene and drew his weapon—Kline's body on the floor and three figures in contractor uniforms holding suppressed short-barreled rifles.

The LifeCore guard squeezed his trigger, and a gun battle erupted in the confined server room.

Ryder felt the familiar calm of combat settling over him. Each action flowed into the next as his Delta Force training superseded conscious thought.

The first guard took two rounds to the chest and collapsed against the elevator door. His partner managed one shot before Kendrick's marksmanship ended his threat.

Silence returned to the server room, broken only by cooling fans and the steady countdown of explosives preparing to destroy evidence of LifeCore's algorithmic murder.

"Check them." Ryder moved to the stairwell door.

Will confirmed both guards were dead while Kendrick secured their weapons and credentials. Standard security protocol following a firefight, transforming enemy equipment into useful resources.

"Three minutes." Will checked the detonation timer. "We need to move."

They entered the stairwell and began climbing toward the executive floor. Each step carried them closer to Andre Atwood and the last confrontation that would determine whether LifeCore's corporate predators faced justice or continued their systematic destruction of vulnerable lives.

Ryder's muscles remembered the countless training runs with full equipment. His breathing remained controlled despite the combat and rapid movement. Behind him, Will and Kendrick matched his pace with the intense determination to achieve mission success.

The stairwell stretched upward toward forty-two—only four more floors. Then justice would find Andre Atwood.

CHAPTER 39

The stairwell lights died the instant the servers exploded. Ryder's night optical device activated, transforming the concrete passage into a tunnel of grayscale clarity. Will and Kendrick flanked him, their NODs also active, as the three shadows ascended toward the forty-second floor through the darkness.

Emergency sirens pulsed through the building as the alarm system responded to the destruction in the server room. Red emergency strips along the stairwell baseboards provided the only light, casting faint crimson patterns across concrete walls.

On the fortieth floor, a door crashed open above them.

"Lock it down!" The voice belonged to Brandon Crane, unmistakable even through layers of concrete and distance. "Nobody gets to forty-two!"

Ryder's pulse quickened. The head of Richter security was here, directing his forces. It was time for the former Navy SEAL to face Ryder's specialized administration of justice.

Multiple footsteps echoed from above, boots hammering against stairs as security guards descended. Ryder raised his fist, halting the team two steps above the fortieth-floor landing. He pressed against the wall, signaling Will and Kendrick to do the same.

Through his NOD, Ryder watched six guards emerge from the forty-first floor doorway and form a defensive line in the stairwell. Their rifles swept the darkness, searching for targets their unaided eyes couldn't see. More footsteps echoed from below, a second element climbing toward them.

They were about to get caught between two forces.

"Bail out." Ryder's whisper carried just far enough for his team to hear. "Fortieth floor. Now."

He pushed through the door, rolling left as suppressed rounds from his Rattler stitched the first guard who tried to follow. The man dropped without a sound, his rifle clattering against concrete.

Will and Kendrick burst through behind him, securing the immediate corridor as the stairwell door slammed shut. The fortieth floor stretched before them, an open floor plan interrupted by glass-walled conference rooms and cubicle farms. Emergency lighting near the exits resembled streetlights on a lonely stretch of highway, casting tiny pockets of dim light between pools of darkness.

"Cover right." Ryder moved toward a reception desk twenty feet ahead.

Glass shattered behind them as security guards from the stairwell opened fire through the door's window. Rounds punched through drywall, sending plaster dust into the air. Ryder dropped behind the reception desk, his Rattler already tracking toward the stairwell entrance.

Six guards emerged, their rifle-mounted flashlights cutting through the darkness. Their beams marked their positions like signal flares on the battlefield.

Ryder squeezed his trigger and unleashed a three-round burst. The lead guard collapsed. He sent another burst, taking out the second guard.

Will engaged from behind a cubicle partition twenty feet to Ryder's right, his suppressed rounds dropping a third guard. Kendrick's controlled fire from behind a conference room wall eliminated a fourth.

The remaining two guards dove for cover behind overturned desks, their flashlights extinguished.

"Moving." Ryder sprinted left, using the cover of cubicle walls to flank their position. His NOD revealed both guards huddled behind a desk cluster, their attention fixed on his team's last known positions.

He put two rounds through the first guard's temple, pivoted, and dropped the second with a controlled pair to center mass.

The floor fell silent except for the shrieking alarms.

"Clear left," Ryder called.

"Clear right," Will responded.

"Clear center," Kendrick confirmed.

The lights turned on, and Ryder flipped the NOD up to let his eyes adjust. The ding from the elevator on the opposite end of the floor was barely noticeable above the sirens. Ryder heard the sound of furniture moving. He dashed through the employee breakroom to see at least six security guards forming a defensive line behind overturned tables and chairs.

"Contact front, fifty yards." Ryder dropped behind a cubicle wall as automatic fire erupted from the line of guards. Rounds chewed through cheap furniture, sending foam and fabric fragments into the air. "Sustained fire, multiple shooters."

Will dove behind a filing cabinet as bullets stitched the wall above his head. "I count seven. Maybe eight."

Kendrick rolled behind a conference room's glass wall, which exploded as rounds hammered through it. "They're flanking left!"

Ryder spotted three guards moving through the cubicle rows, attempting to envelop their position. He squeezed off four controlled bursts, dropping two. The third guard stumbled backward, hit but not down, returning fire.

The tactical situation was deteriorating. Too many guards, too much firepower, and limited cover pinned his team in a kill zone.

"Smoke!" Ryder pulled a canister from his vest and tossed it from his position in the break room. Gray smoke billowed through the open floor plan.

He moved right, using the smoke as concealment, flanking wide toward the guard's fortified position.

A massive boardroom table lay on its side near the bank of elevators, providing solid cover. Ryder slid behind it, his breathing controlled despite the adrenaline flooding his system. From this angle, he could see five guards clustered behind their makeshift barricade, their attention focused on the smoke where Ryder's team had been.

Movement beyond the guards caught his attention. A familiar figure stood at a distance from the men defending the building. Brandon Crane, leading from the safety of the rear, positioned himself for his typical maneuver—a swift, clean escape the moment the battle turned.

Ryder didn't have an angle, but he had an idea of how to get Crane into his sights.

"Cover me while I move," Ryder shouted.

Kendrick and Will laid down suppressive fire while Ryder stood, exposing himself to the guards' fire, and sent a barrage of rounds toward Crane's position.

It worked. Crane abandoned the battle and sprinted toward the open elevator.

Ryder tracked Crane through his optic, compensating for distance and movement. Rounds snapped past his head, so close he felt their displacement. He exhaled, finger tightening on the trigger.

The Rattler barked once.

Crane stumbled, his right arm jerking as the round impacted just above the elbow. The former SEAL's SIG Sauer P226 tumbled from his grip, skittering across the polished floor tiles. Crane collapsed, his hand clutching the wound, crawling toward the elevator with desperate speed.

Bullets whined past Ryder's head, with three rounds narrowly missing. He dropped back behind the conference table as return fire intensified, wood splintering above him. The former Delta Force operator peeked around the table and saw the elevator door close with Crane inside.

Ryder charged forward, using cubicle walls for partial cover, rounds chasing him across the open floor. His legs pumped, carrying him toward Crane's pistol while his peripheral vision tracked muzzle flashes.

He dove, sliding across smooth tile, his hand closing around the SIG Sauer as bullets stitched the floor beside him. The pistol grip was still warm from Crane's hand.

Ryder rolled behind a support column, his new position providing a perfect angle on the guards' flank. Three guards were exposed, their attention fixed on the rounds from Will and Kendrick slicing through the dissipating smoke.

His Rattler spoke in controlled bursts. Two rounds each. The first guard dropped. The second spun, trying to locate the new threat. Ryder put him down with a headshot. The third started to turn, but Will's fire from the opposite angle caught him center mass.

"Last two breaking east!" Will's voice cut through the chaos.

Ryder spotted them, both guards sprinting toward the emergency stairs on the building's opposite side. Kendrick was already moving, her rifle up, tracking. Two controlled bursts. Both guards collapsed.

The fortieth floor fell silent except for the alarm's continuous shriek and the wet sounds of dying men struggling for breath.

Ryder ejected his Rattler's magazine, checking the remaining rounds. Six left. Not enough for sustained combat. He dropped the empty magazine, slapped in a fresh one, and moved toward the break room.

Will emerged from behind a cubicle wall, his face flushed with adrenaline. "Everyone okay?"

"I'm good," Kendrick called from across the floor.

Ryder scanned the carnage. Seven guards down around the boardroom table barricade. Six more scattered throughout the floor—thirteen total. More than half of LifeCore's security force was eliminated in three minutes of brutal combat.

Ryder removed Crane's SIG Sauer from his pocket, checked the chamber, and secured it in his vest. It was the pistol that would execute Andre Atwood and frame Brandon Crane in one move.

He moved toward the break room, stepping over bodies and spent brass. The refrigerator stood intact, its white surface still smooth and clean after the carnage surrounding it. Ryder pulled it open, scanning shelves stocked with employee lunches and drinks.

He grabbed three water bottles, tossing one each to Will and Kendrick.

"What the hell were you thinking?" Will demanded. "Charging after Crane like that? I thought you were dead."

Ryder held up the SIG Sauer. "This belonged to Brandon Crane. Now it's going to be the murder weapon that puts him at the top of the Chicago PD's suspect list."

Understanding dawned across Will's face. "The ballistics will lead straight to him."

"And every camera in this building will show him here during the timeframe of the attack." Ryder took a long drink from his water bottle. "Combine that with the footage you doctored of him casing the place in advance, and detectives will be all over Crane like a dog on a bone."

Kendrick leaned against the break room wall, catching her breath. "How many guards are left?"

"Emma said they doubled security," Will announced. "If we assume twenty guards total before tonight, we've eliminated thirteen. That leaves seven between us and Atwood."

"Let's figure another ten so we're prepared," Ryder stated.

Ryder moved toward a table where someone's abandoned dinner sat beside a laptop. Chicken teriyaki, still warm. The normalcy of it struck him. Minutes ago, employees had occupied this floor, working late, eating dinner at their desks, and planning weekend activities. Now it was a battlefield, bodies cooling in pools of spreading blood.

He pushed the thought aside. Moral reflection was a luxury reserved for after the mission.

"We need to move." Ryder rechecked his magazines. Thirty rounds left, plus whatever they could salvage from the guards' weapons. "Atwood knows we're here now. He's either preparing to fight or preparing to run."

Will moved through the room, retrieving magazines from fallen guards. "They're using 5.56. These won't fit our weapons."

"Check for sidearms." Ryder kneeled beside the nearest guard, took the guard's Glock 17 and two spare magazines, and secured them in his vest.

Kendrick completed her own ammunition check. "I'm down to eighteen rounds."

"That'll have to be enough." Ryder looked at both of them, seeing the exhaustion and adrenaline crash impacting their effectiveness. "We're almost done. Two more floors to Atwood. Then we end this."

They climbed two flights, passing the forty-first floor where bodies from the initial contact still lay. The forty-second floor access was visible above, a reinforced door with a badge reader that Will could override in seconds. Those seconds would give whatever forces remained on the executive floor time to prepare for their arrival.

Ryder glanced at Will, who nodded in understanding. They both looked at Kendrick, whose face showed the weight of the thirteen dead men they'd left in their wake.

"One more floor," Ryder whispered. "Then justice finds its way home."

They'd crossed every line, broken every rule, and paid for this moment in blood and choices that couldn't be undone. But Andre Atwood waited above them, the man whose greed had destroyed thousands of lives, including Nana's.

They were twenty steps and a single door away from completing their mission.

CHAPTER 40

The forty-second floor stretched before them in silence, fluorescent lights humming against the backdrop of distant alarms echoing from below. Ryder moved through the executive corridor with his Rattler at low ready, scanning for threats in the plush carpeted passage where LifeCore's leadership had made decisions that destroyed thousands of lives.

The chaos they'd left behind on the fortieth floor felt worlds away from this sanitized sanctuary of power. Mahogany doors with brass nameplates lined both sides of the hallway. Abstract art hung on cream-colored walls.

Ryder's instincts screamed danger. The calm felt wrong. The emptiness of the floor Crane had vowed to defend less than half an hour ago made little sense. Was it a trap?

He raised his fist, halting the team. Will and Kendrick froze behind him, weapons trained on their respective sectors. Ryder pointed to his eyes, then swept his hand across the corridor, indicating the need for structured clearing.

They moved as a unit, checking offices one by one. Each door revealed the same story. Lights on, computers running, but no occupants. Coffee cups sat half-full on desks. Suit jackets hung on chair backs. The appearance of a recent evacuation, as if executives had fled the building the moment alarms sounded below.

Atwood's corner office stood at the end of the corridor, its double doors ajar. Ryder approached with Kendrick covering his right flank and Will watching their rear. He pushed the door open with his boot, sweeping the massive space with his rifle.

Empty.

The office looked like a scene from a luxury magazine. Floor-to-ceiling windows offered views of the Chicago River with Lake Michigan in the distance. A Brazilian rosewood desk the size of a small car dominated the space. Behind it, shelves displayed corporate awards and framed photos of Atwood with politicians and celebrities.

But no CEO of LifeCore Health Insurance.

"Where is he?" Kendrick's voice carried an edge.

"Not sure."

"He had to hear the shooting. Maybe he's in the penthouse," Will offered.

"Possible." Ryder's jaw tightened. "We need to check every bathroom, every closet, and every conference room."

They continued throughout the executive floor with Ryder on point, using his experience as a Delta operator to clear each room with Will and Kendrick maintaining security in the hallway. A large boardroom where Atwood had presided over countless meetings that prioritized profit over human life concluded the sweep on the north.

A sudden yelp pierced the silence.

Ryder spun toward the sound, his weapon tracking toward a closed office door thirty feet down the corridor. Kendrick emerged from a corner office, her rifle already shouldered. Will appeared from the boardroom, moving fast.

The trio arrived outside the target door seconds later. "Chad Kline, Chief Underwriting Officer" was engraved on the brass nameplate. Another shriek erupted from behind the closed door, followed by the unmistakable sound of shuffling bodies and panicked whispers.

Ryder raised his finger to his lips, then pointed at the door. He used hand signals to indicate he'd enter first, followed by Will. Kendrick moved to the door handle while Ryder and Will stacked on either side.

On his silent count of three, Kendrick turned the handle and pushed.

Ryder swept right, and Will swept left. Their weapons tracked across an office filled with huddled figures pressed against the far wall—three women and two men, their hands raised, their eyes wide with terror. Several were crying. One woman had her arms wrapped around a younger colleague who appeared to be straight out of college.

"Don't shoot!" A man's voice cracked. "Please don't shoot us!"

Ryder lowered his weapon, his tactical mind processing the scene. These weren't security personnel. They wore business casual attire with building access badges clipped to their shirts and blouses. They were all LifeCore employees.

"We're not here to hurt you." Will holstered his weapon, his voice genuine. "You're safe."

A woman in the middle of the group stepped forward. Ryder recognized her face from Will's encounter during their lunchtime reconnaissance a day earlier. Emma Soto. Her eyes met Ryder's with a mixture of recognition and relief.

"Why are all of you still here?" Will moved closer but kept his movements slow. "It's after six."

Emma glanced at the others before speaking. "Mr. Atwood told all of us yesterday that we had to work late on the forty-second floor this week. He said that if we wanted to keep our jobs, we'd have to be here until at least nine every night. Mr. Kline said if we heard anything loud or suspicious, to come into his office, but he left forty minutes ago and hasn't come back."

The pieces snapped into focus.

"He's using them as human shields." Ryder kept his voice low.

Kendrick's sharp intake of breath confirmed she'd reached the same conclusion. Atwood had expected the assault. He'd known they were coming and had taken the most morally bankrupt defensive measure imaginable. He'd forced innocent employees to remain on the executive floor, betting that even vigilantes wouldn't slaughter civilians to reach him.

The move revealed both Atwood's desperation and the depths of his depravity. A man who'd built his fortune on the systematic destruction of vulnerable lives had now weaponized his own employees.

"We need to find Atwood," Ryder growled.

"I'm staying here." Will's voice carried quiet determination. "I'll protect them in case any of the guards come back."

Ryder met Will's eyes and saw the transformation complete. The young man who'd arrived in Chicago eager to kill anyone connected to Phoenix House's enemies had evolved into something better—a protector. Someone who understood that justice required protecting the innocent, not just punishing the guilty.

Pride flickered through Ryder's chest. He gave Will a single nod.

He turned to Kendrick. "My guess is that Atwood is in his penthouse."

"I saw Mr. Atwood rush to the elevator ten minutes ago." Emma's voice was steadier now. "The arrow on the floor indicator showed he went up. I'm sure he's at his residence on fifty-two."

The penthouse. Atwood's fortress and last defensive position.

Ryder checked his remaining ammunition. Two magazines for the Rattler, plus the Glock he'd taken from a dead guard on the fortieth floor. Crane's SIG Sauer P226 rested in his vest, the weapon that would frame the former SEAL for everything that happened in this building.

The former Delta Force operator removed the Glock and turned to Will.

"You may need this if a security team sweeps this floor. Find someone else who can help you if things get sideways."

Emma stepped forward and extended her hand. "I know how to shoot. I can help."

Ryder nodded and handed the Glock to Emma.

"Lock this door behind us." Ryder looked at the employees. "Don't open it for anyone except the police or one of us. Will's going to stay here and make sure you're safe."

Ryder and Kendrick moved back into the corridor, their boots silent on the woven premium wool carpet. The elevator bank waited at the corridor's end, its polished silver doors reflecting their tactical gear and weapons like a mirror showing what they'd become.

They stepped into the elevator. Ryder pressed the button for floor fifty-two.

The doors slid shut. The elevator began its ascent, carrying them toward a confrontation with Andre Atwood. Ten floors to travel. Ten floors to prepare for the moment when justice would find its way home.

Kendrick checked her weapon, her expression unreadable. Everything they'd done tonight pressed down on both of them. The line between justice and vengeance grew thinner with each trigger pull.

The floor indicator ticked upward as the elevator climbed higher. Forty-three, forty-four, forty-five.

Ryder's pulse remained steady despite the approaching confrontation. This was what he'd trained for, what his entire life had prepared him to do.

Forty-eight, forty-nine, fifty.

The elevator slowed. The final two floors stretched before them.

Ryder raised his Rattler, finger indexed along the frame. Beside him, Kendrick mirrored his stance.

The two warriors locked eyes, communicating without speaking. Ryder saw fear intertwined with determination. The Army CID special agent was tough, but this was uncharted territory for the military law enforcement investigator. He wasn't sure how she'd react once it was time for the execution phase of their mission, but he knew he didn't want anyone else by his side when he left the elevator.

The elevator chimed softly, and the doors parted. Shoulder to shoulder, they stepped into the fight, a single, unified force ready for the final confrontation.

CHAPTER 41

The open doors revealed a penthouse of glass and silence. City lights bled through the floor-to-ceiling windows, glinting off marble floors and cold steel accents. Everything stood still, as if the room itself held its breath.

Ryder and Kendrick exited with caution, each covering a sector. The moment Ryder's boots touched the glossy tile, he dove left as suppressed rounds punched through the elevator's rear wall. Brass casings clinked against marble. Kendrick rolled right, her Rattler already firing controlled bursts toward a makeshift barricade.

The first guard took three rounds to center mass before his body slumped behind the couch. The second guard shifted his aim toward Kendrick, but Ryder's burst caught him in the throat. Blood sprayed across cream-colored walls as the man crumpled.

Silence descended except for the ringing alarms from the floors below.

Ryder rose from his position, sweeping the expansive penthouse with his weapon.

The penthouse featured sleek, contemporary finishes that matched its exclusive downtown address. A kitchen designed with professional-grade appliances dominated the far corner, its stainless-steel surfaces gleaming under the accent lights. Abstract sculptures dotted the space between leather furniture and glass tables that cost more than most LifeCore employees earned in a year.

He expected to find more LifeCore security or even Brandon Crane nursing his wound, but there was no more visible resistance. Instead, Andre Atwood stood beside the kitchen island, his hands resting on the granite countertop. He wore dress slacks and a white shirt with sleeves rolled to his elbows. No tie, no jacket. His linebacker build stood out, broad shoulders and thick arms, a warning to anyone foolish enough to physically challenge him.

His expression carried an eerie calm, as if armed intruders murdering his guards represented nothing more than an interesting business development.

"Mr. Ryder." Atwood's voice was steady. "I've been expecting you."

Ryder advanced, his Rattler trained on the CEO's chest. Kendrick moved to flank their target, establishing a crossfire position that left Atwood nowhere to run.

"Hands where I can see them." Ryder's command cut through the space.

Atwood complied, raising both hands to shoulder height. His fingers remained relaxed, with no tension in his posture. The movement revealed complete confidence despite the presence of a known assassin.

Ryder reached into his vest and withdrew Brandon Crane's SIG Sauer P226, the weapon he'd recovered from the fortieth floor. He passed his Rattler to Kendrick, then raised Crane's weapon, centering the front sight on Atwood's sternum.

"You know why I'm here."

"Because my insurance company denied coverage for your grandmother's medical treatment." Atwood's tone carried neither apology nor defiance. "A decision that thousands of health insurance companies make every day based on evidence-based medicine and actuarial analysis."

"You're killing people for profit."

"I'm optimizing resources to help the maximum number of patients." Atwood eased his hands down, setting them on the countertop. "Do you want to hear my story, Mr. Ryder? Or are you going to execute me without understanding what you're destroying?"

Ryder's finger rested on the trigger, a simple squeeze away from ending the man responsible for Nana's suffering. But something in Atwood's calm demeanor suggested this moment was rehearsed, prepared like a business presentation.

"Talk."

Atwood nodded, his expression shifting to something resembling genuine emotion. "I grew up in West Columbia, a tough neighborhood in the capital city of South Carolina. My mother worked two jobs to keep us fed. My older brothers and I shared a bedroom in a house that was always too hot or too cold. Every month, she'd cry over past-due notices. Every day, I'd hear fighting because there was never enough to go around."

He moved around the kitchen island, his movements slow and deliberate. Ryder tracked him with Crane's pistol.

"I was hungry, weak, and desperate, but I had size and speed. Football became my ticket out of poverty. Appalachian State offered me a scholarship as a linebacker. I earned All-Sunbelt Conference accolades, and for a while, NFL scouts talked about me as a day three draft pick. That never happened, but I graduated with a business degree and connections to university boosters who brought me into a club I'd never known existed. After I climbed a few more rungs in life, I vowed to let nothing push me back to the bottom of that ladder."

"Touching story." Ryder's voice carried no sympathy. "Lots of people overcome poverty without becoming murderers."

"I'm not a murderer." Atwood's tone sharpened. "I'm a businessman who built LifeCore from a regional insurance provider into a national healthcare company offering Medicare Advantage plans. We serve twelve million policyholders across thirty-eight states. Twelve million people have access to medical care because of the systems I created."

"Systems designed to deny treatment and maximize profit."

"Systems designed to make healthcare sustainable." Atwood's hands gestured as he spoke, the movements of someone accustomed to boardroom presentations. "Do you understand the economics of health insurance, Mr. Ryder? The average American spends more on medical care in their last year of life than during the previous sixty-plus years combined. End-of-life care consumes forty percent of Medicare spending. Chemotherapy that costs three hundred thousand dollars to extend life by three months. Nursing home care at twelve thousand per month for patients with advanced dementia who no longer recognize their own families."

"And every one of those families suffered the premature loss of a loved one because you decided who deserves to live and who deserves to die."

"No, I created algorithms that optimize resource allocation for the greater good." Atwood's voice rose with conviction. "People will always die from cancer, heart disease, stroke, and accidents. Death is inevitable. What I'm doing is optimizing the number of people we can serve by directing resources toward policyholders with a higher probability for long-term success."

Ryder moved closer, closing the distance to ten feet. The pistol remained centered on Atwood's chest.

"I know about the bounties. You're killing people for bonuses, another vacation home, and a penthouse apartment in the building where you orchestrate mass murder."

Atwood's mask slipped. His jaw tightened, and something predatory flickered in his eyes. The corporate facade cracked to reveal the truth beneath.

"Yes, the money matters. Building something that will outlast me matters." His voice carried an edge now, the rehearsed speech giving way to genuine emotion. "You think you're better than me, Ryder? You're a killer who breaks into buildings and murders security guards doing their jobs. At least I build things. I create jobs. I provide healthcare to millions. How do you benefit society?"

"I hold predators accountable who prey on the vulnerable." Ryder's response was cold.

"Predators?" Atwood's laugh was bitter. "Look around this city. Hospital administrators choosing which treatments to offer. Pharmaceutical executives setting prices for medications. Every insurance company calculating risk versus payout. We're all making the same decisions. The only difference is I'm honest about the benefits."

"The difference is you're trading the quality of life and health of your policyholders for dollars."

"I'm making difficult decisions that someone has to make." Atwood's voice rose. "I didn't create this system. I'm just navigating through it to help as many people as possible."

"By killing thousands."

"By saving millions." Atwood seemed sincere, as his skewed logic led him to believe his own lie. "Every dollar I save on futile treatments funds care for a child with cancer, a mother with heart disease, a veteran who needs rehabilitation. The algorithm optimizes outcomes. It's not personal. It's mathematics."

The confrontation hung in the air between them, two men who'd chosen violence as a tool and convinced themselves their causes justified the means. Ryder saw the parallel and rejected it with every fiber of his being. Atwood chose profit. Ryder chose justice.

The elevator chimed softly.

Ryder's eyes flickered toward the sound, his weapon still trained on Atwood, but his attention was divided.

The doors parted to reveal Brandon Crane clutching a blood-soaked towel against his upper arm. The former Navy SEAL's face was pale, sweat beading on his forehead. His eyes locked with Ryder's for a single heartbeat.

Recognition flashed between the two operators.

Crane's hand shot toward the elevator panel, slamming the close door button.

Ryder pivoted, raising Crane's own SIG Sauer toward its owner. He fired three rapid shots. The first two rounds punched through the closing elevator doors while the third sparked off the steel frame as the doors sealed shut.

The elevator descended, carrying Crane away once again.

Ryder spun back toward Atwood, but the distraction had cost him critical seconds.

Atwood exploded forward like a jaguar launching from jungle shadows.

The former linebacker's athleticism erupted in explosive speed, closing ten feet in less than two seconds. His shoulder drove into Ryder's chest before the Delta Force operator could react. The impact sent them both crashing into a glass coffee table that shattered under their combined weight.

Crane's pistol flew from Ryder's hand, skittering across the marble tile toward the windows.

Atwood landed on top, his size and strength obvious. Three inches taller and forty pounds heavier than Ryder, the former college athlete had maintained his conditioning through years of personal training. His hands grabbed Ryder's tactical vest, pinning him against shattered glass.

Ryder drove his knee upward into Atwood's ribs, but the CEO absorbed the blow and responded with a hammering elbow that caught Ryder's temple. Stars exploded across his vision.

Combat training overrode pain. Ryder bucked his hips, breaking Atwood's mount and rolling away from the broken table. He came up in a combat crouch, his hands raised.

Atwood charged again, this time leading with a straight punch that Ryder slipped. The Delta Force operator countered with a palm strike to Atwood's nose that sent blood streaming down the CEO's face.

They circled each other in the center of the penthouse, two predators seeking advantage. Atwood wiped blood from his lip, his expression shifting from corporate executive to something more primal. The linebacker who'd spent four years delivering brutal hits on college football fields had returned.

"Come on!" Atwood's voice carried feral aggression.

Ryder moved first, closing the distance with a combination of strikes aimed at Atwood's throat and solar plexus. The CEO blocked the first two attacks but took the third punch to his sternum. He grunted, then grabbed Ryder's extended arm and used his superior size to slam Ryder into the kitchen island.

The granite edge caught Ryder's lower back. Pain shot through his spine. Atwood pressed his advantage, delivering a knee to Ryder's midsection that drove the air from his lungs.

Ryder caught Kendrick moving around the room, trying to get in position to break up the melee with her Rattler. He saw the apprehension in her expression and hoped she'd know when to pull the trigger. Atwood also noticed Kendrick and turned toward her when Ryder drove a left hook into Atwood's jaw, but the CEO caught Ryder's wrist with one hand and delivered a brutal cross with the other.

The LifeCore CEO yanked Ryder from the kitchen island, and they crashed into the leather couch where the dead guards lay sprawled, rolling over furniture and bodies in a desperate struggle for dominance. Each exchange left Ryder absorbing more punishment, exhaustion from hours of combat showing in slower reactions.

Atwood drove Ryder against the floor-to-ceiling windows with a linebacker's tackle that rattled the reinforced glass. The Chicago skyline sparkled beyond the transparent barrier, fifty-two stories of empty air between them and the street below.

"You're nothing special!" Atwood's breath came in ragged gasps as he pinned Ryder against the window. "All that military training, and I'll kill you and your girlfriend tonight."

Ryder drove his forehead into Atwood's already broken nose. The CEO's grip loosened. Ryder slipped away, putting distance between them, his back against the windows.

But Atwood was relentless. He charged again, this time getting behind Ryder and locking his massive forearm across Ryder's throat. The chokehold tightened, cutting off blood flow to Ryder's brain.

Spots appeared in Ryder's vision. His lungs screamed for oxygen. Atwood's grip was unrelenting, like a python locked onto its prey.

Ryder's hands clawed at Atwood's arm, but the CEO's size and position provided an overwhelming advantage. The windows pressed against Ryder's back, Chicago's lights beginning to fade as consciousness slipped away.

"Shoot him!" Ryder's voice came out strangled. "Kendrick, shoot him!"

Through dimming vision, Ryder saw Kendrick twenty feet away, her rifle raised, the front sight post tracking their struggle. Her finger rested on the trigger.

But they were too close. Too intertwined and moving too much. Any shot risked hitting Ryder instead of Atwood.

The pressure increased. Atwood's arm crushed Ryder's trachea. The world began to gray at the edges.

Kendrick's hands trembled as she tracked the two fighters locked in mortal combat. Shooting Atwood meant she might also kill Ryder, but doing nothing would lead to his inevitable death by strangulation. The tunnel through which Ryder viewed her began to close as consciousness faded.

Blackness enveloped him like a rapidly rising tide, but Ryder found a desperate surge of breath. He forced one final, rasping command through his crushed windpipe. "Shoot him."

CHAPTER 42

Kendrick's grip tightened until her knuckles went white as she tracked the two titans locked in mortal combat. Ryder and Atwood moved like fighting lions, each blow calculated to maim or kill.

Her rifle stayed trained on the struggle, but the shot wouldn't come. Twenty feet separated her from the two men, yet she might as well have been miles away. They moved too fast, too close together. One bullet could end everything, but which man would it hit?

Atwood slammed Ryder into the kitchen island. The granite edge caught Ryder's lower back, forcing a grunt of pain. The CEO pressed his advantage, driving his knee into Ryder's midsection.

Kendrick shifted position, trying to find an angle. Her finger rested against the trigger guard. One clean shot was all she needed. A single moment when Atwood separated from Ryder by enough distance to ensure the round found its target.

But that moment refused to present itself.

The fighters rolled across the penthouse floor, crashing through furniture and over spent shell casings from the earlier firefight. Each exchange left Ryder absorbing more punishment.

She waited for the Delta Force operator to regain the upper hand and end the fight, so she wouldn't have to make an impossible decision. Kendrick willed Ryder to overcome Atwood, but it never happened.

Everything she'd trained for converged in this moment. Her entire career was built on the foundation that killing outside legal parameters made her no different from the criminals she pursued.

Yet standing here watching Ryder die wasn't justice either.

Ryder drove his forehead into Atwood's already broken nose. The CEO's grip loosened. Ryder slipped away, putting distance between them, his back against the windows.

Kendrick adjusted her aim, tracking Atwood through her sights. Still no shot. The men stood too close, breathing hard, circling each other like wounded animals.

Atwood slipped behind Ryder, locking his massive forearm across Ryder's throat. The chokehold tightened, cutting off blood flow to Ryder's brain.

"Shoot him!" Ryder's voice came out strangled. "Kendrick, shoot him!"

Kendrick's heart hammered against her ribs. The front sight post tracked their struggle. Her finger moved from the guard to the trigger. One pound of pressure. Maybe two. That's all that separated life from death.

But which life?

Internal monologue crashed through her mind like competing radio frequencies. Everything she believed in, fought for, sacrificed for was coming to a crisis point at the worst possible moment.

If she pulled the trigger and missed, Ryder died.

If she pulled the trigger and hit Ryder by mistake, she'd murdered the one man trying to deliver real justice.

If she did nothing, Atwood would kill Ryder, then kill her, and continue his operation. Thousands more would die while algorithms optimized quarterly earnings.

The federal agent inside her screamed about due process, about laws that separated civilization from chaos. You can't just execute people in their homes, no matter what they've done. That's murder. That's the line you don't cross.

But the woman who'd lost Michael York to corporate greed and watched the system fail veteran after veteran, knew something else.

Sometimes the law protected predators instead of prey.

Sometimes justice required action that the system couldn't provide.

Sometimes, choosing not to act was a choice to let violence reign unchecked.

"Shoot him." Ryder's command came more weakly now, his consciousness fading.

Atwood crushed Ryder harder against the window. The CEO's massive forearm compressed Ryder's trachea.

Kendrick's finger touched the trigger and felt the resistance.

She couldn't do it.

Not murder dressed up as justice.

"I'm sorry," she whispered.

Then she shifted her aim, exhaled, and fired three rapid shots into the tile floor six inches from Atwood's back.

The rounds impacted like thunderclaps in the enclosed space. Marble chips exploded upward. The CEO's instincts reacted to the lethal danger. He jerked away, pulling back from Ryder to protect himself from the threat.

It was enough.

Ryder used the break to drive his elbow into Atwood's temple. The blow connected with devastating force. Atwood's grip released. Ryder spun away, gasping for air, his legs wobbly, and his balance uneven.

The CEO stumbled backward, dazed from the elbow strike. He crashed to the marble floor, breathing hard.

Ryder scrambled across the penthouse toward where Crane's pistol had fallen during the initial exchange. His fingers closed around the SIG Sauer grip. He raised the weapon, pointing it at Atwood, who remained on the ground, chest heaving.

"I can't do this." Kendrick's voice cut through the silence. "I'm sorry, but this is still murder."

Ryder kept his weapon trained on Atwood as his breathing steadied. He looked at Kendrick standing twenty feet away, her rifle lowered. The former Delta Force operator must have known from her body language that she had no plans to shoot Atwood or take part in his execution.

"Then step outside."

The words carried no anger, no judgment. Just acknowledgment of who they each had to be.

Kendrick looked at the two men. Ryder, the vigilante, who'd crossed every line to deliver justice the system couldn't provide. Atwood, the corporate executive who'd killed thousands through algorithms and bounties. Two different killers, two different justifications for violence.

She'd made her choice when she fired those warning shots into the tile instead of Atwood's chest. She'd given Ryder the opening he needed while keeping her own hands clean. That compromise was as far as she could go.

Kendrick nodded once, then strode toward the elevator.

Her footsteps echoed across the marble floor. The sound seemed loud in the aftermath of violence. She pressed the button, heard the mechanism engage, and watched the floor indicator climb from forty-two to fifty-two.

The doors opened, and she stepped inside. Kendrick turned to face the penthouse one last time.

Ryder still stood with the pistol trained on Atwood. The CEO remained on the floor, knowing his time had run out. Their eyes met across the distance, and she saw something in Ryder's expression that might have been gratitude.

The elevator doors began to close.

Three shots rang out, each one feeling like it held a specific purpose.

Kendrick flinched at the first shot. She closed her eyes tight at the second and third reports of Crane's pistol.

The elevator descended in silence. She'd made her choice, and Ryder had made his.

***

Ryder stood over Atwood's body, Crane's SIG Sauer pistol still warm in his hand. A crimson puddle formed below him after three center mass shots.

Andre Atwood would never approve another denial. Never destroy another family. Never prioritize quarterly earnings over human lives.

He moved to the kitchen sink and wiped down the pistol, ensuring no fingerprints, DNA, or fibers remained on the surface. He dropped the SIG Sauer in the trash bin under the sink and pocketed the towel to eliminate himself as a suspect and complete the ruse.

The alarms on the floors below had ceased. Emergency responders would be entering the building soon, searching for the wounded or dead. Time to leave. He retrieved his Rattler from where Kendrick had placed it during the fight and limped toward the elevator.

Ryder took the elevator down ten floors to the forty-second floor. Will stood in the executive corridor.

"I wasn't sure you'd still be here." Ryder's voice carried exhaustion.

"Just escorted the last employees to their cars in the parking garage."

Ryder scanned the empty floor. "I guess our plan to frame Crane is no good now. That's five witnesses who saw me go upstairs to Atwood's penthouse with a weapon."

Will's quick chuckle cut through the tension. "Quite the opposite."

"What do you mean?"

"We now have five witnesses who saw Crane with a pistol, screaming that Atwood was going to pay for betraying Richter Enterprises." Will's expression showed satisfaction with the improvised plan. "Brandon Crane is going to be getting some serious heat from detectives."

Ryder nodded and patted Will on the back. Exhaustion was catching up, and adrenaline was fading, leaving only pain and fatigue. "Good work. Let's get out of here."

"Where's Kendrick?" Will asked as they walked toward the elevator.

Ryder shrugged. "I'll tell you on the way down."

They descended LifeCore Tower as Ryder told Will the key details of what had happened on the fifty-second floor, keeping his voice neutral, stating facts without emotion.

"She made her choice," Will said. "Can't fault her for staying true to herself."

"No," Ryder agreed. "You can't."

Sixty seconds after leaving the forty-second floor, they reached the parking garage level. The elevator door opened to reveal Kendrick standing in an empty parking stall, arms crossed, expression unreadable.

Ryder told Will he'd catch up with him at the van.

Will nodded once and headed toward their vehicle.

Kendrick and Ryder stood alone in the parking garage while fluorescent lights hummed overhead. Distant sirens wailed as emergency vehicles converged on LifeCore Tower.

"Are you coming with us?" Ryder asked.

Kendrick shook her head. "No. I'm going to walk back to my hotel."

Silence stretched between them for several seconds.

"Why didn't you shoot Atwood back there?" Ryder's question carried genuine curiosity.

"I told you. That's murder."

"Then why didn't you stop me?"

"Michael." Kendrick's lip quivered, and her voice cracked on the name. "Michael was the reason I didn't stop you."

They stared at each other for a beat, their complicated partnership acknowledged with no further words needed.

Different choices, similar beliefs.

Ryder nodded and watched Kendrick disappear into the Chicago night, walking away from LifeCore Tower and everything that had happened inside. She'd return to her federal badge, her investigations, and her belief that justice could still work within the system.

Maybe she was right. Perhaps the law would eventually catch up with people like Atwood, Crane, and Richter.

But Ryder knew better. He'd seen too much, lost too much, to believe the system could protect people from predators with money, power, and connections.

Sometimes the only way to stop a predator was to become one yourself.

Nana's voice echoed in his memory. "Justice heals, vengeance wounds."

He still wasn't sure which one he'd delivered tonight. But Andre Atwood and Chad Kline would hurt no one again.

Ryder climbed into the van beside Will. They pulled out of the parking garage and merged into traffic, leaving LifeCore Tower and the terminal justice dealt to Atwood and Kline as a memory dissolving into the Chicago night.

CHAPTER 43

The morning after the massacre in LifeCore Tower, Tobias Richter moved from his desk to the leather couch in his office to get a better view of the large-screen television mounted on the wall. His coffee sat untouched on the end table. The Bloomberg anchor's voice carried across the sixty-second floor office with the gravity reserved for market-moving events.

"Breaking news from Chicago. Late last night, a building security supervisor found LifeCore Health Insurance CEO Andre Atwood and Chief Underwriting Officer Chad Kline dead in their offices. The circumstances surrounding these deaths remain under investigation, but sources close to the investigation report that foul play is suspected."

Tobias leaned forward, his knuckles whitening against the armrest.

The screen cut to footage of LifeCore Tower, emergency vehicles still parked outside the building, their lights creating red and blue patterns against the glass facade. Crime scene tape stretched across the lobby entrance.

"In early trading, LifeCore's stock price has plummeted from yesterday's close of ninety-seven dollars per share to thirty-two dollars in pre-market activity. The New York Stock Exchange has issued an emergency trading halt pending further information about the deaths and the company's operational stability."

Tobias grabbed the remote and increased the volume, his jaw tightening as the anchor continued.

"Federal regulators have announced immediate investigations into LifeCore's operations. The FBI's white-collar crime division is examining corporate governance practices, while the Securities and Exchange Commission is reviewing all executive communications from the past eighteen months."

The remote cracked in Tobias's grip. Sixty-five dollars per share was wiped away. Billions in market value evaporated in an instant. His largest equity holding was reduced to rubble by whatever had happened in that Chicago office tower.

His phone buzzed against the mahogany desk. It was Brandon Crane. Tobias let it ring three times before answering, forcing calm into his voice despite the rage building in his chest.

"How did you let this happen?"

Crane's response carried no defensiveness, only cold assessment. "I told everyone Ryder was dangerous. Nobody would listen to me."

"I listened plenty. I hired you to stop him." Tobias stood, pacing toward the floor-to-ceiling windows overlooking Central Park. Manhattan stretched before him, a monument to wealth and power built by men who refused to accept defeat. "You're a former Navy SEAL, decorated combat veteran, and the head of security for my entire enterprise. And you couldn't stop one former special forces operator?"

"Ryder doesn't operate like other targets. He adapts, learns, and exploits every weakness." Crane paused. "I lost two dozen men in the tower and took a bullet myself trying to stop him. Now I am going to a private office to see a doctor. I did all I could with the resources available."

Tobias wanted to reach through the phone and strangle Brandon Crane, but he returned his attention to the stock tickers scrolling across the bottom of the TV screen. The deaths of Andre Atwood and his assistant were a significant setback, but that paled in comparison to the enormous loss of Tobias Richter's personal equity portfolio. His empire, built over four decades of calculated risks and strategic acquisitions, was cracking under the weight of insurance regulators and federal authorities.

"There's more you should know." Crane's voice changed in an instant, something approaching concern. "I heard from my source inside the Chicago PD that I'm a suspect. I think Ryder framed me."

Tobias processed the information, his analytical mind calculating options and probabilities. Making Crane the patsy would be simple. Someone to take the fall for regulatory agencies and law enforcement, providing a clean break between Richter Enterprises and LifeCore's criminal operations.

But Ryder was still out there hunting and eliminating everyone associated with Richter's business interests with surgical precision. Peter was dead. Alexander Novick was dead. Now, Atwood and Kline. The pattern was undeniable. Eventually, Ryder would come for him.

"What evidence do they have?"

"Ryder took my pistol after he shot me, so they'll find a ballistics match between my weapon and slugs found in Atwood. Security footage shows me in LifeCore multiple times in the days before the murders. Multiple witnesses heard me threaten Atwood. The building lost fifty-two minutes of security footage from the night of the killings. Chicago PD suspects I deleted it to cover my tracks."

The setup was professional, almost elegant in its simplicity. Ryder had learned from their previous encounters, adapting his tactics to turn Crane's proximity to LifeCore against him.

Tobias weighed his options. If Crane went down, he'd take secrets with him that could destroy everything. Desperate men made deals with prosecutors, traded testimony for immunity, and revealed operations that should stay buried forever. The former Navy SEAL knew too much about too many things. But despite last night's catastrophic failure, Tobias needed Crane. Ryder was still hunting everyone connected to Richter Enterprises, and Crane's skills, however disappointing they'd proven so far, were still the best defense available.

"I need you operational, not sitting in holding or answering questions from the police."

"Then I need your help to make this blow over."

The pause stretched until the anger boiling inside him slowed to simmer, the silence a negotiation tactic Tobias had perfected over decades of boardroom battles.

"I'll take care of it. Stay in touch. This isn't over."

"Understood."

Tobias ended the call and began working his network of influence, which extended from Manhattan boardrooms to Washington corridors. Senators on his payroll. Congressmen whose campaigns he'd funded. Regulators who owed their appointments to his political contributions. The machinery of power that protected men like him from the consequences ordinary people faced.

His assistant appeared in the doorway, tablet in hand. "Sir, your attorneys are on hold. The public relations firm is requesting immediate guidance on a messaging strategy."

"Tell the lawyers to prepare defensive positions on all regulatory fronts. PR should emphasize LifeCore's cooperation with all law enforcement agencies and the launch of our own internal investigation." Tobias returned to his desk, the initial shock giving way to a calculated response. "And schedule calls with Senator Morrison, Congressman Phillips, and Commissioner Watkins."

The assistant nodded and departed, leaving Tobias alone with the television still broadcasting LifeCore's collapse. The stock ticker at the bottom of the screen showed the trading halt icon beside LifeCore's symbol, a digital tombstone for billions in shareholder value.

His phone buzzed with incoming messages. Board members demanded explanations, investors were threatening lawsuits, and savvy business partners were taking proactive steps to distance themselves from the controversy. The vultures were circling, sensing weakness in an empire that had seemed untouchable twenty-four hours earlier.

Tobias dictated responses to his assistant for immediate distribution, his mind operating on multiple levels. The same skills that had built Richter Enterprises from a regional defense contractor into a multinational conglomerate would preserve it through this crisis.

But beneath the tactical responses and strategic calculations, rage burned with focused intensity. James Ryder had struck at the heart of his financial empire, destroying billions in market value and triggering federal investigations that could expose decades of carefully concealed operations.

For now, his focus remained on preserving the financial health and reputation of Richter Enterprises. He'd mobilize every resource, activate every connection, spend whatever was necessary to protect what he'd built. The storm would blow over. They always did. Public outrage would fade as the news cycle moved forward.

Once the storm passed and his empire was secured, Tobias Richter would turn his complete attention to eliminating James Ryder for good.

***

Brandon Crane sat in his rental car across from the Richter complex, watching Chicago Police Department officers stream in and out of the building's entrance. Yellow crime scene tape stretched across the doorway to his office on the third floor, visible through the glass structure. Evidence technicians in white coveralls carried boxes of materials from his office.

His arm throbbed beneath the sling, the pain a reminder of the round Ryder had put through his triceps during last night's firefight. For a hefty sum, the private doctor on Chicago's West Side had stitched the wound and provided pain medication, no questions asked.

Crane's phone rested on the passenger seat beside him, showing a news alert about the LifeCore murders. The media coverage was extensive, featuring interviews with healthcare advocates demanding accountability and financial analysts discussing the company's collapsed stock price. His name hadn't appeared in reports yet, but that would change soon enough.

He recognized Ryder's tactical genius in every detail of the frame. Using Crane's weapon to kill Atwood ensured ballistics would match. The security footage showed him surveying LifeCore in the days before the massacre, appearing to case the building rather than conduct legitimate security consultations. The deleted surveillance footage from the night of the killings pointed to someone with insider access.

Even the witnesses worked in Ryder's favor. Multiple LifeCore employees had heard Crane admonish Atwood during heated discussions about security protocols. Legitimate professional disagreements transformed into evidence of murderous intent.

A slight smile crossed Crane's face despite the disaster unfolding before him. Professional recognition for a well-executed operation, even when he was the target.

“I have to hand it to you, Ryder. You set my ass up good to take the fall on this one,” Crane said aloud to the empty vehicle.

More police vehicles arrived, including an FBI mobile command unit. His CPD contact texted him that the case was transitioning from a local homicide to potential federal crimes involving interstate commerce and financial fraud. His window for action was closing.

Crane dialed Richter's private line while watching officers stream in and out of his office.

“Mr. Crane, how can I help you?"

"I'm burned. The feds will be the next to come knocking, so I'm going dark for a while."

The pause stretched until Crane felt uncomfortable, a rare sensation for someone who'd survived firefights in four different countries. Richter's silence carried more weight than most people's threats.

"I put in a few calls, but it'll take a couple of days to clear your name. In the meantime, stay in touch. This isn't over."

Relief flooded through Crane. "Understood."

He ended the call, started the rental car's engine, and pulled away from his observation position before the police noticed his surveillance. The Chicago skyline filled his rearview mirror as he drove south, leaving behind his compromised identity and torched professional reputation.

He'd go underground and lay low for a while. Richter's resources and leverage were the only things keeping Crane from multiple murder charges, buying time to regroup and prepare for a future encounter with James Ryder.

And there would be a next encounter. Ryder's pattern was clear. He identified targets, gathered intelligence, executed operations, and moved to the next objective. Crane knew that he and Tobias Richter were at or near the top of Ryder's current hit list.

The rental car merged onto the interstate, carrying him away from the immediate threat of arrest.

Crane stared into his own pale blue eyes in the rearview mirror. Ryder could claim victory in this battle, but Brandon Crane knew how to rise above the abilities of his opponent to win the war.

CHAPTER 44

The morning air carried a hint of dampness as Ryder settled onto Phoenix House's front steps. September had arrived with temperatures that made outdoor sitting enjoyable, a preview of the fall that Chicago would deliver in another month. The street was quiet, except for the occasional rumble of the L train passing over elevated tracks several blocks away.

Shadow sprawled beside him on the concrete, her fur warming in the morning sun. Four days had passed since Andre Atwood and Chad Kline had died in LifeCore Tower, and the world was already a different place.

The coffee tasted bitter and perfect. Ryder let the heat spread through his chest while his mind cataloged recent events. It was his first opportunity to reflect on the mission and savor its success.

Footsteps sounded behind him as Will pushed through the door, carrying his own mug, and settled onto the steps. The jagged, star-shaped cut below his right ear brightened in the sunlight. It was a visible testament to the deadly shrapnel that had sprayed off the exploding cubicles and desks during the fierce battle with LifeCore security.

"Morning," Will said.

"Morning."

They sat without speaking. Minutes stretched between them while they watched Logan Square wake up for another day. A jogger passed on the sidewalk. A delivery truck stopped three houses down. Shadow's ears tracked every sound, but she remained still, content to soak in the sunshine beside Ryder's leg.

Minutes passed before Will broke the silence.

"The FBI investigation into LifeCore is in full swing. Federal regulators descended on the building yesterday afternoon with enough subpoenas to keep their legal team busy for months."

"Good."

"LifeCore's stock price stabilized at twenty-three dollars after the market reopened. Dropped from ninety-seven the day before Atwood died." Will paused. "I took the liberty of closing the short position. You made two point three million before Uncle Sam takes his cut."

Ryder remained still, but he let a quick smile slip before catching it. The money represented justice for Nana, for Ricky, for every veteran and citizen that LifeCore had targeted. A higher balance in his bank account couldn't restore what they'd lost, but it provided resources to rebuild what Atwood's greed had destroyed.

Will noticed the smile.

"You're a rich man now, James Ryder. It must feel good."

Ryder nodded. "If helping Nana regain her independence makes me rich, then I'm guilty as charged."

His encrypted phone vibrated against his thigh. Kendrick's name appeared on the screen.

"Special Agent Kendrick," he answered.

"Ryder." Her voice carried genuine excitement. "I've got news. The LifeCore board appointed Dr. Allison Lee as emergency CEO yesterday."

Ryder straightened. "How's she doing?"

"Still recovering from the broken bones from the hit and run, but she's already making waves. Dr. Lee reversed all denial algorithms as her first act as CEO, then approved all pending appeals. She's going to get LifeCore back on track as the health-oriented company she always envisioned."

"That's great." Ryder meant it. "You sound excited for her."

"I am, but not just for Dr. Lee. Elena Grabowski is getting a new hearing in front of a military review board. The board will probably clear her of all allegations and give her the honorable discharge she deserves. She may even get a settlement."

The words warmed Ryder like a second cup of coffee. Elena had served her country with honor, only to be railroaded by corrupt officers who valued their careers over truth. Her exoneration represented justice delayed but not denied.

"That is good news," Ryder said.

"There's more. Nana's physical therapy has been approved. Dr. Lee personally reviewed her case and authorized comprehensive rehabilitation coverage."

Ryder closed his eyes, letting the relief wash over him. Everything they'd done, every life they'd taken, every line they'd crossed—it had all led to this moment. All deserving policyholders would get the care they needed.

The line went silent for several awkward beats. They had not spoken since Kendrick left Atwood's penthouse the night justice was delivered. Ryder didn't know where they stood going forward, but her phone call meant a partnership was still possible.

"Thanks for the update," Ryder said.

They ended the call. Ryder returned the phone to his pocket and took another drink of coffee.

Will watched him with understanding, recognizing the weight of what they'd accomplished and what it had required. He stood and stretched, his vertebrae popping in sequence like small-caliber gunfire. "I should check on the residents before the day gets away from me. Alex is off to a good start as house manager, but I want to make sure the transition is smooth."

Ryder did not respond. His mind was elsewhere as Will disappeared into Phoenix House.

The morning sun climbed higher, burning off the last traces of overnight coolness. Chicago stretched around him in all directions, a metro area of nine million people going about their lives without knowing how close they'd come to letting corporate predators destroy thousands of vulnerable citizens.

Ryder finished his coffee, called Shadow to his side, and went inside.

***

Ryder arrived at Nana's house two hours later, Shadow pushing through the door the moment it opened. The Belgian Malinois bounded ahead, her nails clicking against the floor as she made straight for Nana's recliner in the living room. The former military canine, having survived multiple combat deployments, had appointed herself as Nana's primary guardian, providing comfort and protection with unwavering loyalty.

Nana sat upright in her recliner and raised her cheek for a kiss from her grandson. She looked stronger than she had in weeks, color returning to her face and clarity sharpening her gaze. The stroke had stolen so much from her, but intensive physical therapy was slowly returning what LifeCore had tried to take.

Karla stepped into the room as Ryder took a seat on the sofa next to Nana.

"Good afternoon, Mr. Ryder."

Karla turned to Nana. "Time for your next session."

"Already?" Nana moaned.

"You know it's helping," Karla said. She waved her hand toward the hospital bed, folded up, and pushed into the corner. "The extensive PT has made a big difference in just a few days, but we still need to keep up with the light PT and stretching."

"Fine," Nana huffed. "Let me visit with James first."

Ryder had to restrain himself from laughing. He loved seeing the fight back in the woman who'd raised him since he was twelve.

Nana squeezed his hand with surprising strength. "Karla says the insurance company finally approved everything. How did that happen?"

"Things changed at LifeCore. They have a new CEO with different priorities."

Nana's expression sharpened. "You have something to do with that change?"

Ryder met her gaze without flinching. "I'm just glad LifeCore has done the right thing."

The silence stretched between them while Nana studied his face. Her eyes, still sharp despite the stroke's damage, searched for something in his expression. The former Delta Force operator knew his grandmother had an idea of his involvement and would never judge him for it. Regardless, the details of his brand of justice were not something he'd place on her soul. The heavy burden it laid on him was enough.

Instead, she squeezed his hand again. Understanding and acceptance were transferred in the silence of the Andersonville living room.

They sat together for another twenty minutes, talking about her physical therapy progress and discussing plans for when she was back to her old self before the stroke. Shadow remained at Nana's feet, content to serve as both guardian and companion.

When Ryder stood to leave, Nana caught his wrist.

"Thank you. For everything."

Ryder nodded. Those words meant more to him than she'd ever know.

Karla appeared in the doorway. "I should get started with your exercises, Mrs. Ryder."

Ryder pulled Karla aside in the hallway. "I want to make this a permanent full-time position with my grandmother. Nana's going to need consistent care during her recovery, so I'll pay you fifty percent more than your current salary."

"I'd be honored." Karla's expression reflected genuine warmth. "She's made remarkable progress in just three days. With proper support, she'll regain most of her independence."

"That's what I'm counting on."

He left them to their afternoon session.

The world felt like it was back on its axis again. Nana was recovering physically, and the fight was returning to the strongest woman he knew. It made all the late-night planning, physical pain, and life-altering actions in LifeCore Tower four nights ago worth it.

***

Will stood in the conference room offering final tips to Alex Serrano, the new house manager. The former Army Logistics Officer listened with careful attention, taking notes on a legal pad while Will explained the daily routine and resident needs.

"Gabe Orosco is your go-to for anything kitchen-related. Steve Walsh handles maintenance issues before they become problems. The important thing here is maintaining structure while respecting everyone's recovery timeline."

Serrano let out a long sigh. "Got it. I appreciate all the tips."

Will clapped him on the shoulder and turned to find Ryder waiting in the doorway. They stepped into the hallway, finding privacy in the quiet space between the conference room and the front entrance.

"Thank you," Ryder said. "For keeping me grounded and keeping this place running like a well-oiled machine with everything else going on."

The moment stretched between them, heavy with everything they'd been through together. Will had arrived in Chicago as an eager hacker, ready to take down anyone connected to Phoenix House's enemies. He'd evolved into something better, a protector who understood that justice required more than vengeance.

"We did all this together." Will gestured around them at the converted recovery center. "You showed me what justice looks like when it's done right."

They left Phoenix House together, climbing into Ryder's sedan for the drive across Chicago. The cemetery waited on the city's northwest side, a peaceful expanse of headstones and mature trees that had witnessed countless final farewells.

Ricky Nelson's grave sat in a quiet corner, marked by a simple headstone that bore his name, rank, and dates of service. Patches of grass had grown over the disturbed earth, nature reclaiming the space where LifeCore's greed had planted one more victim.

Ryder kneeled and placed a small American flag beside the headstone.

"You deserved better than what they gave you."

They stood in silence for several minutes, paying respects to a man who'd served his country only to be betrayed by the systems meant to protect him. Ricky's death had set everything in motion, a senseless loss that had exposed the rot at LifeCore's core.

Ricky Nelson had been trying to rebuild his life, fighting addiction and isolation with the same determination he'd shown in combat. He had deserved more time, more chances, and more support.

"We should go," Will whispered.

They returned to the sedan and drove toward O'Hare International Airport. Traffic thickened as they approached the terminals, travelers rushing toward departures and arrivals.

Ryder pulled to the curb outside Terminal 3. Will gathered his backpack from the rear seat, checking for his boarding pass and identification. The brief goodbye felt inadequate for everything they'd been through together.

"Stay ready," Ryder said. "Richter's still out there, and I may need your help again in the future."

"I'll be ready."

The words were delivered with confidence, and Ryder believed his friend would always be ready if he needed him.

Will turned on his heel and disappeared into the terminal, swallowed by a throng of travelers.

The drive back to Logan Square took forty minutes through afternoon congestion. Ryder let his mind process everything that had happened over the past weeks. Nana's stroke. Ricky's death. The systematic exposure of LifeCore's murder machine. The final confrontation in Atwood's penthouse.

He knew the future would bring new predators who believed they were free from the consequences of their actions. Greed and thirst for power ensured there'd always be another Richter,

Novick, Galindo, and Atwood. Tonight, James Ryder could sleep knowing that justice had found its way home.

Chapter 45

The September evening brought a cool breeze across Nana's front porch, carrying the scent of fresh-cut grass from the neighbor's yard. Ryder sat on the top step, watching shadows lengthen across Logan Boulevard while waiting for Kendrick to arrive. Through the living room window behind him, he could hear the television's muted voices—local news anchors discussing another corporate scandal, another politician's promises, another cycle of the machine that ground people down.

Shadow lay beside him, her amber eyes tracking every passing car with the vigilance of a warrior who had never left the battlefield. Her fur rippled in the breeze, and she pressed closer against his leg when a familiar sedan pulled to the curb.

Kendrick emerged from the rental car looking different from the day of their assault on LifeCore Tower. The tactical gear was gone, replaced by jeans and a Loyola University sweatshirt she must have bought at a local store. Her auburn hair was down, no longer pulled back in the tight bun she'd worn while hunting him. The transformation softened her features—she looked younger and more approachable, like a favorite teacher who was both interesting and fun.

"I'm glad you could make it," Ryder said, standing as she approached.

"You said you wanted me to see Nana." Kendrick climbed the steps, pausing to scratch Shadow behind the ears.

"She's inside watching the news with Karla. Come on."

They entered to find Nana sitting upright in her recliner, a vast improvement from the hospital bed she'd occupied just days ago. The physical therapy had worked miracles. She could grip a coffee mug with her left hand now, and her speech had improved, though fatigue still crept in during the evening hours.

"Jenna!" Nana's face brightened. "James said you might stop by."

Kendrick crossed the room and took Nana's extended hand. "You're looking wonderful, Mrs. Ryder."

She gestured toward the couch. "Sit, sit. Karla was just making tea."

The home health aide appeared from the kitchen carrying a tray with four steaming mugs. Karla had become part of the household routine, arriving each morning to help with exercises and staying through dinner to ensure Nana took all her medications. The insurance company had approved extended coverage after Dr. Lee's reforms at LifeCore.

They settled into comfortable positions. Nana in her chair, Karla perched on the armrest beside her, Ryder and Kendrick on opposite ends of the couch with Shadow sprawled between them on the floor. The television droned on about a warehouse fire on the South Side, the anchor's voice competing with sirens from somewhere distant in the city.

"How long are you staying in Chicago?" Nana asked.

Kendrick pursed her lips and shook her head. "I'm not sure. I should have been back in Virginia a week ago."

"So you're staying here to spend more time with James." Nana fixed Kendrick with the penetrating stare that had extracted confessions from Ryder throughout his childhood.

"Nana," Ryder protested. "Please don't start—"

"It's okay." Kendrick interrupted. "In a way, it's true. I stayed in Chicago to spend more time with your grandson, but I can't stay much longer."

Nana's eyebrows rose. "Oh?"

Kendrick's phone buzzed. She pulled it from her pocket, frowned at the screen, then tucked it away. "Sorry. Work stuff."

"Everything okay?" Ryder asked.

"Fine. I'll deal with it later."

Nana launched into a story about her brief time in Virginia decades ago, when she visited a cousin who'd worked for the US government. Her voice grew stronger as she spoke, animated by memory. Karla occasionally prompted her when a word escaped, but the improvement from even a week ago was remarkable. The intensive therapy sessions were rebuilding neural pathways and creating new routes around the damage.

Ryder watched Kendrick's shoulders relax and her body ease deeper into the couch cushions as Nana wove her tales. Her hand found Shadow's head, fingers working through the thick fur while Nana described a disastrous attempt at making crab cakes that had almost burned down her cousin's kitchen.

"The smoke alarm went off for twenty minutes." Nana finished with a laugh that crinkled the corners of her eyes. "The neighbors thought the house was on fire."

The conversation continued for another hour, meandering through topics like the beautiful weather, the Chicago Cubs, and Ryder's grandfather. Kendrick contributed occasional observations but mostly listened, her phone buzzing twice more with messages she ignored.

Nana's energy waned as the night wore on. Her words came slower, with longer pauses between thoughts. Karla noticed and sprang into action.

"Time for your evening medications," the home healthcare worker announced. "And you should rest."

Nana didn't protest, a sign of her exhaustion. "It was wonderful seeing you again, Jenna. Don't be a stranger."

"I won't," Kendrick promised, though something in her tone suggested she wasn't sure she could keep that promise.

Karla helped Nana to her feet, supporting her weight as they made their way toward the bedroom. Shadow followed, her protective instincts extending to anyone Ryder cared about. The dog would sleep beside Nana's bed tonight, as she had every night since they'd returned home.

Ryder and Kendrick sat in silence until they heard the bedroom door close.

"Want to sit outside?" Ryder asked.

"Yeah."

They sat on the top step, where the evening had cooled further. The streetlights had come on, casting pools of yellow light that attracted moths in dizzying spirals. A mother walked past, pushing a stroller and singing hushed songs to a fussy child.

Kendrick broke the silence first. "I owe you an apology."

"For what?"

"For leaving you at Atwood's penthouse." She stared at her hands. "I know why you had to do it. Seeing your grandmother is proof of all the good that came from what you did. She's doing so much better in a short time. Because of you, Dr. Lee is implementing real reforms, and tens of thousands of policyholders are finally getting the care they need. The system only changed because you forced it to."

"You did what you thought was right."

"Did I?" She turned to face him. "I stood there watching you fight for your life and couldn't pull the trigger. All my training, all my beliefs about law and order, and when it mattered most, I froze."

"You didn't freeze. You made a choice."

"The wrong one."

"There was no right choice in that room." Ryder met her eyes. "Just two perspectives of proper justice."

They sat in comfortable silence for several minutes, shoulders touching. Somewhere in the distance, a dog barked. A television sitcom echoed from the house next door.

Kendrick leaned her head on Ryder's shoulder. His initial instinct was to jerk away, but he caught himself and relaxed. The vanilla and citrus scent of her shampoo taunted his senses, and every sound in Chicago faded as he listened to her breath. It lasted less than ten seconds, but Ryder could swear it was five minutes.

The Army CID special agent's phone buzzed again. This time she looked at it, her jaw tightening as she read the message.

"Bad news?" Ryder asked.

"Sergeant Major Atkins." She showed him the screen. "He knows I stayed in Chicago after being ordered back to Virginia. Says he's reporting me AWOL if I'm not in Quantico tomorrow by noon."

Ryder wanted to tell her to stay. The words formed in his throat, but saying them would be selfish. He couldn't ask Kendrick to abandon everything she'd worked for because he'd grown accustomed to her presence.

“You never shared what you wanted to tell me when you first arrived in Chicago,” Ryder reminded her.

"It was about Atkins." She tucked the phone away. "Something's wrong with him. Has been for a while now."

"Wrong how?"

"He's always been by the book since I've known him, even when he first assigned me to you after the Peter Richter case."

"But something changed," Ryder stated.

Kendrick nodded. "Yeah, right after you killed Alexander Novick, he—"

"No," Ryder corrected matter-of-factly. "He was killed by Marcus Jensen, a member of his security detail."

Kendrick's head snapped toward Ryder until they locked eyes. "Okay. A couple of days after Jensen murdered Novick, Atkins said he wanted to assign fresh eyes to the case. That's unheard of at CID unless the case goes cold."

She rechecked her phone, but this time showed no emotion. "I thought little of it at first, but a week later, I was on a video call with Atkins and asked him if anyone was investigating the abnormally high death rates from RM-5974, which is causing unexplained cardiovascular failure of our troops in military hospitals. Atkins looked confused and said he wasn't aware of RM-5974, and you should have seen his face when I said it was the experimental drug from Richter Pharmaceuticals that killed my fiancé."

Kendrick wet her lips and let her eyes fall to the cracks in the sidewalk. Ryder knew she was reliving the pain of Michael York's sudden death in that moment. Her eyes rose again, and she continued.

"His face turned white as a ghost, and he ended the call. Two days later, he tried to convince me to pull back from pursuing you after he had complained earlier that week that I wasn't moving fast enough to arrest you. Now, he changes his mind with the wind, and I get whiplash trying to keep up with all the new orders. The Sergeant Major Atkins I've known since I started was always decisive and wouldn't sleep until you were behind bars."

She shared the details, laying out a pattern of behavior that suggested Sergeant Major Atkins was protecting someone.

"He seems dirty." Ryder kept his eyes on the passing traffic. "Question is, who's influencing him?"

The question hung heavy, like fog shrouding Lake Michigan on a cool fall morning.

"It could be Tobias Richter. He seems to have friends everywhere," Kendrick stated.

Ryder nodded and bumped her shoulder with his, the casual contact carrying more weight than words. "I know a great way to find out."

Kendrick bumped back, a smile playing at the corners of her mouth. "Oh yeah? How?"

Ryder's attention snapped back to Kendrick, his eyes filled with the unshakeable resolution of a man who'd just made a life-altering decision.

"Let's see how he reacts when I kill Tobias Richter."

The smile vanished from Kendrick's lips. "You're serious."

Ryder nodded. "He won't live to see the new year."

***

If you're ready to witness Ryder going on offense to hunt for Tobias Richter and Brandon Crane, look for **EXECUTION ORDER**, Book 4 in the James Ryder Thriller series

I hope you enjoyed TERMINAL JUSTICE. You can find a bonus chapter recounting Shadow's journey as a military K9 with the Delta Force Kill Team. You'll learn more about Shadow before Ryder became her handler, and you can download now at: **JTPorterAuthor.com/bonus-content/**

JT Porter is the pen name behind a series of gritty, unflinching thrillers featuring morally complex protagonists who battle forces darker than themselves. Porter's books explore the shadowy boundaries of justice, vengeance, and redemption through characters like James Ryder, a ruthless assassin who targets the powerful predators society cannot touch.

Born and raised in America's heartland, Porter's Midwestern roots and military background inform the capable characters and compelling storylines found in each adrenaline-fueled narrative.

Learn more at JTPorterAuthor.com

Made in the USA
Coppell, TX
20 January 2026